Praise for
the Lacys' Novels

"In *The Land of Promise*, the Lacys detail the accounts of three settler families and the unspeakable torments endured by American Indians forced to give up their land to live on reservations in the late 1800s. Well-researched details and engaging characters make this a moving historical novel. The series will please fans of fast-paced, absorbing tales of the American West and may have crossover appeal for those who enjoy Larry McMurtry's works."

—*Library Journal*

"In *The Land of Promise,* the Lacys' love of history and evangelism shine through. The final novel in their trilogy beautifully illustrates the joys and sorrows of life for both the Indians and white settlers during the late-nineteenth-century land rush.... A stirring, intriguing story filled with endearing characters."

—*Romantic Times Bookclub Magazine*

"*The Land of Promise* is a superb historical fiction story that looks at the late-nineteenth-century land rush that caused heartbreak for both races. The key to this saga is that Indians and whites are treated with respect by the authors, who also do not hide from the atrocities that occurred. This is a deep, inspirational historical that shows that even at life's darkest, hope and faith in the promise of the Lord enable people to seek the light of salvation."

—Midwest Book Review

"*Cherokee Rose* overflows with the heart-rending emotion that makes for a true award-winning novel. The way the words are woven will leave readers wondering whether this is fact or fiction, and the characters exert a strong hold on your heart.... A true tribute to the craft of writing."

—MYSELF.COM

"*Cherokee Rose* is intimately intertwined with the history of the Cherokee people. We get a glimpse of the wise chiefs who made such a big difference in the lives of their people, the congressmen and presidents, as well as soldiers who played a part in this very real and very black mark on the historical reality of our nation. This story is also one of God's love, faithfulness, and triumph."

—AUTHOR'S CHOICE REVIEWS

A LINE IN THE SAND

Other Novels by the Lacys

A Place to Call Home series

Cherokee Rose

Bright Are the Stars

The Land of Promise

Dreams of Gold Trilogy

Wings of Riches

The Forbidden Hills

The Golden Stairs

Frontier Doctor Trilogy

One More Sunrise

Beloved Physician

The Heart Remembers

The Orphan Trains Trilogy

The Little Sparrows

All My Tomorrows

Whispers in the Wind

Mail Order Bride series

Shadow of Liberty series

Hannah of Fort Bridger series

Angel of Mercy series

Journeys of the Stranger series

Battles of Destiny series

A LINE IN THE SAND

THE KANE LEGACY
BOOK ONE

AL & JOANNA LACY

MULTNOMAH
BOOKS

A LINE IN THE SAND
PUBLISHED BY MULTNOMAH BOOKS
12265 Oracle Boulevard, Suite 200
Colorado Springs, Colorado 80921
A division of Random House Inc.

All Scripture quotations or paraphrases are taken from the King James Version.

The characters and events in this book are fictional, and any resemblance to actual persons or events is coincidental. Where real-life historical figures appear, the situations, incidents, and dialogues concerning those persons are fictional and are not intended to depict actual events or to change the entirely fictional nature of this work.

ISBN 978-1-59052-924-9

Library of Congress Cataloging-in-Publication Data
Lacy, Al.
A line in the sand / Al and JoAnna Lacy. — 1st ed.
p. cm. — (The Kane legacy ; bk. 1)
ISBN 1-59052-924-9
1. Texas—History—Revolution, 1835–1836—Fiction. I. Lacy, JoAnna. II. Title.
PS3562.A256L56 2007
813'.54—dc22

2007022873

Printed in the United States of America
2007—First Edition

10 9 8 7 6 5 4 3 2 1

This book is dedicated to Julee Schwarzburg, who is a special blessing to us. In the transition of Multnomah Publishers merging with WaterBrook Press to become one publishing company, Julee was appointed our "point person." She has been a tremendous help to us. God bless you, Julee! We love you.

2 Timothy 4:22

PROLOGUE

The series of fierce nineteenth-century battles between the armies of the United States and Mexico, which historians aptly call the Mexican-American War, are sometimes dated April 1846 to February 1848. However, the majority of historians who have written on the subject agree that the war between the United States and Mexico that began in April of 1846 and extended until February of 1848 actually stemmed from the Mexican army's attack on the fighting Texans and their Tennessee friends at the Alamo in San Antonio, Texas, February 23 to March 6, 1836.

This attack, which was led by Mexico's president and chief military leader, Antonio López de Santa Anna, was in retaliation against the Texans for declaring themselves independent of the Mexican government.

In 1835, the people of Texas formed their own government and issued a declaration of independence from Mexico at a large meeting in Washington-on-the-Brazos in southeastern Texas. David G. Burnet was chosen as president of the new Republic of Texas, and General Sam Houston was appointed to be its military leader.

Thus, the majority of historians who have written of these events actually date the Mexican-American War from February 23, 1836, to February 2, 1848.

A bit of history: The land known as Mexico was conquered in the 1540s by Spain. By the 1730s, Spain had sent several expeditions into the land called Texas and claimed it for their own, since Mexico had claimed it before it was conquered by Spain. The city of San Antonio, Texas, which since 1758 had housed a military post and a Franciscan mission known as the Alamo, had become the administrative center.

Anglo-American colonization gained impetus in Texas when the United States government purchased the Louisiana Territory from France in 1803 and claimed title to all the land from the Sabine River as far west as the Rio Grande. All of Texas was then claimed by the Anglo-Americans.

Mexico had remained in Spain's control until 1821, when the Mexican people rose up in determination to be free. They declared their independence from Spain and adopted a federal constitution modeled after that of the United States of America.

There was trouble between the Mexicans and the Spaniards because of this, but no blood was shed. The Spaniards quickly withdrew peaceably when a Mexican revolt in 1833 placed Antonio López de Santa Anna in power. By military might, Santa Anna became the undisputed leader of Mexico.

Thus on February 23, 1836, in retaliation against the Texans for declaring themselves free from Mexico in 1835, Santa Anna attacked the Texans who were fortified at the Alamo defending their freedom. That is why the Mexican-American War actually extended from that date until a peace treaty was signed between the two countries on February 2, 1848.

During the twelve-year period of 1836–1848, it was never the American government's desire to be at war with the Mexican government, but it seemed that the United States was caught in a web of destiny that forced them to fight Mexico, no matter how hard they tried to avoid it.

INTRODUCTION

In mid-1835, when the people of Texas declared themselves independent of Mexico and established their own republic, the government of Mexico was angry. The anger did not subside as time passed. On December 4, 1835, Mexican General Martín Perfecto de Cos brazenly led his 1,400 troops into San Antonio, Texas, and occupied the old Franciscan mission known as the Alamo.

The townspeople were frightened and sent riders to the nearest Texas army outpost to inform the leading officers that General Cos and his troops had taken over the land and buildings of the Alamo. The riders made it clear that the people of San Antonio were in grave danger.

On the morning of December 5, a well-armed band of some three hundred Texan soldiers surrounded Cos and his troops in the Alamo.

Five days of battle ensued, and by December 10, 115 of Cos's men had been killed and 185 had deserted him and run away. Cos and his 1,100 remaining troops threw down their weapons and surrendered to the 290 Texans who were still alive and strong.

When word of the rout reached General Antonio López de Santa Anna in Mexico City, he gathered his military leaders for a joint conference.

News of the conference reached Texas, with reports that Santa Anna had declared that he would personally lead his Mexican troops on a punitive sweep across Texas. He would begin by punishing the people of San Antonio for backing the Texan troops in their attack on General Cos and his men.

At the time, Texas army headquarters under General Sam Houston were located at Washington-on-the-Brazos in southeastern Texas. Houston received the news of Santa Anna's threat and knew at once that he would have to enlarge his army considerably to defeat Santa Anna's troops when they came to punish the people of San Antonio. Knowing they were going to San Antonio, Houston feared they would use the Alamo as a fort as General Cos had.

General Houston knew it would take Santa Anna better than two months to lead his army from Mexico City to San Antonio. He sent word by Texas newspapers and by word of mouth that he needed at least five thousand volunteers to join the army by March 1 so they could meet Santa Anna and his troops head-on when they arrived at San Antonio.

Time passed, and in mid-February 1836, Houston sent Lieutenant Colonel William Travis to go into Texas towns and challenge Texas men to go with him and destroy the Alamo before Santa Anna and his troops got there.

And now begins the story of the Kane Legacy. It begins not in Texas, but in Massachusetts; not in the winter of 1836, but in the spring of 1834. This first story in the trilogy reaches a heart-gripping climax on the afternoon of March 5, 1836, when a line is drawn in the sand with the tip of a sword on the plaza at the Alamo.

ONE

It was a solid, jarring punch and caught thick-bodied thirty-two-year-old Kenton Roach with his mouth open. His head snapped back, and his teeth clacked like a steel trap. He staggered backward; then forty-nine-year-old Abram Kane came after him and sent a powerful right fist to his midsection. Roach made a gagging sound as the wind blew from his mouth. Then the tall, muscular Kane smashed a left to his jaw. Roach dropped to his knees, his eyes rolling back in his head. Wind sawed out of his throat as he fell facedown on the hard wooden dock.

It was a warm spring morning in early April 1834 in Boston, Massachusetts. At this particular section of the docks in Boston Harbor, a large group of men who were employed by the Dixon Ship Lines were in the process of unloading cotton bales from a ship that had sailed from Alabama and berthed the night before.

Three of Kenton Roach's friends rushed up to him as he lay on the dock unconscious. One of them, Hal Ripley, looked up at Abram Kane, who had now been joined by his four sons, Alex, twenty-eight years of age; Abel, twenty-six; Adam, twenty-three; and Alan, twenty. "Abram," Ripley said grimly, "I told him not to test you, but he wouldn't listen."

Abram, who stood six feet four and weighed some 220 muscular pounds, said, "I wish he *had* listened to you, Hal."

"Kenton had to learn the hard way, like so many others here on the docks," responded Ripley. He ran his gaze among the dock workers. "I hope if any more of you want to try to take the title Bareknuckle Champion of the Boston Harbor Docks from Abram, you will forget it. Remember what you just saw here and what many of you have seen in days gone by. It will get the notion out of your head."

"Yeah!" Ben Delsart, an older dock worker, spoke up. "In his twenty years on these docks, Abram has never initiated a fight, but when a fight is forced on him, he does what he has to do. So far, every dumb cluck who has tried to whip him has ended up the loser."

Delsart paused, ran his gaze over the four Kane brothers, who were very close to the same height and muscular build as their father, then looked back at the crowd of dock workers. "Let me tell you somethin' else, in case you don't know it. Abram's four sons here have also proven themselves rugged fighters when they've been forced to do it. Their forefathers came to this country from Ireland, and Abram and his sons are known on these docks as the Fightin' Irishmen."

A few of the men in the crowd smiled and nodded. Most of them showed no feelings, but there were several who scowled at Ben Delsart's words.

Ben frowned at the scowlers and said levelly, "Some of you resent the fact that Abram and his sons are Christians. They remain aloof from those of you who use foul language and drink liquor. Just like I do, because I'm a born-again child of God too. We all know that fightin' among dock workers, no matter where the docks are, is nothin' new, but the Christian witness and standards upheld by the Kanes often makes them targets of both verbal and physical abuse. You'd come after me too, if I wasn't seventy-six years old and a bit crippled. Even some of your best friends would get on you if you picked on this old man."

There was dead silence as Ben stepped close to Abram Kane and his sons.

Finally, another of Kenton Roach's friends, who had been kneeling beside him, stood up. "Kenton's conscious now. We'll have him on his feet in a couple minutes. Let's all get back to work before Mr. Dixon comes out here from the office."

Heads nodded, and the men began to move back to the carts they were using to transport the cotton bales from the ship to the edge of the dock some three hundred feet away.

On this particular day, Adam and Alan Kane had been working close with two brothers, Will and Jack Benson. Will was in his early thirties, and Jack was in his late twenties. Both men, along with their wives and children, had recently come to Boston from Portland, Maine, and joined the same church where the Kanes and Ben Delsart were members. It had been through Abram Kane's influence with John Dixon that Will and Jack had been hired with the Dixon Ship Lines. They had just started with the company that morning.

Will and Jack had been standing beside Adam and Alan since the fight started.

The Kane sons turned to their father, whose sand-colored hair and sideburns were already showing a great deal of silver. Alex said, "Papa, I hate to tell you this, but I was watching that big, burly Lee Nevins while all of this was going on."

Abram's eyebrows arched. "Oh? What was he doing?"

"He kept looking at you with evil eyes."

"I noticed that too, Abram," said Ben Delsart. "I've heard that he's been tryin' to start a fight with you ever since he came to work here. That so?"

"It is," spoke up Adam Kane. "Papa has done his best to keep it from happening, but I'm pretty sure he's going to have to fight Nevins before too long."

Young Alan Kane, whose hair was sand-colored like his brothers', looked at his father. "You really think you'll have to get into it with Nevins, Papa?"

Abram sighed and nodded. "Yeah. He keeps pushing me harder every chance he gets."

"So who is this guy?" Will Benson said.

Alan sniffed and ran a palm over his nose. "Nevins came to Boston five weeks ago and was hired by Mr. Dixon immediately because of his dock experience. Word soon spread among the rest of us workers that he had previously worked on the docks at Port Norris, New Jersey, on the Delaware Bay. He learned to fight on the Port Norris docks, and the last couple of years he apparently took on all challengers and always emerged the victor. He's a big, husky guy, twenty-eight years old. Word is that Nevins himself usually started most of the fights he got into and always put his opponents down."

"Yeah," spoke up Abel, "all the Dixon Ship Lines workers know this about Nevins, and most of them steer clear."

Alex looked at the Benson brothers. "The first day he came to work here, Nevins learned about Papa being dubbed the Bareknuckle Champion of the Boston Harbor Docks twenty years ago. He's been trying to prod Papa into a fight ever since. Let me tell you, Abram Kane has never gone looking for a fight. So far, he has ignored Nevins and, as much as possible, has avoided him. But if the big guy keeps it up, our papa will have to take him on."

"Well," said Adam to his youngest brother and the Benson brothers, "we'd better get back to our job. Those cotton bales won't move themselves."

Abram ran his gaze to all four sons and the Benson brothers. "Ben and I need to get back to our job. See you at lunchtime."

They scattered in three directions: Abram with Ben, Alex with Abel, and the Benson brothers, with Adam and Alan, went back to their cart. Soon Adam, Alan, and the Benson brothers were loading cotton bales together, while Will and Jack asked questions about the Kanes. They wanted to know more about their Irish roots. They were especially interested in learning about when the Abram Kane family had come to know Jesus Christ as Lord and Saviour.

Adam informed the Bensons that the family name *Kane* in Ireland had been *O'Kane.* "We'll explain about the change after we give you some basic information."

"Sounds interesting," Jack said.

While lifting the heavy bales, placing them on the cart, then running the cart across the dock to the big stack and unloading them, Adam and Alan went on to tell the Bensons some family history. Son of Abner and Elizabeth O'Kane, born February 21, 1785, in Dublin, Ireland, their father had crossed the Atlantic to the United States in late 1792 with his parents. They settled in Pawtucket, Rhode Island.

As time passed, they became acquainted with their neighbors, and in March of 1793, some neighbors in Pawtucket invited the O'Kanes to a Bible-believing church. After attending the services for a few weeks, eight-year-old Abram found Jesus Christ as Saviour, as did his parents.

Within a year, Abram's paternal grandparents, Alexander and Maureen O'Kane also moved from Dublin to Pawtucket and soon received Christ as well. Abram was brought up in that solid church and in his Christian home was taught the value of family living and hard work.

Alan paused to take a breath after the four of them had loaded the cart again. "As far back as we can trace the O'Kanes in Ireland, though they were not Christians, they were traditionally honest, hard-working people with strong family ties. At least this part of their lives has had an influence on us Kanes today."

Will Benson smiled. "Mighty good influence, I'd say."

"Sure is," Jack said.

Adam grinned. "Now, about the name change. In December of 1793, our grandparents Abner and Elizabeth O'Kane and our great-grandparents Alexander and Maureen O'Kane decided to change their last name simply to Kane. We've never been able to learn why they decided on this change, but we love our last name."

"We sure do," said Alan. "Then our great-grandfather died in 1795, and our great-grandmother joined him in heaven in 1798."

The Benson brothers nodded. "What a joy to know they are in heaven," Jack said.

Alan grinned. "For sure. We'll all be together again some glad day."

"Amen," Adam said. "More of the story now. In 1804, when our father was nineteen, he married eighteen-year-old Kitty Foyle, who was a member of the church in Pawtucket and a fine, dedicated Christian. Papa and Mama moved to Boston shortly thereafter and found the good, solid church we belong to. And you Bensons now too."

"It's a good one, all right," Will said.

Adam went on. "Shortly after coming to Boston, our father found employment as a dock worker here in Boston Harbor. It was a different company then. Two years later, Alex was born. He was named after our paternal great-grandfather, Alexander. Some two years later, Abel was born. Three years later, I came along. Then eighteen months after that, our parents finally had a girl. Keeping with the O'Kane tradition of always giving their children a name that started with an *A*—which had begun in Ireland over a hundred years earlier—they named their new little daughter Angela."

"Then in 1814, I was born," Alan said.

"I want to say this, fellows," Will said. "In the short time our families have been members of the church, we certainly have come to love all the Kanes a lot. We think a lot of Alex and his wife, Libby, and Abel and his wife, Vivian."

"And, of course, your father too," Jack said. "We're so sorry about your mother's ill health and that she isn't able to come to church. And we've been told that your sister, Angela, is a sweet person too. I guess she stays home with your mother all the time?"

"That's right," Alan said.

Will cleared his throat gently. "Ah...just when did the tuberculosis strike your mother?"

"This tragedy wormed its way into our home in 1830," replied Adam. "Mama is wasting away and dying a little each day before our eyes. The best doctors in Boston tell us they can do nothing for her. The disease is going to take her life." Tears formed in Adam's eyes.

Alan said softly, his own eyes watering, "We're not blaming the Lord for allowing Mama to have this disease. He has a plan for every one of His born-again children. We have prayed for her recovery, but so far she has only grown worse. One thing is for sure: when Mama goes to heaven, she will join our other loved ones there, and one day we'll be with her again."

The Benson brothers now had tears in their eyes. "Bless your hearts," Will said.

"What a sweet testimony you have," Jack said.

As the four men pushed the full cart toward the far edge of the docks once again, Adam Kane said, "Let me tell you more about our precious sister. Angela refuses to leave our ailing mother's side. At twenty-one, she has yet to enjoy the company of young men. Though many would-be suitors in the church have sought her attention, she is so devoted to caring for our dying mother that she simply doesn't have time for romance."

"That's for sure," Alan said. "Angela tends to Mama's every need and takes care of the house, keeping it clean and in order. She also does the marketing and the cooking for Papa and Adam and me. All of this consumes most of her day. She often works late into the night. She"—Alan choked up, swallowed hard, and went on—"she seldom gives any thought to her own needs and dreams, knowing that in God's time she will be able to focus on her own life."

"She's so utterly unselfish," Adam said. "Right now, all her thoughts and energies are centered on our dear mother and her family's needs."

"God bless that sweet Angela," Will Benson said.

"Yes." Alan nodded as he wiped tears from his cheeks.

The conversation ceased as they drew near the place where the cotton was stacked. Soon they drew their cart to a stop between two carts where other dock workers were unloading bales and paying them no mind.

They paused to drink some water from the jugs that were kept aboard the cart.

When they had each devoured a sufficient amount of water and were ready to start unloading the bales, Adam Kane said, "Though we pray daily about this situation, we're human, and Mama's condition keeps everyone in the family on edge...especially Papa. He carries her suffering every waking hour of every day. Papa has said that he knows the Lord has allowed Mama to have this disease for a reason, and though our whole family, our pastor and his wife, and many close friends in the church have been praying for God to heal her of the disease, it becomes progressively worse. Only recently Papa told the family that he knows it is God's will for Mama to go to heaven very soon."

Alan nodded. "And though Papa has accepted this, as a mortal being, the knowledge that his beloved wife will die soon gnaws at his insides."

"I can understand that," Will Benson said.

"But let me tell you this," Jack said. "Will and I and our wives will be praying for God's grace on your whole family in this time of great trial."

Adam smiled. "Thank you."

"Yes." Alan smiled. "This means very much to us. Thank you."

At that moment, all four men saw Abram Kane come around the half-empty cart next to them. "Will...Jack...I want to thank you for praying for our family."

Abram saw their surprise at seeing him appear and said, "Ben and I are working on this cart to your right, along with our other co-workers. I only noticed it was you a few minutes ago. I couldn't help but hear your conversation." He set his soft gaze on his sons. "Adam...Alan...I deeply appreciate your feelings toward me in the burden I carry for your dying mother. It—it is quite difficult for me to face the fact that she will soon be going to heaven and I will not have her love and companionship here on earth in the latter years of my life."

Adam and Alan stepped up to their father simultaneously, as if it had been rehearsed, and wrapped their arms around him. With tears in their eyes, they told him how much they loved him and that they would always stand by him when their mother was gone.

While tears spilled down his cheeks, Abram hugged them back and thanked them for being the good sons they were. As he and his sons let go of each other, Abram said, "See you at lunchtime."

When Adam and Alan rejoined the Benson brothers at their cart, Abram was still on the edge of weeping. He decided to take a little time to gain control of his emotions before returning to Ben Delsart and the other workers at their cart. He made his way along the edge of the dock until he came to the end of it and stood staring beyond narrow Deer Island at the deep blue Atlantic Ocean.

Abram's heart was heavy, but he was not wallowing in self-pity, nor was he bitter toward the Lord for allowing Kitty to have the dreadful disease. He did, however, have grievous feelings toward the situation. Watching his precious wife slowly dying kept him constantly on edge.

Abram Kane's mind went back to the day when he first caught sight of the fair colleen Kitty Foyle. She was standing alone on the beach of Dublin Bay on the Irish Sea, looking out at the sunlit surface of blue. Her Irish red-gold hair glowed in the summer sunshine, and as she turned toward him and smiled, he was struck by her bright, sparkling green eyes. In that instant, his heart leaped toward the beautiful Kitty Foyle.

They began to talk and found that they had much in common, and that evening, on their first date, they fell in love.

As the years rolled by in his mind, a sad smile crossed Abram's features as he pictured his beloved wife on the screen of his mind. Her red-gold hair was now streaked with silver, and her long illness had dulled her once brilliant locks. Her green eyes were now filled with pain, yet her smile still shone whenever she saw him enter the room. The love between them was almost a tangible thing, and in Abram's mind she was as lovely as the first day their eyes met on the beach of Dublin Bay.

Abram raised his eyes toward the azure sky. "Lord, I don't even pretend to understand why this dreadful thing is happening to my precious Kitty. I know that You have allowed it, and that is all that really matters. Please help me accept Your will, and give me Your peace and Your grace.

"Dear Father, You watched Your only begotten Son suffer and die on Calvary's cross, so I know that You can feel my sorrow and pain. Help me to trust and not be afraid. Use me as Your witness to those around me. In Jesus' name, I ask it. Amen and amen."

Squaring his shoulders, Abram Kane turned from the sunlit sea and returned to the men, who were just taking the last bales off the cart.

By the time Abram, Ben, and their fellow workers had returned to the ship with the empty cart, it was noon. A number of cotton bales had been placed on the dock for the workers to sit on while eating lunch. All of them were carrying lunch pails and found places to sit.

Abram was just sitting down with his four sons, the Benson brothers, and Ben Delsart when Adam glanced off to his right, then turned back to his father. "Papa, here comes Lee Nevins. He's got his eyes fixed on you."

The others in their group looked up and saw Nevins's hulking form coming their way.

"Papa," Alan said, "you want me to take him on? He and I are closer to the same age."

Abram shook his head. "No, son. Even if you whipped him, it wouldn't change his insatiable desire to take my title from me."

As Nevins drew near, Abram's sons and friends saw the cocky sneer on his face, a definite signal that he was going to do his best to prod Abram into a fight.

TWO

Lee Nevins stepped up, throwing his bulky shadow over Abram Kane, his big body suggesting something powerful and difficult to stop.

The hostility in his eyes was a still and immobile thing as he looked down at Kane and growled, "Nobody in Boston Harbor is gonna believe you're still the bareknuckle champ on these docks unless you have it out with me and whip me, Kane!"

With every eye in the crowd of Dixon Ship Lines workers on him, Abram Kane rose to his feet and looked down with disdain at the shorter man, who easily outweighed him by forty pounds. "I never asked for the title, Nevins. If you want to tell them you're the champ, go ahead. It won't take long to find out. You'll have plenty of challengers. For that matter, my sons are excellent fighters. Any one of them could whip you."

Nevins shot an ugly sidelong glance at the Kane brothers, who were still seated. All four met his fierce gaze without flinching. Alan said in an even tone, "Any one of us would square off with you right now, Nevins, but we don't have the title. However, if—"

"Forget it!" snapped Nevins as he turned back to Abram. "Well, you gonna fight me?"

Abram gave him a calm look. "Instead of you and I going to fisticuffs, how about we talk about where you're going to spend eternity?"

Nevins's brow furrowed. His eyes went blank. Blinking, he said, "What're you talkin' about?"

"The same thing my sons and I have talked to many of these men about. Are you going to heaven or hell when you die?"

Sudden rage grew like a spreading cancer inside Lee Nevins's chest. "Oh yeah, I've heard about you religious fanatics."

"We're not religious," countered Abram. "We have salvation in the Lord Jesus Christ. People with Christ in their hearts and their sins washed away in His blood have salvation. They go to heaven when they die. People with religion do not have salvation. Hell is their destination. Don't call us religious. We're saved. You can be saved too if you will let me sit down and talk to you with an open Bible in my hands."

Nevins showed his teeth as his eyes flashed in fury. "I ain't interested, Kane!"

Suddenly, Nevins felt the piercing eyes of the four Kane brothers on him. He ran his gaze over their faces then looked back at Abram. His features turned dark with angry blood as he drew a deep breath and snapped loudly, "You're a yellow coward, Kane! You won't fight me because you're old and gray! Why don't you just grab your cane and hobble home to your sickly old lady, and—"

The wicked slur cast on Kitty brought Abram Kane's right fist to Lee Nevins's jaw like a bullet out of a barrel, and Nevins was instantly on his back on the hard surface of the dock.

Some of Nevins's friends knelt over him. One of them, a big man named Jake Bullard, who had become Lee Nevins's closest friend on the docks, was trying to bring him back to consciousness by splashing canteen water in his face. Every man in the area looked on, eyes wide.

Abram stood over the unconscious man and watched his friends hastily attempting to bring him out of it. His temper raged. *Lee Nevins would dare to defame Kitty by calling her a sickly old lady?*

Soon Nevins began rolling his head back and forth, making a groaning sound. Abram watched as the man he had put down finally opened his eyes, obviously attempting to clear them.

Abram's four sons moved up, two on each side of him, and Abel said,

"You did the right thing, Papa. He asked for it when he called Mama a sickly old lady."

Some of the other workers in the crowd heard Abel's words and voiced their agreement.

Nevins lay flat on his back, still stunned and dizzy. He blinked against the brassy glare of the midday sun and tried to focus on the rigid, square-shouldered form of Abram Kane that hovered over him. Several of the dock workers moved up close and looked down at Nevins. Some voices, raspy and garbled, shouted at him to get up.

The circle of faces was a colorless blur to Nevins as he made another groaning sound and rolled to his knees.

Alex and Abel Kane pushed past Lee Nevins's friends, grabbed him by the upper arms, and lifted him to his feet. Holding him tightly so he could not move, they waited for their father to step up close.

When Abram did so, the crowd of dock workers looked on as Abram said sharply, "Lee, you'd better not ever speak of my wife like that again!"

Nevins blinked, shook his head to clear it, and met Abram's level gaze. He licked his lips. "Abram, I was wrong to do that. I'm sorry. Will you please forgive me?"

A soft look came over the tall, rugged Irishman's eyes. A few seconds passed. "Yes, Lee. You're forgiven. The Lord in heaven has forgiven me when I've done Him wrong and asked for forgiveness. I certainly can forgive you."

Nevins's brow puckered. "Thank you, Abram."

Suddenly big Jake Bullard stomped up to Abram and growled, "I'm sick of you poundin' men down, Kane!" As he spoke, he threw his right fist toward Abram's jaw.

Abram adeptly ducked under it and sent a fist to Bullard's midsection. The big man grunted, bent over, and took two steps back. Then suddenly he rushed at Abram, swinging both fists. One of those fists caught Abram's jaw, snapping his head to the side. Bullard leaned in, ready to punch him again, but Abram sidestepped. The big man stumbled off balance, tripped over his own feet, and fell to the dock.

The muscular Irishman looked down at him. "Better just stay there, Jake. I don't want to have to hit you anymore."

Bullard muttered something, jumped to his feet, and dove in a long, flying tackle. But Abram moved swiftly, avoiding him. Bullard hit the hard wooden floor of the dock, made a sound like an angry bear, and leaped to his feet. Balling both fists, he made the same sound again and rushed Abram, who beat him to the punch with a hard left to the nose, then a crack to his jaw with his right.

The big man fell, shaking his head, then got up, blood bubbling from his nose.

Abram stood ready with both fists clenched. "Give it up, Jake."

Bullard showed his teeth, growling like a wild beast, and charged. Abram's left fist slammed his right jaw, staggering him. Then to finish the fight, Abram sent a piston-style blow with his right fist to Jake's left jaw. The sound of it echoed across the docks as the big man went down, unconscious.

Two of Bullard's friends picked him up and dragged him away, giving Abram Kane hard looks.

At the same time, Lee Nevins moved up to Abram and said, "No question about it. You are without a doubt the Bareknuckle Champion of the Boston Harbor Docks." As he spoke, he extended his right hand toward Abram.

A smile curved Abram's lips as he shook hands with Lee Nevins. "Like I told you, Lee, I never asked for the title."

"You don't need to," said Lee. "You've shown it to be true by winning every time some new hopeful comes along with the desire to capture your title."

At this point, the crowd dispersed, and the men went back to work.

The late afternoon sun was setting over Boston when the last of the cotton bales had been unloaded from the ship to the edge of the dock, where they would be picked up by wagons from different companies.

Ben Delsart told Abram Kane he would see him the next day and walked away with three other men about his age.

Will and Jack Benson were still with Adam and Alan Kane, who stood by their father as the other two Kane brothers came their way. When Alex and Abel drew up, Abram said, "Well, boys, since it's quitting time, let's head for home."

At that instant, Alan noticed one of the office men coming toward them. "Papa, here comes Carl Bates. I don't like the look on his face."

"He *is* frowning a bit, isn't he?" said Abram.

A small, thin baldheaded man of fifty, Carl Bates came to a stop. "Abram, Mr. Dixon wants to talk to you. He just learned about your fights today with Kenton Roach, Lee Nevins, and Jake Bullard."

Abram said defensively, "I didn't start any of those fights, Carl. All three of them attacked me."

"That's right, Mr. Bates," Will Benson spoke up. "Jack and I saw all three fights. Abram is telling the truth."

"He sure is, Mr. Bates," said Jack Benson. "Not one of those fights was his fault."

Bates managed a slight smile. "I'm just the messenger. Mr. Dixon wants to talk to Abram."

Abram laid his hands on the shoulders of Will and Jack Benson. "Thanks, Will...Jack, for speaking on my behalf." He turned to his sons. "Alex, Libby is waiting for you to come home. Abel, Vivian is waiting for *you* to come home.

"And Adam and Alan, your sister will be watching for the three of us. Get going now. Tell Angela to go ahead with supper if I'm not there soon. I'll eat my food later."

The Kane brothers and the Bensons watched Abram stride toward the Dixon Ship Lines office building with Carl Bates. They noticed that Bates was taking two steps for every one of Abram's.

The Kanes bade the Benson brothers good night and headed for home. Alex and Libby and Abel and Vivian lived in apartments on the same block as the Abram and Kitty Kane house on Mulberry Street, which was twenty-two blocks from the docks.

As the Kane brothers walked briskly toward home, they talked about their father's three fights that day and shared their joy that Lee Nevins had asked to be forgiven for what he had called their mother. They also spoke of how proud they were of their father, who was nearing fifty years of age, but was still the Bareknuckle Champion of the Boston Harbor Docks...though he had never sought the title.

The conversation then turned to Adam's girlfriend, Mary Sue Bannigan. She and her wealthy parents were members of the same church as the Kanes. Everyone in the Kane family was expecting that Adam would soon ask Mary Sue for her hand in marriage. His brothers told him they hoped it would happen any day now. Adam told them he was waiting for the Lord to show him when he should propose.

As the Kane brothers arrived on the block where they lived, Alex and Abel entered the apartment building, and the other two brothers moved on down the block toward their home.

When Abram Kane and Carl Bates entered the Dixon Ship Lines office building, they went past the two unoccupied desks of the secretaries who worked in the front office. The secretaries had already gone home for the day.

They moved past Bates's office in the hallway and the offices of other men on staff and came to the last office, which belonged to the company owner, forty-one-year-old John Dixon. John had inherited the company when his father, Harold Dixon, had died some four years earlier. John knew the shipping business well, for he had worked with his father since joining the company in 1825.

John Dixon's door stood slightly ajar as Carl and Abram drew up to it. Carl stepped close and tapped on the door. "Mr. Dixon, I have Abram Kane here."

"Come on in, Carl," came Dixon's baritone voice.

Carl pushed the door open, moved in, then stepped aside to allow Abram into the office.

As Abram walked toward the desk where the company owner sat, Dixon looked past him and said, "Thank you, Carl. I'll talk to Abram alone."

"Yes sir." Bates pulled the door closed as he backed into the hallway.

Rising to his feet, Dixon gestured toward a wooden chair that stood in front of the desk. "Sit down, Abram."

A bit on edge, Abram eased onto the chair as his boss sat down. He then looked John Dixon in the eye and waited for him to speak.

"First of all, tell me how Kitty is doing."

A bit surprised, Abram said, "About the same, sir. It is quite apparent that she doesn't have long to live. I appreciate your asking, though."

Dixon cleared his throat. "I know Kitty's tuberculosis has weighed heavily on you. I am so sorry."

"I appreciate your understanding about it, Mr. Dixon."

Dixon nodded. "Well, let's get to the reason I asked Carl to bring you in here."

The Irishman nodded solemnly.

"Abram, I know you've been the bareknuckle champ on these docks for a long time. We've talked about some of your fights before."

Abram nodded. "Mm-hmm."

"I don't recall you ever having two fights on any given day."

Abram nodded again. "Mm-hmm."

Dixon frowned. "But today I understand you had *three* fights. The first with Kenton Roach, the second with Lee Nevins, and the third with Jake Bullard. Correct?"

"Yes sir," Abram responded.

"Who started these fights?"

"Wasn't me, sir. All three of those guys started the fights. I didn't do one thing to cause them."

Dixon drew a deep breath and let it out slowly. "I'm having a hard time believing that you didn't do something to—"

There was a knock at the office door.

Dixon looked past the Irishman. "Yes?"

The door opened, and Carl Bates stepped in. "Mr. Dixon, your two newest dock men are here. Will and Jack Benson. They wish to speak to you while you are talking to Abram."

Dixon raised his eyebrows. "Oh? Why?"

"If you will let them come in, they can tell you, sir."

John Dixon chewed on his lower lip, thinking the situation over. "All right. Bring them in."

The Benson brothers moved into the office past Bates, who backed out and closed the door.

When Will and Jack stepped up beside the chair where Abram Kane sat, Dixon said, "Okay, why are you here?"

"Sir," Will said, "Jack and I felt from all the things we've heard about the fights Abram has been in over these years that you might think he started those fights today."

Dixon ran his gaze between them. "I was just questioning him about that very thing."

"Well, Mr. Dixon," Jack said, "Will and I wanted to make sure you know that Abram did not start any of the fights today. We witnessed all three. Those three men pushed him into it. He was forced to fight them."

Will interjected. "Let me tell you about Lee Nevins, Mr. Dixon. He was pushing Abram to fight him, and when Abram was trying to keep from it, Nevins said—and I quote—'You're a yellow coward, Kane! You won't fight me because you're old and gray! Why don't you just grab your cane and hobble home to your sickly old lady?' It was then that Abram hit him with a powerful punch that knocked him out, Mr. Dixon."

"Wouldn't you have done that if *you* were Abram?" Jack said.

John Dixon's face paled. He looked at Jack, then at Abram. "I can't blame you at all for punching him out. He had it coming."

Both Benson brothers were nodding their agreement as Abram said, "Thank you, sir. That's how I felt about it. But let me tell you this. After Lee had returned to consciousness, right in front of that whole crowd of dock workers who were looking on, he asked me to forgive him for what he had said about Kitty. I told him he was forgiven, and I have no doubt that he and I will be friends from now on."

John Dixon smiled. "Well, I'm glad to hear that." He rubbed the back of his neck. "Will and Jack have testified that you didn't start the other two fights either, Abram. Let me just ask that you try harder not to get into fights here on the job, okay?"

Abram's eyes showed his feelings. "I'll do my best, sir. Thank you for understanding. I—I was afraid you were going to fire me."

Dixon chuckled. "It would take a whole lot more than this to bring me to fire you, Abram. You go on home to Kitty now. I'll see you tomorrow."

Abram thanked his boss one more time for understanding his situation, and when he and the Benson brothers were outside, he thanked them for caring enough to come and tell Mr. Dixon exactly how the fights got started.

Will grinned. "Hey, my brother in Christ, we Christians are supposed to stand by each other."

"Right!" Jack said.

Abram smiled broadly. "Right!"

When Adam and Alan arrived home, Angela was in the kitchen, cooking supper. Hearing her brothers talking, she hurried up the hall toward them. As she drew near, she looked around. "Where's Papa?"

"When we left work," Adam said, "he was going into Mr. Dixon's office, Sis. We need to tell you and Mama what happened today. Is Mama awake?"

"I believe so," Angela said. "Let's go up to her room and see."

Kitty was awake when they entered her room. Adam and Alan told her and their sister about the three fights their father had been forced into that day and explained that he had knocked Lee Nevins out with one punch when Lee called their mother a "sickly old lady." The brothers then related how John Dixon had sent Carl Bates to bring their father to his office, saying that the boss wanted to talk to him about the fights.

Kitty's brow furrowed. "I hope Mr. Dixon doesn't fire your father."

Angela blinked. "I hope not either, Mama."

"We should know soon," Adam said. "However it turns out, Papa won't be long getting home."

"I've got supper on the stove," Angela said.

Worry clouded Kitty Kane's pallid face as she placed the ever-present handkerchief over her mouth, trying to stifle the cough that wanted to erupt into the room.

Getting the cough under control, Kitty turned to her daughter. "Honey, don't set a place for me tonight. I'm just too tired to sit at the table. I'm going to try to take a nap while the rest of you eat supper. I believe I'll feel better if I can get a nap." She smiled affectionately at her daughter.

Adam and Alan looked on as Angela said, "Okay, Mama. I'll check on you later, and if you're hungry then, I'll bring you a tray of food." Angela brushed a hand over her mother's forehead. "You must try to eat."

"I'll try, lass. I promise. Just let me rest a bit, but please, when your papa gets home, I want to know what happened between him and Mr. Dixon."

"We'll see that you find out, Mama," Alan said.

With that, Adam and Alan each kissed their mother's forehead and headed out of the room.

Angela also kissed her mother's forehead and followed her brothers. When she reached the bedroom door, she paused and looked back at her ailing mother. Angela could see the worried look on her mother's face, even though her eyes were closed. "Please help us, Lord," Angela whispered as she headed down the hall.

A half hour later, as Abram Kane entered the house, a tantalizing aroma of hot food brought saliva to his mouth. The first person he saw was Angela, her long blond hair dancing on her shoulders as she came running to him.

Embracing her father, she said, "Oh, Papa! Is everything all right?"

Abram squeezed his daughter tightly in his strong arms, then looked into her blue eyes. "Everything's all right, sweetheart. Mr. Dixon didn't fire me."

"Oh, praise the Lord!" Angela said as Adam and Alan came running up the hall from the parlor.

"So you didn't get fired, Papa?" Adam said.

"No. Will and Jack Benson came to Mr. Dixon's office while he was questioning me about the fights and convinced him I had not started any of them. Mr. Dixon felt bad when he learned what Lee Nevins had called your mother, and said he couldn't blame me for punching him out." He looked at his two sons. "I assume you told Angela and your mother about all of this."

Both brothers nodded. "Yes, we did."

"Angela, how's Mama doing?" Abram asked.

"She's had a bad day, Papa. She already told me she doesn't want any supper."

"Oh. Bless her heart."

"Papa," Alan said. "while you wash up for supper, I'll run and tell Mama that you didn't get fired. She wanted to know about that as soon as you got home."

"Thanks, son, but I'll go up and tell her. I need to see her for a few minutes anyhow." He turned to Angela. "Honey, if I'm not back down here when supper's ready, you and your brothers go ahead and eat."

Abram dashed to the staircase and quickly made his way up to the second floor and down the hall to Kitty's room. She had heard him coming down the hall, and her eyes were on him when he stepped inside. He kissed her forehead, then, holding her hand, sat down on the edge of the bed. "Sweetheart, Mr. Dixon didn't fire me."

"Oh, thank God!" she whispered.

Abram could tell that his dear wife was definitely feeling bad. She was very pale, and her eyes revealed that she'd had a difficult day. He took both her hands and tried to encourage her.

She thanked him for his encouraging words, then sniffed the aroma that was coming up from the kitchen. "Honey, supper smells awfully good. You go on down there and eat with the kids."

Abram managed a smile. He bent over and kissed her cheek. Then he rose to his feet. "I'll be back later."

Kitty smiled. "I'll look forward to it!"

THREE

When Abram arrived in the kitchen, heads were bowed at the table, and Alan was leading his brother and sister in prayer, thanking the Lord for the food. Abram waited silently in the doorway.

Alan also prayed for their mother, asking God to give her strength and to ease the pain she suffered from the tuberculosis.

Abram felt a pang in his heart.

Then Alan asked the Lord to give their father the comfort and grace he needed as their mother drew closer to her last day on earth.

Again, Abram felt a pang in his heart.

When Alan closed off his prayer, the three kids looked at their father as he took his place in his usual chair at the head of the table.

Angela set her soft blue eyes on her father. "Papa, did Mama perk up when you told her Mr. Dixon hadn't fired you?"

"Yes," Abram said. "Her words were, 'Oh, thank God!' "

All three of Abram's offspring smiled, but Angela's smile faded. "Papa, can you tell that Mama's strength is failing rapidly?"

Abram nodded. "Yes, I can tell."

The four of them discussed Kitty's worsening condition for a few minutes; then Angela looked at the older of the two brothers and asked, "Adam, are you going to see Mary Sue this evening?"

"I plan to, Sis. I haven't made a date with her, but I'm going over to the Bannigan house to see her after supper."

When they had almost finished their meal, Alan's heart began to flutter in his chest as his nerves tightened. He ran his gaze over the faces of his father and siblings. "Uh...I have something very important to tell you."

All eyes turned to the youngest son of Abram and Kitty Kane.

Alan's lips quivered. "I—I've been thinking about getting into another line of work. I have decided to quit my job with Dixon Ship Lines and go to Texas."

Abram Kane's jaw dropped open. Angela stopped chewing her mouthful of apple pie. Adam dropped his fork. Suddenly the silence was deafening.

The senior Kane's pale blue eyes seemed to penetrate to the joints and marrow of Alan's soul. "*Texas?* Why Texas, son?"

"I don't want to load and unload freight in Boston Harbor the rest of my life. I want to do something that can one day develop into me being my own boss. I want to have my own business."

Abram blinked. "Loading and unloading freight is honest work, Alan."

"I know that, Papa," Alan said, "but—"

"I'll ask it again, son. Why *Texas*? Why can't you find a way to work for yourself here in Massachusetts?"

"There's no way I could ever do anything in Massachusetts but load and unload freight. Take Adam for instance."

The older brother's head bobbed at the mention of his name.

Angela was chewing her apple pie once more as Alan said, "Here Adam is, twenty-three years old, Papa. He would like to take Mary Sue for his wife, but he can't afford it. If he ever does marry her, they'll have to live as poor as church mice unless Mr. Bannigan forks over some cash now and then."

"Tell you what, Alan," Adam said. "Mr. Bannigan is looking for a young man to work in his store, and he has indicated that if the person he hires does a good job, someday he will be a partner in the business. Maybe you ought to look into it."

Alan locked eyes with him. "If it's such a good deal, big brother, why haven't you taken the job? You are the one who's going to become his son-in-law, not me."

Adam nodded. "This is so, but selling clothes for the rest of my life doesn't appeal to me. Mary Sue keeps begging me to take the job, but I keep trying to get her to understand that it just isn't what I want to do."

"Me neither," Alan said. "What I want to do is become a cattle rancher."

Abram's eyes widened, as did Angela's and Adam's.

Angela gasped. "A cattle rancher?"

Alan grinned at her. "That's right, little sis. A cattle rancher."

Abram cleared his throat. "Well, why go to Texas, son? People in Massachusetts have cattle."

"I know, Papa, but Massachusetts doesn't have cattle ranches. The farmers here who raise cattle only have a few. Nobody makes a living with them. As I said, I want to become a cattle rancher, and Texas is the best place to do that as far as I can see. They have cattle ranches in other states and territories out west, but Texas is the place with the most cattle ranches. I want to have my own ranch out there someday."

The senior Kane rubbed his jaw. "On a dock man's savings? You have very little money, Alan."

"I know, Papa, but Texas has countless numbers of wild horses and wild cattle. Anyone can round them up and take them."

"What about land?" Adam said. "You've got to have land to raise the cattle on if you're gonna have a ranch."

Alan smiled at him. "You've heard of Stephen Austin?"

"Yes. I've read about him in the *Boston Herald* from time to time. In the early 1820s, he founded the principal settlements of English-speaking people in Texas, despite the fact that Texas was still fully under Mexico's rule."

"Right. Well, the *Herald* had an article about Mr. Austin a couple months ago. I read that he has established a colony in southeast Texas. Any family or single man who joins the colony gets 640 acres of land free of charge."

Adam nodded. "I read that article."

Abram smacked his lips. "Six hundred and forty acres *free*?"

Alan Kane's eyes were shining as he looked at his father. "Yes, Papa. Don't you see? This is my chance!"

Abram frowned. "Now, hold on, son. You don't know anything about cattle ranching."

"You're right, Papa, but there's a man in Texas who is willing to hire me as a ranch hand and teach me the cattle ranching business."

Abram arched his eyebrows. "Who might that be?"

Alan pushed his plate away. "You know the ship the *Blue Bayou* that comes up from New Orleans to Boston Harbor frequently? It carries cattle hides for leather workers in Boston and other nearby cities to purchase."

"Mm-hmm."

"I've seen it many times," Adam said. "You've been in the crew that's unloaded it, right?"

"Right. Well, about a year ago I met the man who owns a huge ranch called the Circle C in southeast Texas, where they raise cattle for hides that are brought here by the *Blue Bayou.* His name is William Childress. He was on the ship at that time, and I had been assigned to help unload it that day. He introduced himself and told me that he was in Boston lining up some new customers for his hides. We got to talking about his cattle business, and he told me that he has his ranch hands transport the hides by wagon from the Circle C to the Brazos River. Then they are floated on a boat down to a town called Velasco on the Gulf of Mexico. A small boat carries them from Velasco to New Orleans, where the *Blue Bayou* takes them, along with other cargo, and brings them here."

"Mr. Childress sounds like an interesting man," Angela said.

"He is for sure, Sis. You see, Mr. Childress has been on the Boston docks via the *Blue Bayou* three times since I first met him a year ago. We have talked each time. And let me tell all three of you this. That first time we talked, he said something about the Lord Jesus, and when I told him that I know Him as my Saviour, I learned real quick that Mr. Childress is a born-again Christian. He gave me a clear testimony of his faith in the Lord Jesus."

It was instantly obvious to Alan by the looks on the faces of his father and siblings that they were glad to hear this.

Adam's brow furrowed. "Alan, is he that tall, red-headed man dressed in western-cut clothes I saw you talking to on the *Blue Bayou* about a month ago?"

Alan nodded. "Mm-hmm. Six weeks to be exact. At that time I told Mr. Childress I was interested in going to Texas so I could join Stephen Austin's colony, lay hold of 640 acres of ranch land, and become a cattle rancher. Mr. Childress said before I did that, I should learn the cattle ranching business. He said especially because I am a Christian, he would like to take me to the Circle C and hire me as a ranch hand. He told me about the Bible-believing church that he and some of his ranch hands attend. It is in Washington-on-the-Brazos. That's the capital of the Texas republic. The Circle C Ranch is about thirty miles west of there. He is really serious about me coming to work for him."

"I didn't know Texas had a capital. Did Mr. Childress say he would pay you good?"

Alan nodded. "Yes, Papa. I don't know how much yet, but he said it would be better than dock pay. He told me that he would teach me the cattle ranching business, and when he felt I was ready, he would take me to Stephen Austin, and I could join up and get my own 640 acres of land."

Abram scratched at his left ear. "I take it Mr. Childress will be back in Boston soon."

"Yes, Papa. He told me he'd be back the first week of June. I'm supposed to be ready to sail back to Texas with him if I still want to go."

Abram frowned. "Why, that's less than two months away. Why didn't you bring this up before now?"

Alan's face flushed. "Well, I…uh…I just couldn't find the right moment."

Adam took on a serious look. "I read in the *Boston Herald* not long ago that there's some trouble brewing between the Texans and the government of Mexico."

Angela's eyes widened.

"That's supposed to be all settled now," Alan said. "The last time William Childress was here, he brought the situation up to me and said he believes that the Mexican president, Santa Anna, is going to tolerate Texas as a separate republic within the country of Mexico."

"I've read articles about that myself," Abram said. "I don't believe that beast Santa Anna will put up with that arrangement. Sounds like the lull before the storm to me."

Alan took a deep breath and let it out through his nostrils. "Well, Papa, if the Texans have to fight for their freedom, they won't be the first people on earth to do so."

All was quiet for a moment. Then Angela broke the silence. "Alan, I don't think you're being very considerate. We Kanes have always stuck together. If you go to Texas—"

"Now, Angela," her father said, "Alan is almost twenty-one. He is his own man now. He has every right to think of his future and build his own life."

Alan was stunned but pleased to see his father take it so well.

Adam slowly rolled his hazy blue eyes toward his brother. "What about Mama, Alan?"

The younger brother's face stiffened.

Angela's voice cracked as she said, "Alan, the least you could do is wait till she—" Tears quickly filled her eyes.

"I have already talked to Mama about going to Texas," Alan said, surprising the others.

"And?" Abram said.

"Mama told me to discuss it with Papa, and she said if you feel it's right for me, I should go with Mr. Childress when he comes in June. She told me she was proud that I had the desire to become a cattle rancher and that if Papa felt the same way, I would have her blessing."

"Of course she would say that, Alan. But you know that deep in her heart, she would want you to stay until—" Suddenly Angela pushed her chair back from the table and fled the room, weeping.

Abram skidded his chair back and rose to his feet. He dropped a calloused hand on his youngest son's shoulder. "This isn't easy for your old papa to say, Alan, but you are coming of age. Pray about it, and make your decision for what you feel the Lord would have you do. I can fully understand your desire to become a cattle rancher."

Adam was off his chair by then. Laying a hand on Alan's other shoulder, he said, "I understand too, little brother. You have my blessing."

"You have mine too, son."

Alan reached to his shoulders and squeezed his father's hands. "Thanks, Papa...Adam." He rose to his feet and looked toward the kitchen door and the hallway beyond. "Guess I'd better go have a talk with Angela."

"I'm sure it would help," Abram said.

Alan took a few steps toward the door, then stopped and turned around. "I wish I could stay until Mama goes to heaven, but she urged me to go with Mr. Childress if you approved, Papa."

Abram bit his lower lip, blinked away the excess moisture in his eyes, and nodded.

When Alan was gone, Adam said, "Papa, I'll go up and visit with Mama a few minutes, then go to the Bannigan house and call on Mary Sue."

Abram nodded. "Sure, son."

When Adam had left the kitchen, Abram Kane picked up his cup from the table, carried it to the stove, and poured himself more hot coffee. Then, sitting down, he hunched over the table, sipped at the steaming liquid, and went over in his mind what Alan had just told them.

As he remembered himself at Alan's age, a slight smile lightened his face. "Oh yes," he said in a low voice. "I well recall wanting to be my own man and go my own way. Can't say as I blame the boy at all. Even at my age, starting over again sounds rather appealing. Only the Lord knows what He has ahead for all of us."

He slowly drank his coffee, then rose from his chair, carried the cup to the stove, and filled it again. He stepped to the kitchen window and, gazing at the gathering darkness outside, let his mind go back to when he and Kitty married and the wonderful times they'd had together.

Suddenly his thoughts were interrupted by footsteps in the hallway outside the kitchen. He knew it was Angela. Just as he turned from the window, she entered the room. Abram could see that her eyes were puffy from crying, but there was a smile on her lips.

Angela stepped up to her father. "Well, Papa, it looks like we're going to have a Texas cattle rancher in the family."

Abram set his coffee cup on the counter by the sink and looked deep into his daughter's eyes. "You sound like it's all right now."

Angela nodded. "Yes. When I left crying, I went up to Mama's room. She asked me what I was crying about, and I told her. She had me sit down on the bed and explained that she had already told Alan she wanted him to take advantage of Mr. Childress's offer and go to Texas with him when he returns next time. She said only the Lord knows how long she has in this world, but she didn't want her impending death to keep Alan from this wonderful opportunity."

Abram bit down on a quivering lip and nodded. "Your mother is very special, honey."

"That's for sure, Papa." At that moment Adam came in, and after hearing Mama's attitude about Alan going to Texas, he was all right too. He then left to go see Mary Sue. A couple of minutes later, Alan came in. "Papa," Angela continued, "when Mama talked to Alan about going to Texas right in front of me, I got peace about the whole thing. I feel sure the Lord has something really great for him in Texas, and I want God's best for him."

Abram smiled, gathered her in his arms, and kissed her cheek. He looked down at her lovingly. "Sweet lass, this helps me with the situation too. I really think this Texas opportunity is a good thing for Alan."

Angela smiled. "Good. Knowing you feel like this about it helps me too."

"I'm glad, honey. We need to be supportive of Alan's decision and encourage him in every way we can."

"Yes! We'll all work together to help his dream be realized."

Abram smiled again. "Good girl. I know I can always count on you to do what is right. You not only look like your dear mother, you think just like her too."

"That is a great compliment, Papa. Thank you. There is no one I would rather be like than my sweet mama."

Abram hugged her and kissed her cheek again.

Angela looked up into his eyes. "I'm going to fix Mama a small supper tray. It'll take a half hour or so. Would you take it up to her when it's ready? Maybe she'll eat it if her favorite man in the world coaxes her to do so."

"I'll be glad to try, honey. I'll go on up to her right now while you prepare the food."

"Good! Come back in about a half hour."

"Will do." Abram headed for the door to the hallway.

After he topped the stairs and turned toward Kitty's room, he passed Alan's room and saw the lantern light beneath the closed door, which told him that his youngest son was now in his room.

Seconds later, the tall man entered Kitty's bedroom through its open door. The flame of the lantern on the small table beside the bed exposed the love light in forty-eight-year-old Kitty Kane's eyes. "Hello, my darling. The children told me you approve of Alan's going to Texas."

Abram nodded. "Yes. I think it is a great opportunity for him."

"Me too."

He then eased down and sat on the edge of the bed as usual. It hurt him to look at her. Her once-beautiful face was gray and drawn. Her lips were almost colorless. There were dark circles around her eyes.

Kitty took hold of his hand. "You know, I got to thinking about your three fights today."

"Mm-hmm?"

"All three of those men must have short arms. I don't see any marks on your face."

Abram managed a grin. "Well, each of them only has one arm. And strangely, each one of their belts broke as we started to fight, so they had to use their only hand to keep their pants up. Made it easy for me to punch 'em."

Kitty started to laugh, then broke into a hacking cough. Quickly she yanked a handkerchief from the bed table and pressed it to her mouth.

Abram's heart went cold.

When the coughing spasm had passed, Kitty adjusted her head on the pillow and forced a smile. Abram leaned over and kissed her forehead. Then he lowered his head next to hers and said, "I love you, Kitten."

Closing her eyes, she whispered, "And I love you, my darling."

Abram's breath was warm in Kitty's ear as he said, "Angela is preparing you a small meal. I'm to go down and get it in a few minutes and bring it up to you."

"And you're supposed to get me to eat it even if I don't feel like eating, right?"

He sat up and looked into her eyes. "Yes. Our daughter knows you must eat to keep up your strength as much as possible. You *will* eat it, won't you?"

Kitty made a slight giggle. "Well, all right, since you'll be in trouble with Angela if I refuse."

Abram smiled, lowered his head next to hers again, and gripped her shoulders in his hands. As he held her, the horrid thought of losing her froze his brain and clawed at his heart.

Somehow Kitty knew what was going through her husband's mind. "Darling, I'm sorry you have to carry this burden because of me."

Abram sat up and looked her in the eye. "It's not a burden. When you love someone as much as I love you, it's not a burden. I ache inside to see you so ill. I am deeply concerned, but I don't think of it or *you* as a burden."

Kitty reached up and caressed his rugged face. "For such a big, tough bruiser, you sure are tender, Abram Kane."

Abram leaned down again and held his wife for a long moment.

"Is it time for you to go down and get my supper? I'm hungry."

Abram sat up and smiled. "Since you're hungry, Queen Kitty Kane, your humble servant will hurry real fast to bring your supper!"

Kitty raised her head and watched her husband's broad back as he passed through the door. Settling down on the pillow, she smiled to herself. *Some kind of man is this Abram Kane. He is big, strong, and able to put down every would-be Bareknuckle Champion of the Boston Docks...yet when it comes to Angela, or myself, he is so gentle, kind, and tender.*

The dying wife and mother mused on the family she would soon leave behind. She loved them so very much. Alex and his dear wife, Libby, were so precious to her heart, as were Abel and Vivian. And then there was beautiful, sweet Angela. The dear girl had sacrificed so much in her young life to take care of her mother. The blond, blue-eyed beauty had stepped in and become cook and housekeeper in the Abram Kane home. For her mother, Angela was both nurse and waitress. Unselfishly and cheerfully, she had done her best to make her mother's last days on earth as happy as possible.

And then there were her two younger sons. Like Alex and Abel, Adam and Alan were handsome, just like their father—sandy-headed, blue-eyed, and square-jawed. Adam would probably marry Mary Sue Bannigan soon, but Alan hadn't found the right girl yet. Still, Kitty knew that, like his older brothers, Alan would only marry a dedicated Christian young lady.

Tears were now welling up in Kitty's eyes. She rubbed them with a shaky hand, smearing tears over her sunken cheeks.

Suddenly she heard Abram's footsteps in the hallway.

Using the handkerchief again, she quickly dabbed away the tears and made a smile for her loving and devoted husband.

FOUR

Mary Sue Bannigan had just washed her hair. Clad in a blue and white dress, she was brushing her hair dry in her room on the second floor of the plush Bannigan house when she heard the knocker clatter on the front door downstairs.

When she heard her father open the door and say, "Hello, Adam," she looked at herself in the mirror and turned her mouth down.

Seconds later, Chester Bannigan called from the bottom of the stairs, "Mary Sue, Adam's here to see you!"

"All right!" she called down, making a twisted face that reflected back at her in the mirror. "I'll be down shortly!" There was a look of displeasure in her hazel eyes.

Mary Sue was nineteen years old and very pretty. Her dark brown hair came all the way to her waist. Lifting the hair from the back of her neck, she wrapped it with a ribbon which she tied in a bow. With that, she turned and left the room.

When she reached the top of the stairs, she saw Adam waiting below. She felt her nerves clawing at her stomach as she started downward.

Adam smiled at her but knew by the look in her eyes that she was upset about something. "Want to go for a walk?" he asked.

Stepping off the last stair, Mary Sue replied, "I'd rather just go to the parlor."

"Sure." Adam gave her his arm.

Mary Sue's parents were standing in the hall that led to the parlor. They stared at Adam but said nothing as he and Mary Sue walked past them. Adam knew something was amiss. Her father had been rather cold to him when he opened the door, and her mother had yet to speak to him, even though she had come into the hall as he was walking toward the staircase.

Adam followed Mary Sue into the parlor, and she gestured toward an overstuffed chair. "Sit down there, Adam."

They always sat together on one of the couches. Now, as he sat where directed, Mary Sue pulled up a straight-backed wooden chair and sat facing him.

"Is something wrong?" Adam asked. "You don't seem like yourself."

Mary Sue drew a deep breath and let it out slowly. "Adam, I have something to tell you."

Adam blinked. "Yes?"

"I'm seeing someone else."

"You...you mean we're not going together anymore?"

"That's what I mean."

"Oh. Well, do I know this other guy?"

"Mm-hmm. He teaches the boys' Sunday school class at church."

"Wally Haskins?"

"Yes."

Adam swallowed hard. "Mary Sue, what did I do to deserve this?"

"It isn't what you did. It's what you *didn't* do."

"Huh?"

"You know very well that my father wanted you to ask him for that job that was open in his store. I pleaded with you to ask him for the job, didn't I? I told you that if you did, one day you would be made a partner in Bannigan's Clothiers."

"Yes, but I explained that selling clothes just doesn't appeal to me. Um...you said the job that *was* open. Did somebody take it?"

"Yes."

"Who?"

"Wally Haskins."

"So he gets *you* because he took the job?"

"Well, not exactly, but I'm not going to marry a dock worker. I'm used to living better than I could live on a dock worker's income."

Adam looked her square in the eye. "Did you pray about dumping me for Wally, Mary Sue?"

Mary Sue stood up. "I didn't have to pray about it. I know God wants me to have more than what you could provide for me."

Adam rose to his feet. "Okay. Well, I hope you get what you want. I'll be leaving now."

Mary Sue did not move. As Adam walked toward the parlor door, she sighed with relief. It was over. Now she could marry Wally Haskins.

Heavy of heart, Adam Kane stepped up on the porch of the Kane house, unlocked the door, and went inside. After locking the door behind him, he made his way in the shadows to the staircase and mounted the stairs. As he walked down the hall, he didn't see light beneath any of the doors except Alan's.

Feeling like a whipped dog, Adam wanted to share his disappointment with someone in the family, and Alan would be just fine. He tapped lightly on Alan's door and spoke just loud enough for his younger brother to hear him. "Alan, it's Adam. May I come in?"

"Of course. Come in."

When Adam opened the door and stepped into the room, by the light of the lantern on the small table next to the bed, he saw his brother lying on his back with only the sheet over him, the fingers of both hands laced together behind his head on the pillow. The night breeze toyed with the curtains on the open window.

Adam looked down at Alan as he walked up beside the bed. "How come you're lying here like that?"

"Oh, I was just thinking about what it's going to be like on Mr. Childress's ranch in Texas. So how's Mary Sue?"

Adam sighed. "Happy."

"What's she happy about?"

"She's marrying Wally Haskins."

Alan's hands slipped from behind his head, and he sat up.

"Wally Haskins! Why?"

"Because he took that job at her father's store I told you about. She doesn't want to marry a guy who only makes dock worker's wages."

In the silence that followed this news, a dog barked somewhere out in the night.

Alan licked his lips. "Big brother, I'm sorry she dropped you like that, but I've got an idea."

"What's that?"

"Well, since you won't be marrying Mary Sue, how about going to Texas with me? I'm sure Mr. Childress would give you a job on his ranch too. We could learn the cattle business and then join Stephen Austin's colony and get us a nice big piece of land. We could be partners on our ranch."

Adam smiled. "It's nice of you to want me for a partner, little brother. I'll have to think on that idea for a while."

Alan smiled. "Okay, you do that. And think about this. You've always wanted to see New Orleans, right?"

"Yep."

"Well, Mr. Childress told me that we'll change ships in New Orleans on the way to Texas. If you go, you'll get to see it."

Adam rubbed his jaw. "New Orleans. Maybe we'd run into that Jim Bowie guy there."

Alan knew his brother had read about Jim Bowie in the newspapers and thought he was an interesting figure. "We just might."

"A pilot on one of the Louisiana boats I helped unload a while back told me he saw Bowie in a knife fight once."

"Yeah?"

"Mm-hmm. Said it was on a Mississippi River sand bar near a town called Natchez. A fight broke out amid a crowd of men there, and when Bowie tried to stop it, two guys jumped him and threatened him with knives. Bowie had a butcher knife in a scabbard on his waist. He—"

"Wait a minute! Where was his famous bowie knife?"

"Well, this happened in 1827. He didn't design the bowie knife until four years ago, in 1830."

"Oh."

"Anyway, the pilot told me that with the butcher knife, Bowie nicked both of the guys who jumped him, causing them to drop their knives, and put them both down and out with his fists."

"Whew!" Alan said. "If he was that good with a butcher knife, what would he do with that bowie knife?"

"Who knows? That pilot told me the bowie knife stabs like a dagger, chops like a cleaver, and cuts like a razor. He said Bowie actually keeps his own bowie knife so sharp, he shaves with it every morning."

Alan grinned. "Well, if you decide to go with me, you just might get to meet him."

"I'll definitely think about it, little brother. Well, it's time for me to get to my room and sack out. See you in the morning."

"See you in the morning," Alan echoed as his brother went out the door.

The next morning, Kitty Kane was feeling a little stronger, and sat at the breakfast table with the rest of the family. While they ate, Adam told them about Mary Sue dropping him for Wally Haskins, who had accepted the job offer from her father, which she had wanted *him* to accept, saying she did not want to marry a man who only made dock worker's wages.

Angela set soft eyes on Adam. "I'm sorry Mary Sue hurt you."

Adam forced a thin smile. "Well, if that's all I meant to her, it's best that she did drop me."

"And because she did and Adam won't be marrying her," Alan said, "I suggested that he come with me to Texas. I'm sure Mr. Childress would give him a job on his ranch too. Then when we learn the business, we can get our own land and be partners on our own cattle ranch."

All eyes went to Adam. He grinned. "I told little brother I'd have to think on it, and that's what I've been doing since last night. I've also been praying about it, asking the Lord to show me if that's what I should do. I'm sure He will give me the answer before William Childress comes in June."

"I want Adam to do well in life," Alan said, "and from what Mr. Childress has told me, I feel that cattle ranching is the best thing for both of us."

"Can't argue with that," Abram said.

Kitty nodded. "I can't either. I want the best for both of you boys."

Alan looked at Adam with a tender expression. "Big brother, the Lord has somebody better than Mary Sue Bannigan for you. I'm going to pray that He will send a beautiful Christian young lady into your life and the two of you will fall in love."

Adam grinned at him. "Pray, dear brother! Pray!"

Angela smiled at her youngest brother. "Well, Alan, what about *you*? Isn't it about time some beautiful Christian young lady came into *your* life?"

Alan grinned. "I'll find the one the Lord has chosen for me in Texas, Sis."

Adam's eyebrows arched. "Hey! Maybe I will too!"

Abram, Kitty, and Angela laughed in unison. Suddenly Kitty's chuckles seemed to choke her, and she went into a coughing fit. Angela jumped from her chair, but before she could get to her mother, Abram was already leaning over her, patting her back.

Adam and Alan also got up and gathered close.

When Kitty's coughing eased, Abram said, "Honey, I'll carry you upstairs and put you in your bed."

Kitty swallowed hard and coughed slightly. "You and the boys need to head for work. I...I can just lie down on the sofa in the parlor."

"We've got a little time yet before we have to leave, honey." Abram lifted her off the chair.

"Mama," Angela said, "I'll be up as soon as I get these dishes done."

"We'll help, Angela," Adam said.

The brothers went to work beside their sister with the dishes as Abram carried their mother out of the kitchen.

When Abram had taken Kitty upstairs into her room, placed her on the bed, and covered her up, he sat on the edge of the bed. "Sweetheart, I wish I could stay here. I hate going off and leaving you."

"It's all right, darling," Kitty said. "You go on to work now. We need your paycheck. Angela will be at my side shortly. She takes such good care of me…she's the next thing to an angel. I'll be fine."

Abram nodded. "All right, my love. I'll go to work, but I'd still rather stay home with you." Bending down, he kissed her cheek and lovingly patted the top of her head. "You be a good girl now, and rest, rest, rest. You know that's the very best medicine for you."

Kitty met her husband's gaze and saluted military style with a shaky hand. "Yes sir."

"See you this evening, love." Abram headed for the door. As he closed the door behind him, he leaned against the closed door and bowed his head. In a whisper, he asked for God's care and mercy on his precious wife. Brushing away any sign of tears, he made his way back down to the kitchen.

Adam and Alan were drying dishes. Angela told them to go on to work. She would finish the rest in a few minutes, then go up to their mother.

Adam then said, "Papa, as Alan, Angela, and I have been talking, I've had a real peace come over me about going with Alan to Texas. I'm sure the Lord is telling me that this is His will."

Abram hooked an arm around his neck and squeezed hard. "I feel the same way about it, son. I really do."

Adam blinked at the excess moisture that came to his eyes. "Thank you, Papa. That really helps me."

Father and sons hurried out of the house, and as usual met up with Alex and Abel down the block. As the five of them walked toward the harbor, the two older brothers learned about Mary Sue Bannigan dropping Adam for Wally Haskins and about Alan's initial plans to go to Texas—including Adam's intent to go with him.

Alex and Abel told them they understood about their younger brothers' desire to become cattle ranchers and wished them their best, saying they and their wives would be praying for them.

Alex added, "I'm going to be envious of you two. The idea of being a cattle rancher sounds good to me."

Abel chuckled. "Yeah, me too."

When they reached the docks, the four Kane brothers were assigned to work together some distance from the dock where their father would be working with Ben Delsart and two other men: Lee Nevins and Jake Bullard. When Bullard saw that he would be working with Abram Kane, his face took on a woeful expression and he snorted at Abram with fire in his eye. Abram ignored him.

Before them on the dock were several wooden crates loaded with clothing, canned goods, and tools that were to be loaded onto a ship headed for Savannah that was docked at a loading wharf nearby. The crates were on wooden skids held in place by heavy chains.

Before they began their work, Lee Nevins stepped up to Abram. "I want to thank you once again for forgiving my meanness when I spoke of your wife that way."

Abram smiled. "Well, Lee, the Lord has forgiven me for a lot of wrongdoing, so when you asked for forgiveness, I owed it to you to forgive you."

Lee's brow furrowed. "Abram, before I insulted your wife and you knocked me out cold, you spoke of having salvation in Christ. You said people with Christ in their hearts and their sins washed away in His blood have salvation, and they go to heaven. You said hell is the destination of people without Christ. I'd like to learn more about this."

Abram smiled. "Good! I know we have to get to work now, but how about after work today we just sit down and talk about it? I carry a Bible in a leather satchel that I keep with my lunch pail."

"Yes. Let's do that."

The four men went to work. Two men dragged each skid to the edge of the wharf, where the ship's crew would hoist it onto the deck, the chains were released, and the crates were removed from the skids.

While Abram Kane worked a crate off its skid after Jake Bullard had released the long chain and pulled it free, Bullard let about three feet of the end of the chain dangle from his right hand. Aiming at Abram's hands where they gripped the crate, Bullard swung the end of the chain. Abram saw it coming just in the nick of time and jerked his hands away. The chain clattered loudly as it struck the crate and splintered it.

Abram scowled at Jake. "You tried to break my hands!"

At that instant, Lee Nevins and Ben Delsart ran toward them, having seen what Jake had tried to do.

"Hey, Jake!" Nevins shouted. "Put that chain down!"

Bullard's eyes flashed fire as he bellowed, "Get away, Lee! Kane's got it comin', and I'm gonna give it to him!"

Thunderous rage suddenly possessed Lee Nevins. He balled his fists and headed for the man who was supposed to be his best friend. Bullard set himself and swung the end of the chain at Lee's head. Lee dodged it adeptly and sent a powerful punch to Jake's jaw. The blow whipped Bullard's head to one side. He staggered back, braced himself, and swung the chain at Lee again.

Lee ducked under the hazardous chain and rebounded. He sent two driving blows to Jake's midsection, doubling him over, then pounded him with a powerful left hook and followed with an even stronger right cross. Jake hit the dock hard, out cold. The chain fell from his limp hand.

At that instant, John Dixon, who was running toward them, skidded to a stop. Other dock workers had seen what was going on and were gathering.

Dixon glanced down at the unconscious Jake Bullard, then looked at

Abram Kane, then at Lee Nevins. "I saw it all, Lee. For what you just did to protect Abram from that chain, I'm giving you a raise in pay." He turned to two of the men who had just drawn up. "Howard...Edgar...pick Jake up and carry him to my office. As soon as he comes to, I'm going to fire him!"

At lunch, when the four Kane brothers learned of how their father had been protected from the chain-wielding Jake Bullard, they kindly thanked Lee Nevins. Abram then told his sons that Lee had asked questions about salvation that morning and that the two of them were going to sit down and talk about it after quitting time.

When the workday was over, the Kane brothers waited several yards away on the dock while their father sat down with Lee Nevins on a wooden bench.

"I should tell you, Abram, that when I was twelve years old, my parents were killed in a boating accident right here in Boston Harbor, and I was put in a home for orphan children. A couple of women who worked there were Christians. They read to us from the Bible and talked about Jesus and salvation a lot, so I have heard it before. I was only there for a few weeks before a family in Boston whose teenage son had died with pneumonia came to the home, told the caregivers about their son dying, and asked if there was a teenage boy in the home they could adopt. They chose me. My actual last name was Kaiser until I was adopted by the Nevinses."

Abram nodded. "I see. So you haven't been exposed to Bible truths since you were adopted?"

"No. I got with people who made fun of Christians and what they believed, and my thinking went that same direction."

"Well, it's good that you've heard *some* Scripture anyway." Abram opened his Bible. "You brought up what I had said to you, that people who have Jesus Christ in their hearts have had their sins washed away in His blood go to heaven and that hell is the destination for those without Christ."

"Yes."

"Let me show you briefly about those who die and go to hell. This is Jesus telling about a man who died lost and went to hell, here in Luke chapter 16."

He held the Bible so Lee could see it. "He happened to be a rich man. Look what Jesus says, here in verses 22 and 23. He tells about a beggar who died and went to 'Abraham's bosom,' which was Paradise at that time. 'The rich man also died, and was buried; and in hell he lifted up his eyes, being in torments.' In verse 24, Jesus quotes the man in hell, saying, 'I am tormented in this flame.' The Bible tells us that hell is fire, Lee. People who die without Christ will spend eternity in the fire of hell. Many Scriptures make this clear."

Lee Nevins swallowed hard.

Flipping pages, Abram said, "Now, I want to show you about the blood that the Lord Jesus shed by coming to this world to be crucified on the cross of Calvary. Here in Revelation chapter 1, verses 5 and 6, Jesus is being given glory for something. Look what it says in verse 5. 'Unto him that loved us, and washed us from our sins in his own blood.' "

Lee nodded. "I recall those ladies at the home saying that only the blood of Jesus Christ can wash away our sins."

"Good for them. Now let me show you just when that happens."

Abram flipped pages again. "Look at these words, here in Ephesians 3:17: 'That Christ may dwell in your hearts by faith.' See that? The Christ who died for our sins on the cross, was buried, and rose from the dead after three days and three nights must dwell in a person's heart, and it must be by faith. Let me ask you, Lee. Do you believe that Jesus Christ is the only begotten Son of God?"

"Yes. 'Only begotten' means the virgin birth, like we hear about at Christmas, right?"

"That's right. So you believe that?"

"Sure do. Those ladies at the home planted that in my mind."

"Good." Abram turned pages again. "All right, we just saw that Christ must dwell in our *what* by faith?"

"Our hearts."

"Yes. Now, look at what John 1:12 says about Jesus. 'But as many as received him, to them gave he power to become the sons of God, even to them that believe on his name.' Notice the word *believe*. That is faith. It says to become the sons of God, we must *receive* Jesus. Where to, Lee?"

"Our hearts."

"Right," Abram said, turning pages again. "Now, look here at 2 Peter 3:9. The verse opens saying that the Lord is not slack concerning His promise and is longsuffering toward us. Then it says He is 'not willing that any should perish'—that's to go to hell—'but that all should come to repentance.' So without repentance for their sin, Lee, lost sinners will go to hell. Repentance is simply acknowledging to God that you are a sinner and turning from your sin and unbelief to Jesus for salvation, asking Him to forgive you and save you. Romans 10:13 says you must *call* on the name of the Lord to be saved. Do you understand?"

Lee nodded, and tears were welling up in his eyes. "Yes, Abram, I understand. I want to be saved."

"Wonderful! Then let's bow our heads, and you call on Jesus in repentance, asking Him to forgive your sins, wash them away in His blood, and come into your heart and be your Saviour."

The Kane brothers saw Lee Nevins bow his head, and they could hear him calling on the Lord to save him. When he was finished, they ran to their father and the new Christian and told Lee how glad they were that he was now their brother in Christ and that he was on his way to heaven.

FIVE

The following Sunday, Lee Nevins went to church with the Kanes and walked the aisle at the invitation given by the pastor after the sermon. Abram Kane was at his side. Abram introduced Lee to the pastor, explaining that he had led him to the Lord on the job that week. The pastor then asked Lee to give his testimony of salvation to the congregation, which Lee gladly did. The pastor then baptized him, and the people rejoiced.

When the service was over, Adam Kane noticed that neither Mary Sue Bannigan nor Wally Haskins was in the church service.

Mary's parents were standing at the back of the sanctuary talking to some friends. Adam walked over, and both of the Bannigans gave him a strange look.

"Pardon my intrusion, Mr. and Mrs. Bannigan," Adam said. "I just wanted to ask you about Mary Sue and Wally."

"What's that?" Chester Bannigan said.

"I notice they're not here today. Are they all right?"

"They're fine," Chester said. "Wally has an uncle in Manhattan, New York, who owns a wagon and buggy repair shop, and not long ago, he offered Wally a much higher-paying job than I had, so the two of them eloped and are on their way to Manhattan."

Adam nodded. "Oh. I see. Well, I hope they'll be happy there."

When Adam met up with the rest of his family outside the church, he told them what he had just learned, and Alan said, "Big brother, I'm still praying that the Lord will bring that beautiful young Christian lady into your life."

Adam chuckled. "She's probably in Texas right now."

The whole family had a good laugh.

As the days passed, Kitty Kane grew weaker, and the tuberculosis grew stronger. It was very difficult for the family, knowing that her time on earth was drawing short. Alex and Libby and Abel and Vivian came by the house quite often to spend some precious moments with her.

On Saturday evening, April 26, Angela prepared a meal for the entire family. As Abram, Angela, Adam, Alan, Alex and Libby, and Abel and Vivian were eating together, Kitty was upstairs in her room napping. Since Kitty was so weak and would not be able to eat with the family, Angela had fed her earlier.

During the meal, the subject of Alan and Adam going to Texas was discussed, and both young men expressed how excited they were about being partners on a cattle ranch someday.

Alex chuckled. "Maybe Libby and I should give some serious thought to moving down to Texas too. Lots of room down there, I understand!"

Vivian smiled. "Abel and I have been discussing the idea ourselves. We're wondering if they have docks down there!"

The four of them laughed together, making it out to be a joke.

Angela said, "Well, Papa, maybe you and I could join Stephen Austin's colony and get us a big ol' ranch going! I've never even heard a cow say *moo*!"

Abram smiled but did not comment.

When they were about to finish their meal, Angela said, "Mama asked that all of us come up to see her when supper is over."

"Let's go." Abram pushed his chair back and stood. "I'll help you with the dishes later, Angela."

"No, you won't, Papa," Vivian said. "Libby and I will help her."

Moments later, when the family entered Kitty's room, they found her awake. The men hurried to other bedrooms and brought in a few extra wooden chairs so everyone could sit around Kitty's bed. Though she was obviously weak and not feeling at all well, she talked to them, doing her best to show her love for them.

The family members talked about anything but Mama's serious illness for a while. Then Kitty said weakly, "I know all of you are carrying a heavy load with my illness and knowing that any day now the Lord will be taking me home. I want to tell you something."

Kitty had the full attention of everyone in her family.

She drew a shaky breath. "Earlier today, when I was able to sit up in bed for a while, I was reading my Bible. I read a few of the Psalms, then settled on the Twenty-third Psalm. I want to share with all of you how verse 4 in the Twenty-third Psalm touched my heart. Remember, it says, 'Yea, though I walk through the valley of the shadow of death, I will fear no evil: for thou art with me; thy rod and thy staff they comfort me.' "

Angela's hand went to her mouth, and tears welled up in her eyes.

Not noticing this, Kitty went on. "I kept reading that verse over and over. As David wrote of walking through the valley of the shadow of death, it struck me that there cannot be a shadow without light to *cast* the shadow. Then the words 'for thou art with me' stood out. Jesus is the Light."

She drew another shaky breath, and tears misted her eyes. "Since Jesus is the Light and is with every Christian when they die, it is *He* who makes the shadow. So since He will be with me when I die, I have nothing to fear."

Kitty's words had the rest of her family shedding tears.

When their emotions settled down, Alex and Libby and Abel and Vivian were preparing to leave. One at a time, they bent over the bed and kissed their dear one on her cheek, telling her they loved her.

Before the two couples headed for the door, Alan said, "Tomorrow is my day to stay home with Mama while the rest of you go to church."

Vivian looked around at the others. "Abel and I want the rest of you to have Sunday dinner with us at our apartment after the morning service."

The family gladly agreed that they would be there.

The next day, after church, Vivian had a delicious meal for her guests. They talked first about Lee Nevins bringing a man with him to church who lived in his apartment building. The man had walked the aisle at invitation time and opened his heart to Jesus. Adam especially was thrilled to see Lee growing in grace already.

The subject at the table then went solemn as they talked about Kitty's condition. They all agreed that her time to leave this world was drawing very near. The doctor who had visited her in the home a few days ago had told Angela in private that her mother would not last much longer.

Tears were shed, but Abram and Adam also offered comforting words to the others as they quoted Scriptures about heaven and commented that they would all be together in that wonderful place where no good-byes are ever spoken.

When the meal was over, Angela told Vivian that she was going to stay and help her do the dishes and clean up the kitchen. Libby said she would help too. Abel invited the men to go to the parlor.

As the men headed toward the parlor, a disturbing sense of foreboding crept into Adam's heart. When they entered the parlor, he said, "Gentlemen, I'm going to go on home and relieve Alan so he can enjoy some of this beautiful day."

"All right, son. I'm sure Alan will appreciate that. Angela and I'll be home shortly."

Alex and Abel both smiled at Adam and nodded.

Adam removed his hat from a peg by the door, put it on, looked back at his father and brothers, then stepped into the hall. Once he was on the board sidewalk, he walked briskly toward the Abram Kane house. The foreboding he was feeling prodded him almost to a run.

The closer Adam got to the house that had been his home for as long as he could remember, the stronger the urgency grew. He was indeed running by the time he reached the porch. He went up the steps two at a time, and the screen door squeaked as usual as he passed into the cool gloom of the house and closed the door behind him. He felt as though a dark shadow had come into the house with him and was now hovering over him. His heart was beating rapidly, and he paused to draw a deep breath.

Then he heard it. A low moaning and sobbing coming from the second floor. He could tell it was Alan.

A cold blade of fear stabbed through Adam's heart. The word "No-o-o!" escaped his lips in a half whisper as he bounded up the stairs.

When Adam reached the top of the stairs, he could tell that Alan's sobbing was coming from their mother's bedroom. He hurried down the hall, and when he entered the room, there was a strange stillness, except for Alan's partially muffled weeping.

Slim fingers of light were filtering through the heavy curtains, exposing Adam's younger brother sitting on the bed. Alan was holding his mother in his arms. She was still and quiet, her head laid against his chest.

The elder brother knew his mother was dead. He dropped a firm hand on Alan's shoulder.

Turning his tear-stained face and tilting it upward, Alan said softly, "She's gone, Adam. She had a bad coughing spell."

Alan shuddered. "I picked up her bottle of cough medicine, here on the bedside table. Suddenly she sat up and grasped my shoulders with both hands. When I took her into my arms, she said, 'Alan, I see the Light. It's Jesus. There's a shadow, but I'm not afraid. My Saviour has come for me.' Then she collapsed against my chest and stopped breathing."

Alan sniffed. "She's not in my arms now, Adam. She's in the arms of Jesus."

Two days later, as the Kane family stood together beside the open grave on a grassy hilltop in the Boston cemetery, many of their friends from church were there, as well as some friends from Dixon Ship Lines, including John Dixon. Also in the group were Lee Nevins and Will and Jack Benson.

The pastor brought a heart-touching message, which was designed to strengthen and encourage the Kane family in Kitty's death.

Angela stood on one side of her father, and Alan was on Abram's other side. The rest of the family was pressed close to them. While the pastor spoke, family and friends studied the flower-draped casket and the yawning grave, a fresh mound of dirt beside it.

When the service was completed, the crowd passed by the Kane family, offering their condolences. When everyone had left the grave side, the pastor nodded to the gravediggers, and they lowered the casket into the ground.

As the family made their way slowly down the gentle, grassy slope, the hollow sound of dirt on wood met their ears. Alan looked back over his shoulder and wiped tears from his face. He stayed in step with Adam, who was walking close to him. Abram and Angela were side by side.

Angela moved up close to Adam and Alan and said, "I'm glad both of you were still here when Mama died so you could be present for the funeral."

It was a somber family that gathered at the Kane house to spend time together, especially to show their love to Abram. Angela and her sisters-in-law prepared a simple meal, and soon they were all seated around the kitchen table.

Abram prayed over the food, then glanced around at his solemn family. Taking a large white handkerchief from his pocket, he wiped tears from his cheeks, then cleared his throat. Everyone at the table looked at him.

A thin smile graced Abram's lips. "I know we are all going to miss your dear mother dreadfully. No one can ever take her place in our hearts, that's for sure. But she is home safe with Jesus now, and if she could send us a message, I know she would want us to be celebrating her life, not mourning her death. Let's all honor her wishes and rejoice that she is free from pain and suffering, and let our memories of her be precious and sweet, and praise God for His amazing grace."

Abram's family all stared at him wide-eyed for a silent moment. Then Angela said, "Let's each share a special memory about Mama that is particularly dear to us."

More tears were shed, but they were happy tears as each one told of some precious memory they had of Kitty Kane.

Later that night, Alan welcomed Adam into his room and said, "Big brother, this hurting inside will ease for you when we get to Texas and the Lord brings that special, beautiful Christian young lady into your life. You'll fall head over heels in a hurry and end up married soon thereafter."

Adam turned his head and looked him in the eye. "You think so, eh?"

"Yes sir. Of course, I figure the Lord will give me that special Christian girl in Texas that He has picked out for me too. She and I will fall in love, and wedding bells will ring for us also. You and I will build two of the fanciest ranch houses that Texas ever saw! Our wives will be close friends, and our kids will be kissin' cousins. We'll have a happy life in Texas." Then they talked about William Childress's pending arrival at Boston Harbor in early June.

Still carrying the grief of the day, Alan managed a smile. "You and I are going to do well in the cattle ranching business, big brother. We'll build us a real cattle empire! We'll have to figure out a name for our ranch and a brand for our cattle."

Adam nodded. "We'll have to do that, but we have plenty of time before it's necessary." He rubbed the back of his neck. "I—uh, have something to tell you, little brother."

Alan's brow furrowed. "Yes?"

"Well, with Mama having just died, I feel that I should stay with Papa and Angela for a while before going to Texas."

Alan leaned forward. "I think that is a good idea. Since you're the oldest brother still in the Kane home, you can best help Papa and Angela get settled again in Mama's absence."

Adam nodded. "That's the way I'm looking at it. I'll catch up with you in Texas later."

"Sure," said Alan. "If I gain ownership of a ranch before you come, I'll teach you about being a cattle rancher when you get there. I know we'll do good as partners."

Adam grinned. "We sure will, but you'll no doubt still be at the Circle C Ranch, learning cattle ranching from William Childress when I catch up to you. I figure that I can head for Texas by late July or early August. I hope Mr. Childress will give me a job on the ranch."

"I feel quite sure he will, big brother. When I tell him about Mama dying and all and that you plan to come to Texas, I'll ask him if he will give you a job."

Adam stood up. "You're the best, Alan. Well, it's bedtime. I'd better head for my room."

On Monday morning, June 2, the *Blue Bayou* sailed into Boston Harbor. An excited Alan Kane was there on the dock, anxious to lay eyes on William Childress.

Alan had given notice to John Dixon two weeks earlier that he would be leaving Tuesday, June 3, and why. On the previous Friday, Alan had asked Dixon if he could be assigned to the crew that would be unloading the Circle C Ranch hides off the ship, and Dixon agreed.

Alan's heart pounded in his chest as the ship pulled up to dock and he saw William Childress standing on the deck at the railing. He waved and called out, "Hello, Mr. Childress!"

A warm smile curved the Texas rancher's lips, and he waved back. "Alan! Glad to see you!"

A few minutes later, the rancher reached the bottom of the gangplank, and the two men were shaking hands.

William Childress was a lean, lanky Texan. The red hair that was visible beneath the brim of his hat blended with the freckles on his suntanned face. He stood an inch taller than the six-feet-four-inch Alan Kane.

As the two of them stepped away from the gangplank, Childress said, "Well, Alan, are you coming with me when the *Blue Bayou* leaves harbor tomorrow morning?"

Alan smiled from ear to ear. "I sure am, sir!"

"Good! I'm glad!"

"I've been assigned to the crew that's unloading the *Blue Bayou*," Alan said. "So I'd better join the others."

Childress nodded. "I have appointments with some leather goods people in Boston for the rest of today. I'll meet you right here at the dock in the morning. I assume you already know we shove off at ten o'clock sharp."

"Yes sir. I'll be here, ready to go!" He met Childress's gaze. "Something I'd like to tell you right now, if you have a minute."

"Certainly."

Alan told Childress about the death of his mother on April 27 and that his brother, Adam, who was not married, was making plans to come to Texas with him to become a rancher once he felt he could leave their father and sister.

Childress laid a hand on Alan's shoulder. "I'm sorry about your mother's death. You told me that everyone in your family is a Christian, right?"

"Yes."

"Well, praise the Lord, your dear mother is with Him."

"Amen."

"And when Adam comes to the Circle C Ranch to see you, if he wants to work for me and learn the cattle ranching business as well, he has a job."

Alan smiled. "Oh, thank you, Mr. Childress. I told him I'd ask if you might be able to hire him."

"You tell Adam he's got a job as ranch hand as soon as he gets there."

"I sure will!" Alan said. "Well, I've got to get to work. See you right here in the morning."

"Yes!" the rancher said as he hurried away.

When lunchtime came, Abram, his four sons, Lee Nevins, the Benson brothers, and Ben Delsart ate together, but Alan did not bring up to Adam that William Childress had offered to hire him. Later, when lunch was over, Alan collected his father and brothers privately and told Adam what Childress said about giving him a job when he arrived in Texas. This pleased Adam, as well as his father and other brothers.

That evening Angela cooked a meal for the entire family. There was a mixture of sadness and joy at the table as they talked of Alan leaving for Texas the next morning…and Adam planning to follow him some time later. Abram told his two youngest sons that he would miss them very much, but he was glad for the future the Lord seemed to have planned for them in the cattle ranching business.

Angela, her two married brothers, and their wives all spoke their agreement.

Late in the evening, Libby and Vivian told Alan that since they would not be at the docks in the morning, they would say good-bye now. They both told him that they would be praying for him. Alan wept as he hugged them, saying he loved them.

It was a bittersweet good-bye, but as the rest of the family looked on, they knew that going to Texas to become a cattle rancher was Alan's dream—and now Adam's as well.

The next morning, when Alan and Adam were about to head for the docks with Alan's luggage, Angela had tears in her eyes as she opened her arms to embrace her little brother.

Alan had always been Angela's favorite brother, but she had been careful not to let it show. Tears streamed down her cheeks as she clung to him. Then, stepping back, she looked into his eyes and tried to smile. "I can't tell you how much I'll miss you, Alan. So many things are changing in our lives, but I know that the Lord has His hand on us."

Quickly she wiped away her tears and once again embraced him.

"Who knows, Alan? Maybe all of us Kanes will end up in Texas. Wouldn't that be something?"

A bright smile lit up Alan's face. "That would be just wonderful, Sis! Anytime the rest of the family is ready to come, the welcome mat will be out!"

"I'll be praying for you," Angela said. "Please write and let everyone in the family know how things go for you in Texas."

"I sure will," he said.

Angela kissed his cheek. "I love you, Alan."

He then kissed Angela's cheek. "I love you too, Sis. Bye for now."

SIX

At Boston Harbor, the *Blue Bayou*'s towering masts cast shadows over the dock as the Dixon Ship Lines men loaded cargo aboard for New Orleans.

In the office, Alan Kane shook hands with John Dixon, thanking him for the years he had employed him as a dock worker. Then Adam and Alan left Dixon's office with Alan's two pieces of luggage and headed for the place on the dock where the ship was being loaded.

When the two Kane brothers came near the ship, they found William Childress there in conversation with Alex and Abel, Will and Jack Benson, Ben Delsart, and Lee Nevins. Lee was giving his testimony of having been led to the Lord by Abram Kane.

When Adam and Alan drew up, Alan set his luggage down and introduced Adam to William Childress. They shook hands and Childress said, "I just met your brothers here, and I'd sure like to meet your father. Mr. Nevins was just telling me how your father led him to the Lord."

Alan smiled. "Papa will be here shortly, Mr. Childress, to say good-bye before you and I leave for Texas."

"Good!" said the Texas rancher. "I look forward to that."

The Benson brothers, Ben Delsart, and Lee Nevins quickly stepped up to Alan, saying that they had to get to their assigned ships but wanted to say good-bye first. Moments later they walked away, leaving Alan holding back tears. Alex and Abel then hugged Alan and told him they'd miss him and would be praying for him.

When Alan and Adam were left alone with William Childress, the rancher looked at the older brother. "Well, Adam, I wish you could go with us today, but Alan told me about your mother's recent death and why you need to stay with your father and sister for a while." He paused. "Please accept my condolences in the loss of your mother. Like I told Alan, praise the Lord your mother is with Him."

Adam nodded. "Yes sir. Praise the Lord. She's not in pain anymore."

"Right!" Childress said.

Adam smiled. "I want to thank you for the job offer, sir. I really appreciate it. Are...are you sure you can use me on the ranch?"

"Oh yes. I can use you, all right. I've got a big spread out there in southeast Texas, and even though I have a large number of ranch hands, there is always plenty of work for one more man to do."

"Okay, Mr. Childress. I'll take the job! I'm looking forward to the day I arrive at the Circle C Ranch."

"Well, I'm looking forward to that day too, Adam. And let me say this... I'll have Alan well broken in by the time you get there. In fact, Alan will be a seasoned cattleman in no time!"

Alan chuckled. "I hope I don't fall short of your expectations, Mr. Childress."

"You won't, son. I know it."

William Childress then told the Kane brothers about the wonderful Bible-believing church in Washington-on-the-Brazos that he and some of his ranch hands and their families belonged to. He explained that it was about thirty miles east of the ranch.

"We're glad to hear about the church, Mr. Childress," Alan said. "We've got a real good church here in Boston, but I'm sure we'll like your church, too."

At that moment the Kane brothers saw their father coming toward them.

"Here comes our papa, Mr. Childress!" Alan said.

Alan introduced William Childress to their father, and when they shook hands, Childress said, "Hey, you've got quite a grip there, Mr. Kane! Maybe I should hire you to come and help milk the cows on the ranch!"

Abram chuckled. "Don't tempt me, Mr. Childress. I'm kind of envious of these two boys of mine getting to go and learn the cattle business on your ranch."

"Well, come on!"

Abram laughed, and Childress said, "Mr. Kane, I sure have taken to your boys here. In fact, I really like Alex and Abel too! Anyway…I'm really looking forward to having Alan and Adam living and working on my ranch."

At that instant, the whistle on the *Blue Bayou* blew five times.

Abram looked at Alan. "Well, son, as we all know, that means the ship will pull out in twenty minutes."

"We'd better get aboard soon, Alan." Childress looked down at the two pieces of luggage at Alan's feet. "My luggage is already in my quarters on the ship. I'll carry one of those for you."

"Okay." Alan smiled at him. "I'll let you."

Alan hugged his father and his brother and told them he'd write when he got to the Circle C Ranch and let them know how everything was going. "You'll write me, won't you?"

Both Abram and Adam nodded, saying they would.

Adam turned to the rancher. "Mr. Childress, when I send a letter to Alan, how should I address it?"

"Just address it to Alan Kane in care of William Childress at Washington-on-the-Brazos, Texas. That's the capital of the Texas republic, you know."

Adam grinned. "Yes sir."

"When you write my name, put 'Circle C Ranch' right next to it."

Adam nodded.

"The post office isn't open on Sundays," Childress said, "so we can't pick up our mail when we're in town for church, but we have wagons going into town for supplies quite often that pick up the mail."

Adam nodded again.

"Do you have a pencil and paper on you, Adam? I want to give you some information about what you should do when you make the trip to Texas."

"I don't, sir," Adam said. "But I can run over to the Dixon office and get some. Be right back."

As Adam hurried across the dock, dodging carts, crates, and men handling freight, Abram expressed his appreciation for what William Childress was doing for Alan and Adam. He stopped and pointed with his chin. "Look who's coming, son."

Alan turned and a smile curved his lips when he saw Angela.

Abram flicked a glance at the rancher. "That's my daughter, Angela, Mr. Childress."

William Childress looked on with a smile as the blue-eyed blonde drew up and wrapped her arms around Alan. "I just had to come to the docks and give you one more hug before you leave."

Alan's voice choked with emotion as he hugged her tightly. "This means so much to me, Sis. I love you."

After Alan kissed his sister's cheek, he released her. "Mr. Childress, I want you to meet my sister, Angela. Sis, this is William Childress."

Angela extended her hand, and when the rancher took hold of it, he smiled broadly. "I'm so glad to make your acquaintance, little lady."

She smiled up at him. "And I'm so pleased to meet you too, sir. Thank you for what you are doing for Alan and Adam."

At that moment, Adam walked up with pencil and paper in hand and smiled at Angela, who had an arm around Alan. "Hey, little sis, I'm not at all surprised you showed up here to tell Alan good-bye again."

Angela smiled. "Adam, I dearly love *all* my brothers."

Adam bent over and planted a kiss on her cheek. "And we dearly love our little sister!"

Adam gripped the pencil as he leaned the folded paper on his knee. "All right, Mr. Childress. I'm ready."

The others looked on as Adam began to write. William Childress explained that when he headed for Texas, he was to take one of the many freight ships that went from Boston to New Orleans. He pointed out that the freighters were always glad to take on some passengers, and their rates were quite reasonable.

Childress went on to tell Adam that once a week a passenger boat went from New Orleans, Louisiana, to Galveston, Texas. When Adam got to Galveston, he was to take a passenger boat to Velasco, which was on the southern tip of Texas on the Gulf of Mexico. He explained that a boat went every day from Galveston to Velasco and that the Brazos River emptied into the gulf at Velasco.

Adam was then to take the ferry northwest up the Brazos River to Groce's Landing. The rancher explained that he kept one or two saddle horses there at all times. He had a friend at Groce's Landing named Mel Sibley. Childress said that when he and Alan were there, he would tell Mel that Adam was coming. Adam was to identify himself upon arriving, and Mel would saddle one of the horses for him and give him directions to the Circle C Ranch.

Adam was writing hastily, trying to get it all down. When he had written Childress's words about the horse, he said, "Ah...Mr. Childress, I have only ridden a horse one time in my life."

Childress chuckled. "That's enough. My horses are quite tame. You'll be fine."

Alan cleared his throat. "Mr. Childress, I...ah...I have never been on a horse."

Childress chuckled again. "When I get you to the Circle C, my boy, I'll teach you real quick. After all, Alan, since you're going to be a rancher, you must learn to ride a horse!"

Alan laughed. "That's for sure, sir!"

Childress then looked back at Adam. "Remember I told you that there is a passenger boat that goes from New Orleans to Galveston once a week?"

Adam nodded. "Yes sir."

"Well, unless you happen to arrive in New Orleans on the same day the boat goes to Galveston, you will have a few days to wait. I have a close Christian friend who owns a plantation just outside New Orleans. His name is Justin Miller. His entire family is Christian. Alan and I will be staying with the Millers on this trip. I'll tell them that you will be coming in the not-too-distant future, so they will be expecting you in case you have to wait for the boat a few days."

"I appreciate that." Adam's smile claimed his rugged features.

Childress went on. "All you have to do is use a hired buggy to take you to the Miller place. Believe me, all the buggy drivers in New Orleans know exactly where the Miller plantation is. Justin and his family will put you up in their mansion until you can get on the boat to Galveston."

Adam arched his eyebrows. "*Mansion,* eh?"

Childress smiled, turning his palms up and hunching his shoulders. "What can I say? The Millers are quite wealthy."

Adam scratched behind his ear. "Mr. Childress, one other thing."

"Mm-hmm?"

"I've been hearing and reading about the problem between the Texans and the Mexican government. Do you think there's going to be a war?"

Childress rubbed his chin. "Could be. We all hope not." He sighed. *"Presidente Antonio López de Santa Anna,"* he said in a mock Spanish accent, "is going to have to accept the fact that we Texans will not be dominated by his rule. We are a free and independent republic. Have been since 1824. We aim to stay that way, even if we have to fight."

Just as those words came out of Childress's mouth, there was a single blast on the *Blue Bayou*'s whistle, followed by the clanging of the bell atop the ship's cabin. Crewmen were scurrying about on the deck.

Alan turned and embraced his sister one more time. He kissed her cheek. "I love you, Sis."

Angela's eyes shone with tears. "I love you too, Alan."

Abram's youngest son hugged him, telling him he loved him, and as Abram said the same words back, he choked up.

Alan turned toward Adam, and the two brothers' eyes locked. Both were misty-eyed. After a quick, hard embrace and Adam saying he'd see Alan as soon as possible, Alan picked up one of his bags. William Childress already had the other one in hand.

As the Texas rancher and his new employee hurried toward the ship, Alan glanced back at his loved ones. The two of them hurried up the gangplank, then moved to the railing on the deck and looked down at Abram, Adam, and Angela.

The giant sails of the *Blue Bayou* were hoisted upward as the ponderous guy rope was released from the huge post on the dock.

The harbor winds instantly caught the sails with a popping sound.

As the ship moved slowly away from the dock, a tender smile flitted across Alan's handsome features while his gaze fastened on his precious sister. Angela was striving valiantly not to cry, but it was not working. The tears on her cheeks glistened in the morning sun, and Alan's heart was deeply touched. "I love you, Sis!"

Angela blew Alan a kiss and wiped frantically at the streaming tears, flashing a bright smile at him.

Abram was waving. Alan waved back and called out, "Love you, Papa!"

Abram mouthed his "I love you" back.

Alan then cupped his hands around his mouth and shouted, "Hey, Adam! Remember, I'm praying that you'll find a beautiful Christian girl and get married!"

Adam smiled and waved.

Abram, Angela, and Adam Kane stood on the dock and watched until the *Blue Bayou,* masts tilted by the wind, passed from view.

The *Blue Bayou* docked in New Orleans on Saturday, June 28, just as the sun went down over the western horizon.

As Alan Kane and his new boss loaded their gear into a hired buggy, William Childress looked at the driver. "I imagine you know where the Justin Miller plantation is located."

The driver, a silver-haired man in his late sixties, smiled. "I sure do, sir. Everybody in New Orleans knows where the Justin Miller place is."

"That's what I figured. Before we head that way, I need to go to the Galveston Transportation Company and secure boat passage to Galveston."

"All right, sir," the driver said. "I know where that place is too."

As both men climbed onto the seat behind the driver, William Childress said, "That's what I figured."

The driver laughed and put the horse into motion.

It was only a five-minute drive to the Galveston Transportation Company, which was located strategically near the docks. William Childress hopped out of the buggy. "Alan, you can wait here. I'll be back in a few minutes."

Alan nodded and smiled. "I'll stay right here, boss. Promise."

Childress chuckled as he walked toward the office door.

The driver made friendly conversation, asking if Alan and his father lived in Galveston. Alan explained that Mr. Childress was not his father, but that he was owner of a large cattle ranch in southeast Texas and had hired him in Boston as a ranch hand.

Alan was explaining the whole situation to the driver when William Childress came out of the office, tickets in hand, and hopped into the buggy.

Looking at Alan, William said, "Our trip to Galveston is in four days... next Wednesday, July 2."

Alan nodded and smiled. "Okay, I guess the Millers will have guests until then."

"They sure will."

The driver put his horse to a brisk walk and headed through New Orleans.

As the steel-rimmed wheels rambled over the cobblestone streets, William said, "I haven't really told you much about the Millers except that they are Christians and that they are wealthy. They have two beautiful daughters."

Alan met his gaze. "Oh, really?"

"Mm-hmm. Sally is twenty, and Julia is eighteen."

Alan grinned. "I'm looking forward to meeting them."

"Sally has a young man who belongs to their church that she's been dating steadily for some time, but even though many of the young men in the church have shown interest in Julia, the last I knew, she didn't have a steady boyfriend."

Alan nodded.

William said, "Fine family, Alan. You'll like them."

Alan let his eyes roam to the lamplighters on each side of the street doing their job in the gathering dusk. "I'm sure I will, boss."

A bayou mist was gathering among the moss-covered oak trees as the buggy rolled out of the city. The steel-rimmed wheels were comparatively quiet on the soft dirt road.

As the buggy moved out into the country, William explained to Alan that the Millers had slaves on their plantation and quickly told him that, as Christians, they treated their slaves with kindness and love. All the Miller plantation slaves were fine Christians, he told him, and attended a nearby church that had been established for slaves from various plantations owned by Christian white people.

Alan smiled. "I'm glad to hear this, Mr. Childress. I know that so many slaves are mistreated by their owners."

"That's for sure," Childress said, "but not by the Christian plantation owners around here."

It was dark as the buggy, its own lamps now burning, pulled up to the Miller mansion. A silver moon was rising in the east.

Alan Kane had a momentary feeling of unreality as he stepped from his side of the buggy while Mr. Childress stepped from the other. Alan took a long look at the great white pillars that stood as silent sentinels on the long brick porch. Bars of yellow light streamed from the draped and curtained windows. The sound of countless crickets and the sight of little fireflies flitting about, flashing their luminescent lights, added to Alan's feeling of fantasy.

William and Alan took their luggage from the buggy and set it on the porch near the door. William paid the driver, stepped up on the porch, and rapped the brass knocker beside the door.

The door eased open, and a thin man with white hair and a long, slender face appeared. Light from the chandeliers in the vestibule revealed a familiar face to the butler. He smiled. "Mr. Childress! Hello, welcome! The Millers will be glad to see you. Please come in."

As the two men stepped inside, the butler's gray eyes turned to Alan.

"This is Alan Kane," William said. "He's traveling with me. We'll be leaving on the boat for Galveston next Wednesday. Alan, this is Garth"—William blinked—"I…uh…guess I never have known your last name, Garth."

The butler smiled. "It's not important, Mr. Childress." He then turned to Adam and offered his hand.

As they shook hands, Garth said, "Pleased to make your acquaintance, Mr. Kane."

Alan smiled. "And I'm glad to meet you, Garth."

When Garth let go of Alan's hand, he said to William, "Mr. Miller is the only one on this floor, sir. I will summon him and then bring in your luggage."

As Garth walked away leaving the front door open, Alan said in a low voice, "Boss, we can bring our own luggage in."

William shook his head. "No, Alan. It would insult Garth if we carried it ourselves."

He met William's steady gaze. "Oh. Well, all right."

Alan turned to take in the large vestibule. Rich tapestries lined the walls, which were decked with exquisite paintings and glistening mirrors. Luxurious rugs lay scattered on the marble floor. Every shiny surface reflected the flickering flames from the dazzling chandeliers that hung overhead. Hand-carved doors and woodwork surrounded them on three sides, from one of which Garth had entered. The fourth side was dominated by a spiral staircase that swirled its way upward to merge with a balcony at the top. A wide hallway could be seen behind the balcony. Alan assumed that the hallway must lead to a large number of bedrooms.

William took notice of Alan's veneration. In a low voice, he said, "Some shack, huh?"

"Yeah!" The young Kane smiled. "A real neat shack!"

At that moment, they saw Justin Miller coming toward them from the rear of the mansion. Alan studied him. He was obviously in his early fifties and was dressed as if he were going to some special occasion.

"William!" Justin rushed up and extended his hand.

They greeted each other warmly. Then William introduced Justin Miller to Alan Kane, explaining that he had met Alan in Boston and was taking him home to be one of his ranch hands. He quickly added that Alan was a fine Christian young man from a good Christian family. He explained that they would be taking the passenger boat to Galveston on Wednesday. Miller shook Alan's hand and welcomed him warmly.

While this was going on, Garth passed by them, went out the open front door, and returned, carrying the luggage belonging to the Millers' guests. He grunted some as he went up the spiral staircase and soon disappeared.

William looked Justin up and down and asked, "Ol' pal, why are you dressed up so fancy?"

"Well, ol' pal," Justin said, "we're attending a dinner this evening at the Dardanelle plantation. Sally and the Dardanelles' oldest son, Jeffrey, are going to formally announce their engagement at dinner. Most of those guests are from our church in New Orleans, including the pastor and his wife."

William's eyes widened. "Oh! So Sally's going to marry that steady boyfriend of hers!"

Justin chuckled. "She sure is."

William shook his head in disbelief. "Justin, it seems like little Sally should still be playing with dolls. They grow up too fast, don't they?"

"They sure do. As you know, she's twenty years old now."

William shook his head again. "Both of your daughters have grown up too fast. If I remember right, Julia will turn nineteen next month."

Miller nodded. "Mm-hmm, July 23."

"And it seems like *she* should still be playing with dolls too."

"For sure," Miller said. Then the plantation owner clamped a hand on William Childress's shoulder. "Too bad you don't have a son for Julia to marry, William. Then both of my daughters could live in style." He chuckled. "It worries me sometimes with all these peasant young men from the church pounding on the door, wanting to court her."

William laughed.

Justin laughed too. "William, I'm sorry we have to be gone this evening. I hate to go off and leave you and Alan."

William gave him a warm look. "Hey, it's all right. We both understand. Alan and I will get a good night's sleep."

Justin smiled. "Okay! Myra and the girls will be down shortly. We have time yet for you to see each other for a few minutes this evening at least, and we'll take you and Alan to church tomorrow."

"We'll look forward to it!" William turned to Alan. "You'll really enjoy their pastor's preaching."

Alan's eyes sparkled. "I can't wait!"

At that moment, Garth came down the spiral staircase. "Mr. Miller, Mrs. Miller and the girls said to tell you that they will be down in a few minutes and that they are glad William is here to spend a few days. They are looking forward to meeting the friend he has with them."

Justin smiled and turned to his guests. "Let's go into the parlor and sit down."

SEVEN

When the three men had entered the parlor and eased onto overstuffed chairs facing each other, Justin Miller looked at Alan Kane and said, "I know there are no cattle ranches in Massachusetts. Do you have ranching experience from somewhere else?"

"No sir," replied Alan. "Working on the Circle C Ranch will be my first experience with cattle and horses."

William Childress spoke up. "Alan and his brother Adam are going to work on the Circle C as ranch hands so they can learn the cattle business, Justin. Adam, who is three years older than Alan, will be coming a little later. The Kane brothers plan to one day have a ranch of their own in Texas."

Justin grinned at Alan. "Mighty fine. Mighty fine. There's money to be made in Texas, son. However, it looks like you may have to learn Spanish and talk your way out of a war with Mexico before you can live in peace there."

William looked at Justin. "Have you learned of some new developments in this Texas–Mexico thing?"

"Yes," replied Justin. "According to yesterday's edition of the *New Orleans Sentinel,* the Big Mex, Santa Anna, is about to turn the Mexican government into a dictatorship, and he's going to be the dictator. The article said Santa Anna has publicly stated in Mexico City that he is not about to give up Texas. As far as he is concerned, Texas still belongs to Mexico."

William shook his head and frowned. "Somebody over there in Mexico needs to take Santa Anna down a peg or two. He's getting awfully big for his britches."

"I agree," said Justin, "but I doubt it'll get done. From what I've read about him, the Big Mex has an army that worships him, and the common people of Mexico are scared of him. He's a powerful and dominating man."

William smacked his fist into his palm. "Well, if we have to fight Santa Anna and his army, we'll do it. General Sam Houston is no pushover. He has already stated that he will build the Texas army bigger real quick and chase Santa Anna and his troops back to Mexico City for good."

Justin Miller laughed. "Well, from what I've heard about General Houston, if anybody can do it, he's the man."

William nodded with a smile, then sent the smile to Alan Kane.

At that moment, they heard doors opening and closing upstairs and the sound of female voices.

Justin rose from his chair. "Let's go meet them at the bottom of the stairs."

William and Alan followed Justin into the hall and then to the vestibule. Just as they reached the bottom of the spiral staircase, two exquisitely dressed ladies approached the top of the stairs together and began to slowly descend.

At first, Alan thought it was the Miller sisters, but as they came closer, he could see that one of them had to be the mother. His eyes moved to the face of the younger one. She was strikingly beautiful. He wondered if she was Sally or Julia. Her dark brown hair was in an upsweep, revealing a lovely, slender neck. *The kind of woman a man dreams about,* he thought.

Nearing the bottom of the stairs, both ladies smiled as they set their eyes on the tall Texan.

The mother was the first to speak. "Bill Childress! I was so glad when Garth told us you were here! It's so nice to see you. Justin and I were talking about you just the other day. We were wondering if you might be coming through sometime this month." Myra Miller stepped off the bottom stair.

William smiled. "Well, you don't have to wonder anymore!"

Alan Kane watched as his new boss took Myra's hand, clicked his heels, and bowed. Raising her hand to his lips, he kissed the back of it lightly. "Myra, you are lovelier than ever."

Justin spoke up jovially. "She sure is!"

Myra blushed as William released her hand, then turned to her daughter.

Alan was still wondering which sister this was. His question was answered when William said, "Hello, Sally," then clicked his heels, bowed, and kissed her hand as he had her mother's.

William let go of the lovely young lady's hand. "Sally, you are within a hairsbreadth of being as beautiful as your mother."

"Oh, Uncle William." Sally giggled. "You're such a charmer! Do I still get my usual hug?"

"Time's awasting!" William gathered her in his arms.

Alan Kane was enthralled with the moment. He stood, mouth open, taking it all in. He had heard of this New Orleans custom of men kissing ladies' hands, but until now he had never seen it.

William looked softly into Sally's eyes. "Congratulations on your engagement to Jeffrey. I know you'll be happy together."

Sally's cheeks reddened. "Thank you." She then looked over William's shoulder and set her eyes on the tall, sandy-headed Irishman. "So this is your friend Garth told us about."

William released her and turned to Sally and her mother. "Ladies, I want to present Alan Kane. I met him in Boston some time ago, and now he's going to the Circle C with me. I've hired him as a ranch hand. Alan is a Christian. He and I are going to church with you tomorrow."

Alan was thinking that this Jeffrey Dardanelle was a very fortunate young man to be marrying the charming and beautiful Sally Miller, when Sally stepped up to him and extended her hand. "I am so happy to meet you, Alan."

Sally's hand stayed right there. Alan was about to delicately shake hands with her when suddenly, he realized what he was expected to do. Goose bumps crawled up the back of his neck. Quickly, he took Sally's hand and tried to click his heels, but he only got a dull *whump* sound. Clumsily, he bowed and kissed the back of her hand with a loud smack.

Sally saw that Alan was flustered. The young lady had an abundance of personality and showed no shyness. Smiling, she said, "I see you're not accustomed to kissing the ladies' hands. Well, it's all right. You did fine."

Alan's features tinted. "Th-thank you, Miss Sally."

Myra stepped up and extended her hand and smiled. "Welcome to our home, Alan."

The tall Irishman bungled again with his heels, but the kiss on Myra's hand was a silent one.

In an attempt to ease Alan's tension, William Childress said, "Alan's just never been around New Orleans and its customs, but I'm sure he will—"

The sight of Julia Miller at the top of the stairs cut off William's words.

Lifting his eyes, Alan saw that the Texan had caught sight of another female descending the stairs. Raising his gaze higher, he was suddenly and totally captivated. *This has to be Julia.* Alan swallowed hard and blinked. Julia bore the family resemblance, as did her sister. But on her it looked even better.

Julia's long, dark brown hair swirled around her head and lay softly on her elegant shoulders.

While Alan watched her descend the spiral staircase with ease and grace like a dove descends from the blue, he thought, *Sally is beautiful, but Julia is* stunningly *beautiful*!

Julia's deep blue eyes fell on Alan as she neared the bottom of the staircase, and she gave him a warm smile. Alan felt his heart turn to flame. Somewhere deep within him, a drum seemed to thunder, vibrating his rib cage.

The lovely Julia left the last stair and shifted her gaze to the tall Texas rancher. "Uncle William!" she exclaimed, rushing into his arms.

William hugged the girl chastely as he had her sister, then held her at arm's length. "It's so good to see you again, Julia." He took hold of her right hand, clicked his heels, bowed, and kissed it. Then he gestured toward the tall, ruggedly handsome Irishman. "Julia, I want you to meet Alan Kane."

Alan felt his knees turn to water as the breathtaking Julia Miller gave him her hand. He skipped the heel clicking business but bowed and kissed the lovely white fingers. Then resuming his height, he said, "It's pleasurable—uh—I mean, I'm pleased to meet you, Miss Julia."

William Childress chuckled. "I've explained to your family that I met Alan in Boston some time ago, Julia. Now he's going to the Circle C with me. I've hired him as a ranch hand. He's going to work on the ranch and learn the cattle business. His brother Adam is coming down from Boston shortly to do the same. They plan to one day have a big ranch of their own in Texas."

"Your brother Adam?" Julia giggled. "Is he as tall and handsome as you?"

Alan's face flushed. "He's…uh…he's exactly the same height as me, Miss Julia, but Adam is lots better looking."

She smiled. "I have a hard time believing that."

Alan's face flushed again.

"One's as good-looking as the other," said William. "And I want you to know that Alan is part of a fine Christian family and is dedicated to the Lord. He and I are going to church with all of you tomorrow."

Julia smiled at Alan. "I hope your new career as a cattle rancher works out well for you and your brother, Alan. I am glad to know that you have Jesus in your heart."

Alan matched her smile. "Me too, Miss Julia. It's so wonderful to know Him and to have the promise of heaven when my time is up on this earth."

Julia nodded. "Well put." She paused. "Uncle William said Adam is coming shortly from Boston. How soon will that be?"

"I don't know exactly. You see, my mother died in April, and Adam, who is not married, still lives with my father and my sister. He's going to stay with them until he is satisfied that they can go on without his help. We have two other brothers in Boston, but they are married and of course live in their own homes."

Brow furrowed, Julia touched Alan's arm. "I'm sorry about your mother's death."

Alan nodded. "Thank you, Miss Julia. We all miss her terribly, but she's with the Lord in heaven now, so we know we'll all be together again someday."

Tears misted Julia's eyes. "Yes. Isn't that wonderful?"

"It sure is."

"Alan, please accept our condolences in the loss of your mother," said Justin.

A synchronized "yes" came from the three Miller women.

Alan's lower lip quivered a little. "Thank you."

"Well, family, we need to be going." Justin looked at Garth, who was standing near. "Will you see that my two friends here are fed well and bedded down for the night?"

"Certainly, sir," Garth replied.

Justin ran his gaze between the two men. "William...Alan, we'll see you in the morning at breakfast."

"It's a deal," said William.

"Sure is," added Alan.

As the Millers headed for the front door, the three ladies said their polite good-byes to the guests.

Alan watched Julia step through the door and memorized the last expression on her face as she looked back at him and smiled.

Garth closed the door behind the Miller family. "All right, gentlemen, I will show you to your rooms upstairs. Then while you unpack and freshen up, I will prepare your meal. The Millers have a slave cook and housekeeper, but she is not here right now. She is attending a special service at her church in New Orleans this evening."

"Sounds fine to me, Garth," said William. "If you cook as well as you do everything else, it'll be a delicious meal."

Garth grinned. "Follow me."

He led them to the spiral staircase and hurried up the stairs with William and Alan behind him.

When they reached the top of the stairs, Garth said, "Gentlemen, you each have your own private guest room. I have placed your luggage in your rooms already. Mr. Childress, you will be in the room you usually stay in."

William nodded.

"And Mr. Kane," said Garth, "you will be in the room adjacent to Mr. Childress's."

"Fine." Alan gave him a smile.

"I'll go to Alan's room with him first, Garth, if that's all right," William said. "I want to see his face when he walks in there."

"Of course, sir."

Alan grinned at William. "It must be pretty nice, huh, boss?"

"That's an understatement. You'll see."

As they passed the closed door to William's room, he pointed at it. "That's my room, right there."

"And this is *your* room, Mr. Kane," said Garth as he stepped ahead of them and opened the door. Lanterns were already lighting the room.

As Alan followed Garth into the room with William at his side, he stopped and looked around, eyes wide. "Wow!"

The room was exquisitely furnished, with a huge fourposter bed that was heaped high with a thick feather mattress and lush down coverlets. Soft-colored patterned rugs covered much of the gleaming wooden floors, and a hint of linseed oil lingered in the air. Two overstuffed chairs, upholstered in pale blue brocade, sat by the large window, which was draped in the same fabric. The window was partially open, allowing a soft breeze to sway the sheer curtains.

A large mirrored chiffonier stood against one wall, and a desk and chair were at the opposite wall. Near the chiffonier was a dark-colored dresser with a white china bowl and pitcher filled with water atop it.

William studied Alan's wide eyes.

Garth broke the silence. "You gentlemen just take your time to unpack and freshen up. Dinner will be ready when you are."

William nodded. "All right, Garth. I'll go to my own room now. We'll be down shortly."

As William followed Garth into the hall, he said over his shoulder, "Alan, I'll knock on your door when I'm ready to go downstairs."

"Fine, boss," replied Alan. "I'll be ready."

Thirty minutes later, when Alan heard a soft rap on his door, he rushed to it and pulled it open.

"Ready for some dinner, son?" William asked cheerily.

"Sure am, sir! All that fresh sea air I breathed in on the trip has me hungry!"

"Good. Let's go down and see what Garth has prepared for us."

Downstairs the butler was listening for the sound of footsteps coming from upstairs, and when he heard them, he stepped into the hall at the open dining room door. When they arrived at the bottom of the stairs and headed down the hall, he smiled. "Right this way, gentlemen."

William and Alan followed him into the dining room, which was glowing with lantern light, and saw a small table set for two in a cozy alcove near a large bay window. The food was already on the table, steaming hot, with tall glasses of tea.

Guiding them to the small table, Garth pulled their chairs out. "I thought you two gentlemen would be more comfortable here rather than sitting alone at the big table over there."

"This is just perfect, Garth," said William.

As both men sat down, Garth picked up a small bell he had laid on the table earlier. "If you need anything else, just ring this bell."

William grinned. "We'll do it, Garth. This food smells great!"

"Sure does!" Alan said.

"I hope you enjoy it." Garth headed for the door. When he stepped into the hall, he paused and looked back. "Remember, if you need anything else, just ring the bell."

"Sure will!" said William. "I'm an old bell-ringer from way back!"

Garth laughed and headed down the hall.

Later that night, as Alan Kane was lying in the darkness in the most comfortable bed he had ever been in, a soft evening breeze moved the curtains on the large window. The sound of crickets from outside seemed to unite in a word. In fact, it was a name. *Julia.* Over and over again, that name seemed to float through the night air, hovering over his bed and then settling upon him like a warm blanket.

Alan's heart was pounding like it had never done before.

"Could it be possible?" he asked himself in a low whisper. "Have I done it? I've heard of love at first sight. Has Alan Kane fallen in love?"

Suddenly, a numbness gripped him. Even if he had fallen in love with Julia Miller, what good would it do him? He was one of those peasants her father had mentioned who wanted to court her. As her sister was planning to do, Julia would marry a man of means.

"Someday when Adam and I have our own ranch, I'll be a man of means, and I'll be good enough for her," he whispered to himself. "But that's a long way off. Julia will be married and raising a family with her affluent husband before I have wealth."

His heart sank. "I've just got to cross this whole thing out of my mind. Besides...I'm going to Texas. Julia lives here in Louisiana. It's a hopeless situation. I—I'll just have to forget her."

Alan rolled over in the big bed, snuggled his head deeply into the soft pillow, and soon began feeling drowsy. Finally he drifted off to sleep with the Louisiana crickets outside still singing, "Julia..."

The next morning, Alan Kane awakened with the sun in his eyes. His room was on the east side of the house. Strong shafts of bright sunlight coming through the sheer curtains of the large window streamed across his face.

When he turned his face away from the light, his first thought was of Julia Miller.

He reprimanded himself, knowing that he must stifle his feelings for Justin and Myra Miller's youngest daughter. "Please help me, Lord," he said softly. "I mustn't let my heart reach for her anymore. There's no hope for anything to develop between her and me."

He rose from the bed, went to the dresser, and poured the cold water from the pitcher into the white china bowl. "*Humpf.* I have to go downstairs to get hot water for shaving. I'll just forget it today."

He turned away from the dresser, then stopped. "But I don't want Julia to see me with stubble on my face."

He realized what he had just said and shook his head. "Alan Kane, you must stifle your feelings for Julia."

Alan agreed with himself, but shaved with cold water nonetheless.

Young Kane was putting the finishing touches on his hair when he heard a light tap on the door. "Alan, you up?" came William Childress's familiar voice.

Crossing the large room with the comb in his hand, Alan opened the door. "Good morning, boss. Come in."

Leaving the door open, the Texan entered. "I'm hungry. Smelled breakfast cooking from my room."

Moving back to the dresser, Alan laid the comb down, made a final check in the mirror, and turned. "Let's go. I'm hungry too."

At that instant, Justin Miller appeared at the door smiling. "Good morning, my friends. Breakfast is ready."

"So are we!" exclaimed William.

Still smiling, Justin said, "We have a new cook since you were here last, William. Believe me, you'll love her cooking."

Moments later, as Justin Miller led his guests into the dining room, the aroma of bacon, eggs, grits, and hot coffee greeted them. "Myra and the girls will be down shortly," Justin said.

William and Alan noticed a heavyset black woman dressed completely in white busying herself at the large table. She looked up at the guests and flashed a genuine smile. "Good moanin', gennulmen. Mah name's Hosanna Millah."

"Hosanna," Justin gestured toward the two men, "this is Mr. William Childress, and this is Mr. Alan Kane. Mr. Childress is an old friend of mine from Texas. He is a cattle rancher. Mr. Kane is from Boston, and Mr. Childress has hired him to work on his ranch. Both of these men are Christians. They're going with my family and me to church this morning."

Hosanna released another smile. "Ah's glad to meet both of you. De Lord Jesus lives in mah heart too. Ah invited Him in to be mah Saviour when Ah was 'leben yeahs old."

"That's wonderful, ma'am," Alan said.

Hosanna chuckled, shaking her head. "Oh, Mistah Kane, yo' not s'pose' to call me *ma'am.* Ah's jis' a ol' slave."

Alan smiled. "You're my sister in Christ, aren't you?"

"Wal...yassuh."

"Then I will call you *ma'am.*"

She blinked and smiled again. "Ah likes yo' *real good* already!" She then set her gaze on William. "Mistah Childress, Ah's heard Mistah Justin and his fam'ly talk about yo' many times. They really does think a lot of yo'."

William looked at Justin, smiled, then looked back at Hosanna. "I think a lot of *them* too, ma'am."

Hosanna smiled at William's use of *ma'am,* then moved toward the dining room door. "Ah's got to go to de kitchen, Mistah Justin. Be back in a minute."

When she had left the room, Alan turned to Justin. "Did I hear her right? Did she say her last name is Miller?"

Justin nodded. "Yep."

"Coincidence, eh?"

Justin grinned. "Nope. Here in the South, the slaves who are treated kindly often adopt the last names of their owners. She hadn't been here a week before she asked Myra and me if she could change her last name to Miller."

"That says something for you and your family, Justin," said William.

Justin smiled.

Alan was about to comment in like manner when the sound of female footsteps was heard in the hall, along with the voice of Julia Miller, who was saying something to her mother and sister.

The sound of Julia's voice set Alan's heart to hammering in his chest.

EIGHT

The three Miller women entered the dining room.

Alan Kane's eyes went to Julia Miller like a nail to a magnet. Her long, dark hair was pulled to the back of her beautifully formed head and hung in dainty little ringlets. The mother and Sally looked nice too in their lovely dresses, but Alan's attention was riveted on the youngest daughter.

William Childress had noticed the way his new employee looked at Julia the night before. Here was that look in Alan's eyes again.

As the women moved toward the men, who stood close to the dining room table, Myra ran her gaze between the guests and asked, "Did you two sleep all right?"

"*I* sure did," replied William. "Like a little baby."

"Me too." Alan briefly took his eyes off Julia to look at her mother. He was having difficulty breathing properly.

"Looks like Hosanna has already served breakfast." Myra moved toward the table.

Justin stepped up quickly, took hold of her chair, and proceeded to seat her.

William grasped Sally's chair.

This left Julia's chair for Alan. He was not sure he could quiet his nerves enough to lift it but soon found that he did. As he seated her, he noticed Julia's beautiful dress. Up to that moment, his eyes had not left her face and her hairdo.

Justin's voice caught young Kane's attention as he said, "Alan, will you lead us in praying over the food, please?"

Alan smiled. "Of course."

When the amen came at the close of Alan's prayer, Hosanna was standing there with a tray of hot cinnamon rolls in her hands. She laid the tray on an empty spot atop the large table and smiled, saying, "Ah hopes Mistah Childress and Mistah Kane like cinnamon rolls the way the Millah fam'ly does."

"I sure do," William said.

"Me too, ma'am," said Alan.

Hosanna smiled again at his use of *ma'am,* then turned and headed for the door. "If'n anybody needs anythin', jis' ring de bell!"

Instantly plates of food were handed around the table as everyone took their share. While the meal was being devoured, most of the talk was about the dinner at the Dardanelle mansion the night before. Sally was now officially engaged to Jeffrey, and plans were being made for the wedding in December.

Alan Kane was still having a hard time keeping his eyes off Julia. Unaware of this, lovely Julia continued to do strange things to Alan's heart.

Later that morning, Alan found his heart stirred the more when he found himself sitting between William and Julia at church.

When they went to the evening service, once again Julia happened to sit beside Alan. She had a beautiful singing voice and was pleased when Alan told her so.

That night, Alan Kane had difficulty getting to sleep. He lay on his back, looking at the silvery light of the moon as it shone through his window. Julia Miller had stolen his heart.

He sighed and closed his eyes. "Dear Lord, I need Your help in this impossible situation. I know that these feelings I'm having about Julia have got to stop. There's no way she and I could ever end up as husband and wife.

She'll be married long before I can ever escape the status of peasant in her eyes or in the eyes of her parents. Please help me, Lord. I'm having a real battle in my heart, as You well know."

Alan rolled over onto his side, adjusted the pillow and the light covers, and prayed some more. Finally he fell asleep praying.

The next morning, William and Alan, already in the dining room with Justin, were watching Hosanna setting hot food on the table from a small cart when Myra and her two daughters came in. Alan noticed that the skirt Julia was wearing was different than any skirt he had ever seen.

The mystery was cleared up when William looked at her. "Ahh, Julia, I see you're in a riding skirt."

"Mm-hmm," hummed the lovely young lady. "You may recall that on weekdays, I usually ride my horse on the plantation for a couple of hours."

William snapped his fingers. "Oh, sure. Now I remember. I assume you still have Maisie."

"Sure do. She's almost twelve years old, but she can still put on quite a gallop."

Justin turned to his old friend. "William, I'd like to take you out and show you the acreage I just bought. It connects to this property. Six hundred acres."

William chuckled. "Great! You keep this up, Justin, and you're going to have your own Louisiana Purchase!"

Justin laughed, as did his wife and daughters. The cook also laughed and said, "Wal, ever'body, breakfast is on the table. Have at it!"

As Hosanna was wheeling the empty cart toward the door, Justin said to the group, "Let's eat!"

Chairs skidded on the hardwood floor as the breakfast party took their seats. Justin seated Myra, William seated Sally, and Alan seated Julia.

Justin asked William to pray over the food, and when he finished, everybody dug in.

A few minutes later, William Childress swallowed a mouthful of pancakes, then looked at Julia. "Sweet niece of mine, will you do your Uncle William a favor?"

"Of course."

"Since you're quite a horsewoman, would you take Alan with you today and show him a little bit about riding? He's never been on a horse, and I know you can break him in a little so it'll be easier for him when we get to the Circle C."

Julia's dark blue eyes swung to Alan. "They don't ride horses much in Boston, do they?"

Alan shook his head. "No call for it."

"In fact, Julia," William said, "if you can take Alan riding tomorrow too and break him in good, my job will be a lot easier when I get him to Texas."

"That's a good idea, William," said Justin. "Honey, let's have Alan ride Big Louie."

Julia's eyebrows arched. "Really, Papa? *Your* favorite horse?"

"Sure."

Swinging her gaze to Alan, Julia said, "That's quite an honor, Alan. Big Louie is my father's prize horse. He doesn't let just anybody ride him."

Alan smiled at Justin. "Thank you, sir."

Justin smiled back. "My pleasure, son." He rose to his feet and looked back at his youngest daughter. "Honey, I'll go tell Garth to have Wiley and Simon ready to saddle both horses when our breakfast is over. I want Alan to see them get saddled."

"Who are Wiley and Simon, Mr. Miller?" asked Alan.

"Couple of our slaves. They serve as stable hands whenever needed."

Alan nodded. "Oh."

Justin hurried out the dining room door.

When breakfast was over and Alan was walking beside Julia toward the stables, he could not help himself. He was experiencing indescribable ecstasy, being so close to her.

The sun was burning off what fog was left in the cotton fields. Slaves were moving about on the grounds doing odd jobs.

Many of the slaves watched the movements of Julia and her guest.

When they drew up to the stables, two young black men stood waiting for them. They had already bridled both the stallion and the mare. Julia introduced Wiley and Simon to Alan and started to explain why they were not to saddle the horses until Alan was there to observe.

Wiley shook his head. "Yo' don' need to 'splain, Miss Julia. Mistah Garth already tol' us."

"Oh," she said with a smile. "All right, Alan, watch carefully while Wiley and Simon saddle Maisie and Big Louie."

Alan's eyes went to the horse he was going to ride. He was a large black stallion with a mane and tail so black that their strands shone in the sunlight like slender pieces of silken rope. Big Louie held his head high, giving him a magnificent stance. Alan knew very little about horses, but even an inexperienced eye could tell that this was one splendid animal.

He then looked at Maisie. The bay mare had four white stockings, perfectly matched, and a blaze of white on her face.

Julia stood beside Alan as the two slaves, working on the left side of each horse, placed saddle blankets on them first, then swung the saddles onto their backs. Alan watched intently as they reached under the horses' bellies and ran the cinch straps through the metal rings. Adeptly, Wiley and Simon pulled the straps up and tightened them.

The slaves then stepped up to Julia. Simon said, "There you are, Miss Julia."

She smiled. "Thank you." Then she turned to Alan. "Did you watch closely how they saddled the horses?"

"Sure did."

"Good. Well, it's time to go."

"Have a nice ride," said Wiley, and he and his partner walked away.

Julia said, "Alan, before we mount up, there's something you need to do."

"Yes?"

"Step up to Big Louie, stroke his long face, and talk softly to him. Just tell him you really like him."

Alan grinned. "That won't be hard. I really *do* like him!"

Julia looked on with interest as Alan stepped up to the big black stallion, stroked his face, and told him in soft tones that he liked him and was looking forward to riding him.

Big Louie whinnied and bobbed his majestic head.

Alan then moved to the right side of the big black, reached up, and took hold of the saddle horn.

"No!" said Julia. "Not on the right side! You have to mount him on the *left* side! Only if you want to be the first man to fly do you mount from the right side!"

A sheepish look washed over Alan's face. "Oh. I—I didn't know."

"I don't mean to embarrass you." Julia smiled. "But I don't want to see you get bucked off."

"It's all right, Miss Julia." He matched her smile. "I'd rather be embarrassed than grasping for a cloud." Quickly, he circled Big Louie around the rear. The stallion moved nervously, blowing hard.

When Alan reached Big Louie's left side, Julia said, "Whenever you walk behind a horse, it's best to lay your hand on his rump. That way he knows what you're doing. Sometimes they'll kick if you don't."

"Yes ma'am," said Alan. "I'll keep that in mind. Seems I have a lot to learn before I can be a ranch hand."

"That's true. I'll help you all I can. Now, in order to get the feel of it, go ahead and mount up."

Alan raised his left foot, placed it in the stirrup, then swung his right leg over the stallion's broad back and settled in the saddle. "Now, I know I guide him with the reins and stop him by saying 'Whoa' and pulling straight back. But how do I make him walk? I know to make him run I would punch his sides with my heels. So do I just do it lightly?"

"On a well-trained horse," replied Julia, "you just nudge him with your knees to put him to a walk. Big Louie is the best. Go ahead. Nudge him, and at the same time make a clicking sound with your tongue like this." She made the sound for him.

Alan thumped his knees against the stallion's sides and made the clicking sound. Immediately, Big Louie responded in a rapid trot. The Boston dock worker found himself bouncing in the saddle. It shook his teeth, and he bit his tongue.

Julia shouted, "Alan, pull back on the reins and say, 'Whoa'!"

Quite nervous, young Kane yanked back on the reins, shouting, "Whoa!"

The precision-trained stallion skidded to an abrupt halt. Alan sailed over Big Louie's neck and fell to the turf.

Julia was already running toward him. She knelt at his side quickly. "Alan, are you hurt?" she asked, wide-eyed.

Alan rolled over and shook himself. "Only my pride, I think," he said hesitantly.

Julia's strong hands gripped his own as she helped him to his feet. For a moment, he did not want to let go. He could almost feel an electric current running through her hands into his. He released them quickly, not wanting her to catch on.

"You sure you're okay?" Julia asked warmly.

"Uh-huh," he grinned boyishly. "Can I try it again?"

"All right," said Julia, "only this time, nudge him more gently."

Alan rubbed his back. "How can an animal full of grass and oats be so hard?"

Julia giggled. "That's just the way it is. You ready to try again?"

"Sure."

Mounting Maisie while Alan mounted Big Louie once again, Julia said, "Walk him easy now. I want you to get the feel of riding slowly before we try a trot or a gallop."

This time, Alan was gentler with his knees. Big Louie began a casual walk. Joining him, Julia rode alongside.

As they rode away from the stable, Alan ran his gaze over the land that surrounded them and asked, "What's the size of the plantation, Miss Julia?"

"We have two thousand acres—ah, well, Papa just bought six hundred adjoining acres on the east side of the plantation, so now we have twenty-six hundred acres. Our mansion is situated directly in the center of the original two thousand acres, surrounded by eighteen hundred acres of cotton fields. The land Papa just bought is entirely cotton fields. But back to the original land, the remaining two hundred acres are made up of dense woods, open meadows, and a ten-acre lake, which lies a half mile to the rear of the mansion. A clear, bubbling stream feeds the lake."

"I'd like to see the lake," said Alan.

"I'm going to give you a tour of the whole place. We'll head toward the lake." She then said, "Stop for just a minute."

Alan carefully drew rein.

Julia hipped around in the saddle and pointed past the mansion to the east. "Do you see those cabins over there amid those oak and cypress trees?"

"Mm-hmm. Looks like a village."

"Well, those are the slaves' cabins."

"I see. Well, they look real nice."

"They are. My parents take very good care of their slaves."

"Looks like it. I appreciate that."

Julia smiled. "So do the slaves."

Soon the two riders found themselves moving across a green meadow bedecked with daisies and dandelions. Julia pointed up ahead of them. "See the lake?"

"Oh yes! I can see the stream that feeds it too."

A few minutes later, they drew up to the lake at the spot where the stream poured water into it. "Isn't it just beautiful?" Julia asked.

Alan took a deep breath and let it out slowly. "It sure is!" Julia did not know it, but Alan Kane was secretly admiring another beauty.

Swinging from the saddle, Julia said, "Rest yourself for a little while, Alan. Then we'll continue our tour."

As Alan left the saddle, he became aware of a subtle stiffness working its way into his lower body from the ride. He knew it was the result of being thrown from Big Louie earlier.

Julia took the reins of both horses, led them to the edge of the stream with Alan by her side, and let them drink from the stream.

"I often come here when I want to be alone and just talk to the Lord."

Alan smiled. "It's sure a perfect place for that. I really like it."

There was a moment of silence, except for the lapping of the horses at the stream. Then Julia said, "Alan, I'm sure when you are living on Uncle William's ranch, you'll find your own spot to get alone and talk to the Lord. From what Uncle William has told me, the Circle C is a beautiful place."

Alan smiled. "I'm sure I will, Miss Julia."

"You'll like working for Uncle William, Alan. He's such a kind and generous man."

"I'm really looking forward to working for him," Alan responded with another smile.

Julia looked at him with questioning eyes. "How long have you known him?"

"A little over a year. One day, when the ship carrying Mr. Childress's load of cowhides docked in Boston Harbor, he was on board. I had been assigned to help unload that ship. He and I met there on the dock and got acquainted. I liked him immediately, and he seemed to feel the same about me. From time to time, he came to Boston with his cowhides to try to pick up more business, and the Lord just seemed to work it out each time that I was assigned to help unload the ship with him on it."

Julia smiled. "The Lord has a way of doing wonderful things for His children, doesn't He?"

"He sure does. So anyway, we got better acquainted each time. One of those times, in a conversation we were having, I told him I wasn't going to load and unload freight all my life…that I wanted to get into business for myself someday."

"That's good," said Julia.

"Mr. Childress told me how things were opening up in Texas for obtaining land to raise cattle on, thanks to Stephen Austin and his colonizing. Sounded mighty good to me, so here I am, on my way to Texas to learn the cattle ranching business on the Circle C Ranch."

"And your brother Adam too," Julia said, smiling.

"Oh yes! Adam. I'll sure be glad when he can come."

"And your other two brothers. What are their names?"

"Alex and Abel. Alex is the oldest, and Abel is next oldest."

"You're twenty, right?"

"Yes."

"And Adam is—"

"Twenty-three. You'll like him." A light shone in Alan's eyes. "He's the finest brother a fellow could ever have. Good-looking brute. Strong as a cornfed ox."

Julia giggled. "I hope it works out that when he's heading for Texas he can spend a few days here. I'd love to meet him."

"You'll like him; I guarantee it."

Julia looked up at the position of the sun in the morning sky. "Oh! My, how time flies! If I'm going to give you a full tour of the plantation, we'd better get going!"

It was nearing noon by the time Julia had given her guest the promised tour. The two of them were in their saddles on a small hill looking at a grove of oak trees a short distance from the mansion. "Well, we'd better ride for the house now. Hosanna probably has lunch about ready," Julia said. "Since tomorrow is your last day with us, Alan, we'll go riding again, okay?"

"Sure." He felt the soreness in his body from his earlier fall. "Your Uncle William wants you to teach me as much as possible, remember?"

She giggled. "I remember. Tomorrow we'll trot awhile. Then, if you're game, we'll even gallop a little."

"Sounds good to me," Alan responded as they headed toward the mansion.

"Okay!" she said. "Tomorrow we'll turn Big Louie loose and let you feel the wind in your face."

Alan grinned. "Whatever you say, teacher."

As they put the horses in motion toward the mansion, Julia said, "Actually, Alan, it's easier to ride at a gallop than it is at a trot."

"Really?"

"Uh-huh. You'll see why tomorrow."

A few minutes later, as Julia and her pupil rode up to the backside of the mansion, they saw Justin Miller and William Childress sitting on the back porch.

The men greeted the riders as they pulled rein and swung from their saddles. As Alan and Julia walked toward the porch, both men noticed that Alan was walking a little stiff-legged.

William Childress chuckled. "Hey, Alan, you're walking sort of stiff, aren't you?"

Alan met his gaze and forced a grin. "Yeah. First day in a saddle, remember?"

"I remember." William chuckled. "Well, my boy, if you think you're sore now, just wait till tomorrow morning!"

Justin laughed.

"Well, Uncle William," Julia said, "Alan will work out the stiffness when we go riding again tomorrow."

Alan was glad that Julia did not tell them about his flight from the saddle.

Julia smiled. "Uncle William, I can tell you right now that Alan is going to make a real good horseman."

The rancher grinned and nodded. "I'm glad to hear that, Julia. When I get Alan to the Circle C, I'll have him busting broncs in no time!"

The back door of the mansion opened. Hosanna's toothy smile glistened as she said, "Lunch is ready, folks!"

NINE

On Tuesday morning, after an excellent breakfast cooked by Hosanna that the Miller family and their two guests thoroughly enjoyed, Julia Miller led Alan Kane to the stable, where she told Wiley and Simon that she wanted to let Alan bridle and saddle Big Louie so he could learn how to do it.

Wiley took Big Louie's bridle from a peg inside the barn and led Alan into the corral while Julia and Simon looked on.

As they drew near the backside of Big Louie, Wiley handed the bridle to Alan. "Let's see if yo' can do it without my tellin' yo' how."

Alan took the bridle, and as he moved up to the black stallion, he laid a palm on his rump.

Wiley's eyes widened. "Hey, Mistah Kane, yo' done approached him jis' raght!"

Alan looked back and grinned. "Miss Julia taught me about the approach yesterday."

"Good for her!"

Alan moved up in front of Big Louie and stroked his long face, saying, "Good morning, Big Louie. Want to go for a ride?" The stallion bobbed his head slightly and softly whinnied.

"Good!" Alan raised the bridle up to the horse's face.

Big Louie held absolutely still while Alan slipped the bit into his mouth, then put the bridle on his head and strapped it tightly.

"Ah thinks he likes yo', Mistah Kane," said Wiley.

"He sure does!" called out Julia.

Alan smiled at her. "Don't tell your father, Miss Julia, but I think I'm going to take Big Louie with me to Texas!"

Julia and Simon laughed.

Wiley told Alan to lead the horse by the reins to the barn, where Simon had the saddle lying at his feet. Maisie was standing there, already bridled and saddled. Julia looked on as both slaves gave Alan instructions on saddling the horse. Within a very few minutes, Alan had the saddle in place with the cinch tight. He grinned at Julia. "Well, ma'am, let's go for my riding lesson."

The two slaves watched, smiling, as Julia and Alan mounted up and walked the horses away slowly.

When the two riders were some distance from the stable in an open field, Julia said, "I told you yesterday that riding at a gallop is easier than riding at a trot, but there are more times that you will have your horse in Texas at a trot than at a gallop, so you need to learn to handle a trot."

Alan smiled at her. "Whatever you say, Miss Julia."

She smiled back. "What you have to learn is to blend your body with the horse in a trot. If you don't move with the animal, it will jar you to pieces."

Alan nodded.

"All right," she said. "You stop Big Louie and watch as I show you about trotting."

Alan pulled rein, and the stallion halted.

Julia made the usual clicking sound with her tongue, nudged the mare solidly with her knees, and immediately went into a swift trot. Julia made a couple of large circles around Alan while he observed how she bounced in the saddle in rhythm with Maisie's movements. She drew up beside him. "Well, think you've got the idea?"

"Yes, teacher," he replied.

"Okay. Let's see you do it."

Big Louie responded instantly to Alan's prompting, even as Maisie had with Julia, and made several wide circles around her as she looked on, amazed at how quickly he adapted to the rhythm of the trot.

When he drew up to her, Julia said excitedly, "That's it, Alan! You've got it! You're a natural!"

Alan and Julia rode together at a trot, covering a great deal of ground on the plantation. When they came near a stand of oak trees, Alan followed suit as Julia pulled rein. She looked at him. "Well, are you ready to put Big Louie to a gallop?"

"Sure."

"Okay." She looked off to their right. "The lake is about a half mile beyond that hill over there. Let's gallop to my favorite spot where the stream pours into the lake, and we'll rest for a while."

"Whatever you say, Miss Julia."

"All right. Gouge Big Louie good with your heels, and holler, 'Giddyup!' I'll be right beside you. When we get close to the lake, tug back on the reins gently and holler, 'Whoa!' real loud."

"Got it."

Alan did it perfectly and had the big black stallion at a full gallop as Julia pulled up alongside him on Maisie. She smiled and shouted, "You're a natural, Alan! A natural!"

They galloped speedily toward the lake, and the closer they got to the spot, he was finding that he *was* sore. William Childress was right. Alan hurt in places he did not even know he had! But he would never let anyone know about it.

When they halted the horses at the spot where the stream fed into the lake, and dismounted, Julia said, "I'm not kidding, Alan. You *are* a natural. You have taken to riding like you were born in the saddle!"

As Julia spoke, she noticed that Alan was looking at their reflections in the water at the edge of the lake. He then set his gaze on her face. "Thank you for the encouragement. I guess I might make it as a rancher in Texas after all."

"You sure will. You're going to be a real success."

Alan looked back into the water and kept his eyes on their reflections.

Julia saw a slight trace of sadness on his face. "Alan, what's wrong?"

The tall, muscular Alan Kane looked at her and shrugged his wide shoulders heavily. "Well, Miss Julia, it's—it's—"

"What?" she asked, frowning.

"It's just that I've never enjoyed myself as much in my whole life as I have these past couple of days."

Julia smiled. "I'm glad. You're becoming quite a horseman."

Alan grinned. "Yeah. Thanks to the Julia Miller School of Horsemanship for Greenhorns."

A sweet, feminine giggle escaped her lips. "Alan Kane, you're something!"

Young Kane couldn't help himself. He *had* to let her know a little bit about how he felt. "I—I'm sad, Miss Julia, that I have to leave tomorrow."

She lifted a hand with the palm toward him. "Alan, you don't have to call me 'Miss Julia.' You can call me Julia or even Julie if you wish. That's what my friends call me."

"I...ah...I noticed that at church on Sunday. I'd be honored to—"

"Be one of my friends?"

"Well, I, uh—uh, yes."

"Well, then, that settles it. You, Alan Kane, are hereby inducted into the exclusive circle known as the 'friends of Justin Miller's daughter who have permission to call her Julie'!"

"Thank you, Miss Julie." His heart secretly pounded his rib cage.

She shook her head. "No, no. Not *Miss* Julie. Just Julie."

"I—I am honored, Julie. Thank you."

Julia warmed Alan with a smile and took hold of his hand. "Let's go over here and sit down on that fallen tree. If we sit on the grass, we'll get chiggers."

He raised his eyebrows. "Chiggers? What're chiggers?"

Julia laughed. "I guess they don't have them in Massachusetts. They're little tiny bugs that get under your clothes, bite you, suck your blood, and make you itch like crazy."

"Oh. I sure don't want those."

Alan gladly let her lead him to the dead tree. The touch of her hand on his sent a tingling up his spine. As they sat down, Julia said, "I've been calling you Alan ever since you got here. I assume that's all right."

He chuckled, looking into the eyes that captivated him. "Well, ah…that's what my friends call me."

Julia patted his hand. "Well, then, I hope we can always be friends and maybe get to see each other once in a while, even though I live in Louisiana and you'll be living in Texas."

Alan wanted to tell her that he was in love with her and wanted to marry her someday in the not-too-distant future, but because he was one of those peasants her father had mentioned, he told himself again that she would never marry him. He nodded. "I hope we can too, Julie." In his mind, however, he doubted it would ever happen.

She looked into his eyes. "I'd like to know more about your family. I'm so sorry about your mother's death, but I'd like to hear about your father, your sister, your other two brothers, and their wives. You've already told me a lot about Adam."

Alan then went into the subject of his family, and by the time he had finished, Julia said, "I can tell you miss them a lot."

"I sure do."

"Well, maybe when you and Adam get your big ranch going, they can move to Texas and live there with you."

Alan grinned. "Boy, that would be wonderful!" He thought, *I would like to have you there, as my wife, Julie,* but kept it to himself.

That night, at the Miller mansion, after everyone else in the household had retired, Alan sat at the desk in his room and opened a drawer. The Millers had provided stationery and envelopes for their guests, as well as a pen and inkwell.

He wanted to write to Adam so the letter could be posted from New Orleans the next day. Dipping the pen into the inkwell, he addressed the envelope. Pausing to raise the flame in the coal oil lamp on the desk, he took up the pen and began to write.

Tuesday, July 1, 1834

Dear Adam,

I am presently staying in the home of Justin Miller, whom Mr. Childress mentioned to you. His plantation is outside of New Orleans a few miles. The mansion is beautiful! My room is like a luxury hotel room. If you get to stay here, I guarantee you will love it.

We arrived here on Saturday, June 28. We will be leaving for Galveston tomorrow morning.

The Miller family is really nice. They have two beautiful daughters. I've been learning how to ride a horse. Will get better at it in Texas. (I hope!)

Sure will be glad when you and I are together again. Tell everyone in the family I love them.

Your loving brother,

Alan

Alan Kane wiped tears from his cheeks with the back of his hand and sniffed. He waited for the ink to dry, then folded the letter neatly. Before he put it in the envelope, he unfolded it and read it through. He wanted to tell Adam about Julia, but told himself it would be of no use. Tomorrow he would be gone, and for Alan Kane she would be only a sweet memory.

On Wednesday, the early morning sun was straining to cut a hole through the fog that hovered over the Miller plantation as Garth finished loading William and Alan's gear into Justin Miller's largest buggy. The plantation owner would drive his guests to the docks.

Standing on the front porch of the mansion, William reminded the Millers that Adam Kane would come to the Miller plantation for lodging if he had to wait for the boat to Galveston. The Millers all agreed that Adam would be welcome. Hosanna was also on the porch and assured Alan that she would feed his brother real good if he came to the plantation.

Julia then surprised Alan by speaking up and announcing that she was going to ride in the buggy to the docks with the three men.

Alan wished it was because she felt toward him like he felt toward her. *Foolish boy,* he told himself silently. *It's because of her strong affection for Uncle William and the fact that she is just a kind, thoughtful young lady.*

Justin Miller turned to Alan. "You can sit on the driver's seat with me. Julia will ride with William in the rear seat."

"All right, sir," said Alan.

Myra, Sally, Hosanna, and Garth stood on the porch steps and bade their guests farewell.

William then took Julia by the hand, helped her into the rear seat of the buggy, and climbed in next to her.

When Justin and Alan were settled on the driver's seat, Justin put the team of horses in motion.

As the buggy headed toward the city in the misty fog, Alan twisted on the seat and looked at Julia behind him. "Some fog, huh?"

She smiled. "Mm-hmm. Sometimes it's a lot heavier than this."

William said, "We don't have fog like this at the Circle C. We're far enough from the Gulf that what little fog we get is quite thin."

"That's fine with me," said Alan. "I've seen all the fog I care to see in Boston."

William noticed that Alan's eyes went from him to Julia and lingered there a few seconds before he turned around on the driver's seat.

As Alan turned around, Julia's thoughts drifted back over the few days she and Alan had spent together, and a wistful look claimed her lovely face.

William caught the look on Julia's face. He was fully aware of the attraction Alan had for her. He had seen it many times in the few days they had been at the plantation. Wisely, however, he had said nothing to either one. *Best to let the Lord work His will in this situation,* he thought.

Alan's heart was aching as they got closer to New Orleans. He was going to miss Julie. He stiffened a bit and reprimanded himself for these feelings. He knew that he must weed this attachment toward Julie out of his heart. She could never be his.

The mists were still quite heavy on the waters as the buggy pulled up to the pier where the big sign was barely readable through the fog: Galveston Transportation Co.

Within a few minutes, dock workers had carried the gear belonging to William and Alan onto the boat. Passengers were working their way across the gangplank to get on board.

Justin Miller told both men how glad he was they had been able to spend the few days with him and his family.

Julia stepped up to the tall Texan, hugged him, and they told each other good-bye. Julia then turned to Alan, smiling at him.

Alan looked down at the beautiful young lady. "Thanks for the riding lessons, Julie. You've been a great help."

She maintained her smile. "That's what friends are for," she responded in a delicate manner, then rose up on her tiptoes, kissed his cheek, and gave him a light hug.

Alan's heart pounded as he gently hugged her in return. He wanted to blurt out, *"I love you!"* But he knew that such sentiments must forever remain caged up inside him in case he was unable to weed his feelings for her out of his heart.

Moments later, when Alan Kane and his new boss stood on the boat's deck as it pulled away from the dock, Julia stood beside her father and waved, smiling at Alan.

The foggy mists gave it all a dreamlike effect. Alan sadly told himself that this was all Julie Miller could ever be to him. A misty dream.

At sundown on the fourth day at sea, Sunday, July 6, the boat bearing William Childress and Alan Kane pulled up to the dock in Galveston, Texas. William hired a surrey to take him and his new hired hand into town, where they would stay for the night.

While they were helping the driver load their luggage into the surrey, William said, "Tonight, we're staying at Galveston's finest lodging, Alan. It's called the Austin Manor Hotel."

Alan smiled. "Austin Manor, eh? Would that happen to be named for *Stephen Austin*?"

William smiled. "You got it, son! We'll catch the boat to Velasco in the morning."

As they rode through town, Alan saw that Galveston was a bustling place. He commented on it, and William said, "I'll tell you, Alan, the lure of Texas is like a contagion in the United States and territories. It is quickly gaining momentum. Since the first colonization in 1819, settlers have been coming steadily. The population in Stephen Austin's Republic of Texas is now between thirty and forty thousand and gaining in number daily."

"Well, that's good, boss," said young Kane.

"For sure," nodded Childress. "Most settlers are coming by wagons, but many are arriving by boat, and Galveston seems to be the favorite place to land."

Soon they arrived at the Austin Manor Hotel and checking in to their rooms on the second floor. They were famished, so they stepped past their luggage, which was being delivered by a hotel attendant, descended the stairs, and headed for the hotel's restaurant.

When they entered the restaurant, Alan was amazed at its size and how crowded it was already. Giant chandeliers hung overhead, adding their own touch of finesse to the décor. A band of guitars and brass instruments was situated on an elevated platform on the far side of the large dining room. With the band playing behind him, a well-dressed man with a tenor voice was belting out a song about Texas.

When a waiter had seated William and Alan, William smiled. "Ever see anything like it?"

Alan shook his head. "Nope, there's nothing like this in Boston."

When the waiter returned with steaming cups of coffee, William ordered large steaks for Alan and himself. Later, as William saw Alan wolfing his meal down, he said, "That's the kind of eating you'll be doing from now on, my boy."

Alan stopped chewing long enough to smile and say, "I'm liking Texas real well already!"

When the meal was finished, both men were stuffed, especially Alan. "I have to admit it, boss. I've never been so full after a meal."

"Well, good. Tell you what, Alan. How about we take a short walk on the street before going back to our rooms?"

"Sure!" The night air had cooled somewhat as they came out of the hotel lobby onto the street, and the smell of salt water permeated the atmosphere. As the two men walked along the lantern-lit street, people moved about, talking lightly, laughing, and having a good time.

Suddenly Alan's attention was drawn across the street, where a group of men were roughly taunting one lonely figure, slapping his face and ripping at his shirt.

William noticed it also and saw the look of contempt that crossed Alan's face as he watched the scene.

Alan turned. "I'm gonna look into this." As he spoke, he stepped off the boardwalk.

William hastily moved up beside him and touched his arm. "Better stay out of it, son."

"Can't, boss," the muscular Irishman said from the side of his mouth, still moving toward the scene. "It isn't right for so many men to pick on just one man. Especially as small as he is."

Childress kept stride with Kane all the way across the broad street. As the two of them drew near the tight circle, they could see that the small man, who appeared to be in his early twenties, was a Mexican. As seven rough-looking men jostled him about, the Mexican's eyes were wide. Fear rode his swarthy face.

William paused, but Alan barged in and grabbed a man who was slapping the little Mexican and yanked him back so hard he stumbled and fell.

Alan then inserted his six-foot-four-inch, 220-pound frame into the circle, stood by the Mexican, and, looking around at the group, said stiffly, "What's going on here?"

The man Alan had surprised and thrown to the ground leaped to his feet but remained where he stood. The young Mexican looked up at Alan with relief. His shirt was torn in several places, and his face was bruised. Blood was trickling from the corner of his mouth.

One of the gang bellowed at Alan, "Butt out, mud-brain! This is none of your affair!"

"Oh, yes it is!" snapped Alan, fixing the man with an icy glare. "I just made it so!"

William Childress licked his lips nervously.

A big, thick-chested man in his late thirties with ponderous features hitched up his belt and swaggered over to Alan. Showing his teeth, he hissed, "This guy is a dirty Mex, meathead! We're just givin' him his due!"

Alan felt the quick, red tide of anger. "What has he done?"

"He's a dirty Mex! That's enough! Now, get out of here, or I'm gonna beat you to a pulp!"

"You tell him, Hector!" came a raspy voice.

"Yeah, Buttram, button his lip!" came another.

Alan Kane, who was experienced at fighting bullies on the Boston docks said levelly, "You might want to rethink that, Hector."

"You're stickin' your nose in where it don't belong, Mex lover! I hate Mexicans!"

The big man's friends spoke up in unison, backing him in his hatred toward Mexicans.

Alan ran his steady gaze over their faces. "Since when is it a crime to be born a Mexican?"

The man Alan had thrown to the ground earlier rasped, "We're Texans, mister! And the dirty Mexicans are tryin' to take our Republic of Texas away from us! This dirty Mex doesn't belong in Texas!"

Alan's brow furrowed. "You think this one little guy is going to take your republic away from you?" he asked in a singsong tone.

"He's a dirty Mex!" spat one of the gang. "We don't want him here!"

Alan turned back to the little Mexican. "Where are you from in Mexico?"

"From Mehico Ceety, señor, bot I no wanna go back to Mehico. I was soldier in San' Anna's army. He is bloody tyrant! I defected from hees army. No wanna fight an' keel eenocent people. I jus' wanna leeve in Texas. Be a Texan too!"

Setting his jaw, Alan eyed the gang of men coldly. "Now you've heard it. The man defected from Santa Anna's army and wants to become a Texan."

Hector Buttram rasped, "But he ain't got no right—"

"No right to *what*?" cut in Kane.

"To be a Texan!" rasped Buttram, exposing his yellow teeth in an angry grimace. "He's a furriner!"

"Where are *you* from?" lashed Alan.

"Missouri."

"But *you're* not a foreigner? Texas is its own country!"

A vicious look reddened the man's eyes. "But he's a dirty Mexican!"

One of the things that Alan Kane had learned in his fights and savage brawls on the Boston docks was that every gang has a leader. Take out the leader, and the gang turns to jelly. This huge, beefy man was obviously the leader.

Choosing his words carefully, Alan asked, "How did this man become a Mexican?"

"He was born that way," came the deep-voiced reply.

Alan poised himself, every muscle honed and ready. "Well, he can't help that he was born a Mexican any more than you can help you were born a thick-skulled nincompoop."

It worked. Hector Buttram swung his big right fist. Alan ducked and countered with a vicious blow to the nose. Buttram staggered backward. The others scattered, making room for the combatants.

The little Mexican backed away and bumped into William Childress. The rancher took hold of his arm. "You don't have to leave, partner. I've got a feeling that when this is over, you won't have any more trouble from this bunch."

The Mexican smiled up at the tall Texan and relaxed.

TEN

William Childress and the battered Mexican stepped back a few paces from the scene of the fight, becoming part of the crowd that was gathering from both sides of the street.

At the same time, big Hector Buttram came at Alan Kane with blood running from his nose, his eyes wild and filled with wrath.

Alan dodged two hissing fists. Then his own fists pounded the big man's jaws like mallets, the sound of them solid and hard, like an ax striking a tree.

Buttram staggered backward, shaking his head. His friends were calling for him to finish off the intruder. Buttram spit on the ground. "I'm gonna tear off your arms and beat you over the head with 'em!" He dashed for Kane, his hands open and fingers extended like claws.

Alan avoided the big hands and landed a powerful blow to Buttram's jaw. Again the huge man staggered backward. This time he rebounded and ran toward his opponent, swinging his thick right fist. Alan made him miss the punch, but their bodies collided, and Alan went down, thinking he knew now what it was like to be run over by a rhino.

Tottering a bit from the blows that Alan had put on him, Buttram leaned down to take hold of him, but Alan rolled, evading the stubby fingers, and jumped to his feet.

Big Hector glared at him with fire in his eyes. "I'm gonna cripple you, Mex lover!"

Alan answered by rushing in, dodging the fist that Buttram sent toward his head and smashing the big man's nose again. He followed that with a blow to the chin. Buttram took a backward step, then moved in, popped Alan's temple with his left, and caught him with a hard right to the stomach.

Alan felt like a mule had kicked him. His full stomach reacted with a wave of nausea.

The beefy man's nose was bleeding heavily, but he was coming at Alan again. Ignoring his stomach spasms, Alan set himself and drove a powerful fist to Buttram's jaw. Buttram wavered unsteadily, blinking, but countered with a violent blow to Alan's temple.

Alan saw stars. He backtracked and took another punch in the stomach. A sour taste leaped into his mouth.

Hector came in again. Alan planted a sledgehammer blow on his jaw. The big man was caught flatfooted and went down hard.

Alan stood over him, sucking for air and clutching his stomach. The crowd was roaring.

Buttram was groggily trying to get to his feet. Alan was sure he could knock him out with one more solid punch. As he was looking down at Buttram, waiting for him to get up, a man with a revolver on his hip and a tin star on his vest was elbowing his way through the excited crowd, who recognized Galveston's town marshal, Rex Handford.

Alan Kane's attention was fixed on Hector Buttram as he staggered to his feet, a wild look in his eyes. He went after Alan with both fists ready. Before he could swing a punch, a powerful, hissing fist slammed Buttram again. His head wobbled, and he staggered back a bit. Alan was about to send home the finishing punch when from the corner of his eye, he saw a man coming at him. It never occurred to him that the man was an officer of the law. His attention was glued on Hector Buttram. He did not see the tin star or the holstered gun on the man's hip. His only thought was that one of Hector's friends was coming to his rescue.

The man laid a hand on Alan's shoulder and growled, "That's enough, fella!"

The tall Irishman whirled and landed a savage punch square on his jaw. Galveston's town marshal went down like a poleaxed steer.

Still not noticing that the man he'd just put down wore a badge and a gun, Alan turned back to face big Hector Buttram as he was coming at him, both fists pumping.

He dodged the big fists and countered with an earthshaking blow to Hector's jaw with all his weight behind it. Buttram thudded to the street, out cold.

Alan doubled over and grabbed his full stomach, which was now giving him severe nausea. Moving swiftly, he dived between the two nearest buildings and privately gave up his supper.

At the same time, William Childress and the little Mexican, having seen Alan plunge between the buildings, were worming their way through the crowd while two men who were not part of the gang were helping the dazed Marshal Rex Handford to his feet.

Most of Hector Buttram's group were kneeling beside him trying to revive him.

Childress and the little Mexican waited at the edge of the shadows between the buildings where Alan had gone. Moments later, the tall, muscular Irishman emerged into the light provided by the streetlamps, wiping his mouth with a handkerchief. He was slightly stooped.

Alan saw his boss and the Mexican and stopped. William laid a hand on his shoulder. "Are you all right, Alan?"

Alan coughed into the handkerchief. "Yes sir. I'm okay."

With his hand still on Alan's shoulder, William said, "Son, I want to commend you for your fighting ability. You're going to be a mighty good man to have on the Circle C."

Still bent forward, Alan shook his head. "I'm never gonna do that again."

Childress's brow furrowed. "Never going to fight again?"

Alan gingerly touched his midsection. "Not on a full stomach!"

The tall Texan laughed.

The little Mexican started to step toward Alan when he was shoved aside by the irate marshal.

Alan found himself looking down the black muzzle of Marshal Rex Handford's Colt .45.

William Childress stopped laughing as the glassy-eyed marshal shouted, "Get your hands up! You're under arrest!"

Alan's eyes widened, startling blue against his rugged features. They shifted from the menacing muzzle of the revolver to the tin star to the bruise he had put on the marshal's face.

He swallowed hard, still tasting stomach acid, and blinked. "I—I'm sorry, Marshal. I didn't realize who you were. I thought you were one of that guy's friends."

"Striking an officer of the law is a serious offense!" snapped Handford. "Now get those hands up. You're going to jail!" He motioned with the gun barrel. "Down the street thataway!"

Alan lifted his hands above his head and started down the street with the marshal behind him.

Instantly William Childress moved up beside the lawman, keeping pace with him. "Marshal, punching you was really an honest mistake. I know this young man. He's not the kind who would—"

"Talkin' ain't gonna help, mister!" snapped the man with the gun.

The little Mexican was walking next to Childress. Looking past him at the lawman, he pointed at Alan and said, "Señor Marshal, thees man was helping me! Zoes men were beating up on me! Zey might have keeled me! Zis man, he stop them! When he beat op on that beeg man, he was protecting me!"

"Shut up, Mex," said the marshal, "or I'll take you back there and turn 'em loose on you!"

William Childress could not believe his ears. "Marshal, you're an officer of the law. You're supposed to protect people. How could you—"

"Mexicans ain't people!" rasped the lawman. "And don't you be tellin' me my job, or I'll lock you up too!"

Childress shook his head in disbelief as they reached the jail. He saw by the sign on the wall next to the door that the marshal's name was Rex Handford.

Looking at Childress, Handford said, "Open the door. And no funny stuff!"

William and the Mexican were told to wait in the office while the marshal took Alan to the rear of the building through a narrow door. They heard Alan ask what was going to happen to him. The marshal told his prisoner that he would have an arraignment before the judge in the morning.

The cell door clanked shut loudly, and moments later the marshal entered his office. He threw the waiting pair a frown, picked up paper and pencil off his desk, and returned to the cell area.

Some fifteen minutes passed, then the marshal returned to the office. He eyed Childress disdainfully. "That guy that punched me tellin' the truth? His name Alan Kane?"

Childress nodded.

"He told me your name is William Childress. You're *the* William Childress? The one who owns that big ranch west of Washington-on-the-Brazos?"

"I am."

"And he's from Boston?"

"He is."

"You're takin' him to your ranch? You hired him in Boston to be a ranch hand?"

"That's correct."

A scowl formed on the marshal's face. "You're sure he's not a spy for Santa Anna? That the reason he defended this Mex is because he's on Mexico's side, even though he ain't dark-skinned?"

"Marshal Handford, I'm positive Alan is not a follower of Santa Anna. He's never been nearer Mexico than he is right now."

The lawman wiped a hand over his mouth. "Then why was he so quick to help this Mex?"

Childress bristled. "Look, Marshal, Alan saw Hector Buttram and his gang beating up on this man, who is half the size of any one them."

The little Mexican nodded. *"Sí! Sí!"*

"Alan simply did the honorable and decent thing," continued Childress. "He waded in there against that bunch and stopped it!" He rubbed a palm over his face. "I'm only ashamed that I didn't help him."

The Mexican piped up. "I theenk, Señor Kane need no help! He ees mighty tough hombre!"

"Marshal," said William, "may I talk to Alan?"

"You can have ten minutes," the marshal said coldly. "Then I'm lockin' the place up for the night. I've got some things to take care of here in the office. You be back here in ten minutes."

"May I talk to Señor Kane too, Marshal?" asked the Mexican.

"Oh, all right. But you be back here in ten minutes too."

"Sí, Señor Marshal," said the Mexican as both men headed for the door at the rear of the building.

When they reached the door and stepped into the cell area, Alan left the bunk in his cell and walked to the bars. A single lantern hung from a heavy wire from the low ceiling just outside Alan's cell, throwing yellow light around the small, stuffy area. The Texas rancher and the battered Mexican approached the cell. Alan managed a smile and waited to hear what they had to tell him.

"Alan," said William, "I'm not going to let that judge give you a jail sentence. I happen to know how they do it here in Texas. There'll be a fine or so many weeks in jail because you struck an officer of the law. I'll be there with you when you face the judge, and when he lays out the jail sentence or the fine amount, I'll pay the fine, and you'll walk out with me a free man."

Alan noticed that Marshal Rex Handford was standing in the open doorway behind his boss and the Mexican. Handford spoke as he stepped into the cell area, "There won't be any fine, or jail sentence, Mr. Childress."

William and the Mexican turned around to see the marshal rubbing his jaw where Alan had punched him.

"I—I got to thinking about this, Mr. Childress," said Handford. "You are a very reputable man, and since you said that Mr. Kane here simply did the honorable and decent thing going to this little man's rescue, I've realized you were right. Sure, he hit me when I laid a hand on him, but he didn't know who I was. He certainly could have thought I was one of Hector Buttram's friends. I'm dropping the charges. Mr. Kane is free to go."

Alan let out a sigh of relief. "Thank you, Marshal Handford."

The marshal took the key ring off his belt and opened the cell door. "You're welcome, Mr. Kane."

The marshal led the three men to the front door of his office, and as they walked away in the light of the streetlamps, Alan looked at his boss. "I want you to know how much I appreciate that you would have paid my fine to keep me out of jail."

Childress stopped beneath a streetlamp. Alan and the Mexican halted also. The rancher grinned. "Son, I'd have paid a handsome fee to see a fight like the one you had with big Hector any day!"

Alan chuckled.

The swarthy little man set appreciative eyes on Alan. "Señor Kane, you save my life! Zoes mens might have keeled me! I never forget it! *Gracias! Gracias! Gracias!*"

Alan smiled at him. "What's your name, friend?"

"Juarez Amigo."

"Juarez?"

"Sí."

"That's your first name? Juarez?"

"Sí."

"What's your last name?"

"Amigo."

"*Amigo*?" echoed both Alan and William, looking at each other.

There was a slight pause. "Your name is Juarez Amigo?" asked Alan.

"Sí, señor."

"When you said 'Juarez Amigo,' I thought you were saying, 'Juarez, friend.' "

Juarez snickered. "Wal, because of what you deed to rescue me from zoes mens, I *am* your fran' for zee rest of my life!"

"What are you going to do now, Juarez?" asked Alan.

Juarez shrugged. "I no know. Eef I go back to Mehico, San' Anna will have me shot. I no like heem. San' Anna is a bloody keeler. I come to Texas to escape him. I want to be a Texan."

"Do you have a family in Mexico?" asked William Childress.

"No, señor," Juarez replied sadly. "My family ees all dead. My father, mother, and seester. Zey die of fever epi—epi—"

"Epidemic?" Childress helped him.

"Sí."

"You have no other family? Nowhere to go?"

"No, señor."

"How long have you been in Galveston?" queried Alan.

"Two days. I queet San' Anna's army many weeks ago. I walk from Mehico Ceety to Ciudad Madero. Stow away on feeshing boat. Feeshermen find me after they put out to sea. They Texans. Sell feesh to Mehicanos. Bring me to Galveston."

William Childress pondered the situation. Eying the little man carefully, he asked, "Juarez, do you know anything about cattle and horses?"

"I know how to ride a horse, Señor Childress. I learned that een Mehicano army. Bot I know nothing about cattle." He grinned. "Bot I can learn *muy pronto*! Sí! Sí!"

Childress smiled. "All right. I'm going to take you home with me and hire you as a ranch hand."

The Mexican's face lit up.

"Are you willing to work hard on any job I give you?"

"Oh, sí, señor! Anythang you want deed right, you call on Juarez!" He looked at Alan, then back at Childress. "Señor Alan Kane ees going to leeve on your ranch too, yes?"

William smiled. "Yes, he is. He will be a ranch hand, also. You two can start a new life together."

Juarez Amigo's white teeth glistened in a wide smile as he turned back to Alan. "Oh, *muy bueno*! We amigos be frans forever, sí?"

"Sí!" laughed Alan, and hugged the little man. "Juarez Amigo is my friend forever!"

Tears were in Juarez's eyes as Alan let go of him.

William said, "Juarez, Alan and I are staying at the Austin Manor Hotel, and we're leaving on a boat to Velasco at nine o'clock tomorrow morning. You come with us now, and I will get you a room for tonight too so you can get on the boat with us in the morning."

When they reached the hotel, William was able to get a room next to Alan's. He bade the two younger men good night, reminding them that the boat would leave at nine o'clock in the morning, so they needed to be up early enough to eat breakfast together and get to the docks. He explained to Juarez that the hotel rooms had windup alarm clocks, asking if he knew how to use one. Juarez said he had used them at times when he was in the Mexican army. William suggested that they arise at six thirty. Both young men agreed.

Alan and Juarez then moved to the door of Alan's room, and Alan told Juarez good night. Juarez thanked him again for saving his life and repeated what he had said earlier. "We be frans forever!" Juarez then headed for his room.

As Alan stepped into his room, Juarez's words echoed in his ears. His mind flashed back to Julia Miller's last words at the pier in New Orleans. She too had spoken of them being friends. For Juarez's part, Alan was pleased. With Julia, however, he wished it could be more than friends.

The next morning, Monday, July 7, the boat bound for Velasco left Galveston on schedule at nine o'clock.

On deck, William Childress was standing at the railing with Alan Kane and Juarez Amigo when he saw the boat's captain walking across the deck toward him. William was well acquainted with Captain Oscar Donaldson. He introduced Alan and Juarez to the captain, explaining that he had hired both men as ranch hands for the Circle C. Donaldson shook hands with Alan, then with Juarez. William could tell that the captain was a bit off balance shaking hands with a Mexican, but neither Juarez nor Alan seemed aware of it.

The conversation turned to the problem between Mexico and Texas, and in spite of Juarez's presence, Donaldson asked Childress, "What are you going to do if that lowdown Mex Santa Anna comes to take the Circle C from you?"

Childress's features turned to stone. "Make a stand and fight!"

"Sí!" spoke up Juarez, his black eyes flashing. "We will drive that lowdown San' Anna and those other dorty Mehicanos back to Mehico!"

Captain Oscar Donaldson's head jerked as he looked at Juarez. "Did I hear you right? *Dirty* Mexicans?"

"Sí, Señor *Capitán*. I am a Texan!" Juarez looked up at William. "Thees is so. Correct, Señor Cheeldress?"

William scratched the back of his head. "Well, you are not quite a Texan yet. To be a true Texan, you have to formally establish yourself as such. You must establish residence in Texas, plus show yourself in a definite way to be strictly loyal to the Republic of Texas."

Juarez nodded. "I weel make Texas my home by leeving on your ranch, Señor Cheeldress. That weel establish my reseedence, sí?"

"Yes, it will," William said.

"Then what else must I do?"

William smiled. "We'll talk about it later, all right?"

Juarez matched William's smile. "Sí, Señor Cheeldress. Zat is fine."

"I need to ask you something, Juarez."

"Sí, señor?"

Alan looked on. He was interested to learn what the boss was going to ask the little Mexican.

"How old are you?" queried Childress.

Juarez grinned. "Wal, señor," he replied with a sly look in his eye. "Juarez would be twenny-two, bot I was seeck for a year, so I am only twenny-one."

Childress tried not to laugh, but when the Mexican snorted and broke into laughter, he lost control.

So did Alan. Both men laughed heartily.

The hours seemed to pass slowly as the boat sailed westward on the Gulf of Mexico toward Velasco, on the southern tip of Texas, where the Brazos River emptied into the gulf.

At one point on the journey, Juarez was elsewhere on the boat while William and Alan were sitting on a bench near the stern looking out over the sunlit surface of the gulf. Deck hands were carrying out their duties in several places aboard.

As the breeze wafted over the deck, Alan and William talked about their desire to see Juarez become a born-again child of God.

"Well," said William, "we'll take him to church with us this Sunday. I guarantee you, he will hear the gospel from Pastor Evans. If Juarez doesn't go forward at the invitation for salvation, you and I will see that the gospel is pressed to his heart until the light breaks through."

Alan nodded. "We sure will."

Even as he spoke, Alan saw Juarez coming across the deck toward them. Captain Oscar Donaldson was walking beside him, and they were talking, both with smiles.

Alan said, "Look there, boss. It looks like Juarez and the captain are having a nice talk together."

"I'm glad to see that." William looked that direction.

"Given a chance, that little Mexican could win anybody over and become friends with them."

"That's for sure," Alan agreed. "That's for sure."

ELEVEN

Juarez Amigo and Captain Oscar Donaldson were still chatting as they drew up to where William Childress and Alan Kane sat.

Donaldson looked at William and Alan and said, "Juarez and I were just talking about his defection from the Mexican army, and I was commending him for having the courage to do so."

"Well, it took courage for sure," commented Childress.

The captain looked at the Mexican. "Just one more thing, Juarez, and I won't be asking you any more questions."

Juarez smiled. "Sí, Señor Capitán."

"Being born and raised in Mexico City, how did you learn to speak English?"

"I've been meaning to ask him the same thing," put in Childress.

Alan chuckled. "Yeah. Me too."

Juarez looked at Childress. "You remember I tol' you my father, mother, an' seester died of fever epi—epi—"

"Epidemic," said William.

Juarez nodded. "Sí! Sí! I was feefteen years old when they died. Next door to our home was a neighbor, who was een is feefties. Hees name was Jose Esparza. Hees wife had died almos' a year earlier. Señor Esparza take me eento hees home when my family die. He had leeved in the United States for a few years when he was een his thirties, and he learned English. During the nex' three years, Señor Jose Esparza teach me to read and speak English. He die when I was eighteen. I then enlisted in the Mehicano army."

The three men were nodding. Juarez rolled his eyes and added quickly,

"That was ba-a-ad meestake, joining the Mehicano army. Because of San' Anna. Many of Mehico leaders theenk he great hombre. Greatly patriotic for Mehico."

"Yes, they do," said Childress.

Juarez shook his head vigorously. "No! No! San' Anna ees power-mad, bloodthirsty murderer! He ees not patriotic for Mehico. He ees patriotic for San' Anna! He ees greedy and cruel. An' I tell you right now, Señor Cheeldress, he weel come to Texas! He weel come with thousands of soldiers!"

"That's what I'm afraid of, Juarez," responded Childress. "But if he does, General Sam Houston will have a big surprise for him."

"Yes," said Captain Donaldson. "From what I hear, General Houston is making plans in that direction." He paused. "Well, gentlemen, I need to get back to my cabin. I'll see you later."

As the captain made his way across the deck, William turned to Juarez. "I'm sure glad you can speak English. That will make it much easier for you living and working on the ranch."

Juarez nodded, smiling. "Sí, Señor Cheeldress." He put his hand to his mouth. "Uh—I mean, 'Yes, Mr. Childress.' "

Alan laughed, as did William, who said, "Your English will improve as time passes, Juarez. Don't worry about it."

Juarez smiled again. "Sí, señor."

The forty-mile boat ride from Galveston to Velasco took a full day because the boat made several stops in the afternoon.

The rancher and his two new hired hands boarded a large ferryboat that evening at Velasco. The hundred-mile trip up the Brazos River to Groce's Landing took two full days.

Dawn was coloring the eastern horizon a dull gray when the slow-moving ferry pulled up to the dock at Groce's Landing on Thursday morning, July 10. The cool dampness left by the kiss of night made a misty haze that partially shrouded the small cluster of shacks by the river's edge.

William Childress and his two companions collected their gear and plodded through the haze a quarter mile due west from the river to the home of Mel and Alma Sibley. The buildings took shape as yellow light from the eastern sky cast its first shadows of the day. The mists were thinning out.

"There should be two Circle C horses here," said Childress. "Mel always keeps a few horses around, so we'll have to borrow one from him so we each have one. If we keep a steady pace, we can make it to the ranch by sundown."

Both hired hands nodded.

Childress led them past the stables to a large barn. "At this time of day, Mel is usually milking his cows here at the barn."

A calf bawled from somewhere behind the barn as Childress flipped the latch and opened the barn door. Above the squeak of the hinges, they heard the sound of milk spattering the bottom of an empty pail.

Moving inside the barn, they saw a man sitting on a milking stool next to a cow, shooting white streams into the pail. Looking up at the three men, then fixing his eyes on the tall Texan, he said, "Hey, William! Glad to see you back! Who you got there with you?"

"Mel Sibley," said Childress, "I want you to meet Alan Kane and Juarez Amigo."

Chuckling, Mel Sibley stopped milking long enough to reach out his right hand. "Hello, Alan," he said in a friendly manner.

When Alan shook Sibley's hand, he felt warm milk. "Hello, Mr. Sibley. Glad to meet you."

Juarez was next. When they had shaken hands, with Sibley greeting Juarez in the same friendly manner, Sibley returned to his task while Alan and Juarez wiped milk on their trousers. Sibley looked up at his friend. "New hired hands, William?"

"Yep," said Childress. "Alan is from Boston. His brother Adam will be coming through in a few weeks too. Juarez is from Mexico City. He defected from Santa Anna's army. He wants to be a Texan."

"Well, he came to the right place!" laughed Sibley, who was in his mid-forties.

"Circle C have a couple of horses here, Mel?" asked William.

"Sure do."

"Could we borrow one of yours?"

"Of course. You can take your pick right now while I run into the house and tell Alma you're here so she can cook up more food for breakfast. Believe me, William, she'll want to feed you and your new hired hands!"

William Childress smiled. "I reckon we could force ourselves to gag down some of Alma's cooking!" He turned to his companions. "I'm only kidding. You two are about to enjoy some of the best cooking you *ever* tasted!"

Mel left the pail of milk on a shelf and led the three men to the corral. "You fellas go ahead and pick out one of the horses. Bridles and saddles are in that shed over there. I'll be right back."

Twenty minutes later, when the hungry men entered the kitchen, the tantalizing aroma of hot coffee and sizzling bacon greeted them. Next to greet them was lovely Alma Sibley. She warmly welcomed William Childress, saying that it was good to see him again. William then introduced her to his two new hired hands, explaining their backgrounds and that Alan's brother Adam would be coming through in a matter of weeks.

Alma greeted them cordially and told them she had set places for them at the table. "I've added to what I was cooking for Mel and myself, gentlemen, so there's plenty for all."

The men removed their hats and gathered around the table, where Alma had placed large platters of bacon, eggs, biscuits, and fried potatoes. Mel asked William to thank the Lord for the food. When William's "amen" was uttered, the men sat down.

Alma then came from the stove, carrying a steaming coffeepot.

"Eat up now." She poured coffee into each mug.

When breakfast was over, Alma Sibley gave William and his partners food for their lunch on the trail. The trio expressed their appreciation for the kindness they had been shown by the Sibleys, then mounted up and rode away.

The morning wore on as the three men rode northwest across the grassy Texas prairie. At noon, they stopped beside a small stream, watered the horses, and ate the lunch Alma had prepared for them.

Alan Kane's legs were a bit stiff from the morning's ride. As they mounted up to move on, he settled in the saddle and said to William, "I'm sure glad Miss Julia broke me into this before today."

William chuckled, and they rode on, with Alan between William and Juarez.

As the time slowly passed, Alan's mind was on Julia for a while. Then he concentrated on the wide-open country dotted with patches of mesquite trees, luxurious fields of grass, and rolling hills. He knew he was going to love his new home.

With the muffled sound of hooves on thick grass and squeaking saddles in his ears, Alan's thoughts once again drifted to Julia Miller. His mind rested on those few golden days they had spent together. *Oh, Julie,* he thought, *I wish I could get you to fall in love with me, but—but I know it can never happen. I—I'll never be—*

"What do you think of this country?" asked William Childress, unwittingly interrupting Alan's thoughts.

Alan looked at his boss and smiled. "Beautiful. I love it already."

William smiled back. "I'm glad."

At that moment, Juarez lifted his hand and pointed a finger. "Look!" About a mile off to the west was a herd of cattle clustered in a shallow draw.

Childress watched the cattle for a long moment. He noticed Alan studying them intently. "Those are the kind you'll be rounding up, Alan," said the rancher. "Texas is full of them. If a man is willing to work hard, he can get quite wealthy raising them."

"No sense setting my sights low," said Alan. "I'm willing to work hard at cattle ranching, I guarantee you. Once Adam and I learn from you how to do it, we'll build a spread that'll make anyone sit up and take notice."

"Sí," joined in Juarez. "We weel build a big rancho! We weel call eet zee *Amigo–Kane Rancho*!"

Alan looked past William Childress and frowned at the Mexican playfully. "The *what*?"

"Zee *Amigo–K—*" Juarez's face darkened. "Oh. *Perdón,* Señor Alan. I mean zee *Kane–Amigo Rancho*!"

Alan laughed. "That's better, short stuff!"

William Childress laughed, as did both his new hired men.

As the three men rode, William gave them as much insight into Texas ranching as he could. When William wasn't talking, Alan's mind went to his family in Boston. He missed them so much and hoped Adam would be coming soon.

Moments later, to the sound of clomping hooves, Alan's thoughts went to Julia again. He wondered if he would ever see her again. Probably never. What reason would he ever have to return to New Orleans? It was best that way, he convinced himself. Maybe in time, that powerful flame in his heart would flicker down and die out. Certainly Julia would marry some wealthy young man and live in one of the fancy areas of the city.

As the sun began to lower in the western sky, Alan Kane forced his thoughts from beautiful Julia to *Adam.* Nobody could ask for a better brother than Adam. They were more than brothers. They were best friends.

Alan loved his older brothers, of course, but there was something special between him and Adam. Adam had borne more hurt than Alan had. On top of the grief of having their mother die, Adam had had his heart broken by Mary Sue Bannigan, who had thrown him over for a man with money. Adam, bless his heart, had tried to make it appear a small thing, but it had hurt him deeply.

However, Alan was glad that Mary Sue hadn't marry Adam. She wasn't good enough for him. Not only that, but if Adam had married Mary Sue, he wouldn't be coming to Texas. The two youngest Kane brothers would build a great life together here. The future was bright and promising. Everything would be wonderful on the ranch owned by Adam and Alan Kane.

In his heart, Alan said, *Dear Lord, I've prayed about this a lot, and here I am again. Please bring that special Christian young lady into Adam's life who will love him and give him happiness.*

"...just beyond that ridge," William Childress's words filtered into Alan Kane's ears.

Alan swung his gaze to the tall Texan's face. "What's that, boss?"

With his mind on Adam, Alan had not noticed that the sun was now lowering on the western horizon.

"I said the Circle C is just beyond that ridge." Childress pointed straight ahead.

Alan lifted his eyes. About three miles to the northwest was a long, smooth ridge topped with scattered rabbit brush and mesquite trees.

"Let's put 'em to a lope and get on home!" said the owner of the Circle C Ranch.

Juarez Amigo let out a Mexican-style "Wahoo!" The three horses scattered sod as they took off for the ridge. The last flames of the sun's rim were dipping below the horizon as the trio crested the ridge. They paused to let the horses blow.

Alan Kane sat his horse in awe as his eyes drank in the sight. The Circle C Ranch was nestled among tall cottonwoods and bending willows in the hollow of a broad, sweeping valley. Tall grass, oceans of it, swayed in perfect rhythm to the force of the wayward evening breeze. A winding stream wended its way across the valley floor and reflected the orange and red of the flaming sunset.

Vast herds of cattle dotted the land, gathering for the most part in clusters of ten to twenty. A few strays were scattered about, acting independently but never wandering too far from the others.

Alan let out a sigh. "Boss, there are no mortal words to describe the ranch's beauty."

"Sí!" agreed Juarez Amigo. *"Bella vista!"*

William smiled. "I'm glad you fellas like it. Let's move on in."

As they descended the gentle slope, Alan saw three barns skirted by several corrals. Each corral held numerous cattle and a few horses. His mouth fell open as he set his sight on the huge log building that stood in a grove of cottonwoods. He turned to the rancher and pointed toward the building. "Mr. Childress, what's that big log structure?"

William grinned at him. "That's the ranch house."

"Whew! It's a big one. And it's sure beautiful."

"Sí! Sí!" said Juarez. "Eet is *muy bella*!"

As they rode on down the slope, Alan said, "Mr. Childress, I don't believe you have ever mentioned your wife to me. I've meant to ask you about her before."

"I'm a widower, Alan," William replied softly. "My wife, Elaine, died over four years ago. I live alone in the house."

Alan swallowed hard. "Oh. I—I'm so sorry for your loss, sir."

"Thank you."

"Do you have any sons or daughters?"

"No. Elaine was not able to bear children."

"Oh."

Juarez was listening intently, but made no comment.

As they drew nearer, Alan and Juarez saw that between the huge house and the barns was a long, low-roofed log structure, sided by several outbuildings of different sizes. They also took note of a small community of log cabins. Ranch hands moved about in various directions, carrying out their particular chores at day's end.

Noting the way both men were studying the collection of buildings, William said, "Let me explain about all those buildings, fellas. The long, low-roofed log building is the bunkhouse and mess hall for all the single cowhands. Those buildings alongside it are toolsheds, tack rooms that hold our saddles, bridles, and harnesses for the horses, and sheds where we stack our cattle hides before we sell them. The log cabins are where the married hands and their wives and children live."

"Magnífico!" said Juarez.

Alan asked, "How many ranch hands do you have, boss?"

"Thirty-eight." Childress shook his head and snapped his fingers. "Uh—with you two, I now have forty. Fourteen of the ranch hands are married."

"Wow!" said Alan. "Forty cowboys! That's quite a number of ranch hands. I've never asked you how many cattle you have."

"We have some twelve thousand head at any given time," replied William. "New herds of wild cattle are brought in on a regular basis, and calves are born all year long. But the number of cattle on the ranch stays at an average of twelve thousand, as a large number of the cattle are butchered regularly for their meat and hides."

Suddenly, Juarez Amigo pointed to a pair of hawks wheeling overhead about a mile. "Oh, look up there. Magnífico! Hawks!"

While Juarez was watching and exclaiming over the hawks, Alan whispered to William, "Are all the ranch hands Christians?"

William whispered back, "No, not all of them. Ten of them are Christians. Well, eleven, including you. Three of those ten are married, and their wives are Christians. All of the Christians on the ranch go to the same church in Washington-on-the-Brazos I attend, which is led by Pastor Merle Evans."

Alan nodded and whispered, "The desire to see Juarez come to Jesus is strong in my heart, boss."

"Mine too," breathed William.

The hawks were soon gone, and as the three riders drew even closer they noted a few children playing about the cabins.

The evening breeze stirred the cottonwoods and willows that could be seen in various places on the ranch near the buildings and corrals. The rich red of the fading sunset, along with the purple shadows it was leaving behind, added a touch of magic to the scene.

"Well, boys," said Childress, "this is your new home."

"I'll take it!" exclaimed Alan.

"Me too!" joined in Juarez, smiling. His white teeth gleamed in contrast to his black mustache and dark skin.

Several cowboys gathered quickly when they saw their boss ride up. The three men dismounted, and greetings were exchanged as the ranch owner introduced Alan Kane and Juarez Amigo to the cowboys.

Childress then turned to cowboy Smiley Dunn, who was standing next to him. "Smiley, where's Cort? I want him to meet Alan and Juarez."

"Well, right now, boss," said Dunn, "Cort and a few of the men are roundin' up some wild cattle up by Bender Lake. They should be back tomorrow."

William nodded. "Okay."

As Smiley walked away, Alan looked at his boss. "Who's Cort, sir?"

"Cort Whitney's my foreman. I wanted you and Juarez to meet him right away. But it'll have to wait till tomorrow."

Alan nodded.

William ran his gaze between his two new men. "You fellas are arriving at just the right time. When Cort and his men get back, you'll learn how to brand wild, full-grown cattle and how to dull their horns."

"Sounds great," said Alan.

"Sí!" agreed Juarez.

"Now, let's get you boys situated," said William. "Follow me."

Alan Kane and Juarez Amigo were led to the long, low structure, which they had learned was the bunkhouse and mess hall. William took them inside, where they were introduced to more ranch hands and assigned their bunks. Alan unpacked his gear into a nearby chest of drawers.

Juarez, of course, had no gear. All he owned were the clothes on his back. William Childress had bought him a new shirt in Galveston. Alan had plenty of shaving supplies and had told Juarez he would share them with him.

William then told his two new men that he would show them to the mess hall and then head for the ranch house. When they entered the mess hall, Smiley Dunn and another ranch hand were just sitting down at an empty table.

Smiley called out, "Hey, boss! Are those two lookin' for a place to sit?"

"They will be once they've gotten in line at the kitchen counter and picked up their food."

Dunn smiled. "I'll take them over there and bring them back here to eat with Dakota."

William quickly introduced Alan and Juarez to ranch hand Dakota Smith, then told them he would see them in the morning.

Alan frowned. "Boss, aren't you going to eat supper?"

William grinned. "Yes. I have a dear silver-haired lady who is my cook and housekeeper. She'll have supper for me."

"Oh. Okay," said Alan. "I just didn't want you going hungry."

William chuckled. "Don't worry, son. With Daisy as my cook, I'll never go hungry! See you fellas in the morning."

Moments later, Alan and Juarez were seated at the table with Smiley Dunn and Dakota Smith, devouring their meal. Dunn and Smith proved to be quite friendly and answered questions as fast as the two new men could ask them.

Juarez and Alan were seated across the table from Dunn and Smith. Alan looked at the two cowboys. "What can you tell me about the foreman?"

Dunn and Smith smiled and exchanged glances. Then Smiley said, "I'll tell you this. Cort Whitney is a great guy to work with, but believe me, he's one tough cookie. He's forty-six years old and can whip any young cowboy that's dumb enough to sass him."

"Yeah," chuckled Dakota. "Ask Smiley. He found out the hard way!"

Smiley's face flushed. He cleared his throat gently. "One lesson was all I needed. Cort is good to all the ranch hands, but he won't take any sass, and he demands an honest day's work from every man. I admire him for that."

Both Dunn and Smith told about work incidents they had experienced with Whitney, making it clear that he was an excellent leader and was faithful to William Childress in handling the men. He would not tolerate laziness or disobedience to his commands as foreman.

"Meeting Cort Whitney sounds like it's going to be interesting," Alan said.

Smiley Dunn grinned. "It sure *will* be, Alan. Believe me!"

TWELVE

After a brief struggle on the eastern horizon, the dominant ball of fire in the sky chased away the darkness, and a new day was born. It was Friday, July 11, 1834.

In the Circle C Ranch bunkhouse, Alan Kane and Juarez Amigo rolled out of their bunks. While they shaved and combed their hair, some of the ranch hands stopped by to meet them. Alan and Juarez were made to feel welcome as they explained that they had come to the ranch with William Childress.

Alan told them he was from Boston, how he had known Childress and been hired by him. Juarez explained about being born and raised in Mexico City and how he had joined the Mexican army at eighteen, but had defected recently because of General Santa Anna's thirst for Texans' blood. He told them that he had gone to Galveston, Texas, and there had met William Childress, who hired him as a ranch hand.

When Alan and Juarez arrived in the mess hall for breakfast, Smiley Dunn and Dakota Smith were just sitting down at a table. They invited the newcomers to eat with them once again, and soon all four were downing their breakfasts.

Moments later, a ranch hand in his midtwenties moved up to the table carrying his tray of food, looked at the newcomers, then said to Dunn and Smith, "Okay if I sit here?"

"There's room," said Dunn.

The cowboy took the plates and coffee cup from the tray, placed them on the table, laid the tray on an empty table nearby, then sat down.

Dakota Smith looked at the cowboy. "Batt, I want you to meet these two new ranch hands. The one directly across from you is Alan Kane."

Alan smiled and reached his hand across the table.

Dakota said, "Alan, this is Batt Reger."

"Glad to meet you, Batt," said Alan.

Reger reached across the table and gripped Alan's hand. Smiling weakly, he said, "Kane."

Juarez Amigo, who was sitting next to Alan, laid his fork down, smiled, and offered his hand at an angle across the table.

"This is Juarez Amigo, Batt," said Smiley.

Reger eyed the Mexican frostily and did not shake Juarez's hand. Instead, he fastened his cold gaze on the Mexican's face and slowly lifted the steaming cup of coffee to his lips.

While Reger stared at him and sipped the coffee, Juarez's smile drained away. He withdrew his hand, looked down at his plate, and picked up his fork.

This treatment of his Mexican friend irritated Alan Kane. It was Alan's turn to use a frosty stare. He fixed it on Reger's face and held it there until the cowboy had had a good look at it.

Smiley Dunn and Dakota Smith glanced at each other. Then, to avoid trouble, Smiley struck up a conversation about Cort Whitney and the Circle C men who were supposed to arrive back at the ranch with the wild cattle they had rounded up. The tension eased, and breakfast was soon finished. Batt Reger was the first to leave the table and quickly made his way out the nearest door.

Alan and Juarez thanked Dunn and Smith for letting them eat with them and stepped outside into the brilliant Texas sunlight. They immediately saw William Childress coming their way.

As Childress drew up, he smiled pleasantly. "You boys sleep all right?"

"Sure did," said Alan.

"Sí, señor," said Juarez.

"Good. Well, I want to give you fellas a tour of the ranch's buildings and the corrals. After the tour, I'll put both of you to work."

Alan nodded. "Okay, boss. Let's go."

Juarez grinned. "Sí, boss. Let us go!"

Childress first led them to the blacksmith shed, where Chuck Cooley, the Circle C blacksmith, was instructing a young ranch hand in the art of pounding a red-hot horseshoe into shape.

When they left the blacksmith shed, they moved past some of the corrals. William had to lift his voice above the bawling of the cattle as he said, "Whatever wild cattle Cort Whitney brings in today will be added to these."

Lifting his own voice, Alan said, "So wild cattle like these are just roaming the range, waiting for somebody to round them up, eh, boss?"

"Yep. First come, first served."

"Are they everywhere in Texas?"

Childress laughed. "There's lots of Texas, son, but so far they've proven to be everywhere we've looked. Best we can tell, the Spaniards had cattle with them when they landed in south Texas on the shore of the Gulf of Mexico about three hundred years ago. With the passing of time, some of the cattle strayed northward. These that you're looking at right here are some of their descendants. How far north they migrated remains to be seen."

"Interesting," said Alan.

At that moment they came upon a corral where four ranch hands with knives in their hands were throwing male calves to the ground.

"What's going on here?" Alan asked.

"They're making steers out of bulls," Childress replied. "It's called castration."

Alan nodded. "Oh. I've heard of that."

"Why is thees done?" asked Juarez.

"For two basic reasons," said Childress. "First...as a bull calf grows into maturity, his neck and shoulders develop thick and massive, with heavy cartilage. The tissue in this muscle structure is never any good for meat. It's tougher than boot leather."

"Oh," said the little Mexican. "I have never tried to eat a boot, bot I theenk eet would be very hard to chew!"

Alan laughed, as did William.

"When bull calves are castrated," William went on, "their growth pattern changes. They don't develop heavy shoulders, thick necks, and other fleshy patterns that are undesirable for beef."

"I never realized that," said Alan.

The ranch owner smiled. "Second, bulls are high-strung and temperamental. You keep a bunch of bulls around, and there are constant fights among them. So like all ranchers, we keep a few bulls for breeding, but all the rest of the male cattle are made into steers."

"Fights? So zee bools fight a lot, huh?"

"Well, you're from Mexico," said William. "What's the biggest sport in your country?"

"Ah." The little man smiled. "Ees to fight *el toro*!"

"Right. You've never heard of a matador going into an arena for a *steer* fight, have you?"

"Oh no. Zee matador, he fight zee bool!"

"Mm-hmm. If the matador tried to stir up a fight with a steer, he'd work up a sweat, and the steer would just stand there and look at him."

"Ha!" exclaimed the Mexican. "I never theenk of that!"

"Raising steers," said Alan, "is much easier than raising bulls then?"

"For sure," William said as they drew near the leather shed.

At the leather shed, Alan and Juarez saw men working on saddles, harnesses, bridles, halters, and other leather pieces that were necessary on the ranch.

The ranch owner then took his two new employees on a tour of the corrals that surrounded the barns. They saw various kinds of work being done by the ranch hands. William Childress took the time to show Alan and Juarez the difference between the hooves of cattle and horses. He pointed out that cattle have split hooves, but that horses have solid hooves.

He explained that God made horses with solid hooves so men could put horseshoes on them and use them for heavier work than horses could do.

When they came to a group of cowboys who were clipping the tips of the horns of some bulls, William explained that the bulls were less dangerous with blunt horns.

As they left the corrals and barns, William headed toward the big ranch house. "I want to give you boys a tour of my house. Then I'll put you to work."

"I'd love to tour your house, boss," said Alan.

"Me too," said Juarez.

When they reached the backside of the ranch house, William said, "We'll start in the kitchen and work forward."

Alan and Juarez followed their boss up the steps of the back porch toward the kitchen door. As they entered the kitchen, they saw a small silver-haired lady at the stove. She was clad in a blue and white gingham dress. A snow-white apron covered most of it. She turned toward them, stepped from the stove, and smiled at Alan and Juarez. "Well, howdy-do, gentlemen! Mr. Childress told me all about you at breakfast this morning. Welcome to the Circle C!"

William introduced them to his cook and housekeeper, calling her Miss Daisy. Daisy shook hands with both of them, then looked the new ranch hands over from head to toe. Eying Alan carefully, she gave him a wide smile. "My, my, you're a tall one, Alan, just like our boss! Big as you are, I imagine when you eat a meal, it takes a lot to fill you up!"

Alan chuckled. "Well, I can eat my fair share, ma'am."

She giggled. "I don't doubt that at all!"

Then she turned to Juarez and gave him the same wide smile. "You may not be as big as Alan, Juarez, but I imagine you can still put down a hefty meal!"

Juarez chortled. "Sí, Mees Daisy, I can do zat!"

" 'Scuse me, gentlemen," Daisy said and turned back to the stove.

William grinned at Alan and Juarez as they watched Daisy. At the counter next to the stove, she picked up two hot pads and opened the oven door.

A delicious aroma filled the kitchen, and Alan took a step closer as she pulled a pan full of cinnamon rolls from the oven. He sniffed twice and looked at Childress. "Wow, boss! You are one fortunate man to have this lady for your cook!"

Daisy giggled.

"You're right about that, Alan," said William. "Daisy is a great asset to this ranch."

"I can see why," put in Juarez. "Mees Daisy can sure make rolls that smell good! Sí! Muy bueno!"

Daisy ran her gaze between Alan and Juarez. "Would you gentlemen like to taste my cinnamon rolls?"

Alan chuckled. "You don't have to ask me twice, ma'am!"

"Or me!" said Juarez.

"Me neither!" echoed William.

Daisy's eyes twinkled. "Well, gentlemen, sit down at the table here, and I'll see that you get a midmorning snack!"

William guided Alan and Juarez to the kitchen table, and as they sat down, the sprightly little lady drew up with three plates in hand, each one bearing a large cinnamon roll. She laid a plate before each man. "Just a minute." She dashed back to the cupboard.

All three men watched her pick up a small bowl. She hurried to them and starting with Juarez poured sugar frosting on each roll. "There! Enjoy! I'll be right back with some hot coffee."

Seconds later, she returned with three mugs of steaming coffee and set one by each plate.

Chewing on a mouthful of roll, Alan spoke around it. "Miss Daisy, next time you bake cinnamon rolls, would you save one for me?"

Daisy grinned at the young man from Boston. "You can count on it, young fella! You can count on it!"

When the three men had finished their rolls and coffee, they thanked Daisy. Then William led Alan and Juarez outside. At that moment, Alan and Juarez saw a hay wagon coming their way. William said, "Now, fellas, I'm going to put you to work." He lifted a hand and motioned to the two men on the seat of the empty hay wagon. Alan and Juarez recognized them. Smiley Dunn was holding the reins, and Batt Reger was sitting beside him.

Smiley drew the wagon to a halt. "Yes, Mr. Childress?"

"You're bringing hay to the barns from the stacks over by the south spring, aren't you?"

"Yes sir."

"Grab a couple more pitchforks on your way, and take these boys with you. I want them to learn about pitching hay."

Smiley grinned. "Sure, boss."

William turned to Alan and Juarez. "Climb aboard, boys. Have a good day." With that, William turned and walked away.

Batt Reger shot the Mexican a caustic glare as the two hopped on the wagon. Alan saw it but said nothing, though he wanted to warn Reger not to mistreat Juarez.

Dunn turned the wagon up to a barn minutes later and told Reger to go get two more pitchforks. When Reger returned with the pitchforks, he laid them on the bed of the wagon where Alan and Juarez sat and gave the Mexican a cold look.

As they drove toward the south spring, Alan told Dunn and Reger that Juarez used to be in Santa Anna's army and how and why he had defected and come to Texas.

Smiley Dunn commended Juarez for defecting, but Batt Reger said nothing.

When they reached the huge haystacks near the ranch's south spring,

Smiley handed the new men their pitchforks and said he would show them how to use them.

During the two hours it took the four men to load the large hay wagon, Batt Reger maintained a sullen silence. His antagonism toward Juarez Amigo was plainly evident. This infuriated Alan Kane, but he remained silent.

Later, just as they arrived back at the corrals with the load of hay, William Childress hurried to them. He was asking Alan and Juarez how they took to pitching hay when they saw four riders driving some sixty head of cattle in. It was Cort Whitney and his men.

Within a few minutes, the cattle were in a nearby corral with the gate closed behind them. Whitney's three partners rode on toward the bunkhouse, and seeing his boss, Dunn, Reger, and the two new men standing beside the fully loaded hay wagon, the foreman hurried to them.

Alan looked the foreman over as he drew near. He was tall, muscular, ruggedly handsome, and obviously rawhide tough. There was a spark of dogged determination glinting in his gunmetal gray eyes.

William greeted his foreman and introduced him to Alan Kane and Juarez Amigo. Both men shook hands with him and liked him immediately. William told Cort Whitney that he wanted both Alan and Juarez to learn how to brand cattle. Cort assured him that he would put them in the branding corral right after lunch while the wild cattle they had just brought in were being branded. William then asked Cort to come to the house and have lunch with him, saying he needed to talk to him.

When lunch was over in the mess hall, Cort Whitney appeared and took Alan Kane and Juarez Amigo to the branding corral. There he assigned Alan to work with a ranch hand named Ed Kostis, and he assigned Juarez to work with Batt Reger. Alan was on edge that Juarez would be working with Reger as he went to work with Kostis on the chute right next to them.

The two new men were told to watch the experienced ranch hands as they used the branding irons on the cattle. While they were working at both chutes, Alan heard Reger speaking abusively to Juarez, and it made him angry.

After almost two hours of Reger verbally mistreating Juarez, Alan looked over at the other chute and saw Reger carelessly swing a red-hot branding iron, just missing Juarez's face.

The lithe Mexican jumped back, eyes bulging. "Hey, señor!" he snapped. "Watch what you are doing weeth zat iron!"

Alan watched Batt Reger spit on the hot iron, making it sizzle. "Ah, shut up, Mex!" he hissed. "I didn't come anywhere near you!"

With that, Reger placed the branding iron against the bull in the chute. The hide and flesh hissed, and the bull let out a pained roar. Reger released the bull from the chute, and as the bull darted away, bawling, Alan stepped over to Reger and said levelly, "You come near my friend's face with that iron again, and you'll be sorry."

An insolent sneer curled Batt Reger's lip. "I might just brand you like I did that bull, Mex lover," he growled, waving the smoking iron close to Alan's nose.

Fury heated Alan's blood. "Back off right now, Reger!"

Batt raised the hot iron as if to use it as a weapon. Alan Kane surprised him as he stepped in and slammed him square on the jaw with a savage blow.

Reger went down, dropping the smoking iron in the dirt, and stayed there. He was out cold.

Other ranch hands in the area were watching the scene. Ed Kostis stepped up beside Alan, looked at him and at Juarez, and said, "I'll go get Cort. He's had trouble with Reger before."

The other men in the area looked on as Alan and Juarez stood over the unconscious Batt Reger. Shortly, Ed Kostis returned with the foreman.

Cort looked down at Reger, who was just beginning to awaken, then ran his gaze to the other men around. "Ed told me that Reger brought this on himself by waving a hot iron at Juarez, then threatening Alan with it. That the way you saw it?"

Every man gave him an affirmative answer. Cort then commended Alan for going to his friend's rescue. Moments later, when Batt Reger regained consciousness, he was told to apologize to both Juarez and Alan or he would be fired.

Reger countered by telling the foreman that with Santa Anna and his troops no doubt coming to Texas with plans to take it over, it made him feel shaky to have a Mexican working on the ranch.

Some of the other ranch hands spoke up and said they felt the same way. For sure, when Santa Anna came to Texas, he would seek to capture all of the ranches for Mexico.

Reger made the apology, however. Cort then warned him to never do anything like that again, and Reger promised he wouldn't.

Whitney spoke to all the men gathered there. "I believe you men are right about Santa Anna's plan, but let me tell you what Mr. Childress told me during lunch. He said Juarez was a soldier in Santa Anna's army and defected because he disagreed with Santa Anna's bloody ways. He came to Texas to escape being executed, and his desire now is to become a Texan. You, Batt Reger, and any others who feel the way you do, should take this into consideration and treat Juarez properly."

Smiley Dunn spoke up. "I agree, Cort!"

The others nodded and told the foreman that they also agreed. "Good!" Cort said. "Now make sure you welcome Juarez to the Circle C Ranch!"

Within five minutes, every man in the group, including Batt Reger, had done so.

Two days later, on Sunday, when Alan Kane and Juarez Amigo went with William Childress and the other Christians from the ranch to church in Washington-on-the-Brazos, Alan was pleased to learn that Cort Whitney was a Christian.

As Pastor Merle Evans preached that morning, Alan watched Juarez from the corner of his eye as they sat side by side. He hoped his Mexican friend would see his lost condition and go forward at invitation time to receive Christ as Saviour.

It did not happen in the morning service or at the evening service.

That night, when Alan and Juarez were sitting on their bunks before lights out, Alan said, "Juarez, my friend, what did you think of Pastor Evans's sermons today?"

"Oh. Zey were fine."

"Did you understand that at the end of both sermons Pastor Evans was asking those who are not Christians to come forward so they could be shown from the Bible how to become Christians?"

Juarez smiled. "I *am* a Christian, Señor Alan."

"Oh? When did you become a Christian?"

"I cannot tell you *when* I became a Christian, bot when I was nineteen years of age, a fran' of mine asked me if I believed that Jesus Christ is the virgin-born Son of God. I had been touched in the past at Christmastime, and I liked the story of the virgin birth, so I told him I believed zat. He told me, then, zat made me a Christian."

Alan shook his head. "Juarez, simply believing that Jesus is God's virgin-born Son does not make you a Christian."

Juarez's eyes widened. "What? It does not?"

"No." Alan reached for his Bible, which lay on the small table beside his bunk. "Jesus said that we must be born again to be real Christians and go to heaven when we die."

"Born again? What does that mean?"

"It means you were born wrong the first time. You were born physically alive but spiritually dead. God doesn't allow anything dead into heaven."

Opening his Bible to Ephesians chapter 2, Alan placed it where Juarez could see it and said, "The apostle Paul, who wrote the book of Ephesians under the inspiration of the Holy Spirit, is writing to Christians. Read me what he said in verse 1."

Juarez bent close to the page. "He said, 'And you hath he quickened, who were dead in trespasses and sins.' " He looked up at Alan. "What is 'quickened'?"

"It means to give *life*. Paul is speaking of when they received Jesus as their Saviour. They were born again...given spiritual life by almighty God."

Juarez shook his head. "I have never received Jesus into my heart. I do not know how to do zat. So I am not a *real* Christian."

"That's right," said Alan. "But you *can* be. You want me to show you how right now?"

"Oh, sí! I want to become a *real* Christian!"

Using the Scriptures, Alan took Juarez to Calvary, showed him the blood-shedding death that Jesus died on the cross, His burial, and His resurrection. He explained that this is the gospel. He showed him that Jesus said lost sinners must repent and believe the gospel to be saved. He explained repentance of sin, then took Juarez to John chapter 3, showed him what Jesus said about being born again, and then showed him in John 1:12 that receiving Jesus is what makes a lost sinner a child of God. He then showed him in Ephesians 3:17 that he must receive Jesus into his heart.

With tears in his eyes, Juarez said, "Oh, Alan, my fran', I want to take Jesus into my heart. I want to be a *real* Christian!"

Alan had the joy of leading his Mexican friend to the Lord. The little Mexican hugged Alan and thanked him for showing him the truth. "Now, I am a *real* Christian! And now I know when I became a *real* Christian!"

Alan smiled. "Yes! A real Christian knows when he became a Christian!"

On the following Sunday, Juarez went to Pastor Evans before the morning service with Alan at his side and told him of Alan leading him to the Lord. When the invitation was given at the close of the sermon, Juarez went forward and presented himself for baptism. Before the pastor baptized him, he had him give his testimony to the congregation, and Juarez closed it off by saying he was so happy to be a *real* Christian, and he also wanted someday to become a *real* Texan. The congregation loved it.

As time passed, Alan and Juarez learned to do just about every kind of work on the Circle C Ranch. They were not surprised to see that William Childress had foreman Cort Whitney training the ranch hands how to use a rifle in combat so that, if Santa Anna's troops came to take the ranch, they could fight them. Both Childress and Whitney were pleased to see how good Juarez Amigo was with a rifle and how quickly Alan Kane learned to use both a rifle and a revolver adeptly.

Not a day passed that Alan Kane didn't think of Julia Miller and wish he could see her.

THIRTEEN

One afternoon in late August, Alan Kane was working on a stretch of corral fence near one of the barns when he looked up to see two of the ranch hands coming from the road in a wagon. He knew they had been to town.

The driver, Frank McDonald, waved at him. "Hey, Alan! I've got somethin' for you!"

Alan stepped away from the fence as Frank pulled the wagon to a halt. "Ollie and I stopped at the post office while we were in town." He picked up an envelope from the seat and extended it to Alan. "Here's a letter for you."

As Alan took the letter in hand, he saw that it was from Adam. He hoped the letter was to tell him that Adam would be coming to Texas soon. "Thanks, Frank."

Alan started to turn away, but stopped as Frank picked up another letter from the seat. "I've got one here for Mr. Childress too. Would you take it to him for me?"

Accepting the letter, Alan smiled. "Sure. Be glad to."

As the wagon rolled away, Alan slipped the envelope for his boss into his shirt pocket without looking at the front of it. He paused long enough to quickly read the letter from Adam. His features paled when he read that his father had been injured in a work mishap on the docks. The rope on a loaded pallet being lifted by a crane had snapped, and the pallet fell on him, knocking him down and injuring his back.

Adam explained that the doctors said Papa would get better, but it would take some time. Adam could not leave for Texas until Papa was well. He went on to tell Alan that he would keep him posted by mail on how it was going.

Alan thanked the Lord that it was no worse and told himself that he would write back immediately and inform the family that he would be praying for Papa.

Alan placed the letter back in the envelope, held it in his hand, and headed for the big log house. Moments later, as he approached the front door of the house, he pulled the boss's letter from his shirt pocket and placed it on top of Adam's letter, holding both in his hand. He stepped up on the porch, knocked on the door, and waited.

Slowly Alan's line of sight dropped to the front of the envelope in his hand. Goose bumps rose on his skin. The letter was from Sally Miller in New Orleans, Louisiana. Alan breathed Julia's name.

The door opened, and William Childress smiled. "Howdy, Alan."

"Howdy, boss." He held up the letter from Adam. "I wanted to let you know that Frank McDonald and Ollie Pitts brought me a letter from the post office in town just now. It's from Adam. Papa had a loaded pallet fall on him at work, and it hurt his back."

William's brow puckered. "I'm sorry to hear that, Alan. Is he hurt bad?"

"Well, sir, enough that Adam won't be able to come for a while, but the doctors say Papa will get better in time."

"I'm glad he'll get better, but I'm sad that Adam won't be coming as soon as planned."

"Yes," said Alan. "Me too."

"I'll be praying for your father, Alan. For his sake and for Adam's. I really want Adam to come and work here on the ranch."

"Me too." Alan took the second envelope and held it up. "There's also a letter here for you. It's from Sally Miller."

A smile broke across William's face as he took it in hand.

"I have an idea that this is probably a wedding announcement." He opened the envelope, took out the letter, and nodded as he read the letter. "It is indeed the wedding announcement I've been expecting. Sally is marrying Jeffrey Dardanelle at their church on Saturday, December 6."

Alan's thoughts were on Sally's sister, but he smiled and nodded.

Reading a bit further, William looked at Alan. "Sally wants to know if I can come to the wedding." He paused briefly and smiled. "She is also inviting *you.*"

"Really?"

"Mm-hmm." He grinned. "Of course you probably wouldn't be interested in making the trip just to attend the wedding."

Julia Miller's beautiful face was on the screen of Alan Kane's mind. "Oh, yes I would! I'd love to go, boss. I wouldn't insult Miss Sally for anything!"

Smiling, William said, "Well, let's see…this is August 28. The wedding is barely three months away. We'll plan to leave on November 27. That will give us a few extra days in New Orleans before the wedding. Sally says her parents want us to stay in their home if we can come."

Alan felt warmth swell up within him. "Well, bless their hearts; that's very kind of them."

As the weeks passed, the torch Alan Kane was carrying for Julia Miller burned in his heart. Though he knew he could never have her, his love continued to grow. He knew by this time that, though he had thought absence from her might cause his love to dwindle and fade out of existence, it was not going to happen. His love for her would never die.

During the passing time, Alan learned of letters that came to William Childress from Justin and Myra Miller.

In the newspapers, Mexico's Generalissimo Antonio López de Santa Anna was in the news almost daily. He was showing more and more of a desire to take Texas back as a possession of Mexico.

One day William Childress and Alan Kane were riding fence together, checking for any needed repairs, when they hauled up at a small pool of water that was fed from one of the streams that crossed the Circle C. Both men dismounted, and while they were watering their horses, they heard cattle bawl extra loud near a ridge off toward the west.

As they looked that direction, William said, "I wonder what's got them upset."

Seconds later, they saw two Circle C riders come over the ridge dragging a steer carcass by a rope. The riders had not seen their boss looking on and soon passed by at a distance of about a half mile.

"What do you suppose happened to the steer, boss?" Alan asked.

"Hard to tell," William said. "Those things just happen now and then." He paused. "With all of this Santa Anna stuff in the newspapers, yours truly is living with one eye watching for Mexicans to invade the ranch while the other eye is on the ranch hands doing their work. I thought maybe the cattle were frightened by invading Mexicans."

Alan nodded. "I think a lot about those Mexican soldiers myself, boss."

William sighed. "Any day now, I expect to see Mexican soldiers coming over that ridge with rifles in hand and bayonets shining in the sun."

Alan swallowed hard.

As time continued to pass, Alan exchanged letters with Adam and Angela, as well as his married brothers and their wives. Abram Kane's injuries were slowly healing. Alan praised the Lord for answered prayer.

Alan Kane's thoughts also often wandered to lovely Julia Miller. One night, shortly after he fell asleep in his bunk, he began to dream. He saw himself with Julia. They were holding hands and running through fields of spring flowers, surrounded by Texas mists. Julia was laughing as they drew up to a bubbling stream.

Suddenly her laughter ceased, and she was caressing his face with both hands. There was love and adoration in her tender eyes. Slowly she pulled his face down to hers. In a warm whisper, she cooed, "I love you, my darling. I love you."

Just as their lips were about to meet, Alan awakened. The long bunkhouse was filled with snores and heavy breathing. His heart thundered against his ribs. He sat up in the dark, then eased back down and laid his head on the pillow. "Oh, Julie," he whispered. "Why does it have to be a dream? I love you so much, Julie. Why does it have to be a dream?"

On Thursday, November 27, 1834, William Childress and his young friend Alan Kane embarked on schedule for New Orleans. They arrived at the New Orleans docks at noon on December 2. They took a hired carriage to the Miller mansion and were greeted by Garth, who informed them that the Miller family was visiting the Dardanelles at their plantation but would be home in a while.

Garth then asked, "Have you gentlemen had lunch?"

"No," replied William.

"Well, I will go tell Hosanna you're here, and she'll take care of you. I will then take your bags to your rooms. You will be staying in the same rooms you occupied before."

Hosanna quickly prepared lunch for the guests and fed them in the dining room. They had beef sandwiches, fried potatoes, and green salad, along with hot coffee. For dessert, they were given a plate heaped high with molasses cookies.

At two thirty that afternoon, the Millers returned home. Garth led them into the parlor, where William and Alan were waiting. Sally and Julia hurried ahead of their parents, with open arms. Sally hugged Alan, while Julia hugged Uncle William. Then when Julia turned to Alan, her face lit up, and she gave him a tender embrace that made him feel like someone had just poured liquid fire in his veins. Justin and Myra welcomed their guests warmly. Courteously,

Alan clicked his heels perfectly and kissed Myra's hand. He then shook hands with the man he wished could be his father-in-law. William followed suit, kissing Myra's hand and shaking hands with Justin.

Alan's heart secretly surged over the next few days as he and Julia spent time together. At one point, she asked him if he was adapting to ranch life all right. He assured her that he was and added that his success in horsemanship had come easily because of what she had taught him. This pleased her immensely. Julia brought up more than once what a beautiful friendship she and Alan had developed.

On Saturday, December 6, while the wedding ceremony was in progress at the church, Alan's eyes were glued to beautiful Julia, who was one of the bridesmaids. She was stunning in her lovely dress. He tried to picture what she would look like in a wedding gown, coming toward him on the arm of her father to marry him, just as Sally had been escorted down the aisle by her father to marry Jeffrey Dardanelle.

While Alan feasted his eyes on Julia during the ceremony, he also observed Jeffrey Dardanelle. Jeffrey was right and proper material as a son-in-law for the Millers, Alan thought. Handsome. Mannerly. Rich.

It was then that a grisly thought gripped Alan's mind: someday a rich young man would have the pleasure of marrying Julia. He told himself he never wanted to know who or when she married. He could not stand it.

Monday came all too soon for Alan, and he found himself with William Childress at the New Orleans docks saying good-bye to Julia and her parents.

When William and Alan were about to board the ship to head for home, Julia hugged "Uncle William," then turned to Alan and opened her arms. After a brief embrace, Alan held her hands and looked down into her eyes. She smiled. "Alan, I want you to know that I'll be praying for your father."

Alan smiled in return. "Thank you, Julie."

"And you tell Adam that my parents and I sure hope he gets to come to our place on his way to Texas and spend some time with us."

"I'll tell him."

Julia squeezed his hands, then stood on her tiptoes and kissed his cheek, which caused a tingling sensation to run down his spine.

"Alan, no matter how long it is until we see each other again, the two of us will always be good friends."

Alan smiled, gave her a long, steady look, and said in a low voice, "Yes, Julie. You will always be my good and treasured friend." He was thinking that he wished it could be more than just friendship between them.

She gave him another brief embrace, then stepped back so that he could go up the gangplank with Uncle William.

Moments later, as the ship pulled away from the dock, Alan and his boss waved to the Millers, who waved back. Fixing his gaze on Julia, Alan said in his heart, *I love you, Julie! I'll probably never see you again, but I'll always love you!*

On Monday morning, December 15, William Childress and Alan Kane arrived by ferry at Groce's Landing. They chatted with Mel Sibley while they bridled and saddled their horses, then mounted up and headed for the Circle C Ranch.

As they were riding, William glanced at Alan. "I know I said it while we were on the boat, and again on the ferry, but it sure was an excellent wedding that Jeffrey and Sally had."

Alan nodded. "It sure was, boss."

"Sally was a beautiful bride, wasn't she?"

"Yes," agreed Alan.

"Of course," said William, "as beautiful as Sally is, I have to say that Julia is even *more* beautiful. On the day of her wedding, she will be a real knockout! Whoever has the privilege of marrying Julia is going to be one fortunate man!"

Young Alan Kane felt sure his boss had no idea that he was in love with Julia. He swallowed hard. "You're right about that, boss. He will most certainly be a fortunate man. I have to say that Julie is the most beautiful girl I have ever seen."

William looked at him, eyes wide. "*Julie?* You call her *Julie?*"

"Mm-hmm. Since she and I have become close friends, she allows me to call her Julie."

William turned his head away from Alan, and a furtive grin hovered on his lips for a few seconds.

As they drew near to the ranch just before noon, they pulled rein at the ridge where the entire ranch came into view. The Circle C lay quietly in the peaceful valley.

Alan said, "Well, boss, winter hasn't hurt the ranch's charm. It is still majestically beautiful, even though the cold December winds are turning the grass to a faded brown."

"Home always looks good to me, Alan," replied William, "no matter what time of year it is."

Alan nodded. "It's looking that way to me too because this is home to me now." As those words left his lips, a lonesome feeling passed through his heart. He thought of his previous home, far away in Boston, and a yearning for his family gripped him.

William nodded. "I'm glad you feel that way about the Circle C, my boy." There was a wistful look in the ranch owner's eyes as he studied Alan's handsome, angular face.

When their eyes met, Alan took note of his look and asked, "What is it, sir?"

"I…ah…I was just thinking."

"About what?"

William smiled at him. "Before I tell you what I was thinking, let me say that I am very pleased with the way you have learned every aspect of cattle ranching in the relatively brief time you've been here. I am also amazed at how quickly you've learned how to handle both a rifle and a revolver. It has made me proud of you. What…what I was thinking, was if I'd have had a son, I would want him to be exactly like you."

Alan felt a lump rise in his throat. He forced it down and said, "I am very honored that you feel that way, sir."

William smiled at him again. "I just praise the Lord that He allowed you to come here to the Circle C."

Tears filmed Alan's eyes. "Me too, boss," he said. "Me too."

In late December, Alan Kane received a letter from his brother Adam in which he was told that their father was doing much better. His back injury was bothering him a little less each day. Adam said he figured he could leave Papa with Angela and the married brothers within a month or so. He told Alan that he would write him again within a couple of weeks and let him know how Papa was doing by then.

In the envelope, there were also brief letters from Angela, Alex and Libby, and Abel and Vivian. They all told him that they missed him very much and were jealous that Adam would soon be living at the Circle C Ranch with him.

Alan wrote back, saying how glad he was that Papa was doing so well and how much he missed all of them. Jokingly he added that if they wanted to, they could all come to the Circle C Ranch and live with him.

Time moved on. The new year—1835—came and with it the threat of the Mexican government's greed exploding into war.

Word spread across Texas from Washington-on-the-Brazos that in Mexico City, Presidente Antonio López de Santa Anna was moving toward open dictatorship. He had installed a puppet congress and rammed through law after law, undermining the federal structure established by the constitution of

1824, which had been built on an agreement between Mexico and Stephen Austin that the Texans were free to colonize and to function as an independent republic.

With the threat of Mexico taking Texas back under its control, by early 1835 the Texans found themselves divided into two camps. One was a war party that wanted to revolt immediately and have it out with Santa Anna and his army. The other was a peace party that still hoped to somehow come to a peaceful agreement with the aggressive Mexican dictator.

Sam Houston, who had become the national leader of Texas, sent out messengers who spoke for him, calling for all Texans to remain calm. He warned that the Republic of Texas was not yet equipped or ready for war.

In mid-February, a letter came to Alan Kane from Adam, advising him that as he had told him in previous letters, their father's condition was still improving. Adam told Alan that he would write him again when he had a date set to embark from Boston Harbor and head for Texas.

Late on Saturday morning, February 28, one of William Childress's supply wagons returned to the ranch from Washington-on-the-Brazos, driven by a ranch hand named Hal Pierson.

Pierson drew the wagon to a halt near the corrals, where a large number of men were working. He spotted Cort Whitney among them. Removing his hat and waving it, he called out, "Cort! Cort!"

When the foreman heard Hal's voice, he turned and saw him waving his hat. The men watched as Cort ran toward the wagon.

As he drew up, he said, "Something wrong, Hal?"

Pierson nodded. "Yes"—he placed his hat back on his head—"I've got bad news about the Mexicans! Send someone to tell Mr. Childress that I need to have all available men on the ranch gather around so I can tell them what's happened!"

In less than fifteen minutes, the ranch owner and all the nearby ranch hands, as well as a few women and children, were gathered in front of Hal Pierson as he stood up in the wagon. William Childress and Cort Whitney stood together beside the wagon, facing the crowd.

Speaking loudly enough for all to hear, Pierson told them that he had just returned from Washington-on-the-Brazos, and while there he'd heard people all over town talking about news that had come from seven Texas men who'd talked to some Mexicans who disliked Santa Anna. They told how the blood-hungry Santa Anna, in his dictatorial takeover of Mexico, had assigned a large number of troops under his brother-in-law, General Martín Perfecto de Cos. He sent the general and his troops to the Mexican city of Saltillo to depose the governor of the state of Coahuila, in northern Mexico, bordered on the north by the United States.

Pierson went on to explain that Santa Anna was angry at Governor Rulfo Zapata and the people in Coahuila's capital city, Saltillo, because they had become friendly with Texans just across the border. The Mexicans and the Texans were spending time together in Saltillo and small Texas towns along the border. Leading in it all was Governor Zapata.

Pierson then told that, the day when General Cos and his troops were spotted coming toward Saltillo, Governor Rulfo Zapata and the city's citizens fled toward Texas. Cos pursued them, however, and captured them. They were punished severely for being friendly with the Texans.

Hal Pierson had the rapt attention of everyone in the crowd. Running his gaze over their faces, he said, "There is now talk in Mexico that General Cos is going to invade and retaliate against the Texans for standing against the Mexican government."

The Circle C ranch hands and the women who were gathered around the supply wagon with the ranch owner and the foreman were visibly upset at the news.

William Childress took a step closer to the crowd. "Men, we had better lay up more ammunition. If those Mexican troops come on this property, we're going to show them that they can't take it from us."

"Right, boss!" shouted Cort Whitney, moving up beside Childress. "They'll find out just how stubborn we can be!"

Men were waving their fists and shouting agreement.

Childress said, "Tell you what, men. I've got business to take care of in Washington-on-the-Brazos this afternoon. I'll take a wagon and bring back a load of ammunition."

From where he stood on the wagon, Hal Pierson squared his jaw. "If those Mexicans want a fight, boss, we'll sure enough give 'em one!"

Close to the wagon, standing next to Alan Kane, was Juarez Amigo. "Sí!" he shouted. "We sure will, boss!"

A cheer went up among the men as the women and children looked on in fear.

Noting the fear, William Childress said so all could hear, "I want all the wives and children to listen to me! If you should see or hear Mexican soldiers riding onto the ranch, you are to go inside your cabins, lock the doors, lie down on the floor, and remain absolutely quiet!"

The women nodded, pulling their children close.

Childress then dismissed the crowd, and they stood around in small groups talking about the situation.

At that moment, Hal Pierson hopped down from the wagon and approached Alan Kane. Reaching into his coat pocket, he pulled out a white envelope. "Alan, I stopped by the post office. Here's a letter for you."

Alan quickly took it from his hand. "Thanks, Hal."

As Hal turned back toward the wagon, Alan looked down at the envelope. His eyes widened when he saw that it was from Adam.

As he stared at it, the ranch population dispersed, heavy-hearted over the ominous events taking place in Mexico.

FOURTEEN

Juarez Amigo was still at Alan Kane's side. He smiled. "I weel let you read your mail by yourself, my fran', Alan. See you later."

Alan smiled back at him and nodded. "Sí, señor."

Juarez walked away, saying over his shoulder, "You are catching on, Señor Alan!"

Excited, Alan tore the envelope open and read it eagerly.

In the letter, Adam reminded Alan of his comment in his earlier letter to the family that, if they wanted to, they could all come to the Circle C Ranch and live with him.

Adam then wrote, "Papa and Angela want to take you up on your invitation and come with me from Boston. I know that I will have a place in the bunkhouse, but would you talk to Mr. Childress and see if he would have someplace for Papa and Angela to live on the ranch?"

In the next sentence, Alan was told that Papa had a buyer for the house. If Adam heard back that Mr. Childress had a place for Papa and Angela, he would let Alan know when they would leave Boston for Texas.

Alan Kane was dumbfounded as his eyes perused the letter. He took a moment to let the news sink in. Then he reread the letter.

With a wide grin spreading over his face, he made a dash toward the big log house, saying, "Oh, dear Lord, thank You for this good news! Please work on Mr. Childress's heart so he will agree to Papa and Angela coming and provide them a place to live! I really do miss them. This would just about make my life perfect! The only thing lacking would be that I don't have Julie. But there again, Lord, my future is in Your hands."

At the big log house, William Childress was reaching for the knob on the front door and about to enter the house when he saw Alan coming on the run. Taking a step back, he smiled at young Kane and waited for him to arrive.

As Alan drew near the porch, he waved the letter and said excitedly, "Boss, I've got really good news!"

"Well, let's hear it!" replied William.

Alan bounded up on the porch and shook the letter toward his boss. "This letter is from Adam! He says that Papa and our sister, Angela, want to come with him and live here on the ranch! That is, if you have a place for them."

William's eyebrows arched. "So your father is well enough to come, I assume."

"Yes sir!"

A wide smile spread over William's face. "Alan, this is great news! Of course I have a place for them to live. There is plenty of room right here in this house!"

Shock showed on Alan's ruggedly handsome features. "Wha— Th-this house?"

"Sure! There's plenty of room. I just rattle around in it all by myself. Of course, Daisy has her small apartment in the back, but it would please me more than I could tell you to have your father and sister living here under this roof! I'll have Daisy prepare separate rooms for them, but all of the house—the whole ranch, for that matter—is theirs to enjoy."

Alan's eyes were sparkling. "Oh, thank you, Mr. Childress! Of course, both Papa and Angela will want to help out around here in any way they can. Papa will need to stay busy, especially now that he's feeling better. He's a hard worker. Angela can be a real help to Daisy. She's a great cook and housekeeper. She has been taking care of all of us since she was a little girl because of Mama's illness."

"Sounds good to me!" William replied.

Tears misted Alan's eyes. "I so much want them near me, boss, and I know they'll just love being here as much as I do. I know Papa will thrive once he's here in these wide-open spaces. Thank you so very much."

William laid a hand on Alan's shoulder. "You are more than welcome, son. It will do my heart good to share the blessings the Lord has given me. I can hardly wait to get them here. How soon will they be coming?"

"Well, Adam says that once he knows there's a place on the ranch for Papa and Angela, he'll let me know when they will be coming." He took a deep breath and let it out slowly. "And since you've offered to let them live here in the house with you, I'll write Adam immediately and tell him. We'll be hearing back within about four weeks."

"Swell!" William patted Alan's shoulder, then turned to enter the house. Taking hold of the doorknob, he looked back with a smile. "Tell them to hurry. I want them here as soon as possible."

"Yes sir!" His happy smile was spread from ear to ear. "Ah…boss…"

"Mm-hmm?"

"Since you're going to town to do your business and get a load of ammunition, could you wait a few minutes?"

"Sure, why?"

"Well, I'd like to write a quick letter to Adam right now and have you mail it for me when you go to town."

"I'll be glad to do that. You go write the letter, and I'll be ready to leave when you come back."

Alan hurried away toward the bunkhouse, calling over his shoulder, "I'm a fast writer! Be back real quick!"

Alan Kane received Adam's next letter, dated March 14, on Thursday, March 26. In the letter, Adam spoke of William Childress's generosity in allowing

Papa and Angela to live in the large ranch house with him, then informed Alan that they would be leaving Boston on Tuesday, March 24. There was no way at this point, Adam pointed out, to know whether they would be stopping in New Orleans to visit the Millers. He figured they would arrive at Groce's Landing in late April or early May, then hire a carriage and come to the ranch.

Excited to receive the news, Alan went to William Childress and shared the letter with him. William could see that Alan was extremely excited about his loved ones coming to live on the Circle C Ranch. "Well, son, since it will be a good while before they arrive, I have a trip I want you to make with me."

"Where to, sir?" asked Alan.

"I have some business to take care of in Galveston. I'd sure like to have your company."

Alan's face shone brightly. "I'm honored, sir! Of course I'll go with you! When do we leave?"

"Next Monday."

"I'll be ready!"

On Monday, March 30, William Childress and Alan Kane traveled on horseback to Groce's Landing, took the ferry to Velasco, and boarded a boat for Galveston. They arrived in Galveston just after midnight, and checked in to the Austin Manor Hotel.

On Tuesday, Alan accompanied William to three different stores that dealt in leather goods. At each one, the owner of the Circle C Ranch received orders for cattle hides, which made him very happy. As they headed back toward their hotel, Alan commended his employer for his excellent salesmanship.

That night, after they had eaten supper in the restaurant at the Austin Manor Hotel, William and Alan took a walk together along the city's main street.

Alan went into a boot store to purchase a new pair of boots while William waited on a nearby street corner watching what little traffic there was by the light of the streetlamps.

While William stood beneath a streetlamp, he was unaware that three thugs were standing in the shadows not very far away. They were looking him over.

One of the three said in a whisper, "Hey, guys, that guy is dressed pretty fancy. He's gotta be well off."

"I'd say so, Lenny," commented Jake Mantle. "Let's get his wallet."

"Yeah," agreed the other one, whose name was Wayne Kistler.

"Let's do it," said Lenny Puckett.

Slowly the trio moved up behind their intended victim. Lenny Puckett pulled a hunting knife from a sheath on his waist, stepped in front of William Childress, and pointed the tip of the blade at William's nose. "Gimme your wallet, mister," he said through his teeth, "or I'll cut off your nose."

William had not yet seen Puckett's two companions. He swiftly stepped back, swung his foot out, and kicked the knife from the thug's hand. While his knife sailed through the air, Puckett took a step toward Childress and ran into a hard right punch that dropped him to the boardwalk.

Instantly, Wayne Kistler moved in and cracked William on the jaw while Jake Mantle picked up the knife from the boardwalk.

Staggered by the blow, William was shaking his head when suddenly Mantle stabbed him three times with the knife.

At the same time, Alan Kane was coming out of the boot store, carrying a box with his new boots. When he saw what was happening, he dropped it and dashed toward the scene.

William Childress was down on the boardwalk, and the thugs were trying to find his wallet. Alan kicked Wayne Kistler in the face and sent him rolling. Quickly, he snatched Jake Mantle by the back of his jacket collar and yanked him away, slamming him down hard. The bloody knife slipped from Mantle's hand, and Alan kicked it into the street.

Lenny Puckett let out an angry roar and leaped at Alan, fists swinging.

Alan popped him solidly on the nose, and Puckett staggered backward, shaking his head.

Alan glanced down at William, who was bleeding and barely moving.

A furious Wayne Kistler was on his feet again and came charging in, fists ready. Alan beat him to the punch, slamming him on the jaw. He felt a warm surge of satisfaction as the man slumped to the boardwalk.

Suddenly the other two thugs jumped Alan from behind. Puckett had a death grip on Alan's neck, and Mantle was trying to grasp an arm and pull him down.

A crowd was gathering.

The thugs were unaware that they were in combat with a man for whom fighting had been a way of life on the Boston docks. Alan Kane's six-foot-four-inch, 220-pound frame was a mountain of muscle. His strength was like a caged beast…eager to be released.

The gathering crowd stood in awe as Alan loosened the grip of the man who had hold of his neck and punched him with a powerful blow, dropping him to the boardwalk. Then he grabbed Jake Mantle's right arm and twisted it savagely, flipped him over his back, and slammed him hard into the boardwalk headfirst.

Puckett and Mantle were both unconscious, but Wayne Kistler was now on top of William Childress, going through his pockets, trying to find his wallet. Despite his bleeding wounds, William was trying to fight him off.

Alan dashed to the spot. He made a dive and slammed into Kistler, knocking him over. Quickly, he looked at William, trying to assess his wounds.

At the same time, Kistler, shaking his head, spotted the knife where it lay in the street and scrambled to it. He grabbed it and spun around with fire in his eyes. Alan was coming after him.

Kistler swung the knife at Alan, but his timing was off. Alan drew back his right fist and then fired it like a cannonball onto the thug's jaw. Wayne Kistler went down and out.

A woman in the crowd had begun screaming at the younger men for not jumping in to help the man who was fighting three men alone. No one answered her.

As Alan knelt over William Childress, examining his wounds, an older man stepped up and said, "My brother has gone for help from the law, son."

Even as he spoke, two deputy marshals came on the scene, along with a man who resembled the older man. When people in the crowd told them what had happened, the deputies handcuffed all three unconscious thugs.

While this was going on, a man who had been driving down the street in his wagon and stopped to observe the fight was now offering to take the wounded man to a nearby doctor. Alan pointed out his package of new boots near the door of the store and asked the man to retrieve it for him while he carried William to the wagon.

As Alan laid the bleeding William on the wagon, one of the deputies told him he had plenty of witnesses to the crime. The thugs would be taken to jail and would have to face a judge tomorrow. They would be going to prison. If Alan's friend died, they would be hanged.

Alan explained who his friend was and said if the doctor could save William's life, Alan would be taking him back to the Circle C Ranch as soon as possible. The deputy had heard of the ranch and of its owner. He would see to it that justice was done to the thugs. Alan thanked him, and the deputy headed back to where his partner was watching over the thugs. One of them was beginning to regain consciousness.

A few minutes later, Alan was riding in the bed of the wagon with his boss while its kind owner was driving down Galveston's main street. He introduced himself as Leland Scott and told Alan that he was taking them to Dr. John Partridge's house, which was next door to his office.

William Childress was conscious, though very pale and a bit glassy-eyed. By the light of the streetlamps along the way, William tried to focus on Alan's worried face and spoke in a weak, raspy voice. "Thank you, son, for coming to my rescue. I thought I was a goner for sure." William tried to smile, but it was more of a grimace than a smile.

"I'm sorry I didn't come out of the store sooner, sir."

"Well, you certainly handled those crooks well when you did come out. If you hadn't, they would have killed me."

"I learned a lot about fighting while working on the docks in Boston, sir. My father was the best fighter I've ever seen."

William tried to say something else, but his pain kept him from it.

"The Lord's going to see that you're taken care of, Mr. Childress," Alan said softly. "I'm sure Dr. Partridge will be able to help you."

William tried to smile, but it just would not come.

When they reached Dr. John Partridge's house, Leland Scott jumped out of the wagon, ran up to the door, and knocked. Moments later, the doctor was leading Alan Kane, who was carrying William Childress, into the office. Leland Scott stayed close by Alan's side.

Dr. Partridge went to work on William, with Alan and Leland standing a few feet from the examining table. The doctor had also heard of William Childress and the Circle C Ranch. He quickly found that William had been stabbed in the right side at his waist, in the left shoulder, and the upper right arm.

As the doctor stitched up the wounds, William spoke hoarsely and told the doctor how Alan had saved his life.

When the doctor had finished stitching up the wounds, he said to Alan, "It would be best if Mr. Childress stayed here in my office for a couple of days so I can make sure the wounds are healing properly, especially the one in his right side. It is by far the most serious."

Alan nodded. "Whatever you say, doctor."

"I can let you sleep on a cot in the same room if you wish," said Dr. Partridge.

"Fine," replied Alan. "I appreciate that."

"I do too," said William.

Two days passed, with the doctor watching over William Childress very carefully. On Friday morning, Dr. Partridge stood over William with Alan at his side. "Mr. Childress, I wish your wounds were healing faster, but I will allow you to go home since you have Mr. Kane with you. He has assured me that he will see that you have proper transportation between boats and after you get to Groce's Landing."

William nodded, showing a thin smile. "Alan will take good care of me, Doctor."

Partridge nodded. "But you must be very careful. This wound in your side is quite serious. If you start bleeding internally there, you could die. Do you understand?"

William nodded slowly. "I…I understand."

"I do too, Doctor," put in Alan. "I'll watch over him very carefully. The only walking he will do is to get on the boat to Velasco and the ferry to Groce's Landing. And if he can't do it, I will carry him. We rode our horses from the ranch to Groce's Landing, but I'll find a way to get him home by wagon."

"Good." Partridge looked down at William. "This young man has a good head on his shoulders."

William smiled weakly. "Doctor, if I could have had a son, I'd want him to be just like Alan."

The doctor looked at Alan, whose face tinted. He then turned to William. "I assume you have a personal physician at home?"

"Yes sir. His name is Dr. Dennis Dewitt. His office is in Washington-on-the-Brazos."

Partridge nodded. "You need to have him check you over soon after you get home, just to make sure you're all right."

"I'll do that, Doctor."

When William Childress and Alan Kane arrived back at the Circle C Ranch in a wagon loaned to them by Mel Sibley, everyone at the ranch was upset to learn what happened to the ranch owner.

All of the Circle C people gathered around Mr. Childress as he lay in the wagon in front of the big log house and were stunned at his pallid face and obvious weakness. He looked gaunt and haggard. His skin was ashen gray, like that of a dead man. He was hollow-eyed and spoke in a half whisper when he told them how Alan had come to his rescue and saved his life.

The next morning, William sent for Smiley Dunn and asked him to ride to Washington-on-the-Brazos and tell his attorney, Edgar Phillips, that he needed him to come to the ranch as soon as possible.

Smiley wanted to ask why the boss needed to see his attorney but held his peace.

William then asked Smiley to go by Dr. Dewitt's office while he was in town, tell him what had happened, and ask him to come and check on him when he had time.

Late the same afternoon, Smiley brought the middle-aged attorney into William's bedroom at the ranch house.

William was sitting up in the bed and tried to smile when he saw Edgar Phillips. "I didn't expect you so soon, Edgar," he said weakly.

Phillips smiled as he stood over him. "Well, William, you happen to be one of my very best clients, and when Smiley told me what had happened to you in Galveston, I told him I was coming today."

The ranch owner nodded. "Thank you."

"Mr. Childress," said Smiley, "I saw Dr. Dewitt, and he said he would be here on Monday to check on you."

"Fine. Thank you for your help."

"You are most welcome, boss." Smiley left the room.

William looked at his attorney. "Edgar, I've asked you to come because I want to draw up a will. As you know, since my wife died, I have never set up a new one."

"Yes sir."

"I need to finalize one right away, Edgar. This horrible incident has awakened me to that fact. Should something happen to take my life, I must have the will so that ownership of the ranch and the money I have in the bank at Washington-on-the-Brazos would go to the proper hands."

Phillips opened the briefcase he was carrying and took out paper and pencil. "All right. Tell me how you want the will set up."

The attorney made notes as William gave him the necessary information. When he had all the information, he used pen and ink to write up the will and had William sign it.

When Edgar Phillips rode away, some of the ranch hands who recognized him wondered why he had been there but agreed that no one should ask.

Daisy Haycock attended to William Childress, cooking his meals and meeting his every need.

On Sunday afternoon, William was sitting in an overstuffed chair at the window in his bedroom when he looked up to see Daisy ushering Pastor Merle Evans into the room. Daisy picked up a wooden chair across the room, placed it next to where her boss was sitting, and invited the pastor to sit down. She then left the room.

William learned from the pastor that the Circle C people had told him at church that morning what had happened in Galveston.

Pastor Evans spoke encouragingly, read Scripture, and prayed with him. William thanked him for coming.

When the pastor left the house to mount up and ride for town, he found Juarez Amigo standing beside his horse. Juarez smiled. "Thank you for coming to see Meester Cheeldress, Pastor."

"It's my duty and my privilege, Juarez," the pastor said.

"I sure do like your preaching," Juarez told him. "Eet is wonderful to know that I am going to heaven when my life on earth is over."

"Amen," said Evans. "I'm so glad that Alan led you to the Lord."

The Mexican showed his white teeth in a wide smile. "I am glad for that too, Pastor. Eet is great to be a *real* Christian!"

The pastor mounted his horse, looked down at Juarez, and said, "I'll see you at church this evening."

"Sí, you sure weel, Pastor." He waved to Evans as he rode away.

On Monday morning, April 6, Dr. Dennis Dewitt arrived at the Circle C and did a thorough examination of William Childress. He told William that he seemed to be healing all right, but warned him to be especially careful with the wound in his side.

The next morning, when Daisy entered her boss's room, she found him dressed and sitting in his overstuffed chair.

"Mr. Childress!" she gasped. "What are you doing out of bed?"

"Well, Daisy, it's about time I start trying to get back to normal," William said. "I know you were planning to bring my breakfast on a tray, but I'm going to walk down to the kitchen and eat there. I really need to start walking some."

Daisy knew it would do no good to argue with him. "All right, but I'm walking with you."

Moments later, when William sat down at the table, Daisy set his food before him. "While you're eating, Mr. Childress, I'll go to your room and change your bedding."

As William ate, he heard a knock at the front door of the big log house. He called out to Daisy, but she had already heard the knock and was on her way to the door. Seconds later, Alan Kane and Cort Whitney entered the kitchen. They told him they had come to see how he was doing, adding that all the ranch hands were awaiting a report on his condition.

When Alan and Cort were satisfied that their boss was gaining his strength back, they told him they were glad and wanted to relay the good news to the men.

Later, while Daisy washed dishes, William carefully walked to the front of the big log house, stepped out onto the front porch, and sat down on one of the comfortable chairs.

The sun was shining brightly, and a slight breeze was blowing. The early April air was a bit cool but not uncomfortably so.

William told himself that now that his will had been made out, he could rest easy. He closed his eyes, thinking back for a few moments to the days when he and his wife were enjoying life together. Suddenly the sound of children playing jerked him back to the present. He opened his eyes and saw two small boys—sons of ranch hands—scuffling and playing together in an open area nearby.

Suddenly he heard thundering hoofbeats and saw several head of cattle running wildly and bawling as if they had been frightened by something. They were headed for the very spot where the two boys were playing.

William stood up and shouted, "Boys! Boys! Run! Hurry! Run!"

Both boys froze in their tracks at the sight of the cattle thundering toward them.

With his heart pounding in his chest, William ignored the weakness he was experiencing from the stab wounds and dashed off the porch. He hurried toward the terrified boys, crying out for them to run away. Finally, just as he reached the spot, the boys were able to make their feet move and dashed away, escaping the racing herd.

William Childress, however, was having a spasm of pain and staggered from dizziness. Putting his hand to the sharp pain of the wound, he dropped to his knees just as the thundering, wild-eyed herd of cattle closed in.

They knocked him down, and heedless hoofs pounded him into the ground.

FIFTEEN

After the last of the wild-eyed cattle that had trampled William Childress were out of range, the two boys stood frozen on the spot several yards away, staring at the scene. Four ranch hands, who had seen the incident from a field close by, came running up. At the head of the pack was foreman Cort Whitney.

Whitney glanced at the terrified boys, then skidded to a halt at William's lifeless form, which lay bloody and crumpled on the ground. The other three men formed a circle and looked down at their boss.

As the two boys moved slowly in that direction, Alan Kane came riding up and noticed the three men standing over his boss and Cort Whitney kneeling beside him. The scene stole the breath from his lungs. He pulled rein, leaped from the saddle, and darted toward the spot where William Childress lay in the dust. He dropped to his knees beside the foreman and looked down at the blood and the battered head, face, and body of his boss. "Cort!" he gasped. "What happened?"

Whitney swallowed hard, and while the other men and the two boys stood together and looked on, he told Alan what he and the other three men had observed from the nearby field.

His voice trembling, Cort closed off his story by looking at the boys "Donny…Harlan…Mr. Childress gave his life trying to save yours."

Both boys were weeping. All they could do was stare at the body and nod.

Still kneeling at William's side, Alan took a lifeless hand in his own, and unbidden tears coursed down his cheeks. The other three ranch hands stood in stunned silence.

Alan looked up at Cort through his tears. "Do you know what spooked the cattle?"

Cort shook his head. "No. And we may never know." He sniffed and wiped at the tears on his cheeks. "Mr. Childress was a hero to the very end, Alan."

Alan squeezed the hand he was holding. "That he was, Cort."

Other men were coming to see what happened, and within twenty minutes all the ranch hands had gathered around, as well as the women and children. The parents of the two boys stood together holding them. Daisy Haycock was also there, and everybody was shedding tears.

In a choked voice, Cort asked for everyone's attention and told them that he and Alan would take Mr. Childress's body to the undertaker in town. While they were there, they would go to the church and let Pastor Evans know what had happened and arrange for the funeral.

Cort then looked at Daisy and asked if she could fetch them a blanket from the ranch house, saying they would need to cover the body when they laid it in the back of the wagon. He then asked two men who stood close by to hitch up a team and bring them to him. The two men hurried away.

As Daisy headed toward the house sniffling, Alan stood up and looked at Cort through his tears. "I'll ride in the back of the wagon with the body." He drew a ragged breath and wiped tears. "I can't believe he's gone, Cort. It all happened so quickly." Again tears threatened, but Alan was able to hold them back.

Moments later, the wagon was brought to the spot. Smiley Dunn and Cort Whitney placed the body in the bed of the wagon, and Alan climbed in. Daisy handed Alan the blanket, and he gently placed it over the body of the man who had become his very close friend.

Just before Alan drew the blanket up over William's face, he paused and looked at it again. It was different than a few minutes earlier. He could see peace written there. More tears filled his eyes as he whispered, "Thank You, Lord," and lowered the blanket over the bruised, bloodied face.

Just as Cort Whitney was about to climb up onto the wagon seat, some of the ranch hands stepped up. One of them said, "Cort, we're concerned. What's going to happen to the ranch now that the boss is gone?"

Cort shrugged his shoulders. "Fellas, I'm not sure. I'll contact Mr. Childress's attorney after the funeral and see what he can tell me."

"Sure hope it doesn't mean we've all lost our jobs," one of them said.

"Me too." Cort climbed up and sat down on the wagon seat. He took the reins in hand, put the two-horse team into motion, and gave the men a wave as the wagon rolled away.

As the wagon bounced its way along the dusty road toward Washington-on-the-Brazos, Alan sat beside the blanket-covered body of William Childress. He went back over in his mind how much had happened in his life since he first met the man. What was going to happen now that he was dead? His father, sister, and brother were on their way from Boston to live here. *But what if the new owner of the Circle C doesn't want them here?*

He pondered this upsetting thought for a while, then realized that God already knew all about it and already had a plan for the Circle C's future...including the arrival of Papa, Adam, and Angela. "Lord," he whispered, "I'll just have to leave it all up to You. In Your Word, You tell us to cast all our care on You. So that's what I'm doing right now. Please help me not to worry or be fearful about it."

The funeral was held at the church in Washington-on-the-Brazos the next day, where Pastor Merle Evans preached a clear Bible-based message. The body was then taken to the town cemetery with the mourners following and was buried after a brief, comforting message for the Christians gathered there, assuring them that they would meet William Childress one day in heaven.

Cort Whitney had noticed attorney Edgar Phillips at the church and in the crowd at the grave side. When the pastor had closed in prayer and the crowd dispersed, Cort stepped up to the attorney and shook his hand. "I appreciate your coming to the funeral, Mr. Phillips."

The attorney nodded. "William was one of my best clients. Word of his death spread quickly through town after his body was delivered to the undertaker."

Cort nodded. "I see. Well, sir, I was going to come to your office and ask if Mr. Childress had set up a will concerning the ranch."

Phillips made a thin smile. "He did. Just last Saturday."

"Oh, so that's what your visit was about."

"Yes. I was going to approach you here, but you beat me to it. I'll come to the ranch tomorrow, if that's all right. I'd like to meet with you and Alan Kane since you are both strongly involved in the will."

"Oh? Well, sure. That sounds all right. You have any idea what time you might arrive at the ranch?"

"Mm-hmm. About ten o'clock?"

"All right," Cort said. "I'll tell Alan, and we'll be expecting you."

The next morning, Edgar Phillips arrived at the Circle C Ranch on horseback at precisely ten o'clock, briefcase in hand, and met with Cort Whitney and Alan Kane in the privacy of the parlor at the huge ranch house. Alan had no problem understanding why Cort was involved in the will. After all, he was the foreman of the Circle C. But Alan had no idea why *he* was involved.

When they sat down together, Phillips reminded both men that he had come to the ranch just days ago at William's request.

He explained that William hadn't made a new will since his wife's death but had wanted to do so.

He then opened his briefcase and pulled out the new will. "The simplest thing for me to do, gentlemen, is to *tell* you what it says. Then if you have any questions, I can read you the parts that deal with your questions."

Whitney and Kane nodded.

"It's really quite simple," said Phillips. "First of all, Mr. Childress leaves ten thousand dollars to Daisy Haycock, with provision for her to stay on as cook and housekeeper at her normal salary."

Cort frowned. "But what if the new owner doesn't want her to stay?"

Phillips grinned. "Oh, he will, I'm sure."

"You already know who's going to buy the ranch?"

"I'll get to the new owner in a few minutes. Let me go ahead and explain that Mr. Childress's assets total almost four million dollars."

Cort and Alan looked at each other, eyes wide.

"Now here's how it's set up for disbursement in the will. Each ranch hand is to get five hundred dollars for every year, or portion thereof, he has worked at the Circle C. This, of course, includes you, Cort. Plus, since you are the ranch foreman, you are going to receive an additional fifty thousand dollars in a lump sum."

Cort Whitney's jaw slacked.

"Hey, that's great, Cort!" Alan grinned broadly. "You've been Mr. Childress's foreman for a long time. You deserve to share the riches!"

Whitney's eyes were sparkling with joy.

The attorney squeezed the papers in his hands and looked at Alan. "Mr. Childress did not include you among those ranch hands who get five hundred dollars for every year or portion thereof."

Alan's face lost color. "Oh? Even though I've been here a portion?"

"No." Edgar Phillips struggled at that point to keep a straight face. "Mr. Childress felt a special kinship toward you, Alan, for saving his life when you fought off those thugs that day they attacked him in Galveston."

Alan nodded at Mr. Phillips.

"Mr. Childress left you the ranch, Alan," Edgar Phillips said.

Alan Kane thought his ears must playing tricks on him. Eyes bulging, mouth agape, he stammered, "H-he…h-he *what*?"

"You are now the owner of the Circle C Ranch." Phillips smiled. "To put it bluntly, Alan Kane is at this moment a very wealthy young man."

Cort Whitney stood up and slapped the stunned Alan Kane on the back. "Couldn't have happened to a better man, *boss*!"

Alan could not speak. He only stared up at Whitney glassy-eyed.

Cort frowned playfully. "You *are* gonna be my boss, aren't you? I mean, you're not going to look for a new foreman, are you?"

Alan shook his head. "Yes. I—I—I mean, no! I—I mean, I always want you to be my foreman, Cort!"

Phillips and Whitney laughed. Then Phillips said, "Alan, I have papers here for you to sign. I'll take them with me and see that everything is taken care of with the bank accounts."

Alan's eyebrows arched. "Bank accounts?"

"Yes. Mr. Childress has approximately 1.6 million dollars between the ranch's savings account and checking account at the First National Bank in Washington-on-the-Brazos—and that's *after* all the ranch hands and Daisy receive their money. Then he also has nine hundred thousand dollars in his personal accounts there. Add in the value of the Circle C land, buildings, and livestock, and you are worth well over three million dollars, Mr. Alan Kane!"

Alan shook his head in wonderment.

"Alan," the attorney said, "I advise you to come up with a new name for the ranch. It needs to be identified with *you*. I suggest the Circle K, the Box K, the Diamond K, or something of that nature."

Alan licked his lips. "I like Diamond K the best."

Phillips nodded. "All right. I'll set that up legally for you."

"Ah…Mr. Phillips…"

"Yes?"

"While you're setting things up legally for me, I want my brother Adam to be my partner in ownership of the ranch. Fifty-fifty."

Phillips grinned and nodded. "All right. I'll write out the legal form right now, and you can sign it. Also, I need to go with you to the bank so you can get signed up on all the accounts."

"Just say when you want me to come to town, Mr. Phillips," said Alan, "and I'll be there."

"Okay. How about tomorrow morning?"

"Sure."

"Meet me at the bank at ten o'clock. When you've been put on the accounts, you can get the cash that is meant for all the ranch employees."

"Great! See you then."

That afternoon, Alan Kane moved his simple belongings from the bunkhouse into the big log house, evading questions that Juarez Amigo and Smiley Dunn asked him. He thought it best that all the ranch hands hear the news at once. The whole thing seemed like a foggy dream.

That evening Alan ate supper in the mess hall, but before anyone had finished their meal, he sent Juarez and Smiley to the cabins to ask all the married men and their wives to come to the mess hall. They also brought Daisy Haycock to the mess hall.

When everyone was there, Alan stood before them and gave them the whole story, explaining what William Childress had put in his will. The crowd was surprised but well pleased that they all would be receiving a generous amount of money themselves.

Later that night, when Daisy was in her connecting apartment and Alan was alone in the huge log house, he thought of Julia Miller. Now that he was wealthy, Julie just might marry him. He would make a trip to New Orleans as soon as possible and propose to her. The thought of it made his heart pound. He considered writing her a letter and telling her about his sudden riches, but decided he would wait until he could tell her in person.

Adam, Abram, and Angela Kane arrived at the Justin Miller mansion just outside New Orleans at nine o'clock in the morning on April 20. When

Adam knocked on the door, it was opened by the family butler, Garth. Adam introduced himself, his father, and his sister to Garth, who was aware that Adam might be coming by on his way to Texas but not that he'd be accompanied by Abram and Angela. Adam explained that his father and sister were with him because they had decided to move to Texas so they could live close to him and Alan.

Garth fetched Justin and Myra Miller quickly, and they warmly welcomed all three. Garth explained to the Millers why Abram and Angela were with Adam.

Myra set her warm eyes on Adam. "Our daughter Julia is out riding her horse at the moment, but she has been looking forward to meeting you."

Adam smiled. "Well, I've heard a lot about Julia from Alan. I am certainly looking forward to meeting her too. And it will be a few days before we can catch the boat. We're scheduled to leave for Galveston on Friday."

"Well, that gives us today plus three more days," said Justin.

Myra noticed that Abram looked a bit pale. She stepped closer to him. "Mr. Kane, are you not feeling well?"

Adam patted Abram's shoulder. "Let me explain, ma'am." He then told the Millers about his father's mishap on the job at the Boston docks, explaining that he had been feeling better but that the rigorous trip from Boston had taken its toll on him.

"I just need a little rest," Abram said, his voice raspy with fatigue.

Myra touched his arm. "I'll have Garth take you upstairs to your room immediately, and you can get some rest." She turned to her husband. "In the meantime, Justin, I think you should take Adam and go get Dr. Wilson so he can check Mr. Kane."

She turned back to Abram with concern written on her face. "Dr. James Wilson is our family physician. His office is in New Orleans. I know he'll come to see you real soon when he learns of your injured back."

Abram nodded. "All right, ma'am. I appreciate that. I really do need to lie down for a bit."

Angela spoke up. "I'll go to Papa's room with him if that's all right, Mrs. Miller."

Myra smiled. "Of course, dear. And please let me know if you need anything."

"Thank you, ma'am," said Angela. "I appreciate your kindness."

Angela followed Garth and her father as they made their way up the wide spiral staircase.

And Justin headed out in the family carriage with Adam at his side.

Two hours later, they arrived back at the mansion with Dr. James Wilson following in his small buggy.

Justin and Myra waited outside Abram's room with Angela and Adam while Dr. Wilson checked on him. After some twenty minutes had passed, the doctor came out, black bag in hand. He set his eyes on Adam and Angela. "Your father will be all right after he has had a good rest. I recommend, though, that he rest here at the Miller place for a full two weeks before you take him to Texas."

Adam thanked the doctor, saying they would take his advice.

He then asked how much they owed him.

Dr. Wilson smiled. "Nothing. Mr. Miller has already slipped me more than I would have charged you."

Adam and Angela looked at Justin, who shrugged, spread his open hands, and said, "What can I say?"

Adam looked him in the eye. "Well, sir, *I* can certainly say, 'Thank you.'"

"Yes," Angela said. "Thank you so very much."

When the doctor had gone, Myra told Adam and Angela that they would each be given a bedroom for their stay in the Miller home.

Angela asked that her room be next to her father's so she could be close to him.

Myra excused herself to the kitchen to let the cook know they had guests for lunch. Moments later, she returned and took Angela to the bedroom adjacent to her father's room. At the same time, Garth showed Adam his room, which was the same one Alan had stayed in. Adam then went downstairs to the foyer, where the Kane luggage had been placed, and helped the butler carry it upstairs.

As Angela unpacked her travel bag, Myra said, "We'll have lunch in about an hour, honey. Would your father prefer to have his lunch in his room or join us downstairs?"

"I'll go ask him." Angela hurried out the door. Seconds later she returned. "Papa's asleep, ma'am. I think we should let him sleep as much as possible. I'll keep checking on him, and when he wakes up, I'll bring his food up to him on a tray if that's all right."

"Of course," Myra said. "Well, if you're ready, we can go downstairs. I'm sure your brother and my husband are in the parlor by now."

Angela nodded. "Let's go."

When the two women entered the parlor, they found Justin and Adam sitting in overstuffed chairs facing each other. Garth was standing close by, listening as Justin and Adam discussed the threat of war between Texas and Mexico.

Justin and Adam rose to their feet as the women approached, and when they were seated on a close-by divan, the men sat back down and continued their conversation. Garth slipped out of the room.

Justin and Adam discussed how cruel and bloodthirsty Santa Anna was and how sure they were that he was going to try to take Texas back under Mexican control.

Garth returned with a copy of the *New Orleans Sentinel* in hand. "Mr. Miller, since you and Mr. Kane are talking about Santa Anna and the threat of war with Mexico, I thought you might like to see today's newspaper."

Justin looked up at him. "Something about the coming war?"

Garth handed the paper to him. "Yes. Something quite interesting. Right there on the front page."

Justin looked down as Adam leaned over to see it. "Oh! Look!" Justin said. "There's an artist's sketch of Jim Bowie and an article about him."

"The first part of the article says that Mr. Bowie left Louisiana and came to Texas," Garth said. "At Washington-on-the-Brazos, he met with General Sam Houston and joined the Texas army. I haven't had time to read the rest of the article."

Justin glanced at the headlines and smiled. "Well, this doesn't surprise me. I know that Bowie has a grudge against Mexico."

"I know who Jim Bowie is because of the famous bowie knife," Adam said. "And I know that he was living near New Orleans. Have you ever met him, Mr. Miller?"

Myra laughed. "He sure has, Adam. My husband and Jim Bowie are good friends."

Adam's eyes widened, as did Angela's.

Myra went on. "My husband and Jim Bowie have gone into some business deals together over the years."

Adam shook his head. "Really?"

"Tell him, honey," Myra said to her husband.

Adam and his sister listened intently as Justin explained that since he had this cotton plantation and Jim Bowie and his two brothers, John and Rezin, owned a sugar plantation nearby, they had reason to do some business together.

Justin went on to tell the Kanes that one of the slaves the Bowie brothers had on their plantation was exceptionally loyal to Jim and went everywhere with him. "The slave is in his midfifties. His name is Sam. I have no doubt that Sam went to Texas with Jim and probably joined the Texas army too."

"Honey, the article might mention Sam," Myra said.

Justin quickly ran his gaze down the printed lines of the article and suddenly put a finger on the page. "Yes! You're right, honey! Its says right here at the end of the article that Sam has gone to Texas with Jim Bowie!"

Angela said, "Mr. Miller, how old is Jim Bowie?"

Justin rubbed his jaw. "Well, let's see. I know Jim was born in February 1796 in Logan County, Kentucky."

Angela did some quick arithmetic in her mind. "That makes him thirty-nine years old then."

Justin nodded. "Yes. I knew he was getting close to forty."

Adam looked down at the sketch of Bowie on the page. "That look like him?"

Justin nodded. "Pretty close."

"Well," said Adam, "since the Circle C Ranch is only a few miles from Washington-on-the-Brazos, maybe I'll get to meet him."

Justin smiled. "I sure hope you do. I guarantee you you'd like him."

"From everything I've heard and read about him, I'm sure you're right, Mr. Miller." Adam put his hand to his mouth and cleared his throat. "I'm thirsty. Where can I get a drink of water?"

Justin stood up. "I'll go to the kitchen and get you some."

Adam jumped to his feet, shaking his head. "Oh no. You don't have to do that. Just tell me where the kitchen is, and I'll get it myself. You have so kindly opened your home to our family, but that doesn't mean you have to wait on me!"

Justin chuckled. "All right. Just step out into the hall, make a right turn, and follow the hall all the way to the rear of the house. The last door on your left is the kitchen."

Adam cleared his throat again as he headed across the parlor toward the door that led to the hall. "Be back shortly."

Justin chuckled again and looked at his wife. "Just wait till he meets Hosanna!"

Myra giggled. "He'll love her!"

SIXTEEN

When Adam Kane entered the kitchen he saw the cook at the stove. She was a large black woman and was stirring a pan full of a steaming liquid.

She turned and smiled at him, exposing a mouthful of large white teeth. "Hello, yo' mus' be Mistah Adam Kane."

Adam returned the smile. "You're right."

"Yo' look a lot like yo' brothah Alan."

"I've been told that, yes ma'am."

"Mah name's Hosanna Millah. Ah's a Christian jus' like you an' Mistah Alan an' the Millahs."

Adam's face took on a beam. "Well, my sister in Jesus, I'm glad to hear that."

"Thank yo', deah brotha in Jesus. What c'n ah do fo' yo'?"

"I need a drink of water, ma'am. Mr. Miller said I could get it here in the kitchen."

Hosanna stepped to the cupboard counter and filled a cup from a pitcher of water. As she handed it to him, Adam thanked her and immediately began sipping the water. After taking a few swallows, he lowered the cup and smiled at her again. "Did I hear right? Your last name is Miller?"

"Yassah. Many plantation ownahs give their slaves the choice of takin' their last name, so Ah made dat choice. Ah loves the Millahs, an' Ah loves bein' Hosanna Millah."

Adam took a long swallow of water.

Hosanna made a stab at some humor. "Mistah Kane, if'n de watah didn' quench yo' thirst, yo' money will be refunded!"

Adam laughed. "It quenched my thirst just fine, ma'am, so you can keep the money!"

They both had a good laugh.

"Thank you, again, ma'am, for the water." Adam set the cup on the counter and headed for the door to the hall.

Adam was laughing about Hosanna's remarks about the money as she called to him, "Mistah Kane, if you please, tell evahbody to head fo' the dinin' room. Lunch is almos' ready!"

Adam looked back. "I'll do that, sweetie!"

Hosanna was still laughing as Adam walked down the hall.

As the Millers, Angela, and Adam ate together, Adam learned that Angela had checked on their father, and he was still sleeping.

Angela then set her gaze on the Millers. "How long do you expect Julia to ride her horse before she comes home?"

"Hard to say," Myra replied. "Julia has friends in the rural areas on this side of New Orleans who belong to our church. She often rides with them and eats lunch with them. No doubt that's what she's doing right now."

When lunch was over, Angela rose from the table. "I'll go check on Papa. If he's awake, I'll take some food up to him."

Adam shoved his chair back and told his sister he'd run up and check on Papa for her.

Moments later, Adam returned and told Angela that Papa was still sleeping, adding that he was glad that they were staying longer. This would give Papa more time to catch up on his rest.

The Millers then invited Angela and Adam to go out with them to the front porch of the mansion. As they headed that way, Adam told the Millers how much he liked Hosanna.

"We knew you would," said Myra.

"Mm-hmm," put in Justin. "She's quite the gal!"

When they reached the massive front porch, the four of them sat down on the very comfortable furniture and watched the Miller slaves working in the surrounding fields.

"We want you to know," said Justin, "that we treat our slaves kindly."

"I can believe that," said Adam. "It is quite apparent that Hosanna loves the Millers with all her heart."

At that instant, Angela leaned forward in her chair and pointed toward the road, where a horse with a female rider was trotting onto the property and heading toward the mansion. "Is that Julia?"

Myra smiled. "That's her, all right!"

Adam set his eyes on the bay mare with the blazed face and four white stockings. "That's a beautiful horse."

"Yes," said Justin. "Her name's Maisie."

Adam's attention then went to the rider as Maisie drew nearer. As Julia drew up and smiled at her parents and their guests, Adam was immediately captured by her beauty. She was dressed in a black riding skirt with a red blazer over a frilly white blouse. She wore no hat. Her long dark brown hair was swept up on the back of her head and tied with a red ribbon.

Adam noted her smooth movements as she dismounted.

Justin hurried to his daughter, took her by the hand, and led her up the steps. As they reached the porch, Adam and Angela both stood up. Justin said, "Julia, this is Alan's sister, Angela, and his brother Adam."

Julia lips curled into another smile, and her sky blue eyes twinkled. "Hello, Angela…Adam. I feel like I already know you. Alan talked about you so much when he was here." She took a short breath and looked at Angela. "I wasn't aware that you were coming."

"We'll explain that." Angela walked over and embraced her.

Then Julia extended her hand to Adam, gripped it, and said, "You and Alan look very much alike."

He grinned. "That's what we've both been told."

Adam could hardly breathe as he took in the warmth of soul and exceptional beauty of Julia Miller.

Justin then told Julia about Abram Kane resting in his room and his injury on the Boston docks and why he and Angela were going to Texas with Adam.

Julia smiled at Angela and Adam. "I'm glad Adam and Alan can have their father and sister with them in Texas. It's just so good to get to meet some of the family. Alan told me about your brother Alex, his wife, Libby, and Abel, and his wife, Vivian. I hope someday I can meet them too." She ran her gaze to Angela then Adam. "If your father is awake, may I go up and meet him?"

"Why, of course," Adam replied.

Justin headed for the door. "I'll run upstairs and see if Abram is awake."

While Justin was gone, Julia chatted with Angela while Myra and Adam listened to the conversation. The two young women talked about the fact that they were close to the same age but that neither one was married…or even engaged. They agreed, however, that the Lord had a plan for each of their lives, and when it was time for Him to send the young men He had chosen for them into their lives, He would do so, and they would know it.

As Julia and Angela were talking, Adam Kane noticed the afternoon sun touching the porch. Its refulgent rays shone on Julia's dark brown hair, which seemed to form a halo on the crown of her head. He grinned to himself. *Julia sure is heavenly, all right. I never knew there was anything this beautiful on earth.*

His heart seemed to swell inside his chest, and he felt as if it was reaching for her. Her nose was slender and, in Adam's estimation, perfectly formed. Her chin and cheekbones blended perfectly with the lovely nose. Her full, red lips beautifully complemented her white, even teeth. Highlighting it all were two sky blue eyes. Fringing the captivating eyes were long, curved eyelashes, set beneath perfect eyebrows and an exquisitely formed forehead.

Adam Kane was spellbound.

At that moment, Justin Miller returned, saying that Abram was awake and would like to meet Julia. All of them went up to Abram's room, and

Adam, Angela, and the Millers enjoyed seeing Abram Kane get acquainted with lovely Julia.

Later, during the evening meal, which had been so marvelously prepared by Hosanna, Julia Miller was unknowingly capturing Adam's attention and his heart.

Julia and Adam were seated on opposite sides of the table, and nearly every time she happened to look his way, she found his eyes on her. Julia was accustomed to men staring at her, but this tall, handsome, rugged man from Boston seemed to devour her with his eyes. It was a look of extreme admiration. She recalled that it was exactly the way she had often noticed his brother Alan looking at her.

When supper was over, the Millers invited Angela and Adam to go with them to the parlor. During the conversation, Julia would periodically glance at Adam and smile. He felt like his heart was going to pop through his ribs. He had never experienced the sensations that raced through him each time their eyes met. It was like some mysterious, overwhelming spell was controlling his emotions.

When it came time for everyone to head to their rooms for the night, they mounted the winding staircase together. When they reached the second floor, Justin and Myra stopped at their bedroom door and told the others good night. The next room was Julia's. When she stopped at the door, she bade Angela good night, then did the same with Adam.

Adam smiled. "Good night, Miss Julia."

His gaze followed her until she disappeared through the door. *What's the matter with me?* he asked himself. *I don't want that lovely creature out of my sight!*

Adam and Angela moved down the hall and stopped when they reached the door of Angela's room. Adam kissed her cheek and hugged her. "Good night, baby sis. I'm so glad you and Papa are going to Texas with me. I know Alan is mighty glad you're coming too."

Adam entered his room and sighed as he thought of Julia. He made his way to the big bed, sat down on the edge, and looked at his surroundings. The room was large and expensively furnished. The walls were luxuriously tapestried, with drapes on the windows that blended perfectly.

There were small tables with lamps burning, which he knew Garth had lighted earlier. He noticed that the bed was made of solid brass. In one corner were two overstuffed chairs, a dresser with a large mirror, and a marble-topped washstand beside the dresser. Velvet artificial flowers stood in a glass tumbler on the washstand.

Adam took a deep breath, and his mind went to Julia. Once again, his heart seemed to swell inside his chest. She was without a doubt the most captivating young woman he had ever met. She was indescribably beautiful, but that was only part of her attractiveness. Julia Miller was warm and genuine. There was definite womanly tenderness and obvious intelligence...and yet a keen sense of humor.

Adam took another deep breath, let it out slowly, and said in a low voice, "I never believed in love at first sight, but with what happened to me when I first laid eyes on lovely Julia Miller, I believe it now."

He shook his head. "Adam, ol' boy, even though you and Julia are both Christians, you are not in her class of society. Her parents are obviously millionaires. She would never consider marrying a poor man from the docks of Boston."

Moments later, Adam was snuggling down in the comfortable bed in the darkness. He spent some time in prayer, then settled down to go to sleep.

But sleep wouldn't come. His thoughts were centered on Justin and Myra Miller's beautiful daughter. It was as if he could feel the strings of his heart reaching out to entangle themselves around the captivating young woman.

Adam argued with himself. He was a lowly dock worker about to become a lowly ranch hand. Julia would marry some man with means.

Finally he dropped off to sleep.

The next morning, Adam told Justin Miller that he needed to go to the docks at New Orleans and change the tickets for the rest of the trip. He would set Monday, May 4 as the day of departure from New Orleans. Justin had Garth take Adam to the docks in the family carriage.

When they returned, Adam reported to the Millers and Angela that they were definitely scheduled to leave New Orleans on Monday, May 4. He then informed them that he had volunteered to help Garth move some lawn furniture out of a shed in the backyard so it would be ready for summer company.

Adam and Garth were carrying the fourth piece of furniture from the shed toward a spot on the lawn near the back porch of the mansion when Julia came out the back door and said, "Garth, Papa wants to see you for a minute. He's in the parlor."

"Yes ma'am," said Garth as they placed the wicker couch by the other furniture.

When they'd put it in place, Garth hurried up the steps and went inside, closing the door behind him. Adam moved up close to the porch, his eyes fixed on the young lady who had captured his heart.

Julia walked down the steps and smiled at Adam. "I want to ask you something."

Adam smiled back. "Ask away!"

"Do you know how to ride a horse?"

He shook his head. "Miss Julia, I've only ever been on a horse once—not much more than Alan had been. He told me in a letter that you taught him how to ride and a whole lot more about horsemanship."

She giggled. "Would you like me to do the same for you, since you are going to become a cattle rancher?"

"I sure would!"

"Okay. Tomorrow I'll take you riding and teach you all I can."

Adam's heart throbbed because of the way Julia affected him. "I'll look forward to it."

As Julia climbed the steps and headed for the back door of the mansion, Adam's eyes followed her like metal would follow a magnet. When she disappeared through the door, he said in a low voice, "Adam, ol' boy, you are in love. No question about it."

Alone in his room that night, Adam told himself that there was no way Julia would ever marry him. She was out of his social class.

The next day Julia had Adam ride Big Louie, as she had done with Alan, and she rode Maisie as she taught Adam how to handle the horse. The whole time they were together, Adam was battling his runaway heart, telling himself he didn't have a chance with Julia Miller.

Of course, Adam had no idea that his brother felt the same way about Julia and had experienced the same emotions every time he was in the beautiful young lady's presence.

As the two of them rode across the plantation together, Adam prayed in his heart, *Heavenly Father, would You have allowed this love for Julia to take root in my heart if she wasn't going to feel the same way about me? You know what's going on inside me. Lord, I want Your will to be done in my life, You know that. Please guide me concerning Julia...one step at a time.*

When Adam and Julia returned to the mansion that afternoon, Julia bragged to her parents and to Adam's father and sister about what a natural horseman he was. He had taken to bridling, saddling, and riding very quickly.

Angela congratulated her brother, saying this would make both Alan and Mr. Childress happy.

Julia offered to take Adam for more rides so he could learn better how to handle the horse while trotting and galloping. For the next three days, she took him riding, schooling him at trotting and galloping Big Louie.

Julia was having her own inward struggle. She could tell that Adam was attracted to her, but she wasn't sure how deeply. She was careful to keep close check on her own emotions and prayed for God's will to be done in their lives. She was having strange sensations in her heart and knew that her feelings toward the ruggedly handsome and charming Adam Kane were growing every moment of every day.

On Sunday, Abram Kane was feeling well enough to attend morning services. In the preaching service, as the congregation was singing, Adam and Julia sat together. During offering time, Adam turned to her. "Miss Julia, you have a beautiful voice. I love to hear you sing."

Julia found the strange sensations in her heart again. She set her soft eyes on him and smiled. "Why, thank you, Adam."

Something deep within Adam's chest burst into flame. He wanted to just come out with it and tell her that he was in love with her, but he refrained. He reminded himself that he didn't have the kind of money she was used to. She wouldn't want to marry *him.*

That evening Angela stayed at the Miller mansion with her father, who was a bit weak from going to church earlier.

Adam thoroughly enjoyed the evening preaching of the Millers' pastor, as he had that morning. He found himself hoping that the pastor at the church in Washington-on-the-Brazos preached as well.

When the service was over, people stood around in the sanctuary talking. Adam was with Justin, while Myra and Julia were in conversation with a small group of women nearby. Justin began talking to a couple of men, and Adam turned and looked at Julia. His unruly heart was battering his ribs. He struggled with the emotions that came alive whenever he set eyes on her.

As the days passed, Abram Kane was getting stronger and feeling better. He assured Adam that he would be able to travel by May 4.

Late in the afternoon on Saturday, May 2, Adam and Julia were sitting together on the front porch of the mansion, talking about what it was going to be like for him, his father, and his sister on the Circle C Ranch.

The sun was setting, casting its long amber shadows over the Miller plantation.

Julia said, "I'm sure the Lord has the right man for Angela there in Texas."

"Oh, I'm sure He does," Adam said. "From what Alan has written in his letters, several Christian men work on the ranch. About half of them, he says, are married. So the Lord may have one of those single guys picked out for her, or maybe it'll be one of the single men in the church they attend."

Julia was quiet a moment, then looked at Adam with inquisitive eyes.

He met her gaze. "What?"

"I—I was just wondering. Have you ever been in love?"

Suddenly warm waves of something unnamed washed over Adam Kane like he had seen the Atlantic Ocean do in a summer storm on the Massachusetts shore. The look in Julia Miller's eyes seemed to almost suffocate him. Adam finally found his tongue. "I—uh—thought I was one time."

"A Boston girl?"

"Uh-huh."

"What was her name?"

"M-Mary Sue. Mary Sue Bannigan."

"Did she love you?"

"Well, Miss Julia, she said she did, but—"

"Adam…"

"Yes?"

"You don't have to put the 'Miss' on my name when you address me. In fact, my friends call me Julie. Alan does. Please call me Julie."

Adam grinned. "Well, all right. I'll just call you Julie, Julie."

"Good!"

"Now where were we?"

"You were saying that Mary Sue Bannigan said she loved you."

"Oh, yeah. Well, her parents are pretty well-to-do. Her father owns a large clothing store in Boston. Uptown stuff. I was a dock worker. You know. Much lower social scale."

Julia's expressive eyes registered no change.

"Mr. Bannigan offered me a job in his store. Would've been a partnership one day if I'd married into the family. In one big leap, I'd have hit the top of the social scale."

Julia nodded.

Adam cleared his throat gently. "Well, I didn't like the idea of being shut up in a stuffy old store the rest of my life. I didn't accept her father's offer, and to put it plainly, Mary Sue found herself a new love—a rich guy—and married him."

"Well," said Julia, "the Lord has someone else for you. It would be tragic to marry the wrong girl."

At that instant, Adam felt his heart reach for Julia. He wanted to put his arms around her, tell her he was in love with her, and kiss her. But to do so would be way out of line. She was nice to him and very friendly, but he could not have her. Her parents were millionaires, but he was not a wealthy man. Adam wished things could be different.

SEVENTEEN

On Monday morning, May 4, as the Kanes were about to board the boat for Galveston at the New Orleans docks and good-byes were being spoken, Adam looked down at the Millers' daughter and said, "Julie, could I talk to you alone for a moment?"

She smiled up at him. "Why, of course."

Adam looked at the Millers, his father, and his sister. "We'll be right back."

The Millers were talking to Abram, saying they would be praying for him.

When Adam knew they were far enough away that no one could hear them, he took both her hands in his and looked deeply into her eyes. "Julie, I can't leave without telling you that I have very tender feelings toward you."

Julia, hiding her true feelings for him, was flattered at his words. "Adam, I think a lot of *you* too."

Adam noted from the corner of his eye that Julia's parents were watching them. He carefully embraced her in a show of friendship. Julia smiled and returned the embrace in the same manner.

Adam smiled down at her. "Well…Papa, Angela, and I have got to get aboard."

Moments later, the Kanes were on the deck of the boat, standing at the railing and waving as the sails caught the breeze and the boat floated away from the docks. The Millers waved back.

Angela looked up at her brother. "You really care for Julia, don't you?"

Before Adam could find the words, Abram gripped the railing and said,

"I've noticed it too, son. I see something different about you when you're with her."

Attempting to keep his feelings for Julia a secret, Adam replied simply, "I like her a lot, Papa. Julia and I are friends, just like Alan told us in his letters it is between him and that sweet girl."

Angela gave her brother a strange look and held his gaze for an instant but said no more. Abram started to say something else, but decided to keep it to himself.

On the docks, Justin Miller helped his wife and daughter into the carriage they had used to bring the Kanes to the docks and climbed onto the driver's seat. He took the reins and put the horse in motion. Julia was sitting between her parents.

As the carriage moved slowly away from the docks, Julia turned around on the seat and watched the boat moving toward the Gulf of Mexico. A sigh escaped her lips as she turned forward once again.

Justin and Myra looked past Julia at each other, but decided not to say anything to their daughter.

As the carriage rolled through the city, heading toward the Miller plantation, Justin and Myra struck up a lively conversation about the nice visit they'd had with the Kanes and how they looked forward to seeing them again sometime in the future.

Julia rode in silence, staring blankly at the horse pulling their carriage.

Noticing her daughter's withdrawn mood, Myra leaned close. "Did you have a nice time with the Kanes, honey?"

Her mother's voice finally penetrated her thoughts. "I'm sorry, Mother. What did you say?"

"I asked if you had a nice time with the Kanes. Did you enjoy their visit?"

Julia perked up. "Oh! Oh yes! I enjoyed them very much!"

Myra flashed a smile at her husband.

Once again Julia withdrew into her own thoughts, and for a while all was quiet in the carriage.

Justin looked at his daughter. "Sweetheart, why are you so quiet? Is something wrong? Do you need to talk?"

Julia squeezed her father's arm. "Father, I have developed a tenderness for Adam. I miss him already. The only thing I question is whether you and Mother would want things to grow stronger between Adam and me since he is not from a well-to-do family."

"You really like him, don't you, dear?" said Myra.

"Yes, Mother. I do."

"Well, honey," said Myra, "if there is anything serious between the two of you, the most important thing is his standing with the Lord. And I can say quickly that Adam Kane has a positive testimony of being born again. He not only made that clear to us, but his actions proved out his words."

"That's for sure," said Justin. "Julia, I noticed that you and Adam have an attraction for each other. And let me make this clear, sweet daughter. Adam doesn't have to be a man of wealth in order for your mother and me to approve of him. Of course, if marriage came into the picture, we'd like to get to know him better, but his wealth, or in this case his lack of it, doesn't enter into consideration."

"Your father is right, dear," said Myra. "Our only concern is for your happiness. You have grown up in a mansion with servants and have never known a time when we were short on money, but could you be happy without this?"

Thinking on her mother's question, Julia sat quietly for a moment. Then looking first at her father, then her mother, she nodded emphatically. "Yes! Yes, I could be happy with this fine Christian young man even without all the things you just mentioned, Mother. Though we are a wealthy family, you and Father have always taught me not to be snobbish toward those who do not have what we have."

Justin and Myra looked at each other and smiled.

Julia continued. "Mother, you taught me to work. You taught me how to cook and do housework even though we have had a cook and housekeeper ever since I was born. You and Father have never allowed me to be spoiled just because we had wealth and servants. You have taught me to appreciate every dollar the Lord has blessed us with, and I will always treasure your teachings and put them into practice wherever I am. If the Lord should lead Adam and me to marry and he never becomes a wealthy man, I will love and respect him just the same."

"Oh, Julia," said Myra, "you make me so proud to be your mother."

"Me too." Justin chuckled. "I—I mean, to be your *father*!"

Both women laughed. Julia looked at each of her parents in turn. "I want to ask you something."

"What's that, dear?" Myra asked.

"I've heard of people falling in love at first sight. Is that really possible?"

Both parents smiled and looked at each other. "*We* did, daughter dear," Justin said.

Julia's eyebrows rose. "You did?"

Justin and Myra looked at each other and nodded.

"I've never heard this story! Tell me!"

Together Justin and Myra told Julia the story of falling in love at first sight. When they finished, Julia said, "All right! All right! After hearing this, I really do feel that I have fallen in love with Adam."

It was silent for a few seconds. Then Justin said, "Julia, let me say this about Adam. I've already told you that Adam doesn't have to be a man of wealth in order for your mother and me to approve of him. However, a certain something about him makes me think he will indeed one day make something of himself. I believe he is going to do very well as a Texas cattle rancher. The best thing about him, though, is that he loves the Lord and is a dedicated Christian."

This pleased Julia. She focused on her father. "If it turned out that Adam never did become wealthy, would you still want him as your son-in-law?"

Justin nodded. "I really like Adam, honey. The answer to your question is *yes.* I have no doubt that however well he does financially, he would still be a fabulous husband for you."

"I feel the same way, Julia," said her mother. "I would be proud to have Adam Kane as my son-in-law. Like your father, I am so pleased that Adam walks close to the Lord. In my estimation, he would make you a wonderful husband."

Julia smiled. "I'm glad you both feel toward Adam as you do. Now, we'll just have to let the Lord lead us together if this is His will."

At the Circle C Ranch in Texas, Alan Kane's thoughts ran to Julia Miller many times each day while he was mingling with the ranch hands, working at getting to know each man better.

On Thursday night, May 14, after a long day of laboring at different jobs on the ranch, Alan took a hot bath, then went to his bedroom, turned the covers down, sat up with a pillow at his back, and took his Bible in hand. Before reading it, he thought of his father, sister, and brother, who were journeying to Texas. Adam had written that they would be to the Circle C by late April or early May. It was now mid-May, and Alan was getting a bit concerned. He reminded himself that many things could cause them to run a few days late on the long journey from Boston. He bowed his head, asking the Lord to bring them safely to him soon. He read a chapter in the book of Acts, then spent his usual time in prayer. When he was finished, he doused the lantern and slid down under the covers.

As he lay there awake, his mind was on Julia and the love he had for her. He told himself that after Papa, Angela, and Adam arrived at the ranch and got settled, he would take the trip to New Orleans he had been planning ever since he inherited the ranch and the riches and ask Julia to marry him. He would decide later just when to go.

At almost noon the next day, Friday, May 15, Alan Kane was talking to a couple of ranch hands in front of the ranch house, giving them instructions for work he wanted them to do on one of the barns. As Alan turned to go into the house, his eye caught sight of a wagon coming down the road.

His heart skipped a beat when he recognized his father, sister, and brother in the wagon, with Mel Sibley holding the reins.

When the wagon drew up, Mel smiled. "Got some precious cargo for you, Alan!"

"You've got that right, Mel!" Alan dashed up to the wagon, greeted his family members, then helped Angela down, kissed her cheek, and gave her a hug. Adam helped his father down, and after all the hugs had been shared, everyone thanked Mel Sibley for bringing them to the ranch.

After Mel, Alan, and Adam unloaded the travel bags from the wagon, Mel climbed aboard, wished the trio a happy life on the ranch, and drove away.

Alan then turned to his loved ones. "Let's go inside. I have something to tell you."

Adam and Alan carried the luggage inside and set it down in the foyer. Alan said they would take care of the luggage later and guided them down the hall toward the parlor.

As they were walking down the hall, Adam said, "I hope we didn't worry you being later in arriving than I told you in my letter, little brother."

"Well, I *was* getting a bit concerned," Alan said.

"When we arrived at the Miller plantation, Papa was not feeling well at all," Adam said. "Their family doctor came to the mansion and checked him over. He told us to let Papa rest at the Millers' for a full two weeks. That's why we're later than I had told you we would be."

"I understand." Alan ran his gaze over all three faces. "How did you like the Millers?"

"Wonderful people…" Adam said, his heart pounding at the thought of Julia.

"Yes!" Angela said. "We really took to them."

"That's for sure," put in Abram.

"Good!" Alan turned to his father and laid a hand on his shoulder. "You feeling all right now?"

"Much better, yes. The rest at the Millers' greatly revived my strength."

"I'm glad for that, Papa."

Abram grinned as Alan led them into the huge parlor. "I think I can pull my own weight around here, son."

"Well, I have some news for the three of you. Then you can decide how much work you want to do, Papa."

Alan gestured toward the comfortable-looking overstuffed chairs and couches. "Please sit down."

When the others were seated, Alan sat down in an overstuffed chair facing them.

Adam looked around. "I was hoping Mr. Childress would be here when we arrived. How soon do we get to see him?"

"Yes!" Angela said. "We're excited about seeing him."

Alan's features went slack. "Well, I told you I had some news."

Adam frowned. "You seem upset. What is it?"

Angela's eyes went to Alan, as did her father's.

Alan cleared his throat, and tears misted his eyes. "Mr. Childress was killed on April 7."

Alan's words hit the three of them like a bolt of lightning.

They sat in cold silence, their expressions pale, their eyes looking at Alan blankly.

Alan cleared his throat again and in a weak voice told them the whole story of the wounds William Childress had received in Galveston at the hands of the thugs on March 31 and how he stepped in to protect him. He then told them how, a week later, William was trampled while saving two young boys from a herd of spooked cattle that had come charging toward them.

It was obvious to Alan that the story touched his father, sister, and brother deeply.

Adam blinked. "Wh-what's going to happen to us now, Alan? Will the new owner of the ranch still want me to work for him? Will he let Papa and Angela live on the ranch?"

Alan managed a thin smile. "Yes, to the second question. The new owner has already made plans for Papa and Angela."

"But not for me?" Adam's brow furrowed.

"Well, let me explain. When Mr. Childress and I came home from Galveston, with his wounds bandaged up, he had his attorney from Washington-on-the-Brazos come to the ranch and set up a new will. Mr. Childress's wife died several years ago, and in the will he had then, she was his heir. He hadn't updated it after her death. But coming close to death when he was stabbed by those thugs caused him to see that he needed a new will."

Alan choked up a bit and swallowed hard. "I was not aware of it, but because I saved his life that night in Galveston, he"—Alan paused—"he made me his main inheritor. I was not aware of it until he was killed. His attorney came to me shortly thereafter and told me that I was now the owner of the Circle C Ranch."

All three of them were stunned and just stared at Alan.

He went on. "Mr. Childress left some money to all the ranch hands and to his cook and housekeeper, but the rest of the money and the entire ranch he left to me."

Adam, Angela, and Abram were still speechless.

"Now, Adam," said the younger brother, "I told you that the new owner of the Circle C has already made plans for Papa and Angela to live here."

Adam nodded.

"You see," said Alan, "I had Mr. Childress's attorney set you up as co-owner of the ranch. You and I are now partners. Since you are co-owner, you can decide if you want Adam Kane to live and work here on the Circle C."

Angela burst into tears, and Abram also began weeping.

Adam's eyes filled with tears as he tried to find his voice. Finally, he was able to say hoarsely, "Little brother, you—you are the most generous person on the face of this earth!"

"I don't know about that," said Alan, "but the Lord had His mighty hand in all of this. You and I are now worth well over three million dollars."

Adam's jaw slackened, and his wide eyes fixed themselves on Alan. "Th-three m-m-m—"

Alan grinned. "That's right. That's the value of the ranch and money in the bank accounts. Over three million dollars."

Adam ran shaky fingers through his sand-colored hair. "Whew!"

"Of course, running a ranch the size of this one is going to take a lot of work on our part, Adam," Alan said. "And we want to see it succeed just like it did under William Childress, right?"

"Yes sir!"

"We have a tremendous team of ranch hands to help us, and leading them is the Circle C foreman. His name is Cort Whitney. He's a Christian, Adam, and a swell guy."

"Well, we'll just let Cort Whitney do his job, and we'll be here to supervise," said Adam. "You can count on me to work real hard once I learn about cattle ranching. One thing, little brother…"

"What's that?"

"Well, while we were at the Miller plantation, Julie gave me horse-riding lessons just like she did for you."

Alan's eyes lit up. "Julie? You call her Julie?"

"Sure. She said all her friends call her Julie, even you."

"Well, that's right. And so you're already one big step toward learning how to be a rancher! Adam, I know we're going to do well working together as co-owners, and with God's help and blessings on us, this ranch will be dedicated to Him and used for His glory."

"Amen, little brother!"

"And another amen," said Abram Kane. "I know you boys will do well here. And Alan…"

"Yes, Papa?"

"You said after I heard the news, I could decide on how much work I would want to do around here, right?"

"Yes sir."

"Well, I want to do as much as I possibly can!"

"Me too!" said Angela.

Alan laughed. "Then you're both hired!"

"Amen!" said Adam.

When all four had stopped laughing, Alan said, "Something else. The attorney suggested that I change the name of the ranch to fit the Kane name. So the name of the ranch is now the Diamond K."

"The sign at the gate still says Circle C," said Abram.

Alan chuckled. "Well, we just haven't gotten to that sign yet, Papa. I've got to tell Cort to see to it."

"I like it," said Abram. "Diamond K. Yes sir. I like it."

Adam and Angela agreed.

Alan said, "Now that you know the situation, I want you to understand that you will each have your own room in this big ranch house."

Though Abram, Adam, and Angela Kane were saddened by William Childress's death, there was much joy over what the Lord had done for them in all of this, and they all praised the Lord.

Alan then told them that he was going to write to Alex and Libby and to Abel and Vivian. He was going to offer Alex and Abel jobs on the ranch and pay them well. He would have houses built for them if they came, and they could stay in the ranch house with the rest of them until their houses were completed.

The three newcomers shed happy tears over this news, and Abram said he had no doubt that the two couples would come.

Alan told them he would write the letters that evening and mail them tomorrow. He explained that nearly every day ranch hands drove wagons to Washington-on-the-Brazos for various reasons, and when they did they mailed letters from people on the ranch and picked up the mail at the post office.

Alan brought up the Millers again, saying how much he appreciated their keeping Papa, Angela, and Adam in their home for the full two weeks.

It was all Adam could do to keep from telling his brother that he had fallen in love with Julia…and admitting the same to his father and sister. Adam, of course, had no idea that his brother felt the same way toward Julia.

"Well," Alan said, "let me take you upstairs, and you can pick out the rooms you'd like. Sis, I think I know the one you'll choose, and we'll let Papa and Adam pick from all the others."

Angela smiled. "Okay, little brother! Let's go!"

The four of them headed up the stairs, with Alan leading the way. When they reached the second floor, Alan went to the first door to the right of the staircase. "Right here, Sis."

When Angela stepped up and looked inside, a small gasp escaped her lips, and she smothered it with her hand. She took a step into the room, took her hand away from her mouth, ran a quick gaze around the room, and turned to Alan. Her father and Adam were standing next to him. "Oh, Alan!" she said with a lilt in her voice. "This is the most beautiful room I could ever imagine! It can really be mine?"

"Absolutely! Now, take your time, and look it over. I'll take Papa and Adam on down the hall so they can pick out their rooms. Then we'll bring your luggage up."

When her father and brothers were gone, Angela stood in the middle of the room and turned in a slow circle. The single bed was painted white, and tiny blue flowers adorned the headboard. The crocheted coverlet was white, and a blue bed skirt peeked out around it.

Two large floor-to-ceiling windows, which were open, faced the front of the house, and white organdy crisscross-patterned curtains blew softly in the breeze. A braided rug of blue, white, and yellow lay in the center of the gleaming wooden floor.

Two white wicker chairs with blue and white cushions faced the windows. A small writing desk sat against one wall with a wooden chair pulled up to it. There was a white washstand next to the mirrored oak dresser, with a china pitcher and bowl on top that matched the blue and white of the room's décor. A large cupboard painted like the bed's headboard occupied a corner of the large room.

"Oh, dear Lord," said Angela, "how can I ever thank You enough for Your goodness to us? Please help me to always be thankful, and give me a servant's heart so that You can use me."

Leaving her glorious room, she hurried down the hall to help her father settle in.

EIGHTEEN

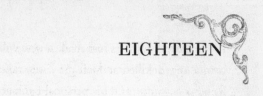

As the newcomers were getting settled in their rooms, Alan Kane brought Daisy Haycock to meet them and bragged about her excellent cooking. Daisy made Abram, Adam, and Angela feel welcome at the Diamond K Ranch.

As the day progressed, they were introduced to foreman Cort Whitney; Alan's close Mexican friend, Juarez Amigo; and many of the other ranch hands. They also got to meet some of the wives and children.

The next day—Saturday, May 16—they got acquainted with more of them, and on Sunday morning and evening, Alan took them to the church services in Washington-on-the-Brazos. The entire family enjoyed the services immensely, and Adam Kane told himself that indeed Pastor Merle Evans could preach every bit as good as the Millers' pastor.

In his room on Sunday night, Adam sat down at the writing desk and took out paper, pen, and an envelope. He dipped the pen into the inkwell and wrote a letter to Julia.

May 17, 1835

Dear Julie,

I cannot keep it to myself any longer. I am deeply in love with you. I must see you again very soon. May I come and see you? It is important that I tell you right now that William Childress, owner of the ranch, was killed April 6 when trampled by a herd of stampeding cattle. I will explain the details when I come—if you allow it—but Mr. Childress had made a new will just a short time before he was killed and left the entire ranch and the money in its bank accounts and his personal bank accounts to Alan. The ranch employees were left some money also, but even then Alan is now worth over three million dollars.

There's something else… Alan had already had an attorney set it up to make me co-owner of the Diamond K Ranch (its new name) and all of its assets. Alan and I are partners, so you can see that I am now a millionaire. The Lord has been so good!

I will wait eagerly to hear from you.

Loads of love, Adam

As Adam signed the letter, his unruly heart pounded against his ribs. He read it over twice to make sure it was the way he wanted it. Then, satisfied with the wording, he addressed the envelope and sealed the letter into it.

The next morning, after a delicious breakfast, Adam told Alan he had a letter to mail and asked if anyone on the ranch was going to town that day. Alan told him of two men who were going to Washington-on-the-Brazos to purchase wood and paint so a sign could be made with the ranch's new name for the front gate at the road. Adam immediately went to his room, picked up the letter, and ran to the bunkhouse. There he found the men Alan had named and asked if they would mail a letter for him. They told him they would be glad to do so.

As Adam headed back to the ranch house, he found his father and brother sitting on the front porch, talking. When he mounted the steps, Alan smiled and stood up. "Big brother, I'd like to take you on a tour of the ranch this morning."

Adam smiled in return. "I'd like that."

"Papa would like to go too," Alan said, "but he's feeling a bit weak after going to both church services yesterday."

"I can understand that," Adam said.

Abram grinned. "I'll let you boys take me on a tour of the ranch some other time."

"We'll do it, Papa." Alan slapped Adam on the back. "Well, cowboy, since Julie taught you how to ride a horse, let's go!"

The Kane brothers left their father sitting happily on the porch and headed to the nearest barn and corral, where Alan let Adam pick out a horse to ride. Adam's eyes fell on a gray stallion.

"All right," said Alan. "I'll ride that bay stallion over there."

Testing his older brother, Alan pointed to the barn. "The bridles and saddles are in there. You *can* bridle and saddle a horse, can't you?"

Adam chuckled. "Of course. The same proficient horsewoman who taught you taught me!"

Alan was pleased to see that Adam bridled and saddled the gray horse expertly. They mounted up, and Alan said, "Let's head west first."

"Sure." Adam looked westward. "Let's go."

While the Kane brothers rode across the wide-open spaces of the Diamond K Ranch, they talked a great deal about their future as cattle ranchers. But there were also silent moments as they rode, and Adam let his eyes roam over the beautiful land.

During the silent moments, Alan was planning in his mind his trip to New Orleans so he could propose to Julia. He planned to leave Monday, June 15. *She's going to be so surprised to learn that I'm now a millionaire,* he told himself.

On Friday morning, June 12, Cort Whitney and Juarez Amigo went in a wagon together to the hardware store in Washington-on-the-Brazos to pick up some tools that Cort had ordered a few weeks earlier.

When they returned to the Diamond K Ranch just before noon, they saw Alan and Adam Kane standing in front of the ranch house, talking. Juarez, who was holding the reins, guided the wagon up to the ranch owners and halted it. "*Buenos días,* señores Kane. We went by zee pos' office while we were in town, and peecked up zee mail. Señor Wheetney has a letter for each of you."

The Kane brothers saw the foreman lift two envelopes from a small mail-bag, which contained mail for others on the ranch as well. "Here you are, boss men."

Alan looked at his envelope and turned to Adam. "It's from Alex and Libby and Abel and Vivian." He tore it open. "I just know they'll be coming!"

Alan read it quickly, and a smile broke out across his face. "They've gladly accepted the invitation and will be here in about a month!"

"Oh, great!" exclaimed Adam. "Praise the Lord!"

"I'm so glad to hear they're coming," Cort said. "It'll be terrific to have the whole Kane clan here on the ranch!"

Juarez popped his palms together. "Sí! Eet sure will!"

Cort looked at Juarez. "Well, Señor Amigo, we'd better go put these tools in the toolshed."

As they drove away, Alan turned to Adam. "So who's your letter from?"

Still totally unaware of Alan's feelings for Julia Miller, Adam grinned. "It's from Julie."

Alan blinked and swallowed hard as Adam took out the letter and read it silently. His face beamed when he looked back at Alan, who said, "Good news of some kind, I take it."

"Sure is. I…ah…I need to tell you something. Julie told me that you and her are real good friends."

Alan felt his stomach lurch. "Why, yes. We sure are."

"You know what a sweet, precious Christian young lady she is."

Alan nodded. "I sure do."

"Well, little brother, I have something to tell you."

Alan's stomach felt like lead now. "What's that?" he asked, trying not to show that his nerves were on edge.

Adam rubbed his chin. "During those two weeks Papa, Angela, and I spent at the Miller plantation, I...I fell in love with Julie."

"Oh?" Alan's mouth went dry.

"Mm-hmm. But—but I didn't tell her my true feelings before we left. Julia had shown me real warmth, Alan, but I wasn't sure exactly how she felt about me."

Alan ran his tongue over the dry roof of his mouth. "You didn't tell her, huh?"

"No. It was eating me up that I hadn't, so shortly after we arrived here at the ranch, I sent Julie a letter and told her that I am in love with her and that I wanted to come see her soon. In her letter here, she says that she is in love with me too and wants me to come see her as soon as possible."

This put the cap on what Alan Kane had feared. It was a severe jolt for him to hear that Julie was in love with his brother.

His brain seemed to be spinning as he struggled with the news. His heart was hurting, but he would not let on. *I'm glad I hadn't gone to see Julie yet and asked her to marry me,* Alan thought. *What a blow that would have been for me, having her tell me she's in love with Adam! No one must ever know that I am in love with Julie. Please, dear Lord, help me to keep this secret!*

Adam's voice penetrated Alan's mind, but the words were incomprehensible. He looked at Adam. "Sorry, I was deep in thought. What did you say?"

"I asked if it's all right with you if I make the trip soon to go see Julie."

Alan forced a smile. "Of course it's all right with me."

Alan's heart felt like it was encased in a block of ice.

Abram and Angela came out the front door of the ranch house at that moment. Angela noted the letters both brothers were holding. "Get some mail?"

They both turned to face their father and sister. Alan had a knot in his throat. He forced it down. "Yes, we did, Sis." He held up the letter in his hand. "This is from Alex and Libby and Abel and Vivian. They're coming here to live! They say they'll be here in about a month!"

Angela squealed with joy and looked toward heaven. "Thank You, dear Jesus!"

"Amen!" said Abram.

Angela looked at her brothers. "Won't it be wonderful to have our family all together again? This is such marvelous news!"

"Yes, it is!" Alan agreed, keeping a guard on the broken heart within him while putting a smile on his lips. "I've got to get the construction going on their houses." He told himself that no matter how crushed he was over the news about Adam and Julie, he must see to the needs of his two brothers and their wives, who would soon be coming to live on the Diamond K.

Angela turned to Adam and looked at the letter in his hand. "Who's your letter from?"

"It's from Julie Miller."

She raised her eyebrows. "Oh? Anything important?"

Abram's curious eyes were on Adam as well.

"Yes," Adam said. "It's actually *very* important. I—uh—I haven't come out and told you and Papa how I really feel about Julie. I'm head over heels in love with her. I wrote to her soon after we arrived here and confessed my love for her and asked if I could visit her soon. In this letter, she says she is in love with me too...and she wants me to come see her as soon as possible. I asked Alan if it's all right if I go, and he said it is. So I'm going to make a trip to New Orleans."

Angela was smiling, and her eyes were sparkling. "Oh, Adam, I'm so glad to hear this about you and Julie!"

"Me too, son." Abram's face beamed. "I sure hope you two end up married. I'd love to have her in this family!"

As the days passed, Alan struggled to conceal his broken heart, not wanting to hurt Adam, who had no idea how he felt about Julie. In his private prayers, he asked the Lord to give him the grace and the strength to never let Adam or Julie know.

On Monday, June 22, Julia Miller was helping Hosanna clean the windows in the kitchen of the mansion when Garth appeared at the hallway door. "Miss Julia," he said, with a smile, "there's some good-looking young man here to see you."

Julia's face lit up. "Adam! He's here!"

Garth nodded. "Yes, Miss Julia. It's Adam Kane."

Hosanna smiled, showing her mouthful of white teeth. "Yo' go on, honey. Hosanna will finish cleanin' the windows!"

By the time Julia arrived at the foyer, her parents had both discovered Adam's presence and were welcoming him warmly. When Adam saw Julia, he smiled. "You just get more beautiful every time I look at you!"

Myra laughed, as did Justin, and they watched as the young couple embraced discreetly. While Julia was in his arms, Adam got a whiff of her perfume. Once again, his unruly heart battered his ribs, and his emotions had come to full life.

Justin stepped closer. "Adam, Julia told us you were coming. Myra and I know that you two need to be alone, so why don't you go out on the front porch and sit down?"

"Thank you, sir." Adam took Julia by the hand.

Together they walked outside, and Garth closed the door behind them.

When they drew up to the porch chairs, Adam continued to hold Julia's hand as he looked down at her.

Then it happened.

Their eyes locked in a helpless look of love. An enchanting, impelling, unexplainable force brought them together, and they embraced each other tightly. For a long moment of sublime ecstasy, there was no one else in the world but Julia and Adam.

Finally, they released each other, and the helplessly-in-love Adam Kane said softly, "Oh, Julie, I love you! I love you!"

"And I love you too, my darling," she whispered. Their lips came together in a phantom kiss that seemed to carry them to another world.

Back in this world, Adam kept his arms around the woman he loved and looked down into her expressive eyes.

Julia smiled. "This is where I belong, Adam darling. In your arms. I've known it since the first moment I met you."

The tall, handsome man smiled. "That was the same moment I fell in love with you, Julie, my sweet."

Julia tilted her head back, rose onto her tiptoes, and gave him her soft, warm lips in a sweet kiss once more.

Adam then took her hand. "Here, let me help you sit down."

When Julia was seated, Adam eased onto the chair next to her and took both her hands in his. "Your parents didn't seem to mind my coming."

Julia smiled. "Of course not. They both really think a lot of you. I told them the day you sailed away for Galveston how I felt about you. My parents agreed that the most important thing was that you were a born-again man. Money, or at that time your lack of it, doesn't enter into the picture. We indeed have my parents' blessing."

Adam's eyes took on a serious look as he rose from the chair, keeping both of her hands in his, and knelt before her.

Along with the serious look was the unmistakable light of love shining in his eyes.

Julia knew what was coming. Tears misted her eyes, and a tender smile graced her lips.

Adam spoke softly. "Julie, I love you more than I could ever tell you. Will you marry me?"

"Yes!" she replied, tears streaming down her cheeks.

"Oh, I'm so happy!" He rose up on his knees. She leaned over, and he kissed her tenderly.

Adam rose back to his feet and sat down beside her again. "I must go inside and ask your parents' permission to marry you."

Julia smiled and palmed the tears from her cheeks. "Darling, when I told them how I felt about you that day you left, they both said they would love to have you for a son-in-law. When your letter came and I read it to them, they were happy to learn about your becoming a partner in owning the Diamond K Ranch and about the money Alan is sharing with you. But as I told you, your lack of money before this didn't enter into the picture. We would have had my parents' blessing to get married even if you hadn't come into the money. They love you because you are a dedicated Christian, and they want me to marry you."

"I'm so glad," Adam said. "But I want to go inside now and formally ask your parents' permission to marry you."

"I understand," she said. "And I appreciate that."

Holding hands, the couple entered the mansion and found Justin and Myra Miller in the parlor. They both rose to their feet with expectant looks in their eyes and waited to hear what Adam and Julia would say to them. It was Adam who spoke up and told them that he was in love with their daughter and had asked her to marry him.

Justin and Myra smiled at their daughter and waited expectantly.

"I told him I will marry him!" Julia said.

Justin clapped his hands. "Then, Adam, you have our blessing! We have prayed much about this, and we feel that the Lord has brought the two of you together."

"That's right," spoke up Myra.

Adam ran his gaze between them. "I have your blessing in marrying Julie, even though it means taking her to Texas so we can build our lives on the Diamond K Ranch?"

Both parents nodded and said in unison, "You do!"

Adam then explained that he had to get back to the ranch very soon so he could be there to carry his part of the load as co-owner.

"We certainly understand that, son," said Justin.

Adam turned to Julia. "Sweetheart, if we could get your pastor to do the ceremony, would you agree for us to get married this Thursday, June 25?"

Julia giggled. "Do we have to wait *that* long?"

All four laughed. Then Justin said, "Adam, I told Julia on the day that you sailed off for Galveston that I'd like to get to know you better. Well, so much for that! I have no doubt that you are God's choice for Julia, so I'll just have to get to know you better *after* you become my son-on-law! Myra and I will just have to make a trip to Texas now and then. Of course, Mr. and Mrs. Adam Kane will always be welcome to come here too!"

Adam hugged Justin and said, "I'm so glad I'm going to become a part of this family!"

"I am too!" Myra wrapped her arms around Adam.

Smiles and happy tears were shared between the four of them.

On Friday, June 26, Mr. and Mrs. Adam Kane stood on the deck of the Galveston-bound boat as it pulled out of New Orleans Harbor and waved to Mr. and Mrs. Justin Miller.

When the Millers had passed from view, Adam said, "Honey, remember when I told you about Mary Sue Bannigan dumping me for that rich guy?"

Julia nodded. "Of course I remember. And I'm so glad she did! What about it?"

"When that happened, Alan told me he was going to pray that a beautiful Christian young lady would come into my life and that the two of us would fall in love."

"Bless him."

Adam smiled. "Later, on the day Alan left Boston aboard a ship for Texas, he stood there on the deck and shouted to me, 'Hey, Adam! Remember I'm praying that you'll find a beautiful Christian girl and get married!' "

Julia giggled and squeezed Adam.

"Little brother will be so happy when he finds out his prayers have been answered!" Adam said.

On Tuesday, July 7, Adam Kane picked up the wagon and team he had left at Groce's Landing with Mel Sibley and drove onto the Diamond K Ranch with his bride at his side.

It was early evening, and Alan, Abram, and Angela were sitting on the front porch of the big ranch house after supper, enjoying the beautiful Texas sunset. When the three of them saw the wagon coming toward the house, Alan was first to recognize the horses pulling the wagon. He jumped up. "It's Adam! And...and he's got Julie with him!"

Abram and Angela were on their feet instantly, and as Adam pulled the wagon to a halt, the three of them stepped off the porch.

Adam hopped out, calling, "Hello, Papa! Sis! Little brother!"

They called back their greetings to him as Adam helped Julia down from the wagon seat.

Wanting to announce in just the right way that he and Julia were married, Adam quickly guided his bride to his father. Abram embraced Julia in a fatherly fashion. "I'm so glad to see you again, honey."

"I'm so glad to see you again too!" she said.

Angela stepped up and wrapped her arms around Julia. "What a surprise! Welcome to the Diamond K Ranch! I sure didn't know you were going to come visit us!"

Julia hugged her tight. "Well, you just never know what I might do, honey. It's so good to see you!"

Angela kissed her cheek. "You too!"

Alan Kane's heart was thudding against his rib cage as he moved up to Julia. She smiled and planted a kiss on his cheek. "It's so good to see you again, Alan!"

With a lump in his throat, Alan said, "It's wonderful to see *you*, Julie!"

Adam's eyes were sparkling with eagerness to share the news. "Little brother, I have some real good news about your friend, Julie, here."

Alan secretly feared what his brother was going to tell him, but forced a wide smile on his lips. "What is it?"

Smiling broadly himself, Adam said, "Little brother, your prayers have been answered!"

"My prayers?"

"Remember the day you and William Childress were on the ship as it pulled away from Boston Harbor, and you shouted something to me?"

Alan thought a moment. "Oh, yeah. You mean about me praying that you'd find a beautiful Christian girl and get married?"

Abram and Angela were observing in great anticipation as Adam turned to Julia and said, "Show him, Julie!"

Julia flashed the shiny gold wedding band in Alan's eyes.

What he had feared was now confirmed. His heart seemed to stop. His blood ran cold. A stiffness ran down his spine, then settled like a cold rock in his stomach.

The smile was still on Alan's face, but it felt as if it had been painted on. He knew he must never reveal his true feelings. Pulling himself together on the inside, Alan said, "It's beautiful, Julie."

Alan turned to his brother. "Adam, I'm so happy for you! Congratulations!" He wrapped his arms around Adam and hugged him tight.

Julia waited for the brothers to part and embraced Alan. "Oh, I'm so happy we're now not only good friends, but we're related!" She kissed Alan's cheek again.

With the thought gnawing at his insides that he would never kiss those sweet lips himself, Alan Kane held his new sister-in-law at arm's length, ran his eyes to Adam and back to Julia, and said, "I'm so glad for both of you. May God give you more happiness than you've ever dreamed possible!"

NINETEEN

For the next three days, Alan Kane struggled with the fact that the young woman he loved would never be his. Having inherited the ranch and William Childress's wealth, he had been so excited about going to New Orleans and asking Julie to marry him. But now that would never happen. She was married to Adam.

Alan prayed diligently, asking the Lord to help him to get over his feelings for Julie. He knew it would no doubt take time, and he prayed that during the process, the Lord would help him never to reveal in any way that he was in love with Adam's wife.

On the afternoon of July 10, the two couples from Boston arrived at the Diamond K Ranch in a wagon driven by Mel Sibley. This in itself helped Alan keep his mind occupied with having Alex and Libby and Abel and Vivian there.

After the Kane family members had been reunited in front of the large ranch house and the Boston couples had met Julia—whom they loved instantly—Alan said to the Boston couples, "Your houses are under construction yet, so you'll have rooms in the big ranch house in the meantime."

"Sounds good to me," said Alex. "Could we take a look at our houses?"

"Oh yes!" said Libby. "We'd love to see them!"

Abel and Vivian agreed that they would like to see the house that was being constructed for them.

Alan smiled and nodded. "Of course! It's just a short walk from here. We'll take you right now."

Abram Kane was feeling much better by now and walked along with the rest of his family as they headed toward the partially built log houses. Quite soon, they could hear hammers pounding and saws chewing wood.

Leading the group, Alan said to the Boston couples, "We started construction as soon as we knew you were coming, but there is still much to do. Libby, Vivian, the interior designs and furnishings will be up to you."

At that moment, they came within view of the houses under construction, and when the Boston couples saw a third house, Abel said, "Three houses! Who else is getting one?"

"Why, Adam and Julie," said Alan.

"Oh! Of course," said Abel. "I should have known."

"Well, now you do!" Julia said.

Everybody laughed. Then Alex commented, "Wow! All three are quite large! They look alike, and I can tell they're well built."

"Nothing but the best for my family!" Alan set his eyes on the Boston couples. "When you're ready to buy furniture and everything else for your houses, I've set up accounts for you in the necessary stores in Washington-on-the-Brazos. Adam and I will be paying the accounts. Feel free to purchase whatever you need."

"That's right," Adam said.

Alex shook his head. "Now, brothers, you are much too generous. I will repay you when I start earning wages here on the ranch."

"Yes, and I will too," spoke up Abel.

"Oh no, you won't," countered Alan. "This ranch was given to Adam and me by the Lord. It'll be a pleasure to share it with you because we love you so much."

Libby's eyes misted. "Thank you, Alan and Adam. Your unselfish generosity is amazing."

Vivian nodded. "That's for sure."

With love for his family showing in his eyes, Alan said, "We will *all* work this ranch together, and God be praised for His abundant goodness."

"Amen, son!"

While the ranch hands who were building the houses kept up their work, the Boston couples were allowed to take a close look at their future homes and were introduced to the workers.

Alex and Libby and Abel and Vivian were then taken to the ranch house and shown their own private rooms. The men—even Abram—carried their luggage, and they busied themselves putting things away. A short time later, at supper, they met Daisy Haycock and found her quite charming.

As the days passed, the Boston couples began meeting the other ranch hands and the families of the married ones. They quickly struck up friendships, especially with those who were Christians.

Of the men on the ranch, they particularly liked Cort Whitney and Juarez Amigo. They loved it when Juarez told them how Alan had led him to Jesus, and with his humor and Spanish accent, the little Mexican kept them laughing much of the time. They very much admired his desire to become a *real* Texan.

The new Kane couples loved the church in Washington-on-the-Brazos and found Pastor Merle Evans's preaching very inspiring.

As Adam and Julia had done, they put their membership in the church.

As time passed, the men continued to work on the ranch. Though Adam was half owner of the Diamond K, he still did his best to put in more work than Alan.

Alex and Abel learned quickly to ride horses and fit in quite well with the ranch hands as they joined in the work on the Diamond K.

News of dictator Antonio López de Santa Anna's desire to take Texas back into Mexico's control was in the newspapers quite often.

One day, Libby, Vivian, Julia, and Angela were sitting in the parlor of the big ranch house having cookies and tea together. They were in conversation about the Mexican threat, and Vivian said to Julia, "I've been wondering about your parents. Did they have any uneasy feelings about your coming to Texas with Adam because of this?"

"Well, they did discuss it with Adam on the day before our wedding. Adam told them he felt sure that General Sam Houston would stay on top of it and keep Santa Anna and his armies away. This made my parents feel better about it, and they simply said they would leave Adam and me in the Lord's hands."

Vivian smiled. "I like that."

Life went on as usual on the Diamond K Ranch. In late September, the three Kane couples moved into their new homes. Alex and Abel had mastered horseback riding by then, as well as all other aspects of working a cattle ranch.

On Monday, December 14, a supply wagon driven by Frank McDonald, with Smiley Dunn at his side, returned to the Diamond K from a trip to Washington-on-the-Brazos. McDonald's first stop was at the big ranch house to deliver the mail to Alan Kane, along with a copy of the *Galveston Daily News,* dated Friday, December 11.

Smiley Dunn jumped out of the wagon, made his way to the porch, and knocked on the door. Seconds later, Alan opened the door and smiled as Smiley handed him the mailbag and the newspaper. "Thanks, Smiley," Alan said.

"You're welcome, boss," Smiley said. "Be sure to take a look at the front page of the newspaper as soon as you can."

Alan nodded. "Will do."

"See you later, boss." Smiley turned and hurried back to the wagon.

Alan went back inside the house and carried the mailbag and newspaper into his den. He laid the mailbag on his desk, then sat down in an overstuffed chair, newspaper in hand. The partially visible newspaper headline had something in large, bold print about Generalissimo Santa Anna.

When Alan unfolded the paper and set his eyes on the headline, a cold shaft lanced through his heart.

Santa Anna Promises Bloody Revenge for Mexican Defeat at San Antonio

Hands trembling, Alan read the article beneath the headlines.

Mexico City, December 10, 1835 — Generalissimo Antonio López de Santa Anna gathered his military leaders for a joint conference earlier today. Displaying his fury while he paced to and fro before eleven generals of the Mexican army, the generalissimo went into a thirty-minute tirade. His anger was directed at the brazen upstart Texans who attacked General Martín Perfecto de Cos and his 1,400 troops after they had ridden into San Antonio, Texas, and taken control of the town. Somehow a citizen of the town had slipped past them and ridden away for help.

The next morning, Saturday, December 5, a small band of 300 determined Texans, who were well-armed, rode toward San Antonio in two columns. When Cos and his Mexican troops saw them coming, they fled from the town and took shelter in the old Franciscan mission, now known as the Alamo, a half mile east of San Antonio. Entrenched in the Alamo, the Mexicans sought to prevail against the indomitable Texans.

The battle went on until Thursday, December 10. By then, 115 of the general's men had been killed and 185 had deserted. Cos hoisted a white flag. He and his 1,100 remaining troops threw down their weapons and surrendered to the 290 Texans who were still alive, strong, and determined to keep Texas free.

The humiliation of such a defeat has led Santa Anna to take extreme measures. The generalissimo has announced that he will personally lead his Mexican troops on a punitive sweep across Texas. In a rage, he shouted that the Texans would pay for this.

Alan Kane ran a sleeve over his brow and let his eyes roam across the page to an article under smaller but heavy-lettered headlines:

SAM HOUSTON DEFIES DESPOTISM OF MEXICO'S DICTATOR, SANTA ANNA

Washington-on-the-Brazos, December 11, 1835 — General Sam Houston, commander-in-chief of the army of Texas, today issued a proclamation to the citizens of the Texas Republic. In part, Houston said, "Citizens of Texas. Your situation is peculiarly calculated to call forth all your manly energies. Under the republican constitution of Mexico, you were invited to Texas, then a wilderness. You have reclaimed and rendered it a cultivated country. You solemnly swore to uphold the constitution and its laws. Your oaths are yet inviolate."

Alan read on, his eyes speeding over the article. His blood heated up as he read General Houston's words, quoting the Mexican dictator's threat to make his punitive sweep across Texas and make the Texans pay for defeating General Martín Perfecto de Cos and his troops.

Houston was asking for five thousand volunteers to join the Texas army to boost its numbers, saying that by the end of the winter of 1835–1836, the Texas army must be ready to meet the enemy with enough troops to defeat them. Santa Anna could possibly come with ten thousand troops, and if the Mexican army was not defeated, they would take over Texas. The Texans would lose everything they had.

Alan Kane shook his head in disbelief. The dreaded nightmare was about to become a reality. *War with Mexico.*

Alan slammed his fist into an open palm. "Why? Why do there have to be greedy, power-hungry men like Santa Anna in this world?"

Alan jumped to his feet and dashed out of the house. He was going to ask whoever he saw first to find Cort Whitney and tell him he wanted to see him immediately. But the first person he saw when he stepped onto the porch of the ranch house was his foreman. Cort was riding his horse past the ranch house, and his eyes fell on his boss, who raised a hand and called his name. Turning the horse that direction, Cort trotted up to the porch. "Something I can do for you, boss?"

"Yes. I want you to get as many men as you can to help spread the word that I want everybody on this ranch to come and gather here in front of the house immediately. This is very important. I need to talk to them. That includes my relatives."

In less than an hour, Alan Kane was standing on his porch with the newspaper in his hand looking at the gathering crowd of men, women, and children, curiosity showing on their faces. Cort Whitney was standing just off the porch, with Juarez Amigo. The rest of Alan's family except for Adam were close to the porch.

At that moment, Adam came running up from the direction of the barns and corrals and hopped onto the porch. "Sorry it took me so long, little brother. I was way out on the northeast corner of the ranch when one of the men found me."

"It's all right. You made it in time."

Adam noted the florid face of his brother. "What's the matter?"

Alan held the newspaper with both hands so Adam could see the front page.

Adam's eyes bulged as he read the headlines.

From the ground, Juarez Amigo spoke. "Sí, Señor Alan. You look like somebody shoot your bes' fran'."

"You're about to find out what's wrong, Juarez," Alan said levelly. Lifting the newspaper above his head with the front page showing, he ran his gaze over the crowd. "This is last Friday's issue of the *Galveston Daily News*! See the headlines?"

Heads were nodding, and eyes were big. Someone shouted, "I see Santa Anna's name!"

"Yes!" Alan said. "Let me tell you what the article says."

While the crowd listened raptly, Alan read them the contents of the article regarding Santa Anna. A mixture of anger and fear consumed the crowd.

Alan then pointed to the article quoting General Sam Houston and told them its contents.

People whispered to each other as Alan said, "This is the thing we have been afraid would happen."

Juarez Amigo said loudly, "Gen'ral Houston is right, Señor Alan! Eef San' Anna an' zee Mehicano army are not defeated, you an' Señor Adam will lose zee ranch!"

Adam could see the fear this news had sparked in Julia and Angela. He left the porch, walked to where his wife and sister were standing, stepped between them, and put an arm around each of them.

"Zat dorty Mehicano, San' Anna!" Juarez said loudly enough for all to hear. "Sawmbody need to take zee starch out of hees breetches!"

"If General Houston can get enough men to join the Texas army, it can be done, Juarez!" Alan said.

"Sí," agreed the little Mexican. "Eef three hondred Texans can wheep zee socks off fourteen hondred, and Gen'ral Houston can get five thousan' new troops, zey can wheep zee socks off San' Anna's army!" Throwing a thumb against his chest, he said, "Juarez Amigo ees not a real Texan yet, bot he weel fight zee dorty Mehicano deectator an' his army!"

The crowd cheered him.

When the cheering died down, Adam still stood with his arms around his wife and sister. "Certainly enough Texans will join the army to help General Houston defeat the Mexicans!"

"I agree!" Alan now held the folded newspaper in one hand. "In my relatively short time here, I have found Texans to have strong wills and a deep love for their republic. Certainly a sufficient number of men will respond to General Houston's request to join the army."

Men and women nodded and spoke their agreement.

Alan dismissed the meeting. The Kane family and the ranch hands and their families were encouraged by the words of Alan and Adam Kane and Juarez Amigo.

Two days later one of the ranch hands who had gone to town brought another edition of the *Galveston Daily News* to the Diamond K. He showed Alan an article that quoted General Sam Houston as saying that he had word from a secret Mexican source that Santa Anna was going to push his troops through winter's cold from Mexico City and be in Texas no later than March 1, 1836. Santa Anna might be coming with ten thousand troops.

Alan showed it to his family and the ranch hands. In the presence of both the Kane family and the ranch hands, Juarez Amigo confirmed that Santa Anna could very easily assemble ten thousand soldiers. Deep concern over this news was expressed by all.

During the next few days, Alan Kane pondered the Texas-Mexico situation. He told himself that Santa Anna must be stopped. If the bloody dictator of Mexico and his thousands of troops marched into Texas and were victorious, the Diamond K would be gone. The wonderful future he and Adam had planned would dissolve like vapor on a freezing day. All that William Childress had built up would be for nothing.

Alan thought of Julia, and his love for her was as strong as ever. But she was Adam's wife, and he wanted her to have a happy life.

And what about all the other people in Texas? Gone would be the fruit of all their labor, and their dreams would be shattered.

As the weeks passed and more news of Santa Anna's war plans were printed in the newspapers, a weight was growing on Alan Kane's mind. He told himself that it was as much his responsibility to join up with General Sam Houston as it was any other Texan's.

This conviction grew stronger within Alan every day, and shortly after Christmas, he made up his mind.

He must do his duty. After all, he had been taught on the ranch how to use a rifle and a revolver. Houston would be glad to get his kind.

Young Alan Kane's mind began to click. He could take a week or so to school Adam on the finances and administration of the ranch. Cort Whitney could handle the men as usual. There would still be ample time for Alan to ride to Washington-on-the-Brazos and sign up before Houston would move his army toward the Texas-Mexico border to meet up with Santa Anna.

The plan was now settled in Alan's mind. He would find the right time and place to let Adam know. Then the rest of the family could be told, as well as the ranch hands and their families.

One day in mid-January 1836, Alan and Adam Kane were riding their horses together on the ranch, checking the condition of the fences in a certain area. Adam could tell that his brother had something heavy on his mind. Alan seemed preoccupied and talked very little.

As they were about to mount up and ride away from one section of fence that had turned out to be in good condition, Adam said, "Little brother, something's bothering you. What is it?"

Knowing that this was as good a time as any to break the news to his brother, Alan said, "With Santa Anna's promise of revenge on us Texans, big brother, I've made a decision."

"Tell me."

"Well, I feel that with the threat of losing everything we have to the

Mexicans if they indeed attack Texas, I should go to General Sam Houston at Washington-on-the-Brazos and join the Texas army."

Alan was surprised when Adam spoke up. "Well, Alan, I'll tell you. I've been having similar thoughts about joining up with Houston myself."

Alan shook his head. "But you shouldn't leave Julie to fight the Mexicans, Adam."

"Little brother," Adam said, "if only single men join up to fight Santa Anna and his troops, there won't be enough Texas troops to defeat them. Texas will be lost. Even though I'm married, it's as much my responsibility to defend our land as it is yours."

The younger brother pulled at his ear. "I can't argue with you on that. How about we agree to pray about it separately for the next few days and ask the Lord to guide us?"

"All right. Let's do that."

Alan nodded. "Okay."

The brothers mounted their horses. As Alan settled in his saddle, he said, "Oh, I need to tell you that Juarez and I are going to ride to San Felipe tomorrow."

Adam met his brother's gaze. "San Felipe? Oh yeah. It's that town on the Brazos River a few miles north of Velasco."

"Right. A *growing* town."

"Why are you and Juarez going there?"

"There's a saddle and harness maker in San Felipe who makes very good products. I want to buy some new harnesses for the horses that pull the ranch wagons and a few new saddles. I've noticed that some of our leather goods are showing quite a bit of wear."

Adam looked him in the eye. "Can I go along with you and Juarez?"

"Well, of course. I'd love for you to go with us."

Before putting their horses into motion, the Kane brothers agreed that after they'd had time to pray about going to Washington-on-the-Brazos and joining the army, they would discuss it again.

At bedtime a few days later, Julia was sitting before the dresser mirror and brushing her hair. In the mirror's reflection, she saw Adam sitting on the edge of the bed, still in his clothes. His brow was furrowed.

Julia turned around on the stool. "Honey, you look worried. Is something wrong?"

"Well, I…ah…need to talk to you about something."

Julia laid the hairbrush on the dresser, slipped off the stool, and sat down beside her husband. She took hold of his hand. "All right, sweetheart, why the worried expression?"

Adam hesitated. "Honey, Alan and I have been talking about joining the Texas army to help General Houston in this war that's coming. We feel that it is as much our responsibility to get in the fight as it is any other Texan's responsibility. If the Mexican army isn't stopped, we'll lose the ranch. Tell me what you think about it."

Julia sat perfectly still, her head lowered, staring down at the floor. After a few seconds, she looked up at her husband, a brave smile on her sweet face. "Darling," she said softly, "I understand why you and Alan feel it's your responsibility to fight for Texas. I don't like the thought of either of you facing Mexican guns, but it has to be done."

Adam stood up, took her hand and lifted her to her feet, then wrapped his arms around her. "Thank you, sweetheart. I knew you'd understand. I don't know just when we'll go, but first I had to know how you felt about it."

"Well, now you know." Julia looked up into his eyes. "You do what you feel is necessary. I'll be just fine here with the rest of the family. I'm so thankful to be your wife and part of this family. With Cort Whitney's help, we'll keep everything running smoothly until you and Alan return home after the Mexican army is defeated. Of course, I'll miss you terribly," she said. "And I'll be praying for your safety all the while."

Adam kissed her tenderly. "Alan and I have already been praying about this, honey. Now that I know how you feel, I'll tell him. I appreciate your support."

Julia smiled up at him. "Well, darling, unless plenty of Texas men join up with General Houston, our future will look pretty bleak. I love you for your courage and your willingness to do your part to save Texas from the Mexicans."

Adam gave her another tender kiss. "I'll miss you terribly too, my love."

TWENTY

Early afternoon on Tuesday, January 19, 1836, Alan and Adam Kane and Juarez Amigo stepped off the ferry at San Felipe.

When they walked up Main Street, they saw a large crowd gathered around a tall, slender man in a dark blue army uniform with gold braids on the jacket, standing in the bed of a wagon, speaking to them.

Juarez said, "Zee gold braid means he ees an offeecer."

"That's what I figured," Adam said.

"Me too," Alan said as they moved closer to the wagon.

The young officer was eloquently attempting to persuade men in the crowd to volunteer to go with him to the Alamo at San Antonio and blow it up so Generalissimo Santa Anna and his troops could not use it as a fort the way General Cos and his men had.

Alan was standing close to a square-shouldered man who was listening with interest. Both Adam and Juarez noticed Alan lean close to the man and ask, "Sir, do you know who the officer speaking is?"

The man nodded. Keeping his voice low, he replied, "That's Lieutenant Colonel William Barret Travis of the Texas army. He was sent here by General Sam Houston from Texas army headquarters in Washington-on-the-Brazos to get volunteers."

While the man was speaking to Alan, a small group of men left the crowd and approached Travis, saying they would go with him.

Travis made a quick count. "I now have fourteen volunteers. I need eleven more. I've got to have twenty-five."

From the back of the crowd, a young man who appeared to be barely eighteen years of age stepped up to the wagon. "I'll go, Colonel Travis."

The fourteen volunteers cheered him.

Travis smiled at him. "Thank you, young man. That's fifteen! Who's next? I need ten more! We've a big job to do! If we can blow up the Alamo, it could make the difference between defeat and victory! General Houston's army must meet Santa Anna's troops in the open field! If they hole up and fortify themselves in the Alamo, they can pick off the Texas troops one at a time! For the future of Texas…for a chance at victory…I must have twenty-five men who will go with me to the Alamo and blow it up!"

"Count me in!" shouted a man standing at the fringe of the crowd.

Another cheer went up from the men who had already volunteered. Adam Kane noted the man as he joined the group. He turned to his brother and Juarez. "He's at least sixty years old."

"That's sixteen!" cried Travis. "Who'll be next? For those of you who weren't here when I first started speaking, the Texas army will provide the horses, the guns, and the food. I've got the guns and the food with me. I've already made a deal with the stable owners here in town to supply horses for those men who need them."

In the silence that followed, Alan Kane said, "Adam, Juarez, I feel in my heart that the Lord would have me go with Colonel Travis. General Houston's order must be carried out."

Adam and Juarez exchanged glances. "How about it?" Adam asked. "I agree with my brother."

Juarez nodded. "Sí! Zee Lord does not want Texas to be in zee hands of zee Mehican government."

"Okay," Alan said. "Let's go tell the colonel we're going with him."

As they walked toward the wagon, Adam said to his brother, "I'm sure glad you took the time over the last few weeks to teach me how to handle a rifle and a pistol."

Alan shrugged. "Like I told you, we had to be ready to battle the Mexican army if they tried to take the ranch from us."

Colonel William Travis saw the three men and said to the crowd, "Here's three more!"

As the trio stepped up to the wagon, Travis extended his hand. Alan shook it. "I'm Alan Kane, Colonel, and this is my brother, Adam. We own a ranch several miles to the west. This young Mexican with us is Juarez Amigo, one of our ranch hands. We're volunteering."

"Thank you." Travis shook their hands. "Can you Kane brothers handle a rifle or a revolver?"

"We sure can, sir," replied Alan.

Travis looked at the Mexican questioningly. "How about *you*? Can you handle a gun?"

"Sí! Sí! Sí!" exclaimed Juarez. "Especially a rifle! Juarez Amigo used to be in San' Anna's army!" Acting as if he held a rifle in his hands, he shouldered it. *"Boom! Boom!"*

Then he pretended to be using a rifle with a bayonet and made slashing sounds with his mouth. "*Xxxt! Xxxt!* Sí, Señor Colonel Travees! Juarez Amigo desert San' Anna, cawm to Texas! San' Anna bloody cutthroat. Juarez wanna be a Texan!"

Colonel Travis lifted his hat and waved it at the crowd. "How do you like that?"

A few of the men in the crowd cheered.

"Do I have some more volunteers?" asked Travis. "I now have nineteen! I need six more! Who'll be next?"

A hush came over the crowd. Silence prevailed for a long moment.

The colonel shook his head and removed his hat. He ran his fingers through his auburn hair. "Men, we're dealing with your futures here. Everything you've worked for and everything you own is at stake!"

A man in the crowd spoke up. "A lot of us ain't convinced the big Mex is really comin', Colonel. Maybe he's cooled off by now and havin' second thoughts!"

"Yeah!" another spoke up. "Maybe Santa Anna's had time to think about the whippin' Cos and his troops got at the Alamo! If three hunnerd could rout fourteen hunnerd, just think what five thousand of General Houston's men could do to the Big Mex's ten thousand!"

Travis shook his head. "General Houston doesn't have five thousand. He's trying to get Texans to join him so he will have five thousand, but he's having a hard time. Too many other Texans are just like you. They coddle the mistaken idea that Santa Anna is not coming. Well, let me tell you. He *is* coming!"

The little Mexican in Travis's group detached himself from the others, stepped up close to the wagon, and raised his voice. "Señor Colonel Travees! May I speak to zee crowd?"

"Sure, Juarez," replied the colonel. "Climb up here on the wagon where everyone can see you."

The swarthy little man bounded into the wagon bed amid whispers in the crowd of "Mexican" and "dirty Mex."

Travis nodded at Juarez to go ahead.

"Ladies an' gennulmen," said Juarez, "I am an ex-soldier of San' Anna's army. I cawm to Texas because I wanna be a Texan. I know zee Big Bull, San' Anna well. I assure you, he *weel* cawm! He weel cawm weeth zee bright colors, an' zee trumpets an' zee drums! An' San' Anna weel cawm weeth cannons an' cavalry, an' foot soldiers zat weel cover zee land like water covers zee bottom of zee Gulf of Mehico! Señor Colonel Travees an' we who have already volunteered need your help. Please join us!"

With that, Juarez Amigo hopped from the wagon and returned to the group of volunteers. They cheered him, pounded him on the back, lifted his hat from his head, and playfully ruffled his coal-black hair.

The ruddy-faced Travis set his eyes on the crowd. "Well, men, you've heard it from a man who knows the Big Bull! I've got nineteen volunteers. I need six more. Remember, we're talking about your homes, your farms, your ranches. Unless the Big Bull is stopped, it's all gone!"

The square-shouldered man who had earlier identified Colonel William Barret Travis for Alan Kane stepped out and raised a hand. "I'll be number twenty, Colonel!"

The other volunteers cheered him as he joined.

Travis asked if any of the other men were going to join him, but nobody moved. "All right," he said sighing. "I'll have to go with the twenty who have volunteered. We'll leave for San Antonio tomorrow morning at dawn. I need to know how many horses we'll need. I've got enough rifles and pistols for those of the twenty who need them, plus plenty of ammunition. I'll have sufficient food for us."

Adam and Juarez followed Alan as he stepped up to the wagon. "Colonel, we really need a day to go set up things at the ranch so it will continue running well without us while we're gone. My brother here has a wife. She needs to know what we're doing, as do the others on the ranch."

Travis smiled at them. "I appreciate your volunteering. We'll leave Thursday morning at dawn instead."

Alan nodded. "We'll be here. And, sir, we'll each need a horse to ride to San Antonio. We'll have to leave ours where we board the ferry to come here."

"I'll have them bridled and saddled for you."

"Señor Colonel Travees," Juarez Amigo said, "zis ees good! When San' Anna cawm to San Antonio an' find zee Alamo ees gone, he weel burp up hees tortillas!"

Travis laughed.

As the three Diamond K men walked away, they heard Colonel Travis announce that they would leave for San Antonio at dawn on Thursday morning.

Later that day, at the Diamond K Ranch, Julia Kane was a bit nervous when the family and Cort Whitney gathered in the parlor of the big ranch house to hear about the three volunteers who were going with Colonel William Travis to San Antonio.

After Alan had made the announcement, explaining what they would be helping Colonel William Travis do at the Alamo and why, Julia spoke up and told her husband, her brother-in-law, and Juarez Amigo that she was very proud they were willing to volunteer to help defeat Santa Anna. Abram Kane spoke his agreement with her, as did the rest of the family and Cort Whitney.

As the Diamond K's foreman was put in full charge of the ranch hands, Alex and Abel said they would do all they could to help him. Angela told Alan and Adam that she would too.

On Wednesday morning, while her husband was shaving, Julia Kane was tying a ribbon in her hair at the dresser mirror. She looked at her reflection and promised herself that she wouldn't cry when Adam left with Alan and Juarez to join Colonel William Travis. *I must be brave so Adam can go with an easy heart,* she thought.

Later that morning, when Alan, Adam, and Juarez led their horses up in front of the big ranch house, they each had their own rifles in their saddle boots and their revolvers holstered on their hips. Adam also had his bowie knife in a sheath on his belt. When Adam and Julia had left New Orleans after getting married, Justin Miller had secretly bought Adam the bowie knife and had slipped it into his luggage. Adam hadn't found it until he and Julia had gotten to the Diamond K and he was unpacking his luggage.

Adam and Alan tenderly hugged their family members. Julia had a lump in her throat that grew larger when Adam kissed her before mounting his horse. So far she had kept the promise she'd made to herself.

As the three men rode away, the small group stood waving at them—with Cort Whitney and many of the ranch people looking on from a reasonable distance.

Alan, Adam, and Juarez were soon rounding a bend where they would pass from view. They waved back one last time, and as they vanished from sight, a tiny moan escaped Julia's lips, and tears began to roll unchecked down her cheeks.

Angela walked over to Julia and wrapped her with loving arms. She held her until the storm in Julia's heart had eased.

Julia looked at Angela through her tears. "Thank you, Angela. I'll be all right now. I just needed to release all of these pent-up emotions." A weak smile became visible. "I promised myself I wouldn't cry, and I kept that promise until Adam was out of sight."

Angela kissed her forehead. "You're a very brave young lady. The most important thing we can do now is hold Adam, Alan, and Juarez before God in prayer."

The three Diamond K men arrived in San Felipe on the ferry late that afternoon and found that Colonel William Barret Travis now had twenty-two other volunteers. He smiled. He had come up with his quota.

Alan, Adam, and Juarez told him they were glad.

The next morning, the wind swept across the low Texas hills as dawn's gray light crested the earth's eastern edge. Colonel Travis was driving the supply wagon. The men knew that in the wagon, along with food and ammunition, Travis had six large boxes of dynamite sticks, sufficient for the purpose of blowing up the Alamo.

The column of riders followed the wagon three and four abreast. His twenty-five men hunched against the biting cold to the sounds of stiff saddle leather squeaking and the wagon rattling. Juarez Amigo rode between Adam and Alan. The raw wind whipping around their upturned collars, the riders anticipated the warmth that would come with the sunrise. The 190-mile westerly trek was launched.

Not wanting to push the horses hard on the cold winter days as they traveled west toward San Antonio with nothing but the brown grass on the ground for them to eat, Colonel Travis allowed an average of only some fourteen miles per day.

The air was frosty at midmorning Wednesday, February 3, 1836, when Colonel William Travis and his twenty-five volunteers drew close to the Alamo. The San Antonio River glistened like a silver ribbon in the bright sunshine, winding its way eastward.

Standing up in his wagon with reins in hand, Travis pointed. "There it is!"

The volunteers peered at the distant sight. Slowly they scanned the entire scene. To the north lay rolling hills of stunted brown grass. The flatland to the south and west was heavy with mesquite and thickets of various description. Along the river were tall cottonwood trees after which the old mission had been dubbed "Alamo." *Los álamos*...the cottonwoods.

As the volunteers and their leader drew nearer, the old stone-walled mission loomed up out of the grassy prairie, casting slanted shadows toward the city of four thousand that stood a half mile west. They rounded the battered walls of the Alamo and drew up to the front.

Cannonball-scarred and bullet-riddled, the place was pockmarked with signs of battle. Time had also taken its toll since the walls, mission building, barracks, and chapel had been built in the mid-1700s. Once white and glistening, it now was a faded dull brown mixed with gray. Part of the chapel roof had eroded away, exposing bare, weather-beaten rafters. Rain and wind had peeled large patches of plaster off the barracks, exposing the crude stones of which they were constructed.

Old and battered as it was, the Alamo was still very impressive to the men and their leader. It seemed a shame to blow it up, but Sam Houston had ordered this for good reason.

William Travis hopped down from the driver's seat of the wagon as the twenty-five men dismounted. Adam and Juarez remained with Alan.

Travis and his men were surprised to hear male voices coming from inside the mission building. Then the double doors opened, and a band of soldiers filed out. In the lead was a tall, slender officer in his early forties with lamb-chop sideburns. The insignia on his coat matched that on Travis's. He spotted Travis and walked over to him. Extending his hand, he said, "You must be Colonel William Travis."

"Yes, I am, Colonel," replied Travis, gripping the officer's hand.

"I'm Jim Bowie," said the colonel as a black man in his midfifties stepped up beside him. Travis noted that the black man was not in uniform.

A blank look captured Travis's features. "I've heard much about you, Colonel Bowie, but I'm a bit confused. Why are you here at the Alamo?"

"I was sent here, along with thirty soldiers, by General Sam Houston."

Travis's head bobbed. "Oh? Why?"

The twenty-five volunteers listened intently as Colonel Jim Bowie explained to Travis that they had been told by General Houston to hurry and get to the Alamo before Colonel Travis and his volunteers did. They were to get there in time to tell Colonel Travis not to blow up the Alamo as Houston had ordered.

When Travis asked why, Bowie explained that Texas army scouts had informed General Houston that Santa Anna was already in Texas and was heading for San Antonio. He presently had at least four thousand troops camped at Saltillo and some two thousand more ahead of them camped on the bank of the Rio Grande near Laredo.

The scouts assumed that Santa Anna was in the camp near Laredo. Both camps were made up of cavalry and foot soldiers. General Houston had told Bowie to tell Colonel Travis that he and his men, along with Bowie and his men, would have to use the Alamo as a fort and fight off the Mexican troops. He would send them more Texas troops as soon as he could.

Travis rubbed his jaw. "Well, Colonel Bowie, I have to say that this doesn't astonish me. Santa Anna wants revenge so much that he would push his men and their horses hard, even in winter, to get it."

Bowie nodded. "I agree." He fixed Travis's men with a look. "General

Houston told me to pass on the word that Colonel Travis is to be in charge here at the Alamo."

The twenty-five volunteers all nodded and smiled.

Bowie turned to Travis. "As I pointed out, Colonel, your men and mine are to fortify ourselves in this old Spanish mission and make ready to fight the Mexican troops."

Travis nodded and drew a short breath. "Well, Colonel Bowie, with you and your thirty men and me and my twenty-five men, that makes only fifty-seven to face the Mexican troops when they come. How does General Houston expect us to withstand such a great number?"

Bowie sighed. "Well, he hopes to have five thousand to send very soon."

"So we have to hope that General Houston's troops get here before Santa Anna and his troops do," Travis said.

Bowie nodded. "Yes sir. You'll be glad to know that there are still rifles, cannons, and plenty of ammunition for both inside the Alamo, which were left here by General Cos when he and his men surrendered to the Texans."

"Good," replied Travis, doing some mental calculations. "With Santa Anna's troops at Laredo, and even if he hurried the cavalry here, they still can't arrive before early March. They will have to move reasonably slow in order for the horses and pack animals to feed on the short winter grass. This will give General Houston time to build his army, and it'll give us time here at the Alamo to fortify ourselves."

"Makes sense, Colonel Travis," said Jim Bowie.

"Sho' does," spoke up the black man at Bowie's side.

"Oh." Bowie looked at Travis. "I want you to meet my slave, Sam. Sam has been with me for many years, starting back when my brothers and I first went into the sugar plantation business."

Adam Kane's ears perked up. He had already planned to introduce himself to Jim Bowie as Justin Miller's son-in-law, and hearing Bowie tell the story just as Justin had gave him a warm feeling inside.

William Travis shook hands with Sam, telling him that he was glad to meet him. Sam smiled and said that meeting Colonel Travis was indeed a pleasure.

Bowie then said to Travis, "Even when we sold the plantation, Sam asked if he could be my partner wherever I go and whatever I do."

Travis smiled at Sam. "Good man, my friend."

"Sam and I have hunted together for years, Colonel Travis. He is a crack shot with a rifle. As you can see, he is not in uniform, but he will make a good soldier just the same."

"Sounds good to me," said Travis.

"I wasn't including Sam when I spoke of bringing thirty men with me since he is not a soldier," Bowie said. "So with Sam, we have a total of fifty-eight men to defend the Alamo right now."

Travis smiled at Sam again. "I'm plenty glad you're here, my friend."

Sam smiled back. "Thank you, suh."

One of Bowie's men who wore a sergeant's stripes on his uniform stepped up. "Colonel Travis, I'm Sergeant Louis Rose, and I just want to say that I agree with what you said about Santa Anna and his troops not being able to get here before early March. That's good thinking, sir."

Travis smiled. "Thank you, Sergeant."

There was a moment of silence between the two colonels. Adam Kane took advantage of it by stepping up to Jim Bowie. "Colonel Bowie, you have a very good friend on a plantation near New Orleans. Justin Miller?"

Bowie smiled. "Yes! Justin is a *very* good friend. How do you know him?"

"He's my father-in-law. I married Julia this past June 25."

"What's your name?" Bowie asked, extending his hand.

Adam shook his hand, introduced himself, and told Bowie that he and his brother Alan now owned the Diamond K Ranch a few miles west of Washington-on-the-Brazos. He then introduced Bowie to Alan and Juarez, explaining that Juarez was one of their ranch hands and had defected from

Santa Anna's army and come to Texas, and he now wanted to fight for Texas.

Bowie shook hands with Alan and Juarez, saying he was pleased to meet them. He then got excited about all the news and poured out accolades on Justin Miller and his family.

Juarez turned to the Kane brothers. "Eef Juarez does hees part to defeat zee Mehicano soldiers, will he be a real Texan?"

Jim Bowie patted Juarez on the back. "You sure will! You sure will!"

"Now you've got it from an authority, Juarez," Adam said.

"Sí! Sí! Gracias for pointing that out, Señor Adam!"

Both Adam and Alan laughed, along with Jim Bowie and William Travis.

TWENTY-ONE

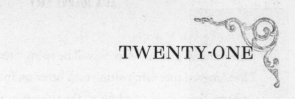

As the four men regained their composure, Jim Bowie's attention was drawn to the familiar handle of the knife in the sheath on Adam's waist.

Bowie stepped close to Adam and eyed the knife. "Hey, where'd you get that bowie knife?"

Adam's eyes lit up. He pulled the knife from the sheath. "You hadn't noticed it before?"

"No! I noticed the Colt .45 in the holster on your right side but just now caught sight of the knife on your left. Where'd you buy it?"

Adam chuckled. "I didn't. Your friend Justin Miller gave it to me sort of as a wedding present when I married his daughter."

Bowie smiled. "Well, at least Justin knows a good weapon when he sees it!"

Adam dropped the knife back in its sheath. "He sure does."

"Good-looking knife," said William Travis. "You just might have to use it on some of Santa Anna's troops."

"That's why I brought it along," said Adam.

"I weesh I had one of those!" said Juarez.

"Well, I just happen to have an extra one in my gear, Juarez," said Bowie. "I'll give it to you. It's in a sheath just like Adam's."

The little Mexican's eyes lit up. "Muy bueno, Señor Colonel Jim Bowie! Gracias!"

"I'll give it to you a little later, okay?"

"Sí! Sí!"

Bowie's slave, Sam, walked up to Juarez. "Ah has one of those knives, too. It's with mah gear, but Ah will be wearin' it tomorrah."

Juarez smiled at him. "Zen we will be twins, Señor Sam!"

They laughed together, patting each other on the back.

William Travis then called for all the volunteers to gather around.

When the entire group stood before Travis in a half circle, he said, "I realize you volunteers came here to help me blow up the Alamo. You didn't sign up to fight Santa Anna and his troops. If any of you want to go on back home, you have a right to do so."

One of the volunteers spoke up. "Colonel Travis, is there mail service from San Antonio to other parts of Texas?"

Travis replied, "I don't know, but I'll find out."

"There is," Jim Bowie spoke up. "San Antonio has a post office."

"Good!" said the man. "I'll write my family and tell them that plans have changed and we're going to use the Alamo as a fort to fight Santa Anna and his troops and that I'm staying to do my part."

"I'm staying too!" called out the square-shouldered man.

The volunteers' voices blended in a loud chorus, stating the same thing. Within seconds, all twenty-five volunteers had made it known that they were staying.

Colonel Travis and his volunteers walked into the Alamo with Colonel Bowie and his men. Bowie led them to the barracks, and each man chose a bunk.

That night the volunteers all wrote letters to their families to explain the new situation. Only Juarez Amigo had no family with whom to correspond.

The next day, after the volunteers had mailed the letters at the post office in San Antonio, Colonel Jim Bowie and his faithful slave, Sam, gave them a tour of the Alamo.

The entire Alamo property was surrounded by hulking stone walls three feet thick and from nine to twelve feet high, with gates of heavy timber.

There was a large rectangular plaza within the walls that covered some three acres. The plaza had a solid-packed sandy surface. On the east side of the plaza stood the largest building in the Alamo—the two-story mission building. The chapel, another stone building, stood some fifty feet from the mission building. Nearby were a few other buildings. One of those was the barracks, which had been built many years previously, when the property was used as a fort during another trying time in the history of the region.

When the tour was over, Colonels Travis and Bowie sat down in a room in the mission building that Travis, as commander of the Alamo, had chosen to use as his office and bedroom.

"Colonel Bowie," Travis said solemnly, "after being given the tour, I have to say that the place is certainly strong enough in a defensive way to withstand anything the Mexicans can throw at it. But when it comes to offense, there are definitely some drawbacks. The walls have no parapets from which riflemen can fight. They have to come up over the walls and leave themselves wide open to shoot. And then there are the cannons. We can't use them effectively when the Mexican army comes. And you know why."

Bowie nodded. "I sure do. General Cos left eighteen cannons here when he surrendered to the three hundred Texans. He couldn't use the cannons to fight off the Texans because there were no platforms to put them on so they could fire over the walls."

"Well, we've got to do something about both parapets for the riflemen and platforms for the cannons."

"Yes, we do," Bowie said. "I haven't introduced you to Major Green Jameson yet. He was a construction engineer before he joined the Texas army. I'll go get him, and as the officer-in-charge you can assign him the task of leading the men in making the parapets and platforms. There is plenty of lumber in some of those buildings we didn't open."

"Sounds good to me, Colonel Bowie," Travis said. "Please go get Major Jameson."

As the days passed, the men in the Alamo worked hard under the leadership of Major Green Jameson to get the place ready for battle.

On Thursday, February 11, Colonel William Travis was walking across the sand-covered plaza ground near the north wall with Colonel Jim Bowie at his side when Sergeant Louis Rose called down to him from atop the wall. "Colonel Travis!"

Both colonels stopped and looked up. "Yes, Sergeant?" Travis said.

"There are some riders coming across the prairie from the northeast. They're heading straight for us. We just counted thirteen of them."

"Mexicans?"

"No sir. Caucasians."

"All right. I'll take care of it."

With Bowie at his side, Travis headed in the direction of the nearest gate, calling to men along the way to bring their weapons and come with him. Some seventeen men had joined Travis and Bowie, including Alan and Adam Kane and Juarez Amigo, by the time they reached the north gate.

Bowie opened the gate, and the men followed Travis and Bowie outside the wall as they made themselves visible to the approaching riders. When the riders saw the men coming through the gate and looking their direction, the leader of the group pointed that way and aimed his horse straight toward them.

"There are indeed thirteen of them," Travis said to Bowie.

"Yep. All dressed in buckskin. I wonder who they are and why they're coming here."

"We're about to find out, I'd say. I'll talk to them."

Bowie nodded and stayed where he was as Travis moved forward a few steps.

When the riders drew up, the leader looked at Travis. "Are you Colonel William Travis?"

"Yes, I am," replied Travis. "And who are you?"

"My name is Davy Crockett, and—"

"The U.S. representative from Tennessee?"

"Yes. You've heard of me, I see."

"Yes," Travis said. "You asked if I was Colonel William Travis. How did you know I would be here?"

"I'll tell you in a minute. How have you heard of me?"

"I've read about you many times in the newspapers. Of course, you're not a representative anymore. Your term was over last year."

"Right. I could have run again and probably would have been elected, but I turn fifty this coming August, so I decided to do something else."

Travis ran his eyes over the men with Crockett, noting the rifles in their saddle boots and the knives in sheaths on their belts. "I see you and your friends here are all armed."

"Yes sir," said Crockett.

"You going to fight a war somewhere?"

Crockett dismounted and faced Travis. "Let me tell you about that."

Travis nodded. "All right."

"These men with me are Tennessee sharpshooters. I call them my Tennessee Mounted Volunteers. They're frontiersmen like me."

Travis nodded. "I've read about some of their exploits with you."

Crockett grinned. "Okay. Well, we recently left Tennessee and rode here to Texas. We came well armed because we've heard about Santa Anna threatening to bring his Mexican army and recapture Texas. We wanted to be prepared if we ran into any of the Mexican soldiers."

"I see."

Crockett continued. "Actually, Colonel Travis, these men and I came to Texas planning to get rich on Texas land grants. You know about them?"

"Yes."

"Well, when we rode into Nacogdoches a few days ago, soldiers from the Texas army were trying to convince men there to join up and go to Washington-on-the-Brazos with them because General Sam Houston was trying to build up his army to stand against Santa Anna. I talked to a captain, and he told me that General Houston had a small number of men at the Alamo near San Antonio under the command of Colonel William Travis who just might be attacked by the Mexican army sometime soon. So my men and I signed up with the Texas army officials in Nacogdoches for six months in the volunteer army, and they told us to get to the Alamo fast. So here we are."

"Well, we're mighty glad to have you, Mr. Crockett!" said Travis. "And... and...those knives you are all wearing. They look like bowie knives to me."

Still standing close by, Jim Bowie grinned.

Crockett nodded. "You're right, Colonel. They *are* bowie knives. Best combat knives in the world!"

Travis turned around, looked at Bowie, and motioned for him. As Bowie drew up beside him, Travis looked at Crockett and said, "I would like for you and your men to meet the one and only *Colonel Jim Bowie*!"

Davy Crockett stepped forward and offered Bowie his hand. While they were shaking hands and Crockett was telling Bowie how glad he was to meet him, the other twelve men dismounted and gathered around Bowie.

When all of Crockett's men had spoken to Bowie and shaken his hand, Colonel William Travis and his men welcomed the Tennessee Mounted Volunteers and their leader.

Doing a little quick arithmetic, Travis told the Tennessee men that their arrival brought the Alamo force up to seventy-one. He then cautioned them that Santa Anna and six thousand Mexican troops were already in south Texas but added that General Houston was working hard to send about five thousand men from Washington-on-the-Brazos.

In front of everyone, Davy Crockett told Travis that he and his sharpshooters would stay right there with them. Seventy-one fighting men, he remarked, would have a better chance against the Mexicans than fifty-eight.

Travis, Bowie, and all the other Alamo troops cheered them, showing their deep appreciation.

On that same day, at the Diamond K Ranch, when the mail was brought in, there was a letter from Adam to Julia and from Alan to the rest of the family. Both letters explained that Santa Anna and six thousand troops were now in Texas, headed for the Alamo, and that instead of blowing it up, Colonel William Travis had been ordered by General Sam Houston through Colonel Jim Bowie and a small band of soldiers sent to the Alamo to use it as a fort to fight the Mexican troops.

Alan, Adam, and Juarez were doing their duty for Texas and staying to fight. More Texas soldiers were supposed to be coming to the Alamo to join the fight.

The Kane family and the other Christians at the Diamond K went to prayer, with Angela and Julia shedding many tears. Alex and Abel Kane rode to Washington-on-the-Brazos and told Pastor Merle Evans about it. The pastor prayed with them and said that on Sunday he would make the entire church body aware of the situation at the Alamo and ask them to be in prayer about it.

The work to prepare the Alamo for the attack continued, and by February 13 still no reinforcements from General Sam Houston had arrived.

Knowing that he must have more fighting men in the Alamo by the first of March, when he was expecting Santa Anna and his troops to show up and with no guarantee that Houston's new men would arrive soon, Colonel Travis sent riders from among the men who were acquainted with that part of Texas to other military outposts in the area asking for help.

By February 16, seventy-nine gallant Texas army men had responded to Colonel Travis's riders and had come to the Alamo to stand against Santa Anna.

Travis expressed his gratitude to the newcomers, saying this made a total of 150 men to face the enemy.

The next day, the Kane brothers and Juarez Amigo were working together on a cannon platform atop the wall when they saw Major Green Jameson coming toward them with another officer by his side. They recognized the young officer as one of those who had come from a nearby army outpost.

As the two officers halted at the base of the wall, Major Jameson said, "Men, I've brought you some help. This is Captain Almeron Dickinson. He knows how to drive nails and saw wood."

"Good, Major," said Alan Kane. "We can use him."

Dickinson climbed the ladder to the platform, and Major Jameson moved on.

The Kane brothers and Juarez Amigo shook hands with Captain Dickinson, saying they were glad to have him working with them.

As they worked together, Dickinson told them that when the group from his outpost near Gonzales, Texas, had come to the Alamo, he had his eighteen-year-old wife and baby daughter with him. Susannah and baby Angelina had been living in a small rented house in Gonzales. He now had them in a another small home in San Antonio.

Adam Kane smiled. "Well, Captain Dickinson, I'm glad you can have your family close to you."

Alan and Juarez agreed.

The next morning, as the Kane brothers, Juarez Amigo, and Captain Almeron Dickinson worked together on another cannon platform, they saw Colonel Travis drawing up to the wall. Looking up at them, Travis said, "Alan, I have another job for you right now."

Alan ran his eyes over the faces of the other three men. "See you later." He descended the ladder. "Don't work too hard, big brother!"

Juarez and the captain laughed.

As the colonel and Alan walked away, Travis said, "Since you know the area between here and Washington-on-the-Brazos, I need you to ride there and ask General Houston how soon he will be sending his troops. I know Adam could have done it for me too, but since I only need one man to go, I decided it would be you."

"I'd be glad to do it, Colonel," Alan said.

Moments later, aboard his horse, Alan rode up to the wall where his brother and the other two men were working and told them the errand he had been assigned. They wished him well, and watched him gallop away.

Colonel Travis then approached Lieutenant Jim Bonham, who had come from one of the outposts and whom he knew well, and assigned him to ride to an army outpost near the town of Goliad.

Travis had not asked for help from this outpost yet, but needed to do so now.

He explained to Bonham that at the Goliad outpost, Colonel James Fannin had an army of five hundred volunteers from some nearby states. They were well equipped and fully trained. He figured that Fannin's five hundred could be his equalizer against Santa Anna until Houston's troops arrived.

On Saturday morning, February 20, the repair and preparation work at the Alamo was almost finished. Eighteen cannons were on the new platforms on all four sides of the wall and were ready for battle. They ranged from four-pounders to one massive gun that would shoot an eighteen-pound cannonball.

In readying this big cannon for battle, having been situated on the southwest corner of the wall, Captain Almeron Dickinson, who had been a metalworker before joining the Texas army, was working with the physically strong Adam Kane at Colonel Travis's request.

As the two men worked together, Dickinson asked Adam if he was married.

Adam smiled. "I certainly am. I'm married to the most wonderful and most beautiful woman in all the world."

Dickinson grinned. "Well now, I will argue that point with you. *I* am married to the woman you just described!"

They had a good laugh together, each contending that *his* wife outshone all others.

While the two men continued their task with the big cannon, Adam told the captain about the good fortune his brother Alan had come into, inheriting the Circle C Ranch, and how Alan had made him partner in the ownership of the ranch, renaming it the Diamond K Ranch.

Dickinson congratulated Adam, and Adam talked optimistically of when the Mexican problem would be settled and how the four Kane brothers would build a great Texas cattle empire.

Breaches in the Alamo's walls had been reinforced with sloped banks of earth, firmly strengthened with huge timbers. Parapets of dirt and timber lined the insides of the walls, which would allow rifle fire in all directions.

Every man in the Alamo was glad that there was plenty of ammunition for all of their weapons.

Juarez Amigo had chosen a fifty-caliber rifle with an attached bayonet, the kind he had used when he was a soldier in Santa Anna's army.

Colonel Jim Bowie, Sam, and Adam happened to be standing near, with Sam at his side, as Adam Kane looked on while Juarez gripped the rifle to get the feel of it.

Bowie grinned. "Juarez, do you know how to use that rifle?"

Juarez grinned back at him. "Sí. I most certainly do." He swiftly brought the butt of the rifle to his shoulder and aimed the muzzle toward the top of the nearby wall. *"Boom! Boom!"*

Then acting as if he was using the bayonet on an opponent, he slashed the weapon and made the sound of a blade slicing the air.

Sam laughed, elbowed Jim Bowie, and said, "Ah thinks Mistah Amigo knows how to use dat rifle!"

Bowie and Kane laughed, as did some other men nearby.

Juarez still gripped the rifle. "Eef I have to, I weel use thees rifle and bayonet to become a *real* Texan!"

There was more laughter, and everyone went back to work. By the end of the day, all preparation work at the Alamo for the battle with Santa Anna's army was finished.

Unbeknown to Colonel William Travis and his men at the Alamo, the Texas sun arose on Sunday morning, February 21 to cast the shadows of two thousand of Santa Anna's men on the banks of the Rio Hondo, just fifty miles south of the Alamo.

That morning, in his quarters at the Alamo, Colonel William Travis was nervously pacing the floor and wringing his hands. It had been three days since Alan Kane had headed for Washington-on-the-Brazos. Riding his horse at a normal pace, Alan would have been back by now. Why hadn't he returned?

And then there was Jim Bonham. If anybody could eloquently convince Colonel Fannin of the Alamo's plight, it would be Bonham. Why wasn't he back from Goliad?

Travis left his quarters and headed for the mess hall to eat breakfast. When he stepped into the mess hall, some of the men gathered around him and asked the same questions about the two riders. The colonel admitted that he did not know but was wondering the same thing.

After breakfast, Adam Kane and Juarez Amigo held a Bible study service in the chapel—with Colonel Travis's permission—and eight of Travis's volunteers joined them in the service. Adam tried to encourage the eight men, as well as Juarez and himself, with the assurance that more help was on the way.

He then gave a Bible lesson on the cross of Calvary and made plain God's plan of salvation through the Lord Jesus Christ. At the invitation to come and receive Christ as Saviour, no one moved, but Adam and Juarez could tell that the message had hit home with most of the eight men.

When the meeting was dismissed, two of the men who had heard the message—Les Waterman and Hank Palmer—came to Adam and Juarez, told them that they were born-again Christians, and gave their testimonies. Adam and Juarez said how glad they were to know this.

Just before noon, Alan Kane came riding up to the Alamo, and the two soldiers assigned to the front gate welcomed him.

As one of them opened the gate, the other ran to Colonel Travis's quarters and told him that Alan Kane was back. Travis stepped outside and called for several men to go round up everybody and gather on the plaza in front of the mission building. He sent the soldier to tell Alan where to meet him.

Moments later the crowd of men gathered at the designated spot, eager to hear what Alan had to say.

Standing before the men as Colonel Travis stepped up beside him, Alan looked at the colonel and said loudly enough for all to hear, "Colonel, the reason I was gone so long is that General Houston detained me because he was expecting a good number of men to come the day after I arrived, to sign up in the army. I could ride here with them. But it didn't happen that way. A few came, but not nearly the number the general was expecting."

A glum look captured Travis's face.

"However, Colonel," said Alan, wanting to encourage their leader, "General Houston told me to assure you that he will come with at least five thousand men as soon as possible."

Travis was visibly upset, but only said, "I know the general is doing his best to build an army large enough to stand with us when we face the Mexican troops." He took a short breath and ran his gaze over the group of men. "Quite possibly, Colonel James Fannin and his five hundred men are already traveling toward us. Maybe Jim Bonham decided to travel with Fannin and his men rather than to gallop ahead of them."

At twilight that very evening, unbeknown to the men at the Alamo, Santa Anna's two thousand troops pitched camp on the banks of the Rio Medina, a scant twenty-five miles south of San Antonio.

Late on Monday afternoon, February 22, the Kane brothers, Juarez Amigo, and two other volunteers, Les Waterman and Hank Palmer, were on the southwest corner of the Alamo's wall, standing by the big eighteen-pounder cannon. It had been a cloudy, dismal day, and they were talking about how much they missed their families.

Suddenly, Jack Waterman's head bobbed as he caught movement out on the southern horizon of the prairie. He turned his head to get a better look and pointed. "Look! A huge crowd coming!"

The other four men quickly saw the soldiers and tensed up.

Juarez Amigo's eyes bulged. "Oh-h-h! Somehow San' Anna's troops have arrived much earlier than Colonel Travees expect!"

The other men squinted at the troops, trying to focus on them.

Alan looked at Juarez. "Are you sure it's the Mexican troops?"

Juarez nodded, swallowing hard. "Sí! I recognize zee tall hats of zee eenfantry! I dunno where zee cavalry ees, bot San' Anna ees bring hees eenfantry!"

Adam Kane gasped. "Let's go tell Colonel Travis!"

The five men hastily descended the ladder and ran to Colonel Travis's quarters.

Alan knocked on the door, and Travis opened it quickly. He looked at them inquisitively. "What's wrong?"

"Colonel," Alan said, "come with us! Mexican infantrymen are coming this way!"

Moments later, when Travis had climbed the ladder, he set his eyes on the large number of Mexican troops who were setting up camp only a few hundred yards to the south. He called out to men who were moving about inside the Alamo's walls and told them to take the message to all the men to meet him at the south gate.

Within less than ten minutes, all the men inside the Alamo were gathered with their commander, standing at the open gate, looking at the Mexican troops who were camped dangerously near.

The hearts of all 150 men were pounding. *Time had run out for the men at the Alamo.*

TWENTY-TWO

Late that night, Adam Kane could not sleep. It had taken some time for his brother and Mexican friend, as well as the other men in the barracks, to get to sleep. While men around him breathed heavily, some snoring—including Alan and Juarez—Adam lay on his bunk wide awake, thinking of his lovely wife. The night wind howled in the eaves outside.

As Adam lay in the darkness, Julia's beautiful face hung sharply like a portrait on the wall of his mind.

Down in his chest, he felt the warmth of his love for her. But accompanying the love was a fear that he might never see her again in this world.

Finally, Adam went to prayer and asked the Lord to give him peace about the present situation and to keep His mighty hand on Julie at home and on him here at the Alamo. He told the Lord that he knew he would only come through this battle with the Mexicans if God willed it. He also prayed for Alan and Juarez and closed his prayer by whispering, "Thy will be done."

Before dawn on February 23, San Antonio was filled with sounds of pounding hoofs, rattling wagons, creaking wheels, and the jangling of pots and pans inside the wagons.

The residents of the town had learned the day before that Santa Anna's troops had been camped at the Rio Medina. Then they had been seen by some of the townspeople making camp in the fields just south of town as night was falling. Fearful that Mexican soldiers might take over the entire town, residents were leaving in a hurry. They had packed up food, water, and other necessities, and wheels rolled before the eastern horizon had grayed.

Colonel William Travis had assigned several men to keep watch from the top of the wall facing the Mexican camp to the south during the night. They were to trade off getting some sleep.

When the men on the wall heard the sounds of the San Antonio residents leaving, one of them hurried to Colonel Travis's quarters by the light of the several lanterns that burned in the Alamo and found that he had also heard them and was about to go to the wall himself.

Just as the colonel was about to leave his quarters, Captain Almeron Dickinson came riding up on his horse. "Colonel, when I heard the wagons leaving San Antonio, I went to the stables and saddled my horse. Is it all right if I bring Susannah and Angelina here to the Alamo? I can't leave them there alone."

Travis nodded. "Of course. You can put them in one of the rooms in the mission building."

"Thank you, sir." The captain wheeled his horse about and galloped toward the west gate.

At the small house in town, Susannah Dickinson stood at the window by the front door and noted that all sounds of wagons leaving had died out. The street was now absolutely still in the gray light of dawn.

Suddenly Susannah heard pounding hoofbeats, and in the vague light, she saw a rider coming up the street. When the rider slowed down and guided his horse into the yard, she gasped. "Almeron!" She opened the door and ran out onto the porch.

As Almeron dismounted, Susannah raced down the steps. He dashed to her and folded her into his arms.

"Oh, Almeron!" she gasped. "We heard last night that Mexican soldiers are camped just south of town! I think everybody has gone!"

"That's why I'm here, sweetheart. Colonel Travis said I could bring you and Angelina to the Alamo. He said you can stay in one of the rooms in the mission building."

Susannah looked up at him. "All right, darling. I'll need to take some clothing for us and some other things too."

Moments later, the captain had his wife and fifteen-month-old daughter in the saddle, and carrying a piece of luggage and a canvas sack, he led them out of San Antonio.

At the same time as the Dickinsons were leaving San Antonio and the bright rays of the rising sun in the east were lighting up the southern horizon, the men at the Alamo stood at the south gate and were amazed that no Mexican troops could be seen.

Colonel Bowie shook his head and looked at Colonel Travis. "Where do you suppose they went?"

Travis shook his head. "I have no idea, but they'll be back. They're planning an attack, I assure you."

Standing a few feet away, Juarez Amigo said, "You are right, Señor Colonel Travees. Thees is San' Anna's way of getting us off balance, as they say. They weel be back!"

Travis nodded at Juarez, then turned to a young Tennessee volunteer named Daniel Cloud who had come with Davy Crockett. "Daniel, I need you to do some lookout work for me."

The twenty-one-year-old Corporal Cloud nodded. "Yes sir."

"You've been in San Antonio since you came here, haven't you?"

"Yes, Colonel."

"You know where the old San Fernando church building is, I assume."

"I do."

"Good. You know it has a bell tower."

"Yes sir."

"All right. I want you to go up into the bell tower and keep a lookout for any sign of the Mexican troops. I mean, keep your eyes peeled, and look in every direction. If you see anything that even looks like Mexicans, pull the rope on the bell, and ring it loud."

"I will do that, Colonel."

While Corporal Daniel Cloud had established himself in the bell tower at the San Fernando church, many of the men in the Alamo were on the walls, doing their own lookout work. Captain Almeron Dickinson, his wife and baby safe in their room in the mission building, was with Adam and Alan Kane and Juarez Amigo gathered around the big eighteen-pounder cannon on the southwest corner. Although Daniel Cloud was perched much higher in the bell tower a half mile away, they wanted to keep sharp eyes on the surrounding land as well.

By ten o'clock that morning, the Texas sun was brilliant in the clear azure sky. Up in the tower, Daniel Cloud's gaze was intent on the rolling landscape all around him. As he squinted against the sun's glare, sudden movement on the western horizon caught his eye.

The refulgent sunlight flashed on shiny cavalry lances.

Cloud's knees went watery. He froze in place, his eyes transfixed on the Mexican troops. His mouth gaped, and his brow furrowed. Abruptly he gained control of his faculties and moved to the bell rope. He closed his fingers around the rope and pulled it with all his might again and again and again. The thunderous warning echoed across the prairie...then suddenly quit ringing.

Colonel William Travis and some of his men who were not on the wall were in a dead-heat run, heading for town. When they reached the old church building, Daniel Cloud was looking down at them from the bell tower.

Colonel Travis and Jim Bowie bounded up the stairs. The men on the ground watched and listened. When Travis and Bowie reached the tower, they looked around the prairie and saw nothing out of the ordinary. "Why did you ring the bell?" asked Travis.

"Because I saw hundreds of Mexican cavalrymen to the west, sir. Then they suddenly galloped away and vanished from sight."

Travis nodded. "You stay here. If you see any more Mexicans, ring the bell again."

The two colonels descended the stairs, and Travis explained to the men what Daniel Cloud had just told them. Travis then told the men—while Cloud was listening from above—that he was sure Santa Anna had both infantry and cavalry waiting to attack whenever he decided to lead them to do so.

Travis said, "But since we all saw the infantry to the south yesterday, I want to send a couple riders westward just to confirm that Daniel indeed saw cavalry."

From the tower, Daniel said, "Colonel Travis, it was cavalry, all right! They were prancing their mounts back and forth, holding their lances straight up in the air! I could see the lances reflecting the sunlight!"

Travis looked up at Cloud. "I'm not doubting you, Daniel, but I simply must confirm it."

Travis then turned to two of his volunteers—Jake Sutherland and John Smith. "I want you two to get your horses right now and ride to the crest of those low hills to the west and see what you find. I'll be on the west wall of the Alamo by then. If you don't see any Mexican troops, ride back at a leisurely pace. But if you do see Mexican troops, gallop back as fast as you can."

As Sutherland and Smith ran toward the Alamo, Travis looked up. "Daniel, we'll head back now, but you watch those two men as they ride west, and if you see them coming back at a gallop, ring that bell real loud!"

"Yes sir," replied Cloud from the tower. "If they come at a gallop, I'll ring the bell!"

Jake Sutherland and John Smith were less than two miles west of the Alamo when they topped a gradual rise and saw the sun's reflection on fifteen hundred polished lances. The Mexican cavalrymen sat at rigid attention in their saddles, striking in appearance with their red waistcoats, vivid blue trousers, and shiny black boots.

Wearing black helmets adorned with black horsehair, they held silver lances bearing bright yellow pennons. On their waists were silver-scabbarded sabers and pistols in black holsters.

The cavalry commander sat straight-backed in his silver-studded black saddle, riding to and fro in front of his men with military precision. Impressive in his indigo blue coat with golden epaulets and red braid, he waved his sword as he rode under a high-peaked, broad black sombrero.

Smith tore his gaze from the awesome scene and looked at Sutherland. "Danny Cloud was right."

Quickly they wheeled their mounts and galloped full-speed back toward the Alamo. Above the wind in their ears and the pounding of hooves, they heard the bell in the tower begin to clang loudly.

When Sutherland and Smith reached the west gate of the Alamo, Colonel Travis and several of his men were there to meet them. Many others were atop the west wall observing. Captain Almeron Dickinson and his wife were standing on the plaza close by. Susannah was holding little dark-haired Angelina in her arms.

"We heard the bell," said Travis as the two scouts dismounted. "Tell us!"

"There are at least fifteen hundred Mexican cavalrymen out there past the rise!" said John Smith.

The men on the ground and on the wall exchanged fearful glances, as did Almeron and Susannah Dickinson.

Travis handed an envelope to Jake Sutherland. "I need you two to take this letter and ride like the wind to Gonzales. It's addressed to Mayor Andrew Ponton. In the letter I've pleaded with Mayor Ponton to challenge loyal Texans in his town to come to the Alamo and help defend it against Santa Anna and his forces. I explained that they are getting very close to us."

Sutherland and Smith were soon galloping at full speed toward Gonzales.

They were just out of sight from the Alamo when they saw a rider coming toward them.

Jake hollered at John, "It's Jim Bonham!"

"Sure is!" John hollered back.

Both men waved at Bonham, signaling for him to stop.

As Bonham drew rein, halting his horse, Sutherland and Smith skidded their mounts to a stop, and Sutherland said, "We've got Mexican cavalry and infantry working their way close to the Alamo! Colonel Travis has the two of us riding to Gonzales to see if we can get some men to come and help us. Are Colonel Fannin and his troops coming?"

Bonham shook his head in disgust. "No, he's not. I argued with him for several days, but he still refuses to bring any of his men to the Alamo."

John Smith squared his jaw and said through his teeth, "This is gonna upset Colonel Travis. He's still hoping Fannin's coming."

Bonham sighed. "I know. Well, you two had better get on to Gonzales. Much as I've been dreading it, I'd better go give Colonel Travis the bad news."

At the Alamo, Colonel Travis was snapping orders, assigning armed men to different positions along the thickly built walls.

Juarez Amigo was glad to be stationed with Alan and Adam Kane beside the Alamo's biggest and most powerful cannon.

Jim Bowie, with Sam at his side, was standing on the west wall, looking at the deserted San Antonio. Davy Crockett and his Tennesseans were mingled with the others along the walls.

"Keep your eyes peeled, men!" Travis shouted so all could hear. "I'll be in my quarters. Let me know the instant you see anything move out there!"

Just as Travis turned to go to his quarters, Captain Almeron Dickinson, who was also on top of a wall, pointed to the prairie and shouted, "Colonel Travis! It's Jim Bonham! He's riding in alone!"

Travis froze in his tracks.

By the time Jim Bonham reached the gate, it was open for him. He rode through the gate, guided his horse toward the spot where Travis was standing, and drew rein. As he dismounted, Travis was looking at him with cautious eyes. His heart pounding, Bonham stepped up to him and said levelly, "Fannin isn't coming, Colonel. I argued with him for days, but he refused to listen to me. He thinks it's more important to stand guard where he is."

The colonel's face turned pale, and he said glumly, "I've heard nothing from General Houston. We've spotted Mexican troops quite close. It looks bad."

Jim Bonham licked his lips nervously. "I'd say so, sir."

The next morning, Wednesday, February 24, Colonel Travis was standing on the sandy plaza talking to Susannah Dickinson, who had her baby in her arms. It was precisely ten o'clock. All of the men in the Alamo were at their stations when suddenly Juarez Amigo jumped to his feet on the wall beside the Kane brothers and the big cannon, waved his rifle in the air, and shouted, "Señor Colonel Travees! Señor Colonel Travees!"

All the eyes in the Alamo swung toward the little Mexican.

Amigo took a deep breath, pointed southwestward, and shouted, "Look, Señor Colonel Travees! Zee Big Bull! San' Anna!"

While everyone on the walls was looking that direction, Travis excused himself from Susannah Dickinson and dashed to the steps that led up to the platform that held the eighteen-pounder cannon. Those on the ground below the walls began clambering up to see the sight.

Standing between Juarez Amigo and Alan Kane, Travis watched the long lines of Mexican troops in a mixture of cavalry and infantry moving back and forth as if in a parade on the crests of the low southwestern hills, just out of cannon range. Out front was a tall, stately Mexican on a high-stepping white horse.

"Look, Señor Colonel Travees!" said Juarez. "Eet ees San' Anna!"

Travis looked at the little Mexican. "You've got it right, Juarez. He's a big bull, all right!"

The men in the Alamo stood in silence and watched the impressive parade. Mexico's dictator and generalissimo was magnificent in his black and white uniform, bedecked with red trim and golden epaulets. The gold stripes on his trouser legs disappeared into the silver guards of his cuffed stirrups.

Travis said to those men close to him on the cannon platform, "I estimate that there are some fifteen hundred cavalrymen out there and five hundred infantrymen."

"Zat ees a good esteemate, sir," said Juarez. "Zees parade is meant to frighten everyone in the Alamo."

Travis nodded. "Yes, I know."

At that moment, Santa Anna waved an arm at his troops, turned his horse, and led them back over the hills. Soon all the Mexican troops had vanished from view.

On the wall where Colonel Jim Bowie stood with some of his men, Sam was at his side. Sam looked at Bowie. "Massa Bowie, if'n we don' get help maghty soon, we's done fo'."

Bowie laid a hand on the black man's shoulder. "Don't you worry now, Sam. Help from General Houston is bound to be on the way."

The next morning, still staying out of cannon range, Santa Anna strutted within sight of the Alamo with his troops for about half an hour. To keep the men in the Alamo nervous, at sunset, they lined up outside of cannon range and fired rifles toward the Alamo. Even though the bullets struck the prairie, kicking up dust far from the Alamo, it was nerve-wracking for the men.

Still, there was no attack. Colonel Travis told his men that Santa Anna was no doubt waiting for the other four thousand troops to arrive.

That evening, the Kane brothers and Juarez Amigo held Bible study and prayer time. Les Waterman and Hank Palmer were in attendance.

Only a few other men attended, but during this time, three men received Christ as Saviour, bringing joy to the hearts of Adam, Alan, Juarez, Les, and Hank.

The next morning, Friday, February 26, Santa Anna and his troops performed another parade for the men in the Alamo, then fired rifles as they had done the previous day. When the rifle firing was over, the Mexicans then spread out on the prairie within sight of the Alamo but out of cannon range, pitching tents on all four sides between the deep gullies and ditches that ran through the land. It was obvious that they wanted the men in the Alamo to know they were now surrounded.

As the sun was lowering toward the western horizon, men on the Alamo's south wall called for Colonel Travis to come and observe what was happening. The rest of the men in the Alamo who were not on the walls crowded up to the south gate to see what the Mexicans were doing.

Colonel Travis made his way up to the platform of the big cannon and observed the scene with the Kane brothers and Juarez Amigo.

Three Mexican cavalrymen were facing Santa Anna as he sat his own horse. The men in the Alamo watched as one of the cavalrymen tied a white flag to a silver lance. The three riders wheeled and galloped toward the Alamo, the white flag flapping in the breeze.

As the trio drew near the Alamo, Travis said, "I know what's coming. They're going to approach us with that white flag of peace and demand that we surrender. Well, we've got an answer for them. General Houston and his five thousand men have got to be coming anytime now. I want you men to light a torch and be ready to fire the cannon. Aim it toward the Mexican troops. They're out of range, but at least we can give Santa Anna our reply so he understands we mean it."

While the Kane brothers and Juarez Amigo followed the colonel's instructions, Travis watched as the three Mexican riders drew up to the wall some distance from where they stood. When the Mexican with the white flag on his lance spoke to the men at that spot on the wall, one of them pointed toward Colonel Travis.

"They're asking for the commander of the Alamo," Travis said to the three men, who now had the cannon aimed as instructed. Adam had lighted a torch and was holding it.

Reining in some thirty feet from where Colonel William Travis stood on the wooden platform, the Mexican on the center horse, who held the lance bearing the white flag, said, "I would speak to you, Señor Commanding Offeecer."

Nodding tightly, Travis met his dark gaze. "All right. Speak."

"As messenger of hees honor, Generalissimo Antonio López de Santa Anna, eet ees my duty to command you to lay down your arms and surrender. As preesoners of zee generalissimo, you weel be treated with kindness and respect."

From his position close by Travis, Juarez Amigo spit. All three riders riveted him with dark eyes. "Kindness and respect! Ha!" growled Juarez. "You mean torture and execution!"

The one on the center horse swung his gaze back to Travis. "Generalissimo Santa Anna expects an eemediate answer."

Without turning his head, Travis said, "Adam."

Adam Kane lowered the flaming torch and touched it to the powder pit on top of the cannon. There was a momentary hiss, followed by the deep-throated roar of the huge eighteen-pounder. The ball hit about eight hundred feet out, exploding and plowing dirt.

The frightened horses reared, whinnying, almost throwing the three Mexicans from their saddles. The center man gained control of his mount, nailed Travis with a hot look, wheeled, and galloped away with the other two behind him.

"Well, I guess they know we mean business now, Colonel," Alan said.

Travis nodded. "I would say so. You men did a good job."

"Bueno!" said Juarez.

Travis looked at Alan. "I need to talk to you in private right now."

"All right, sir."

"Let's go to my quarters."

"Yes sir." Alan turned to his brother and the little Mexican. "See you later."

When Travis and young Kane sat down in his quarters, the colonel told Alan he liked the way he rode a horse and asked if he would be willing to ride to Washington-on-the-Brazos and tell General Houston what was going on at the Alamo and to please send whatever troops he had. Santa Anna was going to attack for sure, as soon as he had all six thousand troops.

Alan nodded. "Of course, sir. I'd be glad to go."

Travis cleared his throat gently. "It's going to be extremely dangerous to make the ride now, Alan. You've got to get past those Mexican troops, who are all around us. But General Houston needs to know what is happening here."

Alan realized the danger. "Well, sir, someone has to do it. I'll go after dark tonight and try to make it past the Mexican troops by riding through the deep gullies and ditches."

The colonel rose to his feet. When Alan followed suit, Travis extended his hand, and as Alan met his grip, Travis smiled. "Thank you for your willingness to make this daring ride."

Alan smiled in return. "Like I said, sir, I'm glad to do it."

During supper that evening, Alan told Adam what Colonel Travis had asked him to do. Other men heard and wished Alan well. The brothers agreed to pray for each other.

Word of what Alan was going to do soon spread throughout the Alamo. When night was falling, Alan said good-bye to Adam, Juarez, and Colonel Travis, then went to the stable and bridled and saddled his horse. When it was totally dark, Alan mounted up and rode past the front of the mission building, where one of the men had built a small fire and was kneeling beside it.

Captain Almeron Dickinson and Susannah were standing by the fire, with little Angelina in her mother's arms. They had seen Alan go to the stable and knew he would be riding past the mission building on his way to the nearest gate.

As Alan rode past the fire, the Dickinsons waved and wished him well. He waved in return, called out a thank-you, and rode on.

As the soldiers slowly opened the gate for Alan to pass through, he turned in his saddle and looked back at the Dickinsons, who still stood together in the glow of the fire.

Alan's gaze zeroed in on Susannah and her baby. A hot lump rose in his throat. He said in a whisper, "I will do my very best to bring troops back with me. Without more men to join us, we don't stand a chance."

The words echoed back to him and sent a shiver down his spine.

In Gonzales, Texas, the next day—Saturday, February 27—thirty-three loyal Texans, including their leader, George Kimball, who had formed a militia company, responded to Colonel William Travis's written request to Mayor Andrew Ponton and rode for the Alamo with Jake Sutherland and John Smith.

TWENTY-THREE

During the next few days, Santa Anna and his troops taunted the men in the Alamo, firing rifles from beyond range, but as yet there was still no attack.

The year 1836 was a leap year. On the morning of February 29, a Monday, Alan Kane arrived at Washington-on-the-Brazos. As he rode into the area that General Sam Houston and his soldiers had occupied, he was shocked to see that there was not a horse in sight, and he could only see one man in uniform, who was standing by a small tent observing him as he rode up.

Alan recognized the man. It was an aging army major named Fred Kitchell. As he drew rein, the silver-haired major said, "Hello, Mr. Kane."

"Hello, Major Kitchell." Alan ran his eyes over the vacant area. "Where did everybody go?"

"General Houston took what troops he had assembled and went to the banks of the Sabine River in an attempt to gain more volunteers from the towns in that area."

Alan blinked. "The Sabine River? That's quite a ways from here, isn't it?"

"Mm-hmm. If you're gonna go there, it'll take you a few days."

"Can you tell me exactly where the general and his men are on the Sabine?"

The major took a slip of paper out of his coat pocket and pulled a pencil from his trousers. "I'll draw you a map."

Late on the night of February 29, Jake Sutherland, John Smith, and the thirty-three Gonzales volunteers arrived near San Antonio and had to use deep gullies and ditches to sneak past the Mexican troops to get to the Alamo.

Colonel Travis and his men warmly welcomed them.

Travis, who was already saddened because Colonel James Fannin and his troops were not coming, was glad to see that, including himself, at least he now had 182 fighting men in the Alamo. He would have 183 when Alan Kane returned…and hopefully a whole lot more when General Sam Houston brought his troops.

Everyone in the Alamo feared that Santa Anna's attack would come soon.

While the Alamo men were in conversation with the Gonzales men, Colonel Travis caught a glimpse of Susannah Dickinson, who was talking to George Kimball with her husband. He thought of how she could have gone to safety with the other people of San Antonio but chose to stay with her husband. He deeply admired her courage.

When George Kimball turned away from the Dickinsons, he stepped up to Travis. "Colonel, I have some news for you. Your men ought to hear it too."

Travis nodded. "All right." He raised his voice above the din of voices and told them all to gather around. Mr. Kimball had news they needed to hear.

Jim Bowie and Sam moved up beside Travis. Everyone listened as Kimball said loudly enough for all to hear that he had received word on February 26 that General Sam Houston had left Washington-on-the-Brazos with his troops and had gone to the Sabine River, where he would attempt to get more volunteers.

William Travis's heart sank. He tried not to show his disappointment, but it was written plainly on his face. Everyone in the Alamo had no doubt that the vicious Santa Anna and his troops would be attacking soon. Houston's move to the Sabine River only placed him and his troops farther away from the Alamo. Travis thought of Alan Kane and wondered if he had made it to Washington-on-the-Brazos yet. If so, Travis told himself, Alan would no doubt be on his way to the Sabine River to take his message to General Houston.

Seeing the effect the news had on Travis, Jim Bowie tried to encourage him, saying that maybe it would be longer than they thought before the Mexican attack came.

Other men also spoke words of encouragement, saying the same thing. Travis thanked them, but warned that none of them should let their guard down. Santa Anna's other four thousand troops had to be getting very close. The attack was imminent.

At early dawn on the first day of March, men on the walls saw several columns of Mexican infantrymen marching across the plains toward San Antonio. Colonel Travis was summoned, and before long all the men in the Alamo were on the walls or at the west gate watching the Mexican troops moving into the town.

The eastern horizon brightened as the last of the Mexican soldiers entered San Antonio, and from the top of a wall, Davy Crockett called out to Colonel Travis and swung an arm, pointing to the rolling prairie in all four directions.

All eyes on the walls turned to the surrounding land, and even more distressing than the Mexican infantrymen marching into San Antonio was the sight of the new entrenchments that had been set up in every direction during the night. Exceptionally strong batteries on the north had been established. More than a dozen cannons were now trained on the Alamo from that direction. Cannons on the west had been moved in as close as three hundred yards.

Captain Almeron Dickinson had his wife and baby in their room inside the mission building, as protected as possible.

At precisely eight o'clock that morning, bombardment by the Mexican cannons began. The Alamo cannons immediately returned fire. The riflemen were in place and ready, but at that point no Mexican troops were within rifle range.

Colonel Jim Bowie was on a cannon platform not far from the big eighteen-pounder. Sam was at his side. While Sam and other men loaded the cannon between shots, Bowie held the torch that set off the powder each time it fired again.

Just as Bowie touched off another cannonball, a Mexican cannonball struck the wall close to the platform, and when the platform shook from the explosion, Bowie lost his balance and fell twelve feet to the ground, landing on his left side.

At the larger platform, Adam Kane had seen Jim Bowie fall and strike the ground hard. He told Juarez Amigo and Almeron Dickinson to keep firing, handed his torch to Dickinson, and hurried down the steps to the ground. When his feet touched dirt, he saw that Sam had picked Bowie up and was cradling him in his arms.

Adam looked into the twisted face of Jim Bowie and above the roar of the cannons asked, "Are you hurt bad, Jim?"

Bowie grunted through his teeth, "I…I don't know."

"Where's your pain?" Adam asked.

Bowie squared his jaw. "My—ribs. Left side."

"May I stick my hand down there?"

Bowie nodded. "Go ahead."

When Adam's fingertips touched the ribs, Bowie let out a howl and ground his teeth.

Adam pulled his hand back. "You've got some broken ribs, Colonel. I'm sure of it. Maybe I should come with you and—"

"I'll take care of him, Mistah Kane," said Sam. "They need you at the eighteen-pounder."

Adam nodded, patted Bowie's arm for encouragement, and hurried back to the platform.

Jim Bowie's slave carried him inside the Alamo chapel to the baptistry room, where the two of them had been staying, and laid Bowie on the cot he'd been using. He did what he could to make Bowie comfortable and ease his pain.

After three hours of cannonade, which had severely damaged the walls of the Alamo, not one man inside had been wounded by the gunfire. Several Mexican soldiers had been maimed in the fields by exploding Alamo cannonballs, and a few had been killed.

Suddenly the Mexicans launched a heavy wave of infantry from the west side of the Alamo. Guns on both sides roared. Mexicans were falling in large numbers, and soon the officers led their infantry in retreat.

At dawn on the morning of March 2, the men in the Alamo awakened to see that Santa Anna had positioned more cannons in the fields, and the Alamo was now heavily surrounded.

The bombardment of the Alamo began just before eight o'clock, and as Mexican cannonballs struck the ground and sometimes the walls, the Alamo cannons fired back fiercely. The air on the Texas plains was filled with clouds of gunsmoke.

The big cannon, manned by Adam Kane, Captain Almeron Dickinson, and Juarez Amigo, did extreme damage to some of the cannons and crews, and soon Santa Anna called his cannons back out of firing distance, specifically away from the eighteen-pounder.

Still...not one man in the Alamo had been wounded by gunfire.

As the day passed and the men in the Alamo continued to watch for the arrival of Santa Anna's additional four thousand troops, Adam Kane sat on the platform beside the big cannon while Juarez told Captain Dickinson stories about his days in Santa Anna's army.

Adam's thoughts went to Julie. He missed her tremendously. He was unaware that many miles away, as his brother rode toward the Sabine River, Alan was thinking of Julie too. But only as her brother-in-law. Although Alan was still very much in love with Julie, he was doing his best not to let that love control his life.

Adam's reverie about Julie was interrupted by Jim Bowie's slave calling up to him from the ground.

Adam looked down. "Yes, Sam?"

"At suppah las' naght, yo' ast me to let you know 'bout Massah Bowie today."

Adam nodded. "Uh-huh."

"He's still in a lot of pain from those broke ribs, but he restin' pretty good raght now."

"Well, I'm glad to hear it. Tell him I said to keep resting, won't you?"

"Yassuh!" Sam said. "I will do dat."

On Thursday, March 3, the day started differently than it had Tuesday and Wednesday. Although more cannons had been added to the Mexican army's prairie battle stations during the night, there was no bombardment.

At about nine o'clock, the haggard men in the Alamo looked on wide-eyed as Santa Anna's additional troops began arriving from the south. The Big Bull was on his white horse, obviously welcoming them.

At the south gate of the Alamo, Captain Almeron Dickinson stood with Susannah looking on, as were the other men beside them. Little Angelina was in her father's arms, wrapped warmly in a wool blanket.

Colonel William Travis was standing on the wall at the big cannon. Adam Kane was on one side of him and Juarez Amigo on the other. Their faces were dismal.

When the troops had all arrived, Colonel Travis looked over the massive crowd. "Juarez, how many new men do you think are out there? It certainly looks like more than four thousand to me."

Juarez nodded. "You are right, Señor Colonel Travees. I am sure there are four thousand cavalrymen. Zee eenfantrymen who came weeth them...there have to be at least five hondred of them."

"So we've just seen some forty-five hundred soldiers arrive," Adam said.

Juarez looked at him. "Sí. Santa Anna is ready to attack full-force. Especially since he has his *zapadores* now."

Adam frowned. "Zapadores? What are they?"

"Zee eenfantrymen. I know zey are zapadores by zeir uneeforms. Zee zapadores are men specially trained in hand-to-hand combat...bayonets and knives."

Adam Kane's left hand instinctively went to the bowie knife strapped to his waist, and he swallowed hard.

"For sure," said Juarez, "zee attack will come soon, now zat zee cavalry and zee zapadores have arrived."

William Travis fixed his gaze on the total of some sixty-five hundred Mexican troops and silently compared them to the mere 182 fighting men in the Alamo, including himself.

Suddenly they could hear trumpets blaring and drums rumbling, and when they looked back at the Mexicans, they saw Santa Anna on his white horse leading a parade in honor of the troops who had just arrived. They were headed toward San Antonio.

Everyone in the Alamo looked on while the band played and the drums rolled. Behind it all tolled the bell in the San Fernando church tower.

On Friday morning, March 4, Santa Anna's cannons, which were out of rifle range on the plains surrounding the Alamo, began a bombardment that lasted nearly all day. The Alamo cannons fired back, and the big eighteen-pounder was taking its toll on the Mexican forces. The Mexican cannonballs, however, did much damage to the Alamo's walls. The Mexican cannonade ceased at sundown, and the Mexican columns quickly withdrew from sight.

Colonel William Travis was both pleased and amazed that as yet, not one man in the Alamo had been hit. Many Mexicans out in the open had been killed, and a great number had been wounded.

Travis left his men at the walls and went to the chapel to visit Jim Bowie in the baptistry room. When he entered the room, he was both surprised and pleased to see Susannah Dickinson helping Sam take care of Bowie. Little Angelina was playing on the floor by a window.

Drawing up to the cot where Bowie lay with Sam seated on one side of him and Susannah on the other, Travis looked at Susannah. "So how's he doing?"

"He's still in a great deal of pain. He can't leave the cot."

Jim looked up at Travis and said weakly, "I heard all that cannonade today. I figure since the Big Bull's forty-five hundred troops are here now, in another day or so, the Mexicans will storm the walls. They want in here."

Travis nodded and said dismally, "You're right. It's going to happen real soon."

Susannah exchanged a solemn glance with Sam.

Bowie said, "If General Houston and his army don't show up in the next twenty-four hours, we're dead men."

Travis nodded silently.

This time the look Susannah and Sam exchanged was full of fear.

Dawn came Saturday, March 5, with a bleak and bitter north wind blowing. The Mexican cannons were in place again and began firing.

The Alamo cannons began firing in return.

This went on for hours. Then suddenly, at three o'clock in the afternoon, the Mexican cannons stopped firing and were quickly withdrawn from sight.

The men remained at their stations, the riflemen still not needing to fire their weapons.

On the wall where the big eighteen-pounder stood on its platform, Juarez Amigo was running his gaze over the area when suddenly his eyes caught sight of activity in San Antonio at the San Fernando church. His eyes bulged, and at the same moment he saw Colonel William Travis walking across the plaza with Sergeant Louis Rose. He stepped to the edge of the platform and called out. "Señor Colonel Travees! Come up here, queeckly!"

"What is it, Juarez?" queried Travis.

"Come up and see! It ees bad!"

Leaving Rose where he stood, Travis scurried up the steps to the top of the wall and looked in the direction where the little Mexican was pointing.

"See?" said Juarez. "On zee church bell tower?"

Travis focused on the tower and quickly caught sight of a large red flag flapping in the wind. His blood turned cold. William Barret Travis knew the meaning of the solid red flag: *No quarter.* Santa Anna would take no prisoners when his sixty-five hundred men attacked the Alamo. Every man in the Alamo would be killed.

Travis met the little Mexican's dark eyes. "No quarter."

"No quarter." Juarez lips were pulled into a thin line.

At that moment, the blare of trumpets and the roll of drums drew the attention of the men on the walls to San Antonio. Travis and Juarez dropped their line of sight to the east edge of San Antonio.

Soldiers at the west gate swung it open, and many men gathered there to look on.

All were stunned to see the Mexican army brass band marching out of town with infantrymen following in an exhibition of rumbling drums and blaring trumpets. Maintaining a safe distance from the Alamo's rifles and cannons, Santa Anna's army presented a dazzling display.

Santa Anna appeared on his white horse, making his own colorful display. He guided his mount to the front of his troops, all facing east toward the Alamo.

Juarez Amigo turned to Colonel Travis. "Thees ees San' Anna's way of declaring that he an' hees army will win the battle that ees defeenently coming tomorrow."

Travis licked his lips and nodded.

In his saddle, Santa Anna was obviously confident that his display of power would demoralize the vastly outnumbered men in the Alamo.

Suddenly the trumpets burst into an ancient Moorish battle march, known as *Èl Degüello*...another military signal of no quarter.

Juarez quickly explained this to the colonel. It was another way for Santa Anna to tell the men in the Alamo that they would die tomorrow. Every fighting man in the Alamo would be killed when the attack came. "An' Señor Colonel Travees?" he said with a quiver in his voice. "Haveeng served under the Big Bull, I know the attack will come at the break of dawn."

A ball of ice formed in William Travis's stomach. General Houston and his troops had not come. Travis and his 181 men would face over six thousand troops. He thought of Jim Bowie's words yesterday: "If General Houston and his army don't show up in the next twenty-four hours, we're *dead men.*"

They were in a deathtrap. Travis knew what he must do.

As the last notes of the Degüello died out in the air, Santa Anna glared toward the Alamo for a long moment, then abruptly wheeled his white stallion and rode back into San Antonio. The band and the troops followed behind silently.

It was four thirty in the afternoon. Colonel Travis descended the stairs from the wall and asked where Captain Almeron Dickinson was.

As Travis hurried to the spot, he heard the men talking about the red flag of "no quarter" and the deadly meaning of the Degüello.

When he found the captain, he told him to gather everybody on the plaza in front of the chapel. He wanted to speak to them.

Within ten minutes, 180 beleaguered men stood together with their backs to the chapel, facing Travis.

Jim Bowie, number 181, his broken ribs giving him much pain, lay on a stretcher on the ground between his slave, Sam, and Sergeant Louis Rose.

Adam Kane was standing with Davy Crockett and his Tennesseans. Next to Adam was Juarez Amigo.

Susannah Dickinson stood in the open doorway of the low barracks close by, holding her baby, who was wrapped warmly in her wool blanket. She could plainly see the haggard faces of the men, including her husband's.

With his face gray and rigid, Travis went over the meaning of the red flag the Mexicans had hung on the bell tower of the church in San Antonio and the meaning of the Degüello the band had so brazenly played. "Men," he said solemnly, "Santa Anna's army of over six thousand will attack the Alamo at dawn. However, there is a choice for each of you. When darkness falls, you can go over the wall. By crawling through the gullies and the ditches, you have a slim chance of making it to freedom. Or you can remain here with me and fight the Mexican troops when they come. If you stay, you will die tomorrow. In death, you will be immortalized. Your names will be cherished in the memories of a free Texas forever."

Adam Kane thought of his darling Julie, his father, his sister, and his two brothers and their wives at the Diamond K Ranch. He also thought of Alan, wondering what had happened to him.

Colonel Travis had the rapt attention of the men and of Susannah Dickinson, whose husband had moved to the low barracks and was now standing next to her.

With every eye on him, Colonel William Travis drew the sword from the scabbard on his waist as he stood on the sand-packed floor of the plaza. Methodically, he plunged the tip of his sword into the sand only an inch or two in front of the toes of his boots. He then moved slowly and drew a line in the sand from left to right some thirty feet in length.

Returning to the place where he had been standing, Travis looked across the line in the sand. "I want every man who is willing to stay and face the enemy to the death to step across this line. The others can wait until dark and go over the wall."

Men quickly crossed the line.

Within thirty seconds, 180 men stood with Travis, who had a grim smile on his lips. Two men remained on the other side of the line. Jim Bowie and Louis Rose.

Unable to get up off his stretcher, Bowie looked at the group of men. "Hey, guys! How about a lift across the line?"

TWENTY-FOUR

Sam and Major Green Jameson dashed to Jim Bowie, picked up the stretcher, and carried him across the line.

Everyone was now staring at Sergeant Louis Rose.

He met their gaze and said in a level tone, "I didn't come to Texas to die. I'll go over the wall when night falls." With that, Rose walked away. All eyes followed him until he entered the mission building and closed the door behind him.

At the low barracks door, Susannah Dickinson had tears in her eyes as she turned to her husband, still holding little Angelina. Almeron wrapped an arm around his wife and held her tight.

Juarez Amigo stepped up. "Meesis Deekeenson, zee Mehicano soldiers weel not harm you or zee baby. I know thees because of my years as a soldier een San' Anna's army. Do not be afraid."

Captain Dickinson said softly, "Thank you, Juarez, for telling Susannah this."

The tears were now coursing down Susannah's cheeks as she looked up at Almeron. He knew the look in her tear-filled eyes. Though her heart was filled with grief, she was proud of him.

Juarez patted Susannah's arm, then turned and made his way to Adam Kane. "Weeth what is going to happen een zee morning, I am so glad Alan led me to Jesus. I know that when I am keeled tomorrow, I weel go to heaven."

Adam nodded. "Praise the Lord, Juarez. And I will meet you there."

Juarez's brow furrowed. "Adam, weel I be considered a *real* Texan when I die fighteeng for Texas?"

Adam nodded. "You sure will, my friend. You sure will."

At that moment, seven of the men who had attended Adam Kane's Bible studies during their time at the Alamo stepped up to him. One of the men said, "Adam, we want to do as you have been telling us. We want to receive the Lord Jesus Christ as our Saviour. We don't want to die lost."

Juarez's eyes sparkled. "Praise zee Lord!"

Adam smiled. "This makes me very happy, men. Let's go to the barracks. My Bible is there. You can all be ready to die and go to heaven in the morning."

Jim Bowie had been carried back to the baptistry room on his stretcher by Sam and Green Jameson and placed on his cot. When the major left the room, Sam stood over the injured man. "Massah Bowie, can Ah do anythin' fo' you?"

Bowie looked up at Sam and nodded. "Yes. First, help me sit up and brace my back against the wall. Then fetch me paper and a pencil."

After Bowie was as comfortable as possible, sitting on the cot with his back against the wall, Sam went to a small desk where he had seen pencils and paper in a drawer.

When Bowie had pencil and paper in hand, he began writing.

Sam blinked. "What is you wraghtin', Massah Bowie?"

"I'll tell you when I'm finished." Bowie kept writing.

"Yassuh."

Moments later, the injured man signed *James Bowie* at the bottom of the page, then looked up at the black man. "Sam, this is an official document releasing you from my ownership. You are no longer my slave. You are a free man."

Sam blinked. "Ah's a free man?"

"Yes." Bowie handed him the paper. "Now, I want you to go over the wall tonight like Louis Rose is going to do and escape. I don't want you getting killed."

Sam looked at the paper. "Massah Bowie, I—"

"I'm not your master anymore, Sam. Don't call me that. But please do what I say. You go over the wall tonight."

"*Mistah* Bowie," said Sam, "since Ah's a free man, Ah can do as Ah pleases, raght?"

"Yes."

"Then, since Ah's a free man, Ah chooses to stay raght heah and die with you!"

Tears filled Jim Bowie's eyes.

Later that night, under cover of darkness when no one could see him, Louis Rose slipped over one of the walls and headed for the gullies and ditches.

In the small room of the mission building where Susannah and little Angelina had been staying, Captain Almeron Dickinson, with a grim countenance, held his wife in his arms. "I love you so much, sweetheart. I wish I hadn't brought you to this place," he said. "I should have found some residents of San Antonio who would take you and Angelina with them."

Her own countenance grim as well, Susannah said, "Hush now, darling. I wanted to be with you as long as possible."

She looked down at the baby, who was asleep in her crib, then looked back at her husband. "Angelina and I will be all right. You heard what Juarez said."

Almeron nodded. "I sure was glad to hear him say that."

Susannah blinked at the tears that were filling her eyes. "I'm so proud of you, darling. You are a *real* soldier."

The captain held her close and kissed her long and lovingly.

He then bent down and kissed the cheek of his sleeping child, saying in a half whisper, "Papa loves you with all his heart, my precious."

When he stood up straight, his eyes were filled with tears. He folded Susannah in his arms and kissed her long and lovingly again. "I love you with all my heart."

"I love you in the same way, darling," she said. "And so does Angelina."

Almeron bit his lip. "I…I have to go now. Every man must be in his place, ready for what's coming at dawn."

The captain gave his wife and daughter one long look, then walked to the door. When he opened the door and looked back, Susannah managed a tearful smile. "I love you, darling."

"And I love you." His lips quivered. With that, he reluctantly stepped out and closed the door behind him.

It was still dark on Sunday morning, March 6, 1836, when Santa Anna's trumpeters blasted the cold air once again with the Degüello. The haunting succession of C notes curdled the blood of the men in the Alamo. Every man was at his post waiting.

Beneath the notes of the Degüello came muffled drums.

While the drums rolled, in the baptistry room of the chapel, Jim Bowie braced himself in a sitting position on the cot with his back against the wall. Facing the door, he had a revolver in each hand and two bowie knives placed by his thighs. The big, heavy door was closed.

Next to Bowie, seated in a wooden chair, was Sam. He also had a revolver in each hand.

In her small room in the mission building, Susannah Dickinson sat on her small bed, wide awake. Angelina was asleep in her arms. Susannah's spine tingled at the sound of the Mexican trumpets and drums.

Out on the fields in the darkness, Santa Anna's troops waited for dawn's light. The Mexican dictator had divided his infantry into four columns on each side of the Alamo's walls. Flanking the infantry at each column were the fierce zapadores. They would go over the walls to finish the rebellious men in the Alamo once the infantry had ruptured their fortified positions.

At the forefront of each column were men with scaling ladders.

The cavalry sat in their saddles behind the infantry, rifles in hand.

On the wall where Adam Kane stood beside the eighteen-pounder, Major Green Jameson and Juarez Amigo were with him, ready for battle. The huge black muzzle was centered on the sounds of the trumpets and muffled drums like a menacing eye.

Adam felt for the Bowie knife on his waist, then in his heart told Julia that he loved her and would meet her in heaven.

Moments later, at 5:10 a.m., the eastern horizon took on a faint glow. The trumpets went silent, but the drums continued to roll in muffled fashion.

Colonel William Travis, sword in hand, stood on the wall at the southwest corner, taking his command position beside a twelve-pounder cannon.

At 5:30, the muffled drums abruptly went silent. The rolling Texas prairie was now slightly visible.

Moments later, at the clear break of dawn, a Mexican bugle pierced the cold air. A single, triumphant cry from thousands of voices lifted off the prairie, "Viva Santa Anna!"

The cry came once more as the thunder of heavy boots beat on the hard earth, coming from all four sides of the Alamo.

William Travis's voice raised above the deep rumble. "Give it to them, men! For Texas!"

The twelve-pounder at Travis's side roared and belched fire. Rifles began to bark. At his place on the wall, Adam Kane unleashed the big cannon on the charging, shouting Mexican troops.

The Alamo was immediately a tumultuous, blustering bedlam of roaring guns and shouting men. The acrid smell of burned gunpowder filled the air. Ladders were quickly raised against the outside of the walls. The stubborn men of the Alamo met the zapadores with rifle butts as they scrambled up the ladders. Knocking the first men off, they flung the ladders backward, spilling the others to the hard ground below.

With the Alamo cannons firing overhead, the riflemen sighted in on easy targets. Mexicans were dropping, some screaming while being trampled by their own men.

As more Mexicans thronged the Alamo on foot, the cavalry charged at Santa Anna's command, firing their rifles at the men who manned the cannons on top of the walls and at the riflemen who blazed away from the parapets just below them.

The bloody battle went on, with men shouting and guns firing.

On the southwest corner of the wall, Colonel William Barret Travis stood tall against the sky, waving his sword and shouting encouragement to the gallant Texans. Suddenly a ladder plunked at his feet. Travis swung his sword down hard, splitting the top two rungs in half.

A swarthy hand reached for a rung that was not there. The Mexican soldier lost his balance and toppled down to the ground.

Travis placed a boot against the top of the ladder and gave it a shove. As it sailed backward, a Mexican bullet struck him in the center of his forehead. The sword slipped from his hand, clattering on the top of the wall. Travis reeled, buckled, and sailed back headlong over the edge. His dead body hit the ground hard at the base of the inside wall.

Two Tennesseans who were changing parapet positions along the wall saw the colonel hit the ground. They dashed to him and saw instantly that he was dead. They shouted to other men close by, above the roar of the battle, saying that Colonel Travis had been killed. The word spread along walls as the battle continued to rage.

Hundreds of Mexican soldiers kept rushing the walls of the Alamo on every side, using the scaling ladders. Many of the ladders were pushed away by the Texans on the walls, but in time, amid blazing guns and bayonets and the hissing swords of the zapadores, the vastly outnumbered men of the Alamo began to fall. Many Mexicans were now inside the walls of the Alamo.

At a parapet, Davy Crockett emptied his rifle at the oncoming Mexican troops, dropping some, then turned to see three Mexicans running toward him. Dropping to the ground, Crockett gripped his rifle barrel and, using it like a club, swung at the trio. He swiftly put one down, then a second one. Before he could swing at the third one, two Mexicans inside the walls saw what was happening and shot him down. He twitched for a few seconds, then lay still.

A Mexican infantryman inside the walls defied Texas bullets and ran toward the gate near the southwest corner where Colonel William Travis lay dead. Bullets chewed into the Mexican's body, but he managed to stagger to the gate. He released the latch on the gate and swung it open before falling down dead. The enemy now flooded through the open gate, rifles barking, bayonets flashing.

Inside the south wall, Captain Almeron Dickinson used his revolver to bring down three zapadores who came over the wall from a ladder. Two other Mexicans came up behind him and shot him in the back. When he dropped to the ground, one word came from his lips as he exhaled his last breath: "Susannah."

Beneath Adam Kane's cannon, Mexicans were still trying to set up ladders and climb them. He had just shot off the last cannonball. The huge weapon was of no more use. Major Green Jameson had taken a bullet a few minutes before the last cannonball was fired and lay dead atop the wall.

Juarez Amigo raised his rifle and fired at a zapador who had just topped a ladder. The zapador fell to the ground with the ladder dropping on top of him.

Above the roar of gunfire and shouts of warriors, Adam said, "Juarez! We need to roll the cannon off the platform and drop it on top of those Mexicans below!"

Juarez nodded. "Sí, I will help you!"

The men on the parapets had to fire in both directions now…toward the front of the walls and at the Mexicans who were inside the Alamo.

As Adam kicked the props from under the big wheels of the cannon, he saw Daniel Cloud take a bullet in the chest a little further along the wall and keel headfirst to the ground.

Juarez had his hands on the left wheel and shook his head when he saw Cloud go down.

"Good soldier," Adam said.

"Sí."

"Okay." Adam took hold of the right wheel. "Let's push this thing off the wall."

Just as the wheels began to turn, a bullet hit Juarez in the chest. He made a grunting sound and fell to his knees. Adam rushed to him and helped him to lie flat on his back. He saw that the slug had hit Juarez on the left side of his chest.

Juarez looked up at Adam with glassy eyes. "Adam," he gasped, "because I…am a *real* Christian…I weel meet you in heaven…an' because I am now a *real* Texan…I…weel die even happier." His eyes closed, and his body went limp.

Adam knew his little Mexican friend was dead. "See you soon, Juarez," he breathed as he saw two more ladders appear at the top of the wall right in front of the cannon.

Stepping swiftly to the rear of the big gun, the muscular Irishman summoned all his strength and pushed the cannon forward. The big wheels rolled, and the Mexican infantrymen working their way up the ladders looked up to see the huge barrel move over the edge, hover for a moment, then come crashing down over the wall's edge.

Amid wild screams, the massive cannon thundered downward, violently taking out the men on the ladders and crushing a dozen or more Mexicans on the ground below.

From ladders several feet away, zapadores were reaching the top of the wall. They had seen what Adam did and raced toward him, swinging their swords. He whipped out his bowie knife, stabbed the first zapador, then was overrun by slashing, glittering swords. When he went down, the zapadores made sure he was dead, then threw his body off the wall.

At the baptistry room, several Mexican soldiers kicked the door open and swarmed in, guns blazing. Knowing it would happen at any moment, Jim Bowie and Sam were ready with their four revolvers. Their guns roared as the Mexicans came in. Bowie and Sam dropped four of them, then died with bullets and bayonets ripping into their bodies.

By nine o'clock that morning, the battle was over. Every man in the Alamo had been killed.

Santa Anna lost over six hundred men in the battle. He assigned several of his men to burn the bodies of all those killed at the Alamo.

A strange hush hovered over the Alamo as Susannah Dickinson, holding little Angelina, was assisted into the saddle of her husband's horse by a Mexican officer, as directed by Generalissimo Santa Anna, who sat on his white horse and watched. The Mexican officer, who spoke some English, said, "You may go now, Mrs. Dickinson."

As Susannah turned the horse in the direction of Gonzales, Santa Anna gave her a white-gloved military salute. The gesture was followed with a like salute from several other Mexican soldiers.

Susannah gave no indication that she saw any of the salutes. As she put the horse in motion, her eyes were fixed on the road ahead to Gonzales.

When she was about five miles out of San Antonio, she saw a crowd of people gathered on the side of the road with tents pitched and horses and wagons all around.

She quickly recognized them as citizens of San Antonio. When she drew up, they gathered around her, calling her by name and asking about the battle. They told her that they had heard heavy gunfire at dawn and that it had stopped completely about nine o'clock.

Susannah noticed one man in the group who she figured was in his midthirties, but he was a stranger to her. The man saw her looking at him and stepped up close to the horse. "You don't know me, Mrs. Dickinson, but I am a reporter from the *Washington Post* in Washington-on-the-Brazos. My name is Michael Stewart."

Susannah held her baby close to her heart. "I am glad to meet you, Mr. Stewart."

"My editor sent me to learn, at least from a distance, what was happening at the Alamo," said Stewart. "When I came upon these people earlier this morning, they told me that the Alamo was under attack."

"It certainly was," said Susannah solemnly. "Every man at the Alamo was killed, including my husband. Santa Anna has his men burning their bodies right now."

Stewart frowned. "Why didn't you leave when these people did, ma'am?"

"Because I didn't want to leave my husband. He was a genuine soldier, sir. I knew when I married him that there were risks. I never imagined there would be anything in his military career like what happened at the Alamo today. When he was at the Gonzales fort, I wanted this little girl to be with her father as much as possible, so when they moved him to the Alamo, Angelina and I came with him."

Tears streamed down Susannah's cheeks. "I—I chose to stay with my husband to the end, Mr. Stewart. And I have no regrets. The Mexicans did no harm to my daughter or to me. I am content in my heart that we had these last few days together."

Susannah hugged her baby close in her arms as the tears continued to flow down her cheeks.

Michael Stewart was making notes as Susannah wept and told the story of the Alamo. She went on to tell him that she was on her way to Gonzales, where she was sure there were friends who would take her in with little Angelina.

Just as Susannah was finishing the heart-ripping story, she saw a rider coming down the road toward them from the east. She recognized him immediately. It was Alan Kane.

It was obvious that Alan also recognized Susannah. As he drew up, he smiled. "Hello, Mrs. Dickinson. What can you tell me about what's happening by now at the Alamo?"

Fresh tears welled up in Susannah's eyes. She choked, gasped, and swallowed hard. "Alan…Alan…Santa Anna's troops have been coming into the area and openly camping near the Alamo for thirteen days. When he finally had about sixty-five hundred troops, he was ready to attack. He made that clear to us last night. They attacked at dawn this morning. By…by nine o'clock, every man in the Alamo was dead—including your brother and my husband. Santa Anna has his men burning all the bodies right now."

Alan's heart jolted in his chest and grew cold. *Adam was dead.* Juarez Amigo was dead.

As tears slipped down his cheeks, Alan said, "Apparently, even Santa Anna doesn't kill women and children. I see you're on your husband's horse."

She nodded. "Santa Anna spared my life and Angelina's and told me I could leave on Almeron's horse."

"Where are you going now?" asked Alan.

"You know we used to live in Gonzales."

"Yes."

"I'm going there because I have friends in Gonzales who I am sure will take in Angelina and me and give us a place to live."

Alan nodded. "I'm glad."

Susannah looked at the crowd. "You folks need to know what Alan Kane, here, did."

She then told everyone that Alan had ridden to Washington-on-the-Brazos to try to get General Sam Houston to bring reinforcements to the Alamo. Alan had risked his life when he rode his horse out of the Alamo at night through the Mexican troops that surrounded it in order to get to General Houston.

Alan then explained about General Houston having moved his army to the banks of the Sabine River, hoping to build up his forces by gaining men from surrounding towns so he would have enough soldiers to go to the aid of Colonel William Travis and his men.

Susannah then said, so all the crowd could hear, "Alan, because of the courage you showed in risking your life to go to General Houston for help, I think your name should be changed from Alan Kane to 'Alamo' Kane."

The crowd applauded Alan, cheering him, and calling him "Alamo." Michael Stewart was writing it all down.

Alan looked kindly at the crowd as the cheers dwindled. "Thank you, Mrs. Dickinson, and all you folks. I like the name. It will always give me a closeness with my brother Adam, who was killed at the Alamo."

The people applauded and cheered again.

Alan turned to Susannah. "Mrs. Dickinson, I will ride with you and Angelina to Gonzales, to make sure you get there safely. After that I'll head for the Diamond K Ranch."

Susannah managed a weak smile. "Thank you, *Alamo.* I appreciate your kindness."

When Susannah had bid all her San Antonio friends and reporter Michael Stewart good-bye, she and Alamo Kane rode on toward Gonzales.

Since Gonzales was some sixty miles east of San Antonio, Alan, Susannah, and little Angelina stopped that evening in a small town on the way that had lodging. Adam paid for Susannah and the baby's room and walked them there, then went to his own room and cried himself to sleep.

The next day they rode into Gonzales in late morning, and Susannah's friends welcomed her and the baby into their home when they heard her story. Susannah expressed her deep appreciation to Alan for escorting them there.

As Alan rode toward the area where the Diamond K was located, he knew he would not get there until the next day. He would camp in the woods that night.

While he trotted his horse along the road, his heart was heavy. He must break the awful news to his family—and especially to Julie—that Adam was dead.

TWENTY-FIVE

As Alan Kane drew near the Diamond K Ranch at midmorning on Tuesday, March 8, sadness filled his heart, and grief was his only companion.

Speaking in a low whisper as his horse walked slowly along the road, Alan said, "Dear Lord, when our whole family finally gathered here, our future looked so bright, and our days were filled with happiness. Now the tragic news I am about to give them will bring heartbreak and sorrow. Lord...why did You spare my life and let Adam be killed?"

At that moment, Alan was on the familiar ridge that gave him a full view of the Diamond K. He pulled rein and stared at the ranch through a film of tears.

Suddenly words filtered into his mind as if spoken from heaven: *My thoughts are not your thoughts, neither are your ways my ways.*

Alan sat quietly astride his horse and let God's holy Word penetrate his mind and his aching heart. "Oh, Lord, please forgive me. I have no right or reason to question Your wisdom or Your authority. Please give me the grace to accept Your will. I know that Your Word says in Psalm 18:30, 'As for God, his way is perfect.' Please lead me, Lord, as I go on in my life, and use me to glorify Thy name. And...and please help my family when I tell them of Adam's death. Especially Julie."

Alan squared his slumped shoulders, prodded his horse into motion, and rode toward home.

When he arrived at the ranch, Alan's plan was to gather the family together and tell them all at the same time about Adam and the fall of the

Alamo. When he drew near the big ranch house, he found Julia, Alex, Libby, Abel, Vivian, and Cort Whitney in front of the house. They were obviously in some sort of conversation with his father and sister.

Abram noticed Alan first and pointed at him. "Look! It's Alan!"

There was an instant smile on every face as Alan pulled rein and dismounted. The family and the foreman gathered quickly, welcoming him home with hugs and words of joy.

Julia was the last to hug him. Then looked into his eyes and asked the question that was on everyone's mind. "Alan, where's Adam? Cort was just talking with us about riding to the Alamo to find out what's happening."

A hot shaft piercing his heart, Alan took a deep breath. "Santa Anna's troops have been coming into the area for nearly two weeks and openly camping near the Alamo. When Santa Anna had finally assembled about sixty-five hundred troops, he attacked at dawn on Sunday morning. By nine o'clock that morning, every man in the Alamo was dead."

Julia gasped. "Ev-every man? Adam?"

Alan nodded, his features pale. "Y-yes. Adam was killed. I wasn't there. I'll explain why later."

Shock quickly spread through the group. Julia Kane's heart seemed to stop. The strength ebbed from her body, and her knees buckled as she burst into tears.

Angela rushed to Julia and put an arm around her, holding her up. Alan moved up and put his arms around Angela and Julia. Both women clung to him as they sobbed.

The rest of the family and Cort Whitney wept, clinging to each other.

After the initial shock was over, Alan explained that he had been sent from the Alamo on the night of February 26 by Colonel William Travis to go to Washington-on-the-Brazos and ask General Sam Houston to bring what troops he had immediately. He told them how he rode away at night to try to get past the Mexican troops who were camped all around the

Alamo. He rode through the deep gullies and ditches and was able to make it safely.

Alan then suggested that they have prayer together. Everyone agreed, and Alan led them in prayer, asking the Lord to give all of them comfort in the face of Adam being killed…especially Julia. When he finished praying, he softly reminded them that they would all see Adam again when they got to heaven.

While silent tears were still being shed, Alan told the family and the foreman about going to the Sabine River, where General Houston was now located. He then told them he had been headed back to the Alamo on Sunday and came upon Susannah Dickinson, who had just left the Alamo on her husband's horse, carrying her fifteen-month-old daughter, and had run into a group of San Antonio residents camped along the road.

He explained that Mrs. Dickinson was headed for Gonzales, where she had friends who would take her and the baby into their home. He then told them of Susannah's suggestion in front of the crowd and a reporter from the *Washington Post* that because of the courage Alan showed in risking his life to ride through the Mexican army camp surrounding the Alamo to go to General Sam Houston for help, he should be called Alamo Kane instead of Alan Kane from now on.

As the family and the foreman exchanged comforting glances, Alan said, "I like the name Alamo because it will give me a special closeness with Adam since he was killed there."

Despite their grief and sadness, the family members all spoke up, saying they agreed.

"I really like that, boss," Cort Whitney said. "From now on, when I don't call you 'boss,' I'll call you 'Alamo.' And I'll tell the ranch hands and their wives to do the same."

Alan managed a smile. "Fine, Cort. I appreciate it."

The group finally broke up and walked away, sadness written on their faces.

Later that day, Alan went to Julia's house. Angela was staying with her in an attempt to be of comfort. Alan told his sister that he needed to talk to Julie alone. Angela hugged her sister-in-law, saying she would be back later, and returned to the big ranch house.

Still secretly in love with Julia, Alan talked to her about Adam, telling her how much Adam had missed her when they were at the Alamo and how often he spoke of her.

This touched Julia's heart. She kissed Alan's cheek, called him Alamo, and thanked him for telling her.

Just the touch of her lips on his cheek set his heart afire.

The next day, at the Kane family's breakfast in the big ranch house—cooked by a saddened Daisy Haycock with the help of Angela, Julia, Libby, and Vivian—the subject at the table was what would happen now, with what Santa Anna and his troops had done in attacking and killing the men in the Alamo.

The man now called Alamo said, "I think eventually there will be an all-out war between the United States and Mexico. And if so, I will enlist in the United States army to fight Mexico."

Alex nodded. "If that happens, I'll be right beside you, Alamo, to enlist."

"I will too," said Abel.

Even though they were a bit shaken by their husbands' words, Libby and Vivian told them they would support them in their decisions.

"I will too," Angela said.

"And as your sister-in-law," Julia said, "I will back you too."

It was almost noon that day when Cort Whitney returned to the ranch from Washington-on-the-Brazos, having gone there to inform Pastor Merle Evans of Adam's death at the Alamo and Alan's return home. He took his horse to the nearest corral and walked up to the big ranch house, where he knew the Kane family was about to eat lunch together.

When Alan opened the front door in response to Cort's knock, the foreman held up the March 8 edition of the *Washington Post.* "Something here on the front page you and the family will want to see."

"Come on in," said Alan. "We just sat down around the kitchen table."

When the two men entered the kitchen, Alan looked at the faces around the table. "Cort just got back from informing Pastor Evans about Adam's death. He has yesterday's edition of the *Washington Post* with him and wants you to see what's on the front page."

They all listened as Cort first read the Alamo battle story of March 6. Then he read them a second article by reporter Michael Stewart, which told about Alan Kane's courageous act in passing through the Mexican lines that surrounded the Alamo on the night of February 26 in order to go to General Sam Houston for reinforcements—and Susannah Dickinson's suggestion that his name be changed to Alamo Kane because of it.

"Well, now that it's in the newspaper," Abram spoke up, "it looks like you'll be known as Alamo Kane for sure, son."

Alamo nodded. "I guess so, Papa."

"Well, folks," said Cort Whitney, "I've got work to do. Pastor and Mrs. Evans will be here shortly."

"Thanks for going to town and letting them know," said Alan.

"My pleasure, boss—uh—Alamo."

Pastor Merle Evans and his wife indeed arrived just as the family was finishing their lunch. They did everything they could to comfort and strengthen the family. Having read the newspaper themselves, the Evanses also felt that Alan should now be called Alamo.

That evening, alone in his room at the big ranch house, Alamo Kane was sitting at his small desk, reading over the newspaper articles for himself, when he heard a knock at the door.

When he opened the door, he was pleased to find Julia standing there. She had eaten supper with him, Angela, and Abram, and they had asked her to stay with them overnight.

"What can I do for you, Julie?" he asked.

She looked into his eyes with a meaningful expression and replied, "I just need some time with you. I've missed you."

Alan smiled. "Well, let's go down to the parlor."

They sat down in the parlor in front of the glowing fireplace, and Alan looked at Julia and waited for her to speak.

"Alamo," she said with a special light in her eyes, "I—I need to know about your plans for the ranch now."

He looked at her questioningly. "What do you mean, Julie?"

"I—I'm asking about *me.* Do I go or stay?"

"Oh, sweet Julie," he said, "I want you to stay. All of us do. And you need to know that Adam's half of the ranch is now yours. We'll work together, you and I, and proceed to build our cattle empire. Half of it will be yours."

"But I don't know anything about cattle ranching."

"Well, I was beginning to learn more about it when I left to go to the Alamo, but we've got Cort and the other men here. They can teach us."

"Then you *do* want me to stay?" Julia said with a quaver in her voice.

"Absolutely, Julie! Absolutely!"

"Well, there's something I need to tell you."

"Oh? What?"

She cleared her throat nervously. "I'm going to have a baby. You're going to be an uncle."

Alan's eyebrows rose. "Really?"

"Yes. I just came to this conclusion a few days ago. I'll have to have Dr. Dewitt come and check me, but I'm absolutely sure of it. The baby will be born in late September or early October."

Alan's eyes filmed with tears. "Oh, I wish somehow Adam could have known."

She formed a smile. "Well, maybe in heaven the Lord has already told him that his little son—or daughter—is on the way."

"Yes, I imagine the Lord has told him," Alan said thoughtfully.

Julia frowned. "And you still want me—and your little nephew or niece—to live here?"

"Sure do," Alan said. "Like I said, the ranch is half yours, and we'll build us a cattle empire that'll make all of Texas sit up and take notice!"

"Bless your heart. Thank you." Julia paused for a few seconds. "Alan—ah, I mean, Alamo. We have been good friends for some time now, and I want you to know how thankful I am for our beautiful friendship."

"I'm thankful for it too, Julie." Alan's heart was pounding just being with her.

They talked for a while. Then Alan walked Julia down the hall to her room.

When he arrived back in his own room, Alamo Kane knelt beside his bed and prayed. "Lord, You know I am still in love with Julie. The love she feels for me is a friendship love. Maybe...maybe someday, Lord, when she is over the jolt of losing Adam and becoming a widow who is expecting a baby, You could change that love in her heart toward me so it is like the love I have felt toward her since I first met her. Maybe...maybe someday she could become Mrs. Alan—er—Mrs. *Alamo* Kane."

ABOUT THE AUTHORS

"PEOPLE OFTEN ASK us how we work together to produce our novels," says Al Lacy of the historical-fiction writing team, "and how we manage to come up with such a variety of story ideas." Al says he and JoAnna pray continually for fresh story lines to come to their minds, and they are amazed at the ideas that surface in frequent plot-outline discussions. Their fifty-plus-year marriage has taught them what teamwork means.

"JoAnna will take the outline and go through it, making notes of things to go into the story that interest women and touch the heart," Al continues. "Then I write the manuscript." Readers agree the result is fiction that appeals to all—and manages to fascinate without shelling out sex scenes, cursing, or compromise.

Al is an energetic man with multiple passions: preaching the gospel of Christ, writing, and studying history. For more than thirty years he has been evangelizing at churches around the country. His love of writing and his zest for history came together when he began writing western novels for the general market—he published forty-seven of these despite editors who insisted his clean writing style was bad for sales.

When Al met with Multnomah in 1992, a perfect partnership was born. Finally a publisher shared Al's commitment to offering entertaining Christian fiction, and he wrote his first book for Multnomah: *A Promise Unbroken.* The novel grew into an eight-book series, and more—much more—followed.

The Hannah of Fort Bridger series marked the debut of Al and JoAnna's writing partnership, to which they added the Mail Order Bride, Shadow of Liberty, Orphan Trains, Frontier Doctor, Dreams of Gold, A Place to Call Home, and their latest series, The Kane Legacy.

Long captivated with the study of American history, the Lacys eagerly conducted the research necessary to write The Kane Legacy series. After poring over historical data about Texas in the mid-1800s, the Lacys have spun a gripping historical-romance collection set in the heart of the Alamo and the Mexican-American war.

With more than one hundred books written and over three million copies in print, Al and his wife, JoAnna, who live in the Rocky Mountains of Colorado, relish their productive life together. "I don't watch a lot of television," Al says, "and I'm amazed I get to do the two things I love most: preach and write. It's even more fun doing these together."

Coming Soon

THE KANE LEGACY

Book Two

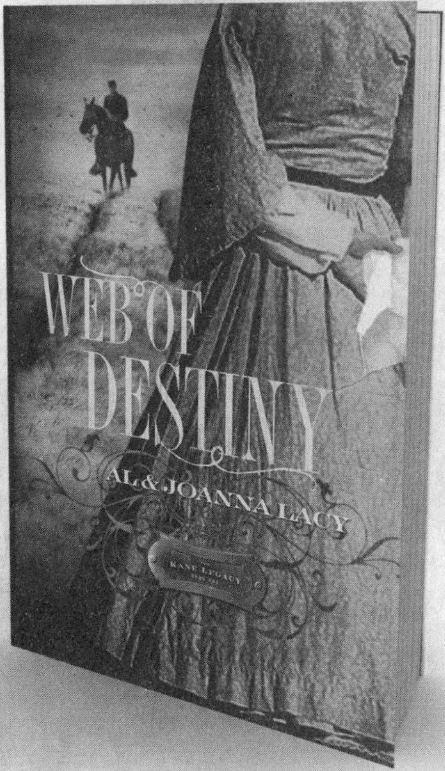

After the battle at the Alamo, the Kane family reunites to recover and grieve their losses. But the war with Mexico is far from over, and as General Sam Houston prepares to face off against General Santa Anna, the three remaining Kane brothers volunteer again, leaving their heavy-hearted wives on the Diamond K Ranch.

Al and JoAnna Lacy once again demonstrate the power of faith and family in an exciting historical story.

Battles of Destiny Series

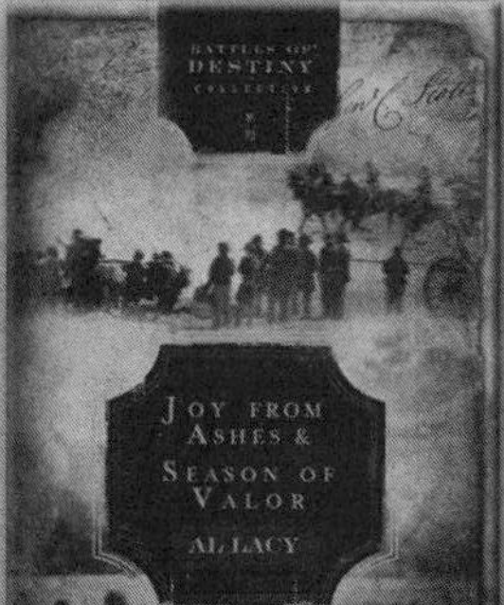

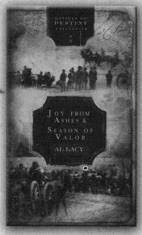

Set during the Civil War, the Battles of Destiny series portrays the lives of families, soldiers, nurses, and spies as they contend with the deadly threats posed by war and the eternal hope that springs from love. Enjoy a thrilling trip back in time with these fast-moving and historically accurate novels.

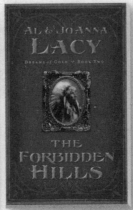

The Orphan Trains Trilogy

The Little Sparrows, book One

Cheyenne, Reno, San Francisco. At each train station, a few lucky orphans from the crowded streets of New York receive the fulfillment of their dreams: a home and family. Yet it is not just the orphans whose lives need mending - follow the train along and watch God's hand bring restoration!

All My Tomorrows, book Two

When sixty-two orphans leave New York City on a train headed West, they have no idea what to expect. Will a real family love and accept them? Future events are wilder than any of the orphans could imagine, and each child learns that their paths are being watched by Someone who cares about and plans all of their tomorrows.

Whispers in the Wind, book Three

Young Dane Weston's dream is to become a doctor. But it will take more than just determination to realize his goal. His family is murdered and he ends up in a colony of street waifs, accused of murder and sentenced to prison. What will become of his dreams and of the girl he loves?